A Most Uncivil War: Lissie's Story

Patricia Diehl

Scripture quotations from the Holy Bible used the King James Version

ISBN: 9781654683849
Imprint: Independently published

Dedicated

T o
The Memory of

My Great-great-grandmother,
Sarah Angeline (Focht) Reber

Chapter 1

January 1, 1921
Palmyra, Missouri

ANNALIESE WINCED AS she sat at her desk. The rheumatism in her hip was more troublesome today than usual. Before setting to work on writing her long-time friend, Eliza, she took the new calendar from Miller's Feed Store out of her desk drawer. Its idyllic picture showed sleek Jersey cows grazing on rolling green hills dotted with white daisies. The sun was shining in a blue sky sporting a few puffy clouds in artistic spots.

The scene was certainly warmer than the blustery weather they were experiencing just now. *A new year,* she mused. *Well, 1920 was a spitfire way to start another decade in America. I still find it hard to believe I got to vote for the president of the United States last November.* She smiled as she thought, *Now, we'll have to see if Mr. Harding does a good job for us.*

She glanced up at the spot she planned to put the new calendar on the wall when she finished her letter. A blast of wind cornered the house and rattled the window at her desk. Annaliese shivered, pushed up the spectacles over the bridge of her nose, and began to write.

Dearest Eliza,

I hope your Christmas was a joyous one with your cousin and her children's family. I imagine Philadelphia is quite the gay place during the holiday season. Did you chaperone any young ladies at Christmas balls or have chaperones gone out of fashion these days? Even here in the rural Midwest we hear of flappers and wild parties in the big cities like Chicago since Prohibition was ratified last January.

Seems like when folks get told they can't *do something is when they try all the harder to do just that. I know Lew would have felt this constitutional amendment to be a good thing as he saw so many families broken and poverty stricken because of alcohol consumption. Many a time he would come home from a preaching circuit full of sorrow at the damage done to a family because of parents drinking to excess.*

Our Christmas Day started quietly with just my son, Landis, and me. However, we were invited to eat dinner with my son, James, and his family. Their younger daughter, Tillie, and her husband and baby Jessie, were there as well as Tillie's older sister, Anna. Little Jessie has provided a bright spot in my life this last year as her birth in April meant I had my first great-grandchild.

Anna says she has come home to stay so she can help her parents. It is true Louisa's health is not the best, but I suspect a love affair gone wrong back in Peoria where she was working. However, Anna has not confided in me.

I seem to find myself living life vicariously through young people like my granddaughters. You would probably tell me you have been doing it for years as you taught your young ladies at the finishing school. I don't recall feeling this way until after Lew died.

My Scripture reading for this morning's devotional came from Psalm 90:12—"Teach us to number our days that we may apply our hearts unto wisdom." Very appropriate for the New Year although as I think over the seventy-two years God has granted me, I wonder about the wisdom I may have gained.

As for the brevity of life, you and I have both experienced that, much to our sorrow.

Annaliese stopped writing for a moment and rubbed her right hand with the left and then stretched and fisted her fingers. Rheumatism there too, but not as painful as her hip.

She thought of Eliza's grief over John's death back in the war days and the loss of her parents a few decades later. Annaliese's acquaintance with shortness of life came with her three babies dead in infancy or childhood and Annie and Linn's lives, snuffed out before they could reach their full potential. Sorrow clogged her throat at the memories and she thought sadly, *Yes, we both know well of the numbering of our days.* She signed off on her letter and placed it to the side of her desk to be mailed in the morning.

Continuing to think about the scripture she had read earlier,

Annaliese pondered the acquisition of wisdom. Perhaps it had come with the years. Bitterness had tinged sadness far too long for Annaliese, but God's grace had eventually triumphed and birthed acceptance. It had been a battle—between her stubborn will and a Love whose compassion had gently dissolved the gall in her soul.

Strange to think, but when she and Lew had been youngsters, the only war Annaliese had thought important was the War Between the States for it would separate them. Her mind wandered back to that time and felt no guilt at the luxury of sitting and remembering because she already had ham and beans cooking for supper. The homey aroma was soothing and mouth-watering at the same time, and would be ready whenever Landis came in from doing chores.

Dear Landis. He was such a treasure.When Lew died, he offered to come live with her and run the farm. Her younger son, Howard, had never taken to farming so she knew he was grateful his help was unnecessary.

Seems like God has always provided, even in the most difficult times, she mused. *I thought our courtship was doomed when Lew told me he had permission from his father to enlist in the Union army.* She closed her eyes and could see plainly the day Lew got on the train headed for Camp Curtin to learn how to fight the Rebels.

Chapter 2

Late July 1862
Cressona, Pennsylvania

THE DISTANCE FROM the Holtschlag farm to the train depot seemed much longer than a mile to Annaliese. She brushed back tendrils of chestnut hair that had worked loose from her braids. Humidity due to the early afternoon heat and the exertion of walking combined to make her naturally curly hair totally uncooperative. Her heart beat faster at the thought of seeing Lew. At the same time, she felt as if tears were lurking, ready to spring forth at the slightest opportunity. She had come to the train station to see young Lew Reber as he went off to war. He had enlisted in the Union Army for a a nine-month stint, excited about the adventures he would have fighting the Rebels.

She knew he still grieved for his mother who had died three months earlier. "Home does not seem like home any more," Lew told her. "Mein vater speaks to me only to assign chores. I feel no love from him. None." Joining the army to save the Union—and escape his father's heavy hand—looked very attractive to Lew.

Annaliese Facht, Lissie to her friends, and LB Reber, known as Lew, had been sweet on each other almost from the time they met in the fifth grade. Consequently, her plea to be allowed to see her beau go off to join the Union Army was not a surprise to her aunt and uncle.

"You may go, Lissie, although why anyone in their right mind would want to be a soldier is beyond me," huffed Aunt Jane. "And how could a parent allow his fifteen-year-old son go off to war?" she sniffed.

"Patriotism, Jane. Hurrah for Old Glory and Uncle Sam!" boomed her husband, Edgar. "The boy is caught up in the hullabaloo. Plus, joining the army is one way to get out from under the thumb of George Reber." Uncle Edgar was referring to common knowledge of the elder Reber's penny-pinching habits and harsh work ethic. "No doubt, George got the bounty money when the boy enlisted, too."

Lissie ignored the dialogue between her aunt and uncle, grateful for their permission to take time from her household chores. She kissed them goodbye and walked the mile to the village of Cressona, finding herself in a bittersweet frame of mind. Happy she could bid Lew farewell, Lissie dreaded his absence and the very real possibility of him never returning.

She saw his tall frame leaning against the front edge of the train depot and called out. "Lew!"

"Lissie!" He bounded to meet her, grabbed her hands and said, "I am so glad you could come see me off." He put his free arm around her waist, the other hand holding the strap of a knapsack that had seen better days.

"Where is your family, Lew?" she asked.

He shrugged. "Busy in the field. Father issued the usual chore assignments this morning and then told me I could leave. So I went before he could change his mind." He grinned, but Lissie could see there was no mirth in his eyes.

She hugged his waist as they walked toward the back of the depot. "I have something for you." She reached into her apron pocket and pulled out a locket containing a tiny mustard seed. "My mother gave me this locket on my tenth birthday, shortly before she died. She said it was to remind me to have faith, like Jesus taught. Maybe it will help you remember me, too, when you feel it around your neck" She looked up at him, her eyes glistening with tears.

Lew pulled her into his arms, kissing her forehead. "Oh, my sweet Lissie. How could I ever forget you?" He bent down so she could slip it over his head.

And then he pulled a small pewter circle from his pocket. "I snitched one of the small household spoons and shaped it into a ring. See," he said, "it has our initials picked out inside. LBR+SAF. Lissie, will you wait for me? Be my fiancée?"

"Yes, I will wait for you, Benjie." Lissie felt her face flush as she promised, using her pet nickname for Lew. She slipped the ring onto her finger. He kissed her again and she hugged his tall frame clinging with all her strength.

The sound of the train whistle effectively broke their embrace.

“Time to go.” He picked up his knapsack and walked her back to the front of the depot. As he got ready to jump on the flatbed car with the other recruits, he turned and said “Please write to me, Lissie.”

“Every week,” she promised in a shaky voice. “You do the same, please.”

“I will try,” he said, just before he turned away. As he found a place to sit, Lissie caught a glint of mid-summer sunlight on the locket she had slipped around his neck.

The next Friday Lissie rode into town with Aunt Jane and the other children all piled into the wagon. They used it to transport eggs and fresh garden produce to trade for other supplies at the general store. The two little girls, Lissie’s sister, Jennie and her cousin, Sally, loved the sights and sounds so different from their farm home. Frederick, at age twelve, welcomed any chance of dodging chores, and Manfred, the seven-year-old, just didn’t want to be left behind.

Lissie was secretly hoping a letter from Lew would be waiting at the post office. After she helped Aunt Jane unload the farm produce to trade to Mr. Murchiston, the owner of The Mercantile, she offered to check for mail at the post office. Keeping an eye on her three children as well as Jennie, Aunt Jane nodded absentmindedly as she fingered some new gingham material Mr. Murchiston had just gotten in.

As Lissie walked rapidly to the post office, she thought back to when Lew first spoke of leaving the grinding toil on his father's farm to join the army. She was upset at his decision and told him so, the tears clogging her throat.

“Oh Lissie,” he said as he reached out with his thumbs and gently smudged at her tears which had begun to roll down her cheeks. “I wish we could be married, but we are too young.” He drew her close and chastely kissed her forehead.

She was brought back to the present when the postmaster handed her two letters. One was for Aunt Jane and--her breath caught in her chest as she caught sight of her name on the other. She tucked Lew’s letter in her pocket to treasure later, her joy making her want to run and jump instead of sedately walking back to The Mercantile.

Later that night after the younger girls were asleep, Lissie lit the coal oil lantern she was allowed to keep on her bedside table in case one of the younger girls needed to get up in the night. She pulled her letter out from under her pillow where she had stashed it earlier that day and sat on the edge of the featherbed she shared with her little sister, Jennie. Edging close to the lamplight she read,

August 8, 1862

Dear Lissie,

Being in the army is sure different than farming. Today a doctor checked me from head to toe. First, my teeth he checked, then my eyes he looked into, and finally, my belly he poked. Next came looking over legs and feet. I guess they do not want any knock-kneed, flat-footed soldiers in the Army of the Potomac.

Despite my size and healthy muscles, it begins to look like the letter of mein vater permitting me to join up even at fifteen years, is not going to work. But by the end of the day only 80 out of 120 of us had healthy eyes, teeth and feet, so my tall frame passed muster despite lack of years.

Next day

Sorry, lights out came before I can finish letter. You should see me in my new uniform. No, you probably should not, for you might have a fit of apoplexy from laughing so hard. I can only say that I am quite overdressed as it appears my uniform was meant for a much heavier man than I.

No matter. I am now a soldier in Company K, 127th Regiment of the Pennsylvania Volunteers. I get the same wage and the same ration of hardtack and salt-horse as any other man who has joined the company.

Just think, Lissie. I am now a soldier! We leave Camp Curtin in a few days for Washington, D.C. but in the meantime, we are learning to drill, practice marksmanship, and drill some more.

Please, please do write, Lissie, for I miss you terrible much. Send your letters to the Army of the Potomac in Washington, D.C. I hear they have mail wagons that go out to the different regiments to

deliver and pick up mail. I kiss your locket as I cannot kiss your face.

With all my love,
Your Benjie

Lissie could imagine Lew's slight German accent as if he had spoken the words he had written. Her eyes misted as she read his loving closing. She tucked the letter back under her pillow, and kissed the pewter ring she had hung around her neck. Lantern out, she snuggled next to Jennie, thinking of her Benjie as she went to sleep.

The next morning Lissie hummed as she worked and Aunt Jane noticed her happier countenance. "You seem to be all smiles today, my dear," Jane remarked as she kneaded the dough for the week's bread supply.

Lissie looked up from slicing vegetables for the evening's stew. "A letter came from Lew yesterday."

"And is he enjoying soldiering?" Jane glanced at Lissie in time to see a tear slip down her niece's cheek.

"Oh, Aunt Jane. Lew is having this wondrous adventure, and I miss him so."

"Wipe your eyes child," her aunt replied. "When you put that pot of stew on to cook, take some time to write a letter back to your beau."

Lissie did not have to be told twice. On her way to the desk where the family kept their writing paper and pens, she hugged Jane and whispered, "Thank you, Auntie."

Pulling out a sheet of paper, she dipped the pen nib into the ink bottle.

August 15, 1862

Dear Benjie,

It was such a treat to receive your letter. Despite what you said of your uniform I should so like to see you wearing it, even if I should laugh just a little.

Your food rations do not sound at all pleasant. Do not break any of your strong white teeth on the substance you called hardtack. As for salt-horse, how truly disgusting! Is our army reduced to eating their worn out horses? I find myself thanking God doubly for the delicious food that comes from Aunt Jane's kitchen as I shudder at the thought of your rations!

Our barn cat, Minerva, moved her new litter of kittens yesterday, carrying each one from her special hiding place. She stalked proudly to her new nest in the straw of the milking shed, the tiny balls of fur looking comical as they hung from her mouth by the nape of their necks. I spied her carrying a coal black morsel while I was milking old Sukey. When I finished, I went over to the cozy spot Minerva had fashioned for her brood. She was licking a tiny calico when I bent closer to look. I believe the little tiger-striped one is my favorite at present.

Aunt Jane has started to help me piece a wedding ring quilt. This is the first large piece of hand sewing I have been allowed to do, so feel quite proud. Is that sinful? She told me when it is finished it can go into my hope chest for our home. I have already sewn two pillowcases decorated with matching embroidery patterns of daisies in a wreath.

I miss you and the walks we used to take through the woods. Please stay safe.

With all my love,
Your Lissie

She sealed the letter, wrote Lew's name, L.B. Reber, and his regiment in her best calligraphic manner and turned to her aunt who was pulling a loaf of bread from the oven. "Aunt Jane, how soon can I get this letter sent to Lew?"

Jane looked over and smiled. "Hiram is taking a load of straw to the livery stable tomorrow. I will see to it that your uncle gets it to him to take by the post office.

"Come finish washing up the bread pans, Lissie, and then it will be time to set the table for supper."

"Yes, Aunt Jane." Then in a lower voice Lissie added, "Thank you for helping me get my letter to Lew."

Her aunt smiled at her and they continued working.

That Sunday the family piled into the wagon to attend church. Aunt Jane, wearing a summery sprigged cotton dress and Uncle Edgar, in his black broadcloth suit and white cotton shirt, sat on a bench seat at the front of the wagon. Lissie and her little sister, Jennie, as well as their three cousins, sat on two additional benches, the girls clutching the wagon's sideboards. Lissie and the younger girls were dressed in their new ginghams, Jenny and cousin Sally, in white pinafores, while Fredrick and Manfred wore freshly starched white shirts and black broadcloth knickers.

As soon as Uncle Edgar got to the churchyard and brought the team to a standstill, the boys began to climb over the back of the wagon, while Aunt Jane and the girls waited for Uncle Edgar to help them to the ground. He tied the horses to a low-hanging oak tree branch and then unhooked the wagon's tailgate which was hinged at the bottom. He had fashioned a clever folding step affair which he pulled out of the wagon and unfolded with a flourish. Then he helped each of the womenfolk step to the ground.

Lissie was headed for the church's entrance when she was halted by the sound of her best friend's voice. "Lissie. Over here."

She hurried over to Eliza Murchiston, who had just dismounted from her parents' buggy. They had not seen each other for two months because Eliza had been visiting relatives since she had graduated from Riverview School in May. Even before that time they had generally used church attendance as a time to re-connect because Lissie's family felt she needed no further formal education once she turned thirteen. She had celebrated her fourteenth birthday in March and still lamented at no longer being allowed to attend school.

The girls hugged each other, both starting to talk at the same time. Lissie prevailed saying, "Eliza, my best friend has blossomed into a fine lady." She eyed her friend's summery dimity gown graced with light yellow and pink blossoms and fashionably flounced with a small hoop beneath the skirt. The pattern and colors accented Eliza's willowy form and blond ringlets.

Lissie could not help comparing her own shorter stature and curly brown hair. Despite her curls being tied back with a ribbon that matched her new green gingham, she felt like a dowdy little wren alongside Eliza. With a mental shake, she reminded herself how much she had missed her dear friend.

As they walked slowly toward the door of the church, Eliza told Lissie of balls, shopping trips, and concerts. "Oh how I wish you could have heard the pipe organ recital in Philadelphia." She knew Lissie had an uncanny knack for picking out melodies and had actually taken a few lessons from their church organist during her last year at school.

Eliza was still bubbling with news when the girls entered the church and spied the minister heading for the platform from a side door. "Looks like I must stop talking," she whispered and Lissie squeezed her hand, smiling, as they slid onto an empty polished pew.

After the service was over, the friends started up where they had left off. "Lissie, I have done all the talking. What has happened in your life while I have been away?"

Lissie's eyes glistened with unshed tears as she told of Lew's going off to be a soldier. "He has asked me to wait for him until we are old enough to be wed," she said with pride, and she pulled the pewter ring up from where it nestled against her heart.

"Oh, my dear, I had not realized you were that serious about each other," Eliza said in a shocked voice. "How romantic!" Then in the next breath, "And how dreadful is the separation of young lovers blighted by this horrid war."

Her dramatic statement struck Lissie's funny bone and she broke into giggles as she wiped her eyes. "You can always bring me out of the doldrums, Eliza." And she elbowed her friend in the ribs. Eliza was ticklish so that brought laughter to both girls.

Then Eliza said, "I feel as if we are both on journeys but we do not know our destinations. You are waiting on Lew to come home safely and then marry. I travel to Philadelphia to attend Madame Ascott's Finishing School." At Lissie's gasp, Eliza continued, "My cousin, Amelia, is already enrolled there, so I shall know at least one girl, but I confess, the prospect is somewhat frightening. Visiting the big city is exciting but living there? I do not know."

"I will miss you greatly," said Lissie, her hazel eyes clouding with tears. "First, Lew goes to war and now you go off to school."

"We must write, at least once a week," declared Eliza. Just then Aunt Jane called Lissie and when she looked over at the wagon, she could see they were waiting on her.

With a desperate hug on both their parts, Eliza whispered, "We shall surely see each other once more here at church before I leave." Lissie nodded and without another word, turned and ran to the wagon.

Chapter 3

IT WAS TWO weeks later when Lissie received her next letter from Lew. That evening, as before with the younger girls asleep, she lit the bedside lantern and opened her Benjie's letter.

August 22, 1862

Dear Lissie,

I am writing this by the light of a campfire as we are now camped on General Lee's homestead in Virginia. Had another fine train ride from Camp Curtin to Washington D.C. but then we practiced marching from that city to where we are now located.

I tell you I was mighty tired from all that marching but it made no difference for I had to stand guard that first night. I was so tired my eyes needed props to stay open so when I heard someone in the brush, I thought it might be another guard and we could visit a bit. After my "hello," the man comes right up to me and tries to take my rifle. I was bounden not to give it up so he draws a revolver on me.

As I think of it now, the sweat pops out on my forehead but right then I felt cool, wondering if the next breath would be my last. Turns out, the fellow was captain of the guards and he lectured me for the next half hour about the duties of a soldier on guard with countersigns and such like. Sure would have saved us both some time and distress if he had told me all that before I was sent out for guard duty!

Being a soldier sure is different from what I thought before. Sleeping on the hard ground does not near measure up to the featherbed at home even with three of us boys sharing it. And the food does not measure up so well as the vittles at home either. Set your mind at ease, sweet Lissie, we have not taken to eating our old horses. The salt-horse I mentioned is salt-pork, although I must say it has been a long time since any of it was part of a live hog!

Tell me more about Minerva's kittens and if her tiger stripe is still your favorite. All the tales you can share of home will be most welcome. Since we mainly march from here to there it helps while away the time to think of you and what you might be doing.

I keep your letter in my breast pocket close to my heart and I kiss your locket as I close.

All my love,
Benjie

She pressed his letter to her chest, slid it under her pillow, turned down the lantern wick and nestled close to young Jennie.

A letter soon sped its way from Lissie's hand to the young soldier. Time passed as life went on at the farm. Eliza left for Philadelphia and Lissie felt as if her link to carefree, golden school days was well and truly gone with her two best friends, Lew and Eliza leaving her behind. It did not help when a visit to the post office yielded no letter from Lew. Three weeks stretched into four, then five. Lissie stopped humming as she worked and she began to actively imagine Lew's body lying on some cold, lonely battlefield.

The next trip in to Cressona yielded one piece of mail for the Holtschlag household—addressed to Annaliese Facht. It was a dirty, creased missive written in an unfamiliar hand. Lissie's heart turned to icy fear in her chest. Afraid to open it but knowing she must, she leaned against the building's wall for support and read:

September 27, 1862

Dear Lissie,

Please do not be alarmed at not seeing my handwriting. My friend, Jack, who is somewhat healthier than I at the moment, has kindly consented to write for me. I have been quite sick with the fever and did not know whether I was alive or dead for some time. It now appears I am not dead.

I have been in this hospital for nigh on three weeks but am still as wobbly as a newborn colt belonging to mein vater. I disremember how the saying goes as to whether a fever should be fed or starved. This particular fever is being starved as we are lucky to get some thin gruel once a day.

At any rate I am alive and miss you much. I even miss the dismal toil on the farm of mein vater and for sure the good grub. Please write and tell me how things go on there.

Your loving Benjie

Sobbing as she made her way back to Aunt Jane's wagon, she came close to being hit by a horse and buggy on Main Street. The driver's shouts roused her to the fact that she needed to get out of the middle of the street and she mopped at her eyes with the palms of her hands.

"Goodness, child. Whatever is the matter?" Aunt Jane's fright showed in her shrill tone . She took Lissie's arm and drew her close. "Have you been took ill?"

"No, Aunt, but Lew has," and Lissie began to cry again. "He has been sick with a fever and is in hospital and I cannot be there to nurse him."

"Be sensible, girl. You are not a nurse. The army will take care of its men," assured the older woman. "Now dry your eyes and let us be on our way home."

That evening after supper was eaten and cleared away, Lissie asked permission to write a letter to Lew. Aunt Jane was quick to allow it and Uncle Edgar said he would deliver the letter to the post office the next day. He planned to drive one of his shoats to sell to another farmer who lived on the outskirts of Cressona.

She wrote:

October 5, 1862

My dearest Benjie,

I just today received the letter telling me of your dreadful fever. Oh, how I wish I could be there to nurse you back to health. I promise I would feed you more than thin gruel once a day. I cry for your discomfort but how I thank God that you survived this dreadful sickness.

Now for news of home. Minerva's kittens are all darling but the tiger stripe is still my favorite. They are really getting fat because I save a little pan of warm milk for them when I strip out old Sukey. Minerva likes that milk too.

Aunt Jane and I have been canning tomatoes this week. Manfred and Sally help pick the tomatoes although he complains it is women's work and begs to help with the haying instead. We have canned twenty-seven quarts of tomatoes by cold pack and are not finished yet. They will taste so delicious in Aunt Jane's tomato soup this winter.

I must close as the family is getting ready for bed. I kiss your ring, dear Benjie, and pray for your health. I should so prize a letter in your own hand, asking God to give you strength to write.

All my love,
Lissie

She felt somewhat guilty as she sat down the next morning to Aunt Jane's griddlecakes, inhaling the delightful aroma of bacon and knowing there was an ample amount of scrambled eggs to satisfy her appetite. Realizing she could not help Lew's lack of good food so many miles away, she shrugged and forked a mouthful of honey-soaked cake, enjoying the taste.

The garden continued yielding its produce for the table, some vegetables being taken to town for sale, but the bulk of it being preserved for winter. The Holtschlag orchard included some Bartlet pear trees that had outdone themselves. Pears appeared in all sorts of forms—pear and cheese salad, baked pears with whipped cream and pear and dried cherry pie. Another half bushel of pears was stored in the cool cellar for eating later. Lissie helped Aunt Jane can forty-two quarts of pears in Mr. Mason's newfangled glass jars with reusable lids. In addition, there were several tumblers and crocks of pear butter and preserves topped with brandy-soaked paper to guard the product from mold.

Once again, Lissie's fear increased each week as no word arrived from Lew. Finally, about five weeks later, she heard from him again. The letter was written in his own hand, and she rejoiced in that fact.

November 15, 1862

Dear Lissie,

Your soldier boy has progressed from hospital tent to marching here and marching there. I am most grateful to say we received orders today to build winter quarters here so maybe we can stop marching.

Herewith is the account of this weary soldier since my last letter. I was in hospital for another four weeks after Jack wrote my letter. I was then released but was so weak I could not even do a full night's guard duty. Picture your Sukey's newborn calf and it's wobbly legs and you will know how I felt and likely how I appeared. The captain had pity on me and let me rest partial days. I am grateful to say I have my appetite back in full force and can now eat my full ration of raw salt pork and hardtack with the best of them!

It has rained a lot and the march through mud stirred up by many feet, both human and animal, adds more than a mite to the weight of my boots. In addition to the mud we accumulate along our march, we carry a sixty-pound pack. You can understand why the idea of winter quarters with shelter and warmth is very attractive.

By now harvest is all set by and all are snuggled in there, ready for wintry winds and snow. I never in a million years thought I should miss my farm home but I do so yearn for the sound of logs popping in the fireplace and the biscuits mein mutter made when I was a boy. Those days are gone and I am a proud soldier in the Army of the Potomac.

Please tell me of the homey things you are doing so I might picture your sweet face as you go about your tasks.

I kiss your locket since I cannot kiss your face, mein liebchen, my dearest.

All my love from
Your Benjie

Lissie wasted no time in answering Lew's letter.

November 21, 1862

My Dearest Benjie,

My heart near flew out from my chest when your letter finally arrived. I must confess my faith was not even the size of the mustard seed you carry around your neck, I was that afraid the fever had carried you off.

It is good news that your appetite has returned, but for such rations? They truly sound disgusting and I wonder you can eat it despite your gain in health. It is also good that you can end this ridiculous marching around to nowhere and are building shelter for the winter.

As for us Pennsylvania Dutch farmers, we are snuggled up for the winter with hay and straw in the barn lofts and grain in the bins for the cattle. Aunt Jane and I have canned beans; peas, tomatoes and all manner of fruit and the carrots, potatoes, onions and apples are nestled in the cellar awaiting our needs. God has blessed us with a good harvest this year. How I wish to be able to share it with you.

Minerva's kittens are now young cats, all sleek and fat from keeping the mice population depleted. I have trained Tiger—for the tiger-stripe kitten has remained my favorite—to jump onto my shoulder when I go to the barn. He curls around my neck, careful not to scratch me, and purrs in my ear. Some mornings he takes his position on my shoulder as I milk old Sukey and he feels like a living fur collar. Such a luxurious sensation!

I kiss your ring, sending all my love.

Your Lissie

The Holtschlag family was soon deep into preparing Christmas gifts for each other. Aunt Jane held very definite ideas on what constituted a proper Christmas from trimming the perfect evergreen tree with cranberries and popcorn garlands to making the perfect gift for each member of the family. This had been true from the time Lissie and little Jennie had joined the family after their mother, Catherine, had died three years earlier.

Beside all the excitement of making gifts, and of course, keeping them hidden away from curious eyes, Aunt Jane also had specific ideas on what food must be prepared for the proper Christmas dinner. Lissie knew that it would not be long before a certain goose would become the beautifully roasted center of attraction on the Hostschlag table. But before that time, there would be special breads baked—potica bread with its yummy nut-raisin-honey filling plus butterhorn rolls so tender and flaky just one look made your mouth water. There would be apple strudel and banbury cakes made from Aunt Jane's British grandmother's recipe, as well as mincemeat pie and peach pie with fresh whipped cream to garnish as one wished.

With all the hubbub of extra activities, there were also Christmas programs at the school and at church. Lissie had little time to think about what Lew might be doing as a soldier for the holiday. Consequently, when a letter arrived five days before Christmas, she was surprised at how much time had elapsed since his last missive. This letter was dated December 10, 1862 and she felt a tendril of fear creep up her spine. Rumors had reached Cressona of a terrible Union loss at the Battle of Fredericksburg which had begun the day after Lew's letter was written.

Dear Lissie,

Your soldier boy is tired tonight as we have marched many long days. Just as we had thrown up decent winter quarters, some log dwellings and some halfway comfortable lean-to's, we got orders to prepare to leave. With five days rations we have marched more than seven. Raw salt pork and hardtack looks mighty good to a starving man.

The scarce rations we have lived on the past few days make me long for the peach mush we brought into camp some time back. Me and two others were sent off for picket duty four miles distant with two days rations. One man had some field glasses and come the third day we spied no relief. Toward mid-afternoon with our bellies rumbling, the man with the field glasses said, "Men, there is a peach orchard over there just waiting for us." We out-flanked those peach trees, filled our bellies and then our knapsacks. By sunset we were finally relieved and when we got back to camp we discovered those fine, ripe peaches had turned to mush. Oh, how wondrous just one of those squashed peaches would taste right now.

The noise of battle is something fierce here. We are camped near the north bank of the Rappahannock River and I will soon be fighting in my first, real battle. I pray I shall get some sleep, dear Lissie, but my mind seems to be part fearful and part ready to fight. I hear we must cross this river somehow to get to the town of Fredericksburg and then on to fight General Lee's army.

I must trust you are praying for me as there is no one else to do so. I once again pull out your locket from under my shirt and kiss it.

Good night, my sweet Lissie.

With all my love,
Your Benjie

It was the third day of January that Lissie heard the dread news. Uncle Edgar came from town after delivering another load of hay to the livery stable at Cressona. It was not yet time to do evening chores but he came to the house and sat heavily on a chair by the kitchen table. Lissie was humming as she peeled potatoes while Aunt Jane was cutting up a chicken to fry for supper.

"Are you ill, Edgar?" asked Jane in a concerned voice. His shoulders were bowed and his face, pale and pinched-looking.

"My body is not ill," he sighed, "but my soul is pained within me." He sighed even deeper and continued, "Lissie, leave your potatoes for a bit and come sit." She laid down the paring knife and came to the table, puzzled at his request.

He put his big hand over her small one and said, "There ain't no easy way to say this, so I will just be plain. Word has come that Lew Reber was kilt in the Battle of Fredericksburg. One of the boys from his regiment who lived through the battle sent word home that he saw Lew go down. Since he did not make it back over the river when the army was routed, it would seem 'tis true."

As he spoke, Lissie gasped, putting her free hand over her mouth to stifle the rising sobs as tears welled up. Jane wiped her hands on a towel and moved to her niece's side, hugging her and making comforting sounds.

Edgar continued. "The news is pretty bad from that battle. Near 13,000 on the Union side kilt, including three men from around here besides Lew, one of them being my brother's boy, Tyson." That name was said with a strangled sound because Tyson was his oldest nephew and a great favorite of Edgar's.

With that, Jane moved to Edgar's side, put her arms around him and kissed his temple. "This is a hard day for the house," she stated. Glancing over at their niece, Jane said, "My dear, if you wish, you may go to your room for a time."

"No, Aunt Jane, I must stay busy." *I must keep my hands at work to make my mind blank,* she thought. She pulled a handkerchief from her apron pocket, wiped her eyes, blew her nose, and returned to her potato peeling, tears tracking a crooked course down her cheeks.

That night Lissie tossed and turned in her bed. Thoughts of Lew lying wounded in the damp Virginia cold, perhaps moaning with pain from a bullet in his chest, made her muscles stiffen and the tears clogged her throat. She would doze, then waken with a start, seeing another scenario of Lew being wounded in the head or slashed with a bayonet.

That sort of traumatic sleeplessness brought her stumbling downstairs the next morning to milk Old Sukey, her head and shoulders aching, feeling like she had been through a battle herself. Actually, Aunt Jane said as much when she caught sight of her.

"Land sakes, Girl, you look like you were the cat in a dog fight and the dog won! Did you sleep at all last night?"

"I mostly remember seeing Lew shot in the head or slashed in his chest," she replied in a dull tone. As she put on her coat to go to the barn, her aunt's voice seemed like a buzz in her ears, not understandable at all.

Leading the cow to the stanchion and fastening her, Lissie sat down to milk. The musical sound of the streams of milk hitting the bottom of the metal bucket and gentle Sukey allowing her milkmaid to lean against her warm flank, lulled the girl to sleep. She woke with a start at the vibrating sound of the cow's low moo.

As Lissie finished her milking chore, she wondered how she could manage to live with the pain she was feeling. The tightness in her throat and chest as she thought of Lew being gone, threatened to suck the breath from her lungs. She picked up her milking stool and bucket of milk, and then loosened Sukey to make her way out to the water tank. A great sob racked her body as she walked back to the house to pour the milk into the separator.

Aunt Jane had breakfast almost ready by the time Lissie hung her barn coat on the hook by the kitchen door. The warm air from the cookstove, the aroma of sausage frying, and the homey sound of the two younger girls talking as they set the table, eased the raw edges of Lissie's grief a bit. No one mentioned her red, puffy eyes, and Aunt Jane set her to work as soon as breakfast was cleared away.

"This cold weather seems to make the males in this household eat double the usual amount of bread," declared Jane. "Lissie, you start the bread dough to rising while I bake some apple pies." The younger children had left for school so the girl and her aunt worked together in comfortable silence.

That stillness was broken by a quiet sob coming from the direction of the counter where Lissie was washing up the last of the pans. "Do not try to hold back your grief," advised Aunt Jane. "The tears cleanse and heal the pain, somehow."

"I seem to have a never-ending stream of tears," gulped Lissie. "It hurts even worse than when Mama died."

"It has only been three years since Catherine died," replied Aunt Jane. "It may well be that the news of Lew's death has re-opened that old grief wound from her death as well."

"Will this hollow pain ever leave me?" Lissie whispered.

For a moment there was a faraway look in her aunt's eyes. "The pain and tears will lessen," she said gently. "Remember, our Savior, himself, wept over the death of his dear friend, Lazarus. And in Matthew's gospel, Jesus told his followers to come to him and he would give them rest when their burdens were too heavy to bear alone. Think of our Lord helping bear your grief as you lay your head on the pillow tonight."

That evening as Lissie lay down and once again imagined Lew in gory battle scenes, she whispered, "Please help me, Lord Jesus, to bear this awful loneliness."

She awoke from a seamless sleep to a bright January morning, sunlight streaming through their east window. "I thank you, Lord," she whispered.

Life went on, as it must on a busy farm, for cows must be milked, chicken and hogs fed. Household work, though different from spring and summer tasks, still continued as three meals must be prepared each day for two hungry men since Hiram, the hired hand, worked for room and board plus a dollar a day. Two of those three meals also fed two growing boys with their sister and younger cousin who were not shy at the table. Besides all the work connected to meals, there was sewing, mending, laundry and ironing to be done for the seven people in the household.

Lissie worked side by side with Aunt Jane but life was a blur and as flavorless as the food she put in her mouth, dutifully feeding her body while her heart felt like a rock in her chest. Valentine's Day drew near and she remembered the first valentine she received from Lew when they were both attending Riverview School.

This Valentine's Day 1863, Lissie sat on her bed as she opened the box holding her "precious things." It was made from her father's discarded cigar box and covered with bright blue gingham material scraps from one of her mother's dresses. Seeing Lew's first valentine to her, a sob gripped her throat. He had water-colored a heart and penned beneath "Be my valentine" in flowing penmanship. She kissed her pewter ring and held his card to her chest whispering, "I am your valentine forever. But you can no longer be mine." She turned abruptly, the box sliding off her lap as she buried her face in her pillow, trying to smother the sounds of her sobs.

Chapter 4

A WEEK BEFORE Lissie's birthday in March, Uncle Edgar came to the house at midday after an early morning trip into town. His face was glowing with excitement. "Lissie," he shouted. "You have a letter!"

It was crumpled and dirty, but it bore Lew's handwriting. Lissie had never been inclined to swoon, but the air in her chest seemed to whoosh from her body and the shape of Uncle Edgar's face appeared to alter. *Was this a letter from the grave* she wondered as Aunt Jane steadied her and led her to a chair. Her heart thumped so fast she thought it might jump from her chest. *Could Lew be alive?* Her shaky fingers fumbled at opening the letter. She read aloud:

January 5, 1863

Dear Lissie,

I am writing this letter to let you know I am very much alive and not wounded.

She stopped reading and just sat there, not visibly breathing. Then, as if the words on the crumpled piece of paper became understandable, she jumped up and screamed, "Lew is alive! He is alive!" and she hugged Uncle Edgar. Then she ran to her aunt. "Oh, Aunt Jane, God has given me a miracle," and she sobbed with joy in Jane's arms.

After the excitement calmed a bit, Uncle Edgar asked, "Well, Lisssie, are you going to read the rest of Lew's letter?"

"Edgar," Jane scolded, "it *is* a letter addressed to her, not the family."

"No," the girl replied. "I will share whatever miracle Lew has written," and she sat back down, wiped her eyes again and began to read.

The battle was going full tilt when we arrived at the Rappahannock River but we had to finish building a pontoon bridge to get across to Fredericksburg.

As we were crossing on the swaying, bobbing bridge, I felt a whisper of air pass my ear. A second later I saw a man several feet in front of me slump and fall into the river. A minute later a shell hit the pontoon mooring shaking the surface so bad we all scrambled for our balance. Despite the extra twenty pounds of ammunition on our backs, we ran for the riverbank. Shells and bullets seemed to fall on us from every direction. Many were wounded or killed just in that crossing.

We stayed in Fredericksburg that night, all the townsfolk having deserted their homes. In the morning the battle, now known as Burnside's Slaughter Pen, began.

Lee's army was behind a long stone wall and earthworks with their cannon located up on a hill overlooking a meadow. Our army would have to cross this meadow in order to engage the rebels. Regiment after regiment was sent in to no avail, those living through the advance toward enemy lines turning and running for their lives. My regiment was no exception.

That night we slept in another deserted house. The next day was Sunday decreed by both sides as a day of rest with no fighting. That night the Union Army silently stole back across the river. Unfortunately, our regiment was not told of the retreat as our captain had been killed in battle.

The next morning we awoke looking for someone to command us. As the town appeared deserted, we headed for the river and ran right into the 17th Georgia Regiment who ordered us to surrender. We did so without any sort of argument as the Union army seemed to have disappeared as had the pontoon bridge across the river.

I have no more paper at present, dear Lissie, so will continue my story when I can get some. I praise God for not having any holes shot in my body. However this imposed fast is not appreciated by my hearty appetite.

Your loving Benjie.

Lissie looked at her audience as she clasped the ragged piece of paper to her heart. "He *is* alive," she murmured.

Turning to her uncle, she asked, "What did Lew mean by an imposed fast?"

"I am thinking he had not had much to eat when he wrote that letter," he replied.

"How dreadful," sighed Aunt Jane. "I wonder when he will be paroled or exchanged for some rebel soldier?"

"He obviously had no idea when he wrote," said her husband.

Rising from the table, he headed for the barn, patting Lissie's shoulder as he passed. "This should lift your heart, little one."

"Yes, Uncle." Her smile enveloped her face, eyes shining with joyous tears and full-blown happiness.

That night after household chores were finished, Lissie sat down with pen and paper to write to her Benjie.

February 25, 1863

My dearest Benjie,

Your letter arrived "from the grave" today and you have no idea the joy I knew at reading of you being alive!

It has been more than a month since you wrote the letter. I pray that the "fast" you mentioned is long broken and you have had adequate rations since that time.

All are well here and I am better than "well" if that is possible, now that I know you are alive and whole. I so wish I might see your smiling face before me on my birthday which is March 1. What a wondrous gift your presence would be.

But until we can be together again, I am

Your loving Lissie.

She hoped against hope that Lew might be exchanged and sent home by her birthday, but that day came and went with no word from him. She put on a happy face for the family as Aunt Jane had baked an angel food cake especially for her day and Jennie had painted a card with her watercolors and Sally had printed a birthday greeting inside. Lissie was sure Aunt Jane had superintended the offering which made it that much more precious. The card joined

Lew's letters as well as the other precious items in her keepsakes box.

Life continued in routine fashion with a spark of hope kindled in Lissie's chest each time someone went to town which always included a stop at the post office. Jane still had family members in England as well as in New York state and Massachusetts. Edgar's family members were not such prolific letter writers, but he stayed abreast of up-to-date agricultural practices and current events by subscribing to two newspapers.

More than a week had passed since her birthday when Edgar returned from town with several envelopes in his hand. He breezed into the kitchen where his wife and niece were working and announced, "This household has been well served by the US Postal Service. My dears, come sit at the table and read your letters."

Jane had been preparing pie crusts and Lissie was punching down the dough in preparation for bread and rolls, some of which would appear at that evening's meal. They dusted their hands off on their aprons and hurried to the table.

"I daresay this one is from your sister, Susan, my dear," said Edgar as he handed the top letter to Jane. "This rather ragged missive is addressed to Miss Annaliese Facht," Edgar's eyes twinkled as he handed it over. "I wonder who the sender might be?" he teased.

Lissie slid a fingernail under the flap, and tuning out the dialogue between her aunt and uncle, read:

March 1, 1863

Dear Lissie,

I am sorry I cannot be a live birthday present for you so I shall write to you of my heart's longing from here at Camp Parole. This begins the third month I have been here waiting to be exchanged for some Rebel soldier. It seems the battles are somewhat lacking during winter as are the prisoner exchanges. Rumors around camp say many exchanges should occur soon as spring nears.

In the meantime, we parolees must invent ways to keep our minds and bodies busy. We are kept by law to do nothing "soldierly" and that often means irregular rations. We are free to wander the town of Annapolis but since we have not been paid our wages recently, the wandering is only beneficial for exercise. There is much skullduggery here, but I have managed to steer clear of such goings-on.

I truly do wish with all my heart to be able to celebrate completing my sixteenth year of life with you, dear Lissie. Let us pray toward that end.

Your loving Benjie

The older adults were watching her when Lissie looked up from her letter. She sighed and said, "Lew still does not know when he will be exchanged, and it sounds like he is still hungry." The last phrase ended with a sad gulp.

Jane leaned over and patted her hand. "Try not to worry, dear. Lew may well be hungry, but he is still a growing boy. I daresay he would be hungry even if he were here at home. Just think of the food Frederick manages to tuck into every time he sits at the table."

They all laughed, releasing the tension because Frederick at age 13 was rapidly nearing the height of his father, if not the breadth, and seemed to be in a perpetual state of hunger.

Lissie decided to write Eliza about Lew's latest adventure connected with his army life as she had done previously. Eliza had replied with sympathy and then with joy, but her interest was plainly focused on a young man she had met at a cotillion ball in Philadelphia. Lissie understood, but she still missed the closeness she and Eliza had once enjoyed.

March 13, 1863

Dear Eliza,

Your accounts of balls and French classes and embroidering table runners sound quite elegant. Perhaps you can teach me some new stitches on your next visit home. However, the French is no doubt much beyond my ability.

News from Camp Parole is not particularly cheerful as Lew has no idea when he might be exchanged. I pray it will happen soon.

Aunt Jane has agreed to allow me to take organ lessons from

Miss Mauldin, the organist at the Lutheran church. I so love the sound of that majestic pipe organ and the thought of actually making music on such an instrument causes my innards to tremble. My mother taught me some hymns on the pump organ we had at home, but of course, I have not played much since Jennie and I came here to live with Uncle Edgar four years ago.

I await with joy your next visit home. (Did I write that in proper Finishing School style?)

Your Best Friend Forever,
Sarah Annaliese Facht

Underneath her formal name written in her best calligraphic style, she signed "Lissie."

She waited in vain for more letters from Lew. One warm April night she awoke to the sound of pea gravel tinkling against her bedroom window. After the second handful sounded, she knew she was not dreaming and jumped out of bed, puzzled.

Looking down at the ground she was astonished to see a young man, and as a cloud moved on past the full moon, she realized it was Lew. In a flash she threw on her night robe and slippers and ran silently down the stair, grabbing a shawl off the coat pegs as she went.

Later, she wondered at her presence of mind as she shut the front door softly, her heart beating so wildly she was sure it would fly from her chest.

"Benjie! Oh, Benjie. I thought I might never see you again," she sobbed as she flung her arms around his waist. With her next breath tumbled out the words, "You have grown inches for my head no longer reaches your chin," and she laid her cheek against his chest and squeezed his ribs.

"The better to kiss your sweet-smelling hair, mein liebchen," he murmured. Then taking her hands, he kissed each in turn and then said, "I fear you may have become a loose woman, dear Lissie. Do you often fly out the door in the dead of night clothed in your nightwear?" The moonlight caught the twinkle in his eyes and she pulled one hand away and swatted at him with it.

"I only act this way with soldiers who are pronounced dead in battle and arrive home in quite a lively fashion," she jibed.

Then leading him to the swing on the front porch, she scolded, "Why did you not let me know you were coming home? No one seemed to know of your exchange when I saw your family at church two weeks ago."

"I, myself, did not know," he answered. "Last week a group of us were mustered to headquarters at Camp Parole and told to pack our gear to go home. We were exchanged. I was able to ride by train to Cressona and then walked home that night."

He continued. "All were in bed but Father opened the door at my knock and told me to spread my bedroll on the kitchen floor which I thought odd. The next morning I was awakened by a strange woman preparing breakfast. She informed me she was my father's new wife. It turns out her two young sons now occupy my former bed at night."

"I did not know this," gasped Lissie. "I have not seen your father and younger brothers and sister for many weeks. Only your sister, Maria, and her family. Does this new wife seem kind?" she asked, uncertainly.

"Much kinder than Father," replied Lew, "for he assigned me to chores and fieldwork on the morning of my return as if I had never left. Except that he made sure I understood my bed was now to be in the barn," he added wryly. "I think New Wife feels badly that her sons have taken my bed, but no one goes against what Father says."

Suddenly the front door opened and Edgar appeared carrying an old flintlock. When his eyes fell on the two young people, Lissie could see his scowl clearly in the moonlight. Apparently, Lew did too, for he jumped up and in serious tones said, "Sir, I can explain this unseemly visit."

"I think you should," said Edgar in a stern tone. Then his face relaxed and he chuckled. "Welcome home, Soldier Boy." Then looking him up and down, he amended that with, "No boy any longer, eh, Lew." And he stepped forward with an outstretched hand.

Edgar leaned against a porch pillar as Lew summarized what he had just told Lissie. "It seemed unfair for Lissie not to know I was home," the young man explained earnestly. "But Father has me working every minute of the day--barring meals." A grin crept over his face as he admitted, "New Wife is a good cook." Then in a more serious tone, "I did not know when I would see Lissie, so I thought up this plan tonight. I guess it was not such a good plan," he muttered.

"It is a mite unseemly," agreed Edgar, "but I think we can come up with a more proper one. Perhaps we can set a standing invitation for you to join us at table every Thursday evening."

"That is most kind of you, Uncle Edgar," chimed in Lissie. "Do you think you should write to Mr. Reber so he will allow Lew to join us?"

"Seems a rather strange request," replied Edgar. "Any man grown enough to be a solder should be able to decide where he wants to eat. What do you think, Lew?"

Embarrassed, the young man answered, "I think your message might make matters easier for me to come here. Mein vater does not like the thought of any labor time wasted, but he should be happy my appetite is not present during one meal of the week."

With that statement Lew was on his feet. Grabbing Lissie's hand, he kissed it and said, "I shall see you next Thursday, Lissie." Turning to Edgar, he shook his hand again, saying, "Thank you, Sir, for your kindness."

Niece and uncle watched the young man's long stride carry him rapidly down the lane and over a rise out of sight. "Enough excitement for one night, Lissie," said Uncle Edgar as he opened the door for her.

She stood on tiptoe and kissed his cheek. "Thank you, Uncle," and she ran upstairs to her room.

Life settled into a pleasant rhythm, at least for Lissie. Her uncle's farm was a prosperous one and he and Jane were kind, generous people. The younger children continued their schooling and Lissie continued to learn all the homemaking skills her aunt exemplified.

As for Lew, his lanky frame filled out due to his stepmother's cooking as well as the weekly visits to the Holtschlag household, but his dissatisfaction at his father's treatment grew as autumn neared.

One sultry August evening, Lissie and Lew were sitting in the swing on the front porch and she asked him how the crops were coming along.

"I judge them to be doing quite well. The corn is tasselling, and the cattle are looking sleek and fat. The clover will soon be due for another cutting—and Father cannot seem to get enough work from me. That is why I was so late to come tonight," he explained. "I cannot do enough to please him. I cannot work fast enough to please him. I find my life there to be so unbearable it makes me want to leave!"

"Dear Lew, I am sorry your father is so harsh." She scooted closer to him, hugged his arm and patted his hand. "You are only sixteen and I am even younger. I do not believe Uncle Edgar would consent to our marriage. And besides that, we have no money."

"I know this, Lissie. I know this." And he put his head in his hands.

As the days turned into weeks and harvest time was in full gear, Lew missed coming to supper. The next week he came, looking exhausted and apologized profusely to Jane. He explained that he and his brother Albert had "cradled" fifty acres of oats that week.

After supper as Lew and Lissie sat on the swing outside, she said, "Lew, you look so tired and unhappy."

He was silent for a moment and then spoke. 'Lissie, I think I must leave my father's farm so I can actually make a living. For all the work I have done since I returned from the army, I have only received room and board, the room being a bed in the hay mow." He continued in a bitter tone. "Father bought one change of clothing and one pair of shoes for each one in our family—except me!"

"How unfair," cried Lissie, aghast at the injustice done to her Benjie. "Can he not see you have grown taller these past months?"

"He pays me no mind at all," said Lew in a deadened tone. "It is as if I were a fence post in the back woodlot. I have bought new trousers and two shirts as well as a new pair of boots from the Mercantile in Cressona but now my salary from the army is all spent."

He turned to her with a determined tilt to his chin. "I truly believe I must leave here. I have heard of work on the railroads in Reading, so I shall head there first."

Lissie forced back the dread she felt rising in her throat. "If you believe this is best, Lew, you must do so. When do you think you might return?"

"Once I am settled and have steady employment, I can give you a better answer. Right now, I have no idea, but I cannot imagine returning to my father's farm. I promise to write to you as soon as I can."

He left with a jaunty lift to his step after kissing her goodbye. Lissie realized her Benjie was off to another adventure, the location unsure. *But at least he is not going where he could be shot,* she consoled herself.

Chapter 5

A WEEK LATER, Hiram came into the farmhouse with the mail. "Here is a letter for you, Miss Lissie." He grinned at her as she dropped the mop handle to the floor and hurried to him with an outstretched hand.

Sitting down, she read:

Dear Lissie,

Reading is a grand place. Although I was not able to get work on the railroad, I am working for a large livery stable. I am paid one dollar a day and have found a comfortable room at Mrs. McIntyre's Boarding House. I am happy to report that she is almost as good a cook as your Aunt Jane.

I miss you, Lissie. Please tell me all your interesting tidbits and how you are getting on with your organ lessons.

I have met the other fellows here at the boarding house, but they all appear to be older than me. I plan to find a church to attend this Sunday as I do not have to go to work until after noon on that day.

Please remember me to your aunt and uncle for they have been most kind to let us see each other and feed me, also.

Your loving Benjie

Lissie smiled to herself as she folded his letter and placed it back in the envelope.

"You are smiling so your letter must contain happy things," said her aunt. "Is Lew doing well, wherever he is, now?"

"Thank you, Aunt. Lew sounds much happier. He is living in a boarding house in Reading and works at a livery stable. You know how he enjoys good food and it seems the woman who runs the boarding house is almost as good a cook as you." She laughed and her aunt joined in.

"Yes. That young man of yours does like good food and plenty of it. Sort of seems like he might have a hollow leg." Jane chuckled.

The weeks rolled on and Lissie detected a hint of underlying loneliness in Lew's letters. *Or maybe that is just because I miss him so,* she scolded herself.

It was nearing Christmas and Jane's household was busy preparing for the holiday with baking and secretive crafting by both adults and children. Lissie had fashioned a housewife sewing kit even though Lew was no longer soldiering. It included needles, thread, buttons and scissors so he could do his own mending since he was not in a home environment. When she finished fashioning the felt pouch with pockets of varied sizes, she inserted a tender note. Preparation for her next gift had to, by necessity, be done at the last minute.

Lew loved molasses cookies and Lissie had asked Aunt Jane to share her secret recipe. The cookies, topped with sugar crystals, sparkled in the sunlight. Lissie felt sure the sight would gladden Lew's heart just as the taste would delight his stomach.

Two days into the new year of 1864, Uncle Edgar blew in from town with the household mail, stamping snow from his boots and heading for the fireplace. "There is a letter for you in this pile, Lissie," he said, rubbing his hands together after laying the pieces of mail on the kitchen table. "It is cold enough out there to freeze the pond 'most down to the mud. I hope it does not kill off the bass I stocked there last summer."

"How can the cattle get water," asked Jane.

"Hiram and I will need to keep chopping a spot at the spring," he replied, continuing to rub his hands. The spring feeds into the pond back of the barn."

While this conversation was going on, Lissie sat at the table, opening her letter from Lew. As she removed the message, she could feel something lumpy in the bottom of the envelope. She pulled out a thin chain threaded through a pewter heart. She laid it in her lap and read her letter.

Dear Lissie,

Your cookies arrived in fine shape with only three broken—so I ate them first. They were first rate pieces! I tried to parcel them out careful like but my appetite reminded me that a cookie is never better than when it is fresh. I regret to tell you that my discipline only lasted through the second day past Christmas. But, oh, how my stomach rejoiced!

I hope you like the "locket." The blacksmith here at the livery stable does filigree work besides hammering out horseshoes and the like. Truly an uncommon mix, but he lets me work with some of his metal scraps. That is how I came to fashion the heart. Let it be a symbol of my heart that beats only for you.

Your loving Benjie

Lissie picked up the locket, kissed it, and placed the chain around her neck. Putting Lew's letter in her apron pocket, she rose and returned to work in the kitchen, humming as she went.

A month later, another letter arrived from Lew.

Dear Lissie,

I am so happy that you like the locket I sent. Perhaps you will be happy also for the news I now have.

My brother Levi sent me word that our brother Gideon is coming home for several days on furlough at the end of March. He intends to re-enlist so I greatly wish to see him before he returns to the army. I am very homesick here and miss you so much, my sweet Lissie.

I am counting the hours until I see your sweet face, mein liebchen.

Your loving Benjie

Lissie jumped from her chair, for she was sitting at the kitchen table, and ran to hug her aunt.

"Aunt Jane, Lew is coming home! Lew is coming home! "

Her aunt patted her back. "That is wonderful news, Lissie." She led the girl back to the table, poured them both cups of tea and proceeded to attempt to piece together the details of the homecoming from her excited niece.

The closer March 31 neared, the more excited Lissie became. Jane caught her more than once standing before the dry sink, holding a potato in one hand, the paring knife in the other, and gazing out the window, immobile.

"Lissie, we need those potatoes to be cooked for tonight's supper, not next week some time."

At her aunt's humorous remark, the girl jerked, startled. "Yes, Aunt Jane. My mind was wandering miles away, it seems."

"No doubt somewhere on the road from Reading with a tall young man named Lew," remarked Jane with a chuckle.

Night fell with no sign of Lew. The family went to bed, but Lissie could not get to sleep thinking she might hear gravel thrown against her window, heralding the appearance of her sweetheart.

She awoke the next morning to the sound of the younger girls getting up and she realized she had overslept. Except she was so tired she didn't feel like she had slept at all. When she got downstairs, she discovered Uncle Edgar had taken pity on her and sent Hiram to milk Sukey.

"Jane looked in on you when we got up and said to let you rest," explained Edgar in a kind voice.

"You had dark circles under your eyes and tear-streaks on your face," whispered Aunt Jane. She had brushed by Lissie on her way to the kitchen to drain the bacon and pour the scrambled eggs into some of the reserved grease to cook. "Come slice some bread for toast. I did not make biscuits this morning," Aunt Jane stated.

Lissie knew her face must look puffy because her eyes felt swollen. Surely Lew was all right but she still worried. Why had he not sent word? Her imagination whirled with dreadful scenes.

That evening she glanced out the dining room window and glimpsed a stoop-shouldered Lew walking up the lane to the Holtschlag house. She ran to the door and out to meet him. "Lew, Lew, are you well? I was so frightened something had happened to you." Her words tumbled over themselves in her excitement.

His face brightened when he saw her and he asked, "Perhaps I could come and sit a spell?"

Then she noticed how exhausted he looked. Lew told her of his trip home, of how wonderful it was to see Gideon again. He concluded with the simple statement, "Father set me to work plowing today. I thought nothing of it at the time, but I see I have become a soft city dweller." His tone was rueful as he showed her the blisters on his palms from the plow handles. "I did not realize four months of town living would soften me up so," he continued. Old Dobbin pretty much ended up pulling me along with the plow by sunset."

"Lew," Lissie exclaimed, "please come inside and let me ask Aunt Jane what remedy she might have to ease those blisters."

"Very well," he agreed and groaned quietly as he rose from the swing where he had seated himself.

Jane clucked her tongue at the sight of the blisters and went to fetch her concoction of tea tree and sunflower seed oils. After cleaning Lew's hands, she dabbed the blisters with the oil mixture and said sternly, "Tell George Reber to let those hands of yours rest until the blisters heal up."

Lew shuffled his feet and replied, "I greatly doubt he will allow me to stay on if I cannot work in the field."

Edgar joined in on the conversation at that statement. "Talk with your brothers who have left home. Maybe they will be able to provide you aid. Or at least some understanding to your father," he muttered, shaking his head in disbelief.

Lew soon took leave of the family, thanking Jane for her medical kindness and Edgar for his advice.

Lissie walked with him to the lane, wondering aloud when she might see him again. "I do not know, Lissie," he sighed. "But I will do my best to return in a few days."

It was more than a week before Lew made his way to the Holtschag farm on a Thursday evening. The family had finished supper and was sitting in the parlor, Edgar and the younger children reading. Jane and Lissie were darning the never-ending supply of socks that seemed to delight in wearing thin and fraying into gaping holes. A knock was heard at the front door as Jane had just finished complaining about Manfred needing to cut his toenails. "This hole is big enough to push your entire big toes through it," she scolded

Edgar went to the door and admitted Lew who greeted the family and then asked to see Lissie. The two went to sit on the porch swing.

"I have missed you, Lew," said Lissie in a wistful tone. "What has kept you away for so long?"

"My brother Gideon and I went to visit our older sister, Susanna. Neither of us had seen her since we joined the army, and Gideon had been away for near three years. Then when we got back to the farm, Gideon tried to persuade Father to pay me a decent wage for he told Father he intended to re-enlist in the Army. Father started bemoaning the fact it was impossible to find farm hands with the war continuing so long."

"Did you father agree to pay you a living wage?" she asked.

Lew shrugged rather sheepishly and answered, "Gideon told Father other fellows are making at least $2 per day on the railroad and other public works." He gave the swing a vicious push with his foot. "The best mein vater would agree to pay me was $9 per month and board through harvest and just board during the winter.

"Lissie, if a stranger had offered me that kind of wage, I would have turned my back on him and walked away. But instead, I accepted Father's offer," he sighed.

Lissie's heart sank at his news for she could see he was making little progress in building a nest egg for their future. She did her best to be encouraging as she patted his hand and said, "I think you did well in honoring your father, Lew. He needs help on the farm."

"This is true," he replied, "but he only remembers the 'old country,'" referring to the family's immigration from Germany twenty-five years earlier. "A fair wage for an honest day's work did not happen in the family there, so I have heard tell. He thinks the same way for me now."

That spring Lissie often saw Lew each Thursday evening after sunset but they ate no more evening meals together. First came preparation of the fields for planting corn, oats and wheat. Next, the crops were planted. Alfalfa and clover had to be cut and stored as the months rolled on, and Lew seemed to get taller and thinner. Finally the crops were all harvested and the following Thursday evening Lew once again visited the Holtzschlag household.

After he greeted the various family members, Lissie led Lew outside to the porch swing. The October air was nippy so she snuggled close to her sweetheart's shoulder. A pumpkin colored moon, almost full, had risen above the ridge of trees across the pasture and Lissie could see the fatigue and discouragement etched in Lew's face.

"What has you looking so dejected tonight, Benjie?" she asked, in a soft voice.

"The crops are nearly all harvested and stored in the barns," he stated with a tired sigh. "There are five more acres of corn to shuck and then we are finished."

"Is that not a good thing?"

"For Father, yes. But from the month of November until spring, I shall be earning no money. Just being a servant on mein vater's farm for a roof over my head and food to eat." His tone was bitter as he continued. "At this rate, Lissie, we shall never be able to marry."

His fists were clenched on his knees and she reached over and tenderly covered the one nearest her with a warm hand. "Please do not despair, Benjie. We will be able to wed when the time is right. You have honored your father in helping with the farm from planting through harvest, and I am sure God will bless you for such honor."

He raised her hand to his lips and kissed it. "You always know what to say to make me feel better." He smiled and she saw the lines around his mouth smooth away.

The next time they were together, Lew brought exciting news. "They are saying in town that a new regiment is forming in Harrisburg. I intend to go there next week and join up."

Lissie gasped, "Oh, Lew. You had such a horrible time in the army before, getting sick and then getting captured. And I thought you had died," she finished in a whisper.

"But do you not see, Lissie? I made it through all that and being in Camp Parole was the easiest living I have had since I left Riverview School," he laughed. Then he sobered, took her nearest hand in both of his and said, "Please understand. This is a way to earn good money. If I stay with Father this winter I earn nothing."

She could tell he was excited about his enlistment prospects and she also understood the futility of staying the winter on his father's farm. Their leave-taking was bittersweet and Lissie's eyes blurred with tears as she waved goodbye to Lew and watched his figure disappear over the ridge.

She heard nothing from him until he showed up on the Holtschlag doorstep one blustery December evening. Edgar opened the door to admit him.

"Come in, Son, before you freeze your toes." Then turning toward the kitchen, Edgar called, "Lissie, there is someone here to see you."

When she saw Lew, she ran to him. "Oh Lew, how cold you must be. Come sit by the fire and warm yourself," and she took his outerwear, leading him to a chair by the hearth.

As he was plied with a cup of steaming hot tea, Lissie urged him to tell of his adventures since she had last seen him. He did so.

"Like I told you, I headed for Harrisburg to see about joining up with a cavalry company I heard about. We stayed in camp for about a week but then the officers wanted us to join the infantry instead. Our entire group refused, so the company was disbanded. There I was, among strangers with no money and an uncertain future."

He stopped and sipped more of his tea. Then he continued his tale. "I found a job in a rail car shop for $2.35 per day and kept body and soul together besides saving enough to travel to Philadelphia where I heard of new companies I could join. When I arrived, the offers were not pleasing as I had had my fill of drilling and wanted to join a veteran regiment. I inquired at the Navy but their quota of men was full. The Marines offered me $800 to join them for a four-year contract but that long a time did not appeal to me.

"So I decided to make my way back home and was able to get on a coal train for about ten miles. Then it was pulled onto a side spur and I was told to get off. I started walking and soon came upon some men working along the track. They told me a fast freight would be coming along soon and if I wanted to jump on, it would be all right.

"I had never jumped on or off a moving train but decided to try it. Soon the freight roared up. I tried to judge the speed and spotted the boxcar I was aiming for. Making a running jump, I managed to grab hold of the wooden doorframe but that was all. I could feel my legs actually flying in the wind as I hung on to that doorframe, almost by my fingernails. My hands were getting numb and my right arm began to quiver so I knew I must somehow hoist the rest of my body up onto the floor of that boxcar. Otherwise, I would be flung off the speeding car down a rocky embankment. I took a huge breath, tensed every muscle, and lunged upward."

His audience gave a great sigh for they were all holding their breath by this time.

Jane broke the silence. "Lew, all I can say is your guardian angel must have been extra busy that day."

"Yes, ma'am," he answered. "After I managed to crawl onto that boxcar, I just sat on the floor and shook. Then I cried. Then I thanked God for saving me from a broken leg or worse."

Teacups were re-filled, the younger children sent to bed, and Lissie sat close to Lew, happy he was back home, but horrified at his adventure. The heat was relaxing and Lew yawned.

"I must be getting back to the farm," he said. "Perhaps we may meet at church on Sunday."

"We will be there," Edgar assured him, and Lissie helped Lew pile on his heavy clothes to return home.

That night she lay in bed, unable to sleep. As she replayed the scene of Lew hopping the freight train, she wondered, *am I ready to share my future with a man who seems to seek out danger? What sort of future* do *I want?* With a sigh, she turned over and went to sleep.

Chapter 6

February 1, 1921
Palmyra, Missouri

JANUARY'S SUBZERO WEATHER lasted about six days but by the first of February, temperatures seemed quite pleasant in comparison. "It's time for me to start mending harness and checking farm equipment," said Landis. "I will be out in the barn until supper time, Mother."

Annaliese sat in her rocker after she had cleared up the dinner dishes and put her kitchen to rights. Her eyes fell on the calendar and she realized this was the day she and Lew had married back in 1865. *How many years ago?* she asked herself. *M-m, fifty-six.* She sighed. *Well, Lew, we did not quite make it to forty-nine years together, but what a journey it was. 1865. The War had not yet ended. Oh, yes,* she sniffed, *that was the reason I insisted on being married. What a nervy girl I was!*

Annaliese smiled to herself and began conjuring up those scenes from long ago, soon drifting to a state of drowsiness.

Chapter 7

Winter 1864
Cressona, Pennsylvania

LISSIE SEARCHED THE faces at church that next Sunday, but Lew was not there. Her distress eased when she heard Eliza squeal her name in excitement. Her blond hair done up in a sophisticated chignon, Eliza was dressed in a full-skirted cobalt-blue taffeta with lace trim at her neck and sleeves.

The girls hugged and Lissie spoke first. "When did you get home from Philadelphia?"

"Just this Friday, but oh, Lissie, I have so much news to tell you." She waved a diminutive hand in front of Lissie's face with a sparkling blue sapphire set squarely on the fourth finger of her right hand.

The confidences had to stop as the minister walked up the steps to take his place on the stage signaling the service to begin.

Afterwards, Eliza asked Jane if Lissie might be permitted to come home with her. Jane knew her niece felt somewhat adrift with her friend so far away at school and never knowing what Lew might choose to do next. So she allowed the girl to spend time with her friend, particularly as the Holtschlag household did its best to observe the Sabbath by not doing any unnecessary labor.

After eating a delicious roast beef dinner with apple tarts for dessert, served by the Murchiston cook, the girls retired to Eliza's room. Eliza had much more to tell her friend. Whenever there was a lag in her recitation of happenings at Madame Ascott's Finishing School, Lissie would ask another question, which in turn would generate another story.

Of course, the main topic of interest was Captain Maxwell, the young Union officer who had stolen Eliza's heart and placed the lovely engagement ring on her finger. After hearing how handsome her captain was and how esteemed he was in his company, Lissie asked, "Have you set a date for your wedding?"

"No," sighed Eliza. "John does not want to marry until this dreadful war is over and he feels sure it will be soon. Perhaps we may be married on Christmas of this next year. I shall be seventeen by that time. Oh, Lissie, would not a Christmas wedding be just the thing!"

Then she realized she had done most of the talking. "What of you and Lew? Do you still consider yourselves engaged?"

"Indeed, yes! But Lew's earning prospects have been so poor, working on his father's farm will never give us enough to start a life together as husband and wife. And recently he has attempted to re-enlist in the army!"

Her dejected tone led Eliza to hug her friend and speak in a comforting fashion. "Do not fear. Lew loves you and he is a good worker. He has done a man's work for several years, yet he has seen only seventeen birthdays. That speaks well of him."

As Eliza's father's hired man drove Lissie to the Holtschlag farm in the family buggy, she thought about the comparison between Eliza's life and her own. Money seemed to be the main difference. She could see no way for Lew to earn a reasonable nest egg in order for them to marry any time soon.

Christmas 1864 saw frequent snowstorms which continued into the New Year. When Lew came to see Lissie at the Holtschlag farmstead in mid-January, he had exciting news. At least, as far as he was concerned.

"Lissie, I just heard yesterday General Grant has called for 100,000 men to join up for one year or until the war's end. I should be able to join a veteran regiment or perhaps even re-enlist in my former one."

She was less than excited about this prospect and said so. "Lew, I know you can see no future working on your father's farm. But why can you not work on the railroad or work as a blacksmith? I beg you. Please do not go back into the army! You nearly died from a fever. And remember the close encounters with bullets whizzing by your ear? Truly, I cannot bear the thought of overhearing someone mention your name as missing or thought dead. Or of reading a newspaper account of soldiers killed in battle and seeing your name." She turned from him with a sob as she remembered the rending grief she had suffered at hearing of Lew's supposed death two years earlier.

He took the hand she had raised to wipe her eyes and squeezed it. "I think I do not understand this grief. But I do remember how I mourned mein mutter. I wish not to give you such pain."

The young lovers had been given the parlor for privacy, so they felt no qualms at speaking their thoughts, freely.

They sat in silence for a moment. Then Lissie turned to Lew with a very determined look. "Lew, since you are set on this course of soldiering, if something were to happen to you, I would much rather be your widow than your girlfriend."

He gasped in surprise and then grinned. "Why, Lissie. Are you proposing to me?"

She ducked her head, blushing, not finding his comment at all amusing. Head now raised, spine straight, she looked directly at him. "Do not joke, please! I am sixteen so am now allowed to marry. We have spoken much of marrying so I see no reason to wait. If you were to get sick or wounded, I could go to you, even to the front lines, and nurse you." She remembered with horror his tale of being in hospital during his bout with fever and nearly starving to death. "Please, dear Benjie, consider this possibility for my peace of mind."

Back at the Reber farm, Lew tossed and turned on the straw mattress laid on his brothers' bedroom floor. *I cannot stay here,* he mused. *Re-enlistment seems to be the only honorable, truly patriotic answer for me. Is it fair to keep Lissie waiting for me just as my sweetheart? I* do *want to marry her, but am I ready for that commitment?* Then he remembered the hollow loneliness he had felt since his mother died. When he was with Lissie, that empty feeling seemed to be filled.

He sighed, turned over one more time and went to sleep.

The next morning Lew informed his family he was re-enlisting. His stepmother patted his shoulder as she walked by with a pot of coffee. His younger siblings buzzed with excitement at the prospect of his soldiering. His father, looking up from his plate said, "Very well," and continued eating. Lew was grateful his father had allowed him to finish his breakfast before he walked to Cressona to re-enlist in the 50th Regiment of the Pennsylvania Volunteers.

"See to it that you are in Philadelphia to join your company on February 12," stated the clerk. "You have ten days to get there.

Here is a voucher for $500 as bounty for joining up." He handed Lew a slip of paper.

The young soldier wasted no time taking it to the Cressona State Bank and received a Certificate of Deposit. Tucking the paper safely into his shirt pocket, Lew started down the road to the Holtschlag farm. He intended to give Lissie the deposit certificate and formally ask Edgar for her hand in marriage.

When Lew appeared on their front porch after dinner, Jane opened the door. "Lew, what brings you here mid-day?"

Shuffling his feet a bit, he stammered, "I come to ask Mr. Edgar for marriage with Lissie—with Annaliese."

The girl in question walked up behind her aunt in time to hear his explanation and giggled. "Lew, you always get your English tangled when you are nervous."

Jane turned to her niece and in a stern tone, but with a twinkle in her eye, said, "Hush, Miss. Go fetch your uncle from the barn. He said he would be mending harness there this afternoon."

Edgar duly fetched, and all settled in the parlor, Lew managed to speak forth his wish to marry Lissie.

"Is this also your wish, Lissie?" asked her uncle in a formal tone.

She clasped her hands over her heart and nodded. "Oh yes, Uncle Edgar. I do so want to be Lew's wife."

"I have seen that you are a good worker, son," stated Edgar. "But I wonder at the timing of this marriage as you are heading for the battle field. It would seem to me…"

"Uncle," interrupted Lissie, "we know the perils, for Lew has experienced war already. And I have experienced mourning from that time. Were something to happen to dear Lew, I far prefer to be a widow than a mere fiancée."

"It appears you have seriously considered this unusual situation," stated Edgar, rubbing his chin thoughtfully, "and since these are unusual times, I see no reason to stand in your way."

Lew was instantly out of his seat, shaking Edgar's hand and saying, "Thank you, sir," while Lissie jumped up and hugged his neck, whispering, "Thank you, Uncle."

Ever the practical one, Jane asked, "When do you intend to take this step?"

The two young people looked at each other, mystified. They had not thought that far ahead.

"I suggest that I take you two sweethearts into visit Pastor Jamison in the morning to get a marriage license and arrange for him to conduct the ceremony the next day. Is that a workable plan, Jane?" Edgar asked, looking at his wife.

She pursed her lips and said, "It does not leave much time for baking in preparation for a reception after the ceremony. But yes, my friends will help make this a joyous celebration."

And so it was that on February 1, 1865, Sarah Annaliese Facht married Lewis Benjamin Reber. Friends and neighbors came to the Holtschlag farmhouse to wish the newlyweds a long life together. Lew's stepmother attended the reception along with his younger sister, Amanda, but his father and younger brothers did not come for it was a week day.

In order to allow for privacy for the newlyweds at the Holtschlag home, the boys were moved to pallets on the kitchen floor next to the hearth.

Lissie entered the bedroom hand in hand with Lew and he turned her to him, tipping up her chin and looking into her eyes. "Mein liebchen, I kiss your lips as my sweet wife. I think this day never come, but I thank the good God it is here."

Taking care to disrobe with their backs to each other, Lew was under the covers first, enjoying the pearly sheen of his new wife's skin and watching her brush the waves of hair from the braided coronet she had fashioned for her bridal day.

Lew turned out the lamp and then lay down, reaching for his love. Their coming together was clumsy and tender, painful and ecstatic.

The next morning Lew woke up to see Lissie looking at him with tender eyes. "Good morning, wife," he smiled and took her in his arms.

Some time later, Lissie, nestling close to him, whispered in his ear, "I do believe Aunt Jane's adage of 'Practice makes perfect' may be true in many ways." She giggled, and he rolled over and kissed her again with enthusiasm.

That day, their first as a married couple, Lissie and Lew prepared for his leave taking the following day. He had his knapsack from two years ago at Camp Parole which they began to fill. First, they fitted in rolled clothing articles. Lew's extra cotton shirt was folded and rolled around an extra pair of flannel undergarments and the pair of woolen socks Lissie had knitted for his Christmas gift.

Folded into a handkerchief she had fashioned from Aunt Jane's quilt scraps, Lew laid a bar of lye soap his stepmother had given him, a "brick" of twelve matches, and his comb. Aunt Jane gave Lew a pencil from the household's supply as well as five sheets of paper. These along with the "housewife's kit," of needles, thread and buttons, was stuffed into the very bottom corner of Lew's knapsack.

He declared himself ready for the trip and the two then made themselves useful to Lissie's aunt and uncle.

"Lew, go to the barn and ask Edgar how you might help," suggested Jane. "Oh, and take the milk pail with you as he may put you to milking Old Sukey. That will allow Lissie to stay in the warm house with me as we finish preparing supper."

Lew left the house, whistling, and Lissie started toward the dish shelves to begin setting the table for the next meal. Her aunt stopped her with a touch on her shoulder. "Come sit for a bit and we shall have a cup of tea, child. The beef is roasting along with the carrots and potatoes, so we have a minute."

"How have you fared as a young wife, my dear?" Jane asked in a kind voice.

Lissie blushed and then smiled, "I think I have fared well, Aunt." But the next minute tears glistened in her hazel eyes. "When I think of Lew leaving me tomorrow, my heart hurts so much, I feel I may die."

The older woman arose and hugged her, whispering, "That is love, my dear. Much joy and much pain often wrapped up in one all-encompassing emotion."

That night the young couple snuggled under the covers once Lew had turned off the lamp. He hugged his young wife to him so tightly she squeaked and then giggled."Oh, Lissie," he sighed, "I do not know how I can leave you. Your warmth, the feel of you," he nibbled at an ear, "the taste of you...."

Their lovemaking was at first frantic and then slow as if to make the sensation and expression of their physical love last for a lifetime. Finally, they slept, in blissful exhaustion.

Lissie woke first, smelling the aroma of frying bacon wafting up the stairway. She realized she was clamped by a muscular arm holding her tight to a warm body. Sensing impending action if she did not disengage herself immediately, she threw off the covers and grabbed her night robe.

"Aunt Jane has let us sleep in. Can you not smell the bacon frying and the bread toasting?"

Lew made a half hearted grab at the covers as he opened one eye then the other. "What a cruel wife you are to expose me to the elements in this cold bedroom," he teased. "Come. Give your soldier husband a morning kiss," he commanded.

"I am quite busy dressing for the day, husband," retorted Lissie. "I believe you shall have to come to *me* for that good morning kiss."

With that, Lew launched himself from his side of the bed and grabbed Lissie who had been sitting on her side, rolling on her stockings.

With a playful growl, Lew pinned her to the bed and began kissing her face, then moving to whatever areas of skin might be available to caress. She squealed in laughter.

Their love play halted with a jolt when Aunt Jane's voice was heard from the bottom of the stairway. "Anyone awake enough to play is awake enough to work!"

"Yes, Aunt Jane," came a masculine and feminine duet in answer. Minutes later, the two were downstairs where Jane pointed Lissie to the kitchen to oversee frying potatoes and Lew was directed to the barn to clean stalls and spread fresh straw for the cows.

That homey scene plus a warm, filling breakfast ushered in the hour for Lew's leave taking. The train to Philadelphia was due in Cressona at 11 o' clock and Edgar planned to drive his niece and her new husband into town so she could bid him goodbye at the depot.

They arrived about thirty minutes before the train warned of its appearance. Lissie and Lew had been sitting on a bench inside the depot with their arms around each other's waists, saying very little, just holding on to each other. The thrumming sound of wheels on the tracks alerted them to the train's approach. But when Lissie heard the whistle, it seemed to cleave her heart and for a moment she stopped breathing.

Then Lew stood, shouldering his knapsack, pulling her up to stand beside him. Exiting the depot, they walked hand in hand to the car where Lew would climb aboard. He tilted up Lissie's chin, and looking intently into her soft hazel eyes, he said, "I so love you, my sweet Lissie. I will be counting the hours until we are together again." He leaned down and kissed her, hard, then turned sharply and climbed aboard the train.

She watched him progress through the car, until he settled by a window and waved, blowing her a kiss. The train began to move, both of them waving, the cold February wind cutting through Lissie's cloak, chilling her arms and face as much as Lew's leave taking had driven icicles of dread through her heart.

Chapter 8

THE FAMILY WAS relaxing in the parlor the next Sunday afternoon. The sunshine streaming through the front windows and the warmth coming from the pot-bellied stove in the corner gave a snug, comfortable feeling to the room. Edgar was dozing in his easy chair and Jane was knitting socks The younger children were playing a marble game and Lissie sat in a corner of the horsehair sofa with a linen napkin she was hemming for her hope chest. Actually, the material lay in her lap, half finished, as she gazed into space, trance-like.

Jane looked up from her work and over at her niece. "Lissie, Mrs. Braintree stopped me to visit for a minute after church this morning."

Edgar roused at the sound of her voice and said, "I did not realize you and Mrs. Braintree were such bosom friends." He winked at his wife for he knew Jane felt the lady in question seemed to be overly proud of her social standing in the community. Just because her husband was the mayor did not mean she put her shoes on any differently from anyone else--that is, one at a time.

Jane laid Manfred's half-finished sock in her lap."As I was about to say when I was interrupted," and she glared at Edgar, "Mrs. Braintree said her elderly maiden aunt who is somewhat crippled needs a live-in companion. She said as how Sally and Jennie appeared to be grown to the age of mother's helpers, perhaps Lissie might be willing to hire on as her Aunt Madge's companion."

"How much are they willing to pay Lissie? What do you know of this old woman, Jane? Would live-in companion mean Lissie would get no free time?"

After firing all these questions at Jane, Edgar turned to his niece. "What do you think, Lissie? Is this something you would like to try?"

She looked at her uncle, hands folding and re-folding in her lap. "I never thought to leave your home, Uncle Edgar, except to go wherever my husband might go." Her voice cracked. "And I for sure cannot follow Lew to war." She cleared her throat then, and said, "I should be glad to meet Miss Madge. If she and I deal well together, I will work for her." Bravado gone from her voice, she added, "I should certainly miss all of you."

"It is not like you will have gone to live at the end of the world, should you get this job," remarked Aunt Jane. "I shall take you to meet this woman and be certain you are paid a fair wage and given comfortable working conditions."

The next day after the younger children left for school and the house set to rights for the next meal, Jane asked Edgar to hitch the horses to the buggy and she and Lissie set out for Cressona. Conversation was sparse as Lissie was busy imagining all sorts of dark possibilities. The thought of leaving the loving, comfortable home she had known for five years was truly frightening.

Soon they were standing before the door of a gabled cottage. At Jane's knock, Mrs. Braintree opened the door.

"Do come in, Jane," she said. Then peering past Jane, the lady continued, "And this must be Lissie."

Lissie nodded in assent, thinking, *I almost feel as if I should curtsey*. She nearly snickered at the thought of what a clumsy mess she would make of that.

They were led through a hallway to a brightly lit room opposite the parlor, with vases of flowers and shelves full of books. An elderly woman sat in a winged easy chair with her feet propped on an ottoman. She looked up from the embroidery she had been stitching.

"Aunt Madge, this is Mrs. Jane Holtschlag and her niece, Lissie. The girl I mentioned to you this morning," she added.

"How do," said the old dame. "Sit," and she pointed at a sofa to her left.

"Lissie. What kind of name is that?"

"My given name is Annaliese," replied Lissie.

"Long name, Girl," retorted the old woman. "How old might you be?"

"Sixteen, ma'am."

"And what manner of things have you learned to do in those sixteen years?"

Lissie looked at the old woman, puzzled.

"Do not sit there like a ninny, girl! Have you gone to school? Can you cook and mend? Do you stitch fancy work?" and the old woman touched the doily on her lap.

"Oh, yes, ma'am." I finished sixth grade at Riverview School and was granted the reader's award in grade five. I can play the organ—a little. And Aunt Jane has taught me to bake breads and pies and roast meats and vegetables. I have started stitching a Wedding Ring quilt and have knit socks for Lew. And I milked our cow, Old Sukey most mornings.

"Well," the old woman remarked with dry humor, "You will not be milking a cow at my house, but the reading and the sewing, and perhaps the baking might be welcome. I need a young person to fetch things for me." She nodded to her feet which Lissie now saw were swollen. "I do not move around like I once could and my eyes are not as sharp as yesteryear. They tire easily, as well."

"What do you think, Girl?"

Before Lissie had a chance to answer, Aunt Jane entered the conversation. "I believe we need to know what sort of accommodations Lissie would have as well as what salary she would receive. Then she can give you her answer."

Miss Madge gave her a dark look but replied. "She would receive room and board plus $5.00 per week with a half day off on Sunday. Lest you think this is a princely sum for reading to an old lady, you would be a constant companion—which includes helping me get into bed and seeing me comfortably settled at night. The job requires that we both deal well together. Now, what do you say, Girl?"

"I am willing to try," replied Lissie.

Aunt Jane was not quite finished with her questions. "Will Lissie be required to cook and do laundry, also?"

"Good heavens, no," snorted Miss Madge. "I am not hiring a drudge. I am hiring a companion."

"Very well, then," said Jane. "Since Lissie is willing, I believe you have a new companion."

"Splendid," said Mrs. Braintree, for she had been substituting for the last companion who had moved to Ohio two weeks earlier. "When can you begin work, Lissie?"

"I should think someone from the farm can bring me with my belongings tomorrow morning," she answered, but looked at Jane for agreement. Jane nodded.

"Very well," said Miss Madge. "Glad that is settled."

As Mrs. Braintree ushered them out, they could hear Madge's querulous voice command, "Florence, bring me a cup of tea once the door is closed."

Jane and her niece had plenty to talk about on the way home. "Do you think you can be happy working there, Lissie?"

"I shall miss all of you at home," replied the girl, "but I believe I can do what is required. Besides, whatever I earn can be put aside for a nest egg when Lew comes home from war."

Jane reached over and patted Lissie's hand. "That is a good outlook to have, my dear. A worthwhile goal." She squelched the thought, *if young Lew makes it back from the war.* Such a negative idea would help no one.

That night Lissie folded her blue serge wedding dress/church dress into a small trunk. She and Jennie had packed their belongings in it, back when they moved to the Holtschlags after their mother died. Also included were her extra work dress and apron, one good dress and one work dress for summer as well as her sunbonnet and her extra pairs of stockings, drawers, petticoats and chemises. On top of them all, nestled her "Precious Things." Lissie opened the box again to be sure Lew's $500 certificate of deposit was safely stowed there. It was.

Breakfast the next morning was a bittersweet experience. First, Lissie made her way to the barn and milked Sukey for the last time, also saying goodbye to her tiger stripe cat.

The younger girls were quiet as they set the table for breakfast. Lissie had always been a part of Jennie's life and her little sister was finally realizing she would be seeing very little of Lissie after today.

"May I sit in your lap before I must leave for school?" whispered the little girl.

"Of course you can," whispered Lissie, bending down to look into her sister's eyes. Taking her hands, Lissie kissed them both and said, "I will be back to eat Sunday dinner with you and everyone else."

"Yes, but my bed will be lonely tonight," said the eight-year-old with tears threatening to spill.

"Oh, sweet Jennie. My bed will also be lonely tonight," and

Lissie hugged her little sister. "We must each go to the window before we get into bed and tell Mr. Moon that we are both looking at him so we will not feel so forlorn." That idea satisfied Jennie and she scampered off to search for her pencil box.

Once the younger children were off to school and the kitchen cleaned from breakfast, Jane sent Lissie to the barn to fetch Edgar. He hitched up the horses to the wagon because he intended to sell some hay to the livery stable that day in addition to delivering his niece to her new place of employment.

Lissie looked around the bedroom she had shared with her little sister and cousin and felt a lump rise in her throat. She swallowed it down and was strangely grateful she was not leaving the room where she and Lew had spent two magical nights before he left—even if that room was in the same house. She spotted her hair ribbons, pins, and combs. How did she manage to forget to pack them? Opening her trunk she swept them onto the top of her clothing. Giving the room one last fond glance, she turned just as Edgar came up the stairs.

"All ready, Lissie?"

"Yes, Uncle. My trunk is packed and locked. I will meet you out front as soon as I grab my cloak and bonnet."

She ran downstairs and went first to Jane. "Aunt Jane, I already miss you and I have not yet left. Thank you for your kindness and your teachings."

Jane patted her shoulder and said, "You and Jennie are easy to love. And I have practiced teaching housewifely skills to you so that they might be perfected with Sally and Jennie." She smiled but Lissie could see the tears glistening in her eyes.

As Lissie put on her cloak, bonnet and gloves, Jane said, "Remember, you are allowed a half day free on Sunday. We shall plan to have you to ourselves each Sunday after church until you must return at nightfall."

The girl hugged her aunt and as she kissed her cheek, she whispered, "I will be counting the hours until I see you all again." Then she was out the door and had jumped into the wagon beside Uncle Edgar.

Upon arriving at Miss Madge's house, Lissie and Edgar were duly admitted, her trunk on her uncle's shoulder. Mrs. Braintree ushered them in and led the way to the upstairs bedroom Lissie would occupy. Edgar lowered her trunk to the foot of the bed, gruffly said goodbye to his niece and hurried off to the livery stable.

She did not have time to be tearful at Edgar's leave taking. Mrs. Braintree was anxious to get Lissie settled with Miss Madge so she could return to her own household. When they entered what was called the Morning Room, Miss Madge was dozing. At the sound of their footsteps, her head snapped up and she appeared to be the sprightly minded dowager Lissie had met previously.

"So, you are finally here," she remarked. "I am sure that relieves your mind greatly, Florence," she said to her niece. Directing her attention back to Lissie she said, "Are you well settled in your room, Girl?"

Lissie took a deep breath and said, "No, ma'am. There was no time as I have just arrived these few minutes ago."

"You are in quite a tizzy to be gone from my house, Florence." As her niece opened her mouth to protest, Madge continued. "Never mind. No excuses need be made. You have your own household to run and I am thankful for your aid with mine these past few days. Go on now," and she made a dismissive gesture with both hands.

Florence Braintree decided she should leave on a good footing with her aunt, so she kissed her withered cheek and said, "Send Minnie to fetch me if this arrangement does not work out." Nodding at Lissie, she turned and left the room.

Miss Madge cleared her throat and said, "I forget your name, Girl, but I would like some tea. Go to the kitchen and tell Cook what I need."

"Yes, Ma'am. And my name is Annaliese."

"Too long a name. I shall call you, Girl. Go on now," and the old lady waved her away.

Lissie left the room, hoping she would have no trouble finding the kitchen. The house was not laid out in the straight forward manner of the Holtschlag farmhouse and to confuse matters further was larger than it appeared from the street. After two false starts, she opened the door to a sunny room lined with shelves and counters and a cook stove and oven alongside a window.

When she spoke to the large woman who had her back to her, rolling out piecrust, Lissie was startled to see a Negro. She managed not to blurt out in shock, but she apparently did not mask her surprise, for the woman laughed and said, "Ain't you seen a black woman afore?"

"Yes ma'am," said Lissie. "I guess I was just startled."

"What you need, Missy?" asked the cook.

"Miss Madge sent me for a cup of tea."

"I got the teakettle on the stove. Give me a minute to git the tea trolley ready." The cook went into immediate action, tea leaves in a fancy pot with hot water poured over them, delicate cups and saucers, a bowl of sugar cubes, and a small pitcher of creamy milk. In less than five minutes, it was all assembled and Lissy was told, "There you is, Missy. Roll it on in to Miss Madge."

The day continued with new experiences for Lissie ranging from fetching shawls guarding against drafts to reading to the sleepy dowager. By the time the old lady was ready for bed, Lissie felt as tired as if she had helped Aunt Jane with the household laundry.

When Miss Madge was comfortably tucked into bed with her hot water bottle just so and the drapes closed tightly against any night drafts, Lissie was free for the evening. She yearned to look over her new domain, but was so tired from the stress of newness--people, tasks and surroundings--she was asleep only minutes after her head touched the pillow.

The next morning Lissie awoke, wondering if she had overslept, but she had not been told when she was to rise and begin waiting on Miss Madge. She sat up, stretched, and looked around. The bedroom was pleasant appearing with pink-sprigged flower wallpaper and white cotton drapes at the window, sporting an elegant eyelet edge. An oaken chiffarobe stood in one corner consisting of a tall section for hanging clothes and a marble-topped chest of five drawers with a mirror. Lissie hugged herself at the thought of such elegance just for her. Sitting on the marble top was a china washbasin decorated with pink rosebuds and a matching china pitcher. She checked the pitcher but it was empty.

Further along the wall facing her bed was a fireplace with a clock sitting to one side on the mantel. The last items to be explored were a desk and chair beside the window and the bedside table she had not noticed when she fell into bed last night.

Deciding she needed to dress and go downstairs to get her marching orders, Lissie slipped on the same dress she had worn yesterday but pulled a freshly washed and ironed apron from her trunk. *I must unpack my things,* she thought, *but I had best get downstairs right now.*

Drawn to the kitchen and the aroma of coffee brewing, Lissie entered to find Cook pulling a baking sheet out of the oven, loaded with cinnamon rolls.

"Those rolls smell heavenly," exclaimed Lissie, for cinnamon rolls ranked number one as her favorite pastry.

"Yo' breakfast ain't ready yet, Missy," said the cook.

"Oh, I do not mean to interrupt your work, ma'am. I failed to ask when I was to start fetching things for Miss Madge."

"Ole Miss generally wants her morning tea real soon here, but she don' get up and 'round 'til mid-mornin'. You sit right here while I fry up some bacon and scramble some eggs," and she pointed to a chair alongside a table situated out of the way.

"I would be happy to help," Lissie said.

"Ol' Mame don' need no help makin' breakfast, Missy," stated the cook in a steady tone, "but that teakettle is 'bout to boil. You can fix yourself a cup of tea," and she nodded toward the tea caddy.

"Would you like some tea, also?" asked Lissie.

"I b'lieve I would. Thank you, Missy."

The girl settled herself into the chair she had been directed to and sipped the hot tea. "Mame," she said, "I would like you to call me by my name."

The cook looked over at her as she turned a slice of bacon. "What might that be?"

"My name is Annaliese, but my friends call me Lissie," she replied.

The cook just nodded.

Soon Mame had scrambled the eggs and was ready to carry Lissie's breakfast plate to the dining room.

"Are we not going to eat together here at the table," she protested, pointing to where she was still sitting.

"Kitchen help don' eat with reg'lar folk, generally speakin'," the cook replied in a reproving tone.

"Well, Mame, I really do not relish eating alone so I would ask you to sit down and eat breakfast with me. I am not so sure I am regular folk in this house, anyway."

The cook stared at Lissie for a moment and then decided she

would allow this break in tradition. "Very well, Miss Lissie, but I think this be the only meal where we should sit down together. Ol' Miss most likely not look kindly on me eatin' with white folk."

"I do not wish to make trouble," said Lissie, "but Pastor Jamison was just preaching about how God does not consider our appearance or even if we are male or female. If He considers us as equals, I believe I should follow His example."

The cook grinned at her as she joined her at the kitchen table, but merely said, "Help yourself to some bacon with those scrambled eggs."

Lissie had taken two bites of egg when she heard a bell ring from the far recesses of the house. She gave Mame a quizzical look.

"Yes, that be Miss Madge wantin' her first cup of tea." The cook started to get up but Lissie stopped her.

"Please just tell me what cup she prefers."

By the time she had made Miss Madge comfortable sitting up in bed as well as happy with her cup of tea, Lissie's breakfast had gotten cold. She slipped into the chair she had vacated a quarter hour before, grateful for the food as well as the refill of tea Mame had poured without her request.

Later that morning during the middle of reading to Miss Madge, Lissie heard a knock at the front door. Her employer told her to answer it, and to her surprise she saw Uncle Edgar standing there. She hugged him and drew him into the foyer.

"Are things going well for you, Niece?" At her nod, he continued. "I just stopped by the post office to check on our mail and saw you had a letter."

"Oh, Uncle, it must surely be from Lew." She could almost feel her body vibrating with excitement.

Just then a querulous voice came from the Morning Room, "Girl, who is that at the door?"

"Do you want to come in and pay your respects to Miss Madge?" she asked her uncle.

"No, I had best be getting back home. I was glad to have an excuse to see how you were faring.

Lissie thanked him and hugged him goodbye, then shutting the door, she hurried back to her employer.

"Who was at the door, Girl?"

"My Uncle Edgar came by with a letter for me," Lissie

answered.

"Humph," was all the old lady said, and dropped the subject.

That night after her duties were finished with Miss Madge, Lissie hurried upstairs, eager to read Lew's letter.

February 10, 1865

My dear little Wife,

I must stop and look at that line for when I think of it, I scarce can believe we are married, Lissie.

I sit here by the fire and listen to my stomach grumble for better food than the hardtack we had to resort to this evening. Makes me miss you and the wonderful vittles your Aunt Jane served up the evenings I came courting you.

We are presently sheltered at Fort McGilvorey not far from the rebels' fort. In fact, our regiment cooks have to make cook fires outside our fort and when they come up out of the sheltered area where the cook fires are located, the rebels take great delight in aiming shells at them, causing our pots of beans and other vittles to drop on the ground as the cooks run for their lives. Makes me glad I am an infantryman.

Our trip to this spot from Washington D.C. was the most unusual train ride I have ever taken, ranking up there with the first time I hopped a freight train. General Grant's Railroad is unlike any other in the world, I vow. There is little grading done before the ties are laid and rails nailed down. Rather a "lay as you roll" sort of operation. The trackmen laid ten miles of track over hill and dale. We then availed ourselves of a flat car and held on for dear life as the engine led us, bucking and jumping over hillocks and hollows.

I am scratching the bottom of my ink bottle, dear Wife. I send you kisses on the breeze that just passed. It is a clear night and I like to think you are gazing at the moon just as I am. It seems to help me feel closer to you.

Your loving Husband,
Benjie

Lissie refolded the letter, kissed it and tucked in under her pillow. She sighed, remembering how she had comforted Jennie by referring to a moon watch and smiled at the same reference in Lew's letter. Tonight, the moon would have to wait, for her body was tired. She turned off her bedside lamp and snuggled under the covers. Her beginning dreams were filled with train engines that bucked and jumped like Uncle Edgar's stallion, but then her brain relaxed into seamless rest.

The next evening Miss Madge retired earlier than before, so Lissie had time to sit at the desk and write Lew. She wanted to tell him of her adventures since he had gone off to war.

February 25, 1865

Dear Husband,

Your letter arrive two days ago and what a prize it was! I cannot imagine riding on a train such as Grant's Railroad that bucks and jumps over hill and hollow. I do believe you must have enjoyed the strange experience it provided despite the danger of being thrown off.

I thank the good Lord you are not a cook for your regiment. The close proximity to the rebel fort seems a rather strange circumstance. But who am I to think herself above the commander's plans?

I daresay you think I am writing from Uncle Edgar's farmhouse but that would not be true. Shortly after you left for Philadelphia to join your regiment, Mrs. Braintree, the mayor's wife, spoke to Aunt Jane about the possibility of acquiring my services as lady's companion to her elderly aunt, Miss Madge Benson.

The thrilling news, my sweet Benjie, is I am to be paid $5 each week plus my own room and meals. And I shall be allowed a half day free on Sunday so I may visit my family after church. Truly, when I think of the money, I can imagine I am in a sort of paradise. Then Miss Madge rings her bell and I must leave off dusting the trinkets in the parlor to fetch her shawl from her bedroom or such like.

The work is not hard, just tedious at times. I read to Miss Madge several times a day, working away at a different book morning, afternoon, and evening. I have never seen so many books, not even at Riverview School. Miss Madge told me yesterday afternoon her father was a minister and had traveled abroad which I took to mean over the ocean.

I know the parents of my mother came from a country called Germany and Aunt Jane's grandparents moved to America from England, but countries like Italy and France I had not heard.

Getting back to my tasks, I keep Miss Madge's bedroom neatened, and mine of course, but a laundry woman comes in to wash and iron clothes, would you believe? How wondrous! And a woman comes to the house on Saturday to clean.

A most *fascinating Negro woman named Mame is the cook. I have never been in the same room with a Negro person much less known one, personally. To say that Mame has proved most interesting would not do her justice. Besides that, she is a very good cook, almost as good as Aunt Jane. I hope to learn from her as time goes on, for I am often free when Miss Madge naps.*

I must describe the darling bedroom I inhabit in one of the front dormers here. But I shall save that until my next letter as this one is getting too lengthy and my eyes grow heavy.

Despite my busy life, I miss you dreadfully, my sweet Husband.

Sending all my love,

Your wife,
Lissie

Lissie's days began to achieve a comfortable rhythm as she became accustomed to Miss Madge's foibles. Mame was not averse to letting Miss Lissie help her bake. The young woman began learning new ways to use seasonings other than salt and pepper in roasted meats and vegetables. Mame was born in Louisiana. She and her mother, also a cook, had been sold to a planter in Kentucky, and from there she had become a free woman in Pennsylvania. Mame had learned much from her mother and added to her culinary skills over the years.

The week after Lissie's birthday, Hiram, Uncle Edgar's hired man, knocked on the door of Miss Madge's home. Lissie opened the door and greeted him, surprised.

Before she could say more, Hiram handed her a letter, saying, "This come for you, Miss, along with the family mail." With no further words, he turned and fled back to his wagon.

Lissie had never heard Hiram say anything more that, “Please pass the ‘taters” or “Thank ‘ee,” so she was not surprised at the brevity of his explanation upon arriving with a letter for her.

What did surprise her was that the letter was not from Lew, for she knew his handwriting well. Then she noted the black edges on the envelope and fear slammed her chest. One hand across her mouth to keep herself from screaming, she stumbled to the nearest chair to sit down.

Chapter 9

TEARING AT THE envelope with trembling fingers, Lissie removed a single sheet and read, *My Dearest Friend*, and sighed with relief—and then consternation.

Please forgive the tear blotches on my letter as I write to you of my dreadful loss. My darling John has been killed in battle. They tell me he was shot in the chest, but was my brave hero to the end for he rallied his troops as he lay on the ground.

"Forward, men. Avenge my wounds and those of your comrades."

Alas. I always knew John was brave, but at the moment they brought news of his death, I wished he was less brave and holding me in his arms!

At this point Lissie saw a blob of ink which she took for a tear track. A sob escaped her throat as she grieved for her friend, Eliza.

Despite the fact we were not wed, I shall wear black to honor my beloved John. Nor can I imagine even desiring to wear bright colors again as my heart is so sorely grieved.

Lissie knew Eliza was heartsick but she also knew her friend thrived on drama. And besides, wearing black was a perfect foil for Eliza's blonde loveliness. Then Lissie had to chide herself for being so uncharitable in thought towards her friend. There but for her forthright persistence, could *be* her. For what had happened to Eliza was what Lissie had dreaded for herself—mourning for a dead sweetheart and not accorded the respect and rights as the dead soldier's widow. She wiped her eyes and read on.

I shall remain at Madame Ascott's Finishing School until the term ends in April. Mother felt my studies and activities here would help alleviate my grief at John's death—although I fear I shall never recover from my broken heart. Another ink blot.

Oh, how I wish John and I had married instead of planning a Christmas wedding—one that will never be. I almost envy you,

Lissie, for even if something should happen to Lew, at least you knew a few nights of wedded bliss before he left for the battlefield.

I must draw this sad missive to a close. Please remember me in your prayers, for I sob myself to sleep each night and daily grow more haggard.

Your grieving friend,
Eliza

Lissie was glad she had taken the time to write Eliza a short letter right after Lew left for the army, although as she remembered it now, she was feeling pretty downcast at the time. She shrugged her shoulders as if to erase the thought of that time and tears came to her eyes as she imagined the grief Eliza must be feeling.

The sound of Miss Madge's voice beckoned from the Morning Room and Lissie's usual morning routine resumed.

Lew's next letter arrived about a week after Eliza's. Hiram was once more the bearer of the prized postal gift. As always, he did his delivery duty with as few words as possible and hightailed it back to his wagon and horses. Lissie tucked the letter into her apron pocket hoping Miss Madge would doze soundly once she started reading to her. This would give her some unscheduled free time to read Lew's letter.

After eating an unusually large meal in the early afternoon, Miss Madge retired to the Morning Room. Lissie settled her comfortably into her easy chair, footstool positioned just so, and commenced to read one of Fannie Burney's satiric journals aloud. Soon Miss Madge was nodding and once she was gently snoring with her head nestled in the corner of her winged chair, Lissie placed a marker in the book, laying it down and pulling out her letter from Lew.

March 22, 1865

My Dearest Wife,

I still marvel at the writing of that word, wife. How I miss you, Lissie.

I daresay since you are living and working in what sounds like the lap of luxury, you do not miss your lonely husband.

Perhaps lonely is not the right word for I am surrounded by many men in this fort. Because the front lines of both armies are but a quarter mile or so apart, we must have pickets out, day or night. And because the front lines are so close, there are no countersigns. If we see someone coming from the front, we are to fire at them.

My first night of picket duty was a great learning experience. Shortly after I began standing guard, one of the men from the First Michigan located somewhere to my right fired a shot. This began a barrage of bullets and I had to hit the ground as bullets were coming at me from both directions. I lay there for what seemed like an eternity but was only two hours, sand and mud flying into my face and covering my uniform as bullets struck nearby.

When the volleys finally died off, I made a beeline back to camp where my comrades greeted me with great joy for they were sure I was either dead or grievous wounded. One of the men who had been there for a longer time informed me that as soon as a picket heard shooting, he should immediately return to camp. Staying low to the ground, I might add. You can be sure I have followed that advice religiously from that time on.

The fire is dying down and my body is feeling mighty tired so I shall draw this to a close.

I kiss this letter knowing your sweet fingers will be the next to touch it and I look forward to the day when I can once again hold you in my arms, my dear wife.

Your loving Husband
Benjie

Lissie gulped back a sob as she read of Lew's close encounter with Rebel bullets. "Thank You for protecting my Benjie—again," was her whispered prayer.

It was almost a week before Lissie had time to write a return letter to Lew. Miss Madge decided she wanted to visit a cousin in Reading and insisted Lissie accompany her.

The girl was more than ready to return to the little house in Cressona because Miss Madge's cousin seemed as helpless as she, and Lissie ended up being lady's maid to two elderly women instead of one.

She described the visit to Mame at breakfast the morning after she and Miss Madge returned home. "It seemed that Cousin Ellen had let her attendant go the week before and Miss Madge was going to visit her offering sympathy—or taunting her because she had an attendant and Ellen did not. At any rate, I was fetching shawls and lap robes all day long, adjusting window shades and screens, either to promote more sunlight or lessen it, or to admit fresh air or eradicate a chilling draft." She sighed. "It seemed what one lady wished, the other felt in opposing fashion."

Then she giggled. "Mame, you should have heard them argue over what books I should read to them. Miss Madge wished me to continue with Fannie Burney's journal, but Cousin Ellen felt that was much too worldly a book and promoted a volume on theology by a Reverend Cavendish. I never read anything to them except items from the Pittsburg Sentinel as Cousin Ellen has a subscription to that daily newspaper." Both women laughed, and Lissie ate her scrambled eggs taking a bite of crisply fried bacon with each forkful.

Miss Madge was tired from her journey which gave Lissie ample time to write to Lew that evening.

March 31, 1865

Dear Husband,

I first must apologize for not having written you sooner but it was impossible. The day after your last letter arrived, Miss Madge decided she must visit her cousin in Reading. What a bustle it is to prepare a wealthy, elderly woman for a journey! I declare, if I were in such a situation, I should never stir from my comfortable home. We stayed there only two days but I vow, that was more than enough visit for me as I was maid in waiting on two elderly women instead of one. And I shall stop complaining with that.

Oh, my dear Benjie, how your letter frightened me when I read of you lying flat, spitting sand and mud, while bullets flew over your head from friend and foe alike. How dreadful! How I pray this horrible war would end.

Which leads me to another sad subject. A few days before I received your last letter, a grief-filled message came from Eliza Murchiston. Her fiancé, Captain John Maxwell, was killed in a battle at the end of February. She is heartbroken and I can share her grief as I remember the desolation I felt when I received word of your death some two years ago. Despite the great danger around you, I can but rejoice that you are my husband. Not my fiancé.

And with that I shall end this missive for my lamp is sputtering. I need to trim the wick tomorrow but I confess I, too, am tired though I am not as aged as Miss Madge.

Sending you all my love as I kiss your ring,
Your loving wife, Lissie

Spring had definitely come to Cressona, Pennsylvania. The daffodils were blooming in buttery yellow brightness when a message came from Eliza Murchiston delivered by a grubby-faced grocer boy from Mr. Murchiston's store.

When Lissie opened the door, she was startled by the young boy who immediately asked, "Be you Annaliese Facht?"

"I am Annaliese Facht Reber," she replied. "I was married to Lew Reber in February."

"I reckon that be all right, then," and he handed her a piece of paper folded in half. "Miss said I was to wait for an answer," and he gazed at her, standing motionless.

She read, *"Dear Lissie, I have returned home from finishing school as my heart is no longer interested in being schooled for finishing. Please say you will come visit at your soonest opportunity.*

Your friend in mourning,
Eliza.

It was Friday morning and Lissie knew she could not leave her employer until Sunday. Bending so she was eye level with the boy, she asked, "What is your name?"

"I be called Albert."

"Do you think you can remember some words to tell Miss Eliza?"

"Oh yes, mum. I 'member things real good. Mr. Murchiston says he only has to tell me something once and I never fergit it."

"All right. I am depending on you and so is Miss Eliza. Please tell her I will visit her after church this Sunday. Now what will you tell Miss Eliza?"

"Miss says she will visit you after church this Sunday."

"Well done, Albert. Now, off with you to Miss Eliza."

Lissie settled Miss Madge comfortably beside her niece, Mrs. Braintree, in the second pew from the front, center section, where she always sat on Sunday mornings. Then Lissie gave a quick glance over the congregation entering before she sat down by the Holtschlag family.

"Who are you looking for, dear?" asked Aunt Jane as she scooted closer to her husband to make room for their niece.

"Eliza. She sent me a message to come see her as soon as possible and I replied that I would visit with her after church today. I thought perhaps she would be here by now."

"I do not see her parents," replied Jane. "If they truly are not in attendance, we can stop by their house to inquire as to their well-being after service."

None of the Murchistons were at church, which greatly worried Lissie. Her uncle drove them to the Murchiston home and as Lissie hopped out of the wagon, she promised not to be more than a moment.

When she knocked at the door, Mr. Murchiston opened it and greeted her warmly. "So glad you could come, Lissie. Eliza has been asking for you."

"Is she ill?"

"Sick at heart, more like," he replied. "You knew her fiancé was killed in battle a month ago?"

"Yes sir. Eliza wrote to tell me of that sad occurrence.

"But I can stay for only a moment," she continued. "My family waits for me on the street for we have just now left church."

Lissie hurried up the stairs to Eliza's room and was aghast at seeing her in bed looking most unhealthy. Kissing her friend's pale cheek, she said, "I was on my way home with the family, but I wanted to check on you as you were not at church today."

Just then the maid came in with a tray of food for the invalid and Lissie excused herself. "I shall return this afternoon if you feel up to a visit."

"Please come back, Lissie," begged her friend. "I daresay I am not good company, but I so long for someone to talk with besides Mother and Father." She waved her hand in a weak farewell and Lissie skipped down the stairs, heading for the door to rejoin her family.

Mr. Murchiston, acting as doorman once again, assured Lissie he would see to it that she was driven to Miss Madge's once her visit with Eliza was finished.

Lissie shared what she had discovered about Eliza with her family as they gathered around the dinner table that afternoon. "Eliza looks so thin and pale. Not at all the frolicking friend I have always known before." She continued in a whisper, looking through tear-blurred eyes at the buttered turnips on her plate. "Of course, when one's heart is broken, I know any joy seems impossible."

"Remember, Lissie, thinking of 'what if's' will do you no good, and a dismal countenance will be of no aid to Eliza," reminded Aunt Jane.

"I know what you say is true," replied the girl, "but I truly fear for Lew's safety. Yet I must trust him to be in God's hands for I cannot protect him."

"Well said, Niece," stated her uncle.

As soon as the girls helped Jane clean up the kitchen from their meal, Edgar prepared to return Lissie to town and the Murchiston home.

"I am sorry to cut my visit short with all of you," Lissie said to Jane, "but I feel that Eliza truly needs me. Although I do not know how I can be of help," she added.

"Just being willing to listen to her sorrowing words will aid in healing her grief," said Jane as she hugged her niece goodbye.

Soon Edgar pulled up in front of the Murchiston home. Lissie bade him farewell, jumped out of the buggy and ran to the door.

She was ushered upstairs to Eliza's room by Mrs. Murchiston. "Here is Lissie to see you, dear," said her mother and then she left the room.

Eliza was sitting up in bed, propped by a myriad of pillows. She reached out a thin arm to Lissie and said, "I am so glad you came back to visit me." She pointed to a chair by the window. "Please drag that over so you can sit and we can talk comfortably."

Lissie did so and sat looking at her friend's wan face. Finally she spoke. "Eliza, has grief brought you to this low state? I have never known you to be so pale and thin."

Eliza's brows rose slightly as she answered in a shade of her old self. "Ever the plain spoken friend, are you not?" Then she sighed. "After I received word of John's death, it felt as if my heart no longer wanted to beat. Then a bout of rheumatic fever swept our school and I was one of the recipients. The wreck you see before you is the result of fever and heartbreak," she said with a twist at the corner of her lips.

Lissie impulsively grabbed her friend's hand and kissed it. "Eliza, you must not give up on living! If for no other reason, I feel sure I shall need your friendship throughout this life, for I have no other friend like you." She settled back in her chair with a sigh.

As the two girls eased into confidences, Eliza told Lissie of the sweet meetings she and her John had shared. Tears flowed again, but somehow, they seemed to be more healing and less painful—for both the young women. Lissie told of Lew's adventures and mishaps, shuddering again as she repeated his tale of burrowing into the mud while bullets whistled overhead from both sides.

"I cannot understand why men go to war. Why can they not just talk through their disagreements?" asked Eliza in a plaintive voice.

"After witnessing two brothers in one family come to fisticuffs over whose marble is whose, I truly do not find it surprising," answered Lissie in a sage manner. "That is not to say I understand it. I merely know it is a fact. Males seem to feel that the only real answer to a conflict is to hammer it out and the strongest must surely be the one in the right."

Eliza wanted to hear more about her friend's duties at Miss Madge's house. "I cannot imagine what it must be like to actually be paid for performing household duties," exclaimed Eliza.

She was beginning to gain a hint of pink in her cheeks, so Lissie told stories of chasing thimbles, reading a multitude of dull pages to an often-dozing elder, and forever adjusting window shades and fetching shawls.

"Do you think we shall ever be that old," queried Eliza after a particularly healthy giggle.

"I am not sure I should wish to attain that age," replied Lissie, "for I know Miss Madge suffers in her joints. She calls it her lumbago and groans often that it is her 'cross to bear.'"

Just then the door opened and Eliza's mother entered. "It is nearly six o'clock, Lissie and I remember you said you needed to be back at Miss Madge's house by that time."

"Thank you, ma'am. I do need to go." Turning to Eliza, she leaned over and kissed her friend's cheek. "I hope to see you at church next week, Eliza, so you must start eating good nourishing food and moving about."

"Yes, Nurse," replied Eliza, in a prim voice, but there was a smile on her lips and even a hint of a twinkle in her eyes.

As Mrs. Murchiston walked Lissie to the door, she said, "Thank you for brightening the day for Eliza. Perhaps she will begin to heal now." She gave the girl an impulsive hug and sent her on her way.

The next week was uneventful for Lissie, but Eliza did manage to attend church the next Sunday. She still looked very thin but showed much more color in her cheeks.

Chapter 10

IT WAS WEDNESDAY of the next week when a frenzied knocking was heard at Miss Madge's front door. "For goodness sake," fretted the elderly woman. "Who can that be, trying to knock down my door. Well, go on, Girl. See who it is before they tear the knocker clear off the plate."

Their guest was Mrs. Braintree, Madge's niece. She walked straight past Lissie as if in some sort of trance, heading straight for the Morning Room. When she saw Miss Madge, she broke into tears, saying brokenly, "They have killed him--the greatest man of our century. They have shot our father," and the rest of her sentence was obliterated by her sobbing.

"Florence, for goodness sake, sit down and get hold of yourself. Girl," and Madge motioned to Lissie, "go fetch some tea and do not let Mame skimp on the sugar and cream! Now, Florence, has the mayor been shot? I know it is not *your* father for he has been dead these five years. Come, woman. Stop blethering and talk sense!"

By the time Lissie had returned with the tea tray, Florence Braintree had composed herself and was telling her aunt the dreadful story.

"The news came by this morning's train—the Washington Evening Star. President Lincoln was shot at Ford's Theater last night and he died this morning. Whatever will our country do? Here we are with General Lee surrendering at Appomattox less than a week ago and this dreadful war looking like it will be over—and our president is dead!" And she began weeping again.

Lissie crept away to a corner in the front parlor. *The war was over? Maybe? Did that not mean Lew would soon be home?* Her heart leapt with joy and then she felt guilty at the sound of Mrs. Braintree's sobbing. She was sorry the president had been shot but she knew nothing of him having seldom seen a newspaper. She wondered if Mrs. Braintree somehow knew the dead man and his family.

Before the time of national mourning was over, Lissie began to understand the rudderless feelings of her fellow citizens. As she became acquainted with the sad events in the lives of the Lincoln family since they had come to Washington, D.C., Lissie wondered how Mrs. Lincoln could bear the pain of losing two sons and now her husband. Would that not tear one's soul to shreds?

The president's assassination was the main topic of conversation everywhere. When Lissie went to fetch mail at the post office or checked the progress on Miss Madge's latest order at the milliner's, all spoke as if a family member had died.

Feeling somewhat guilty, all of Lissie's thoughts were of Lew. *When will Lew come home? Where is Lew? Why does Lew not write?* And then she was surprised one day to receive *two* of his letters at once. Both were dog-eared and grimy, but thankfully, still readable.

April ~~9~~, 1865

Dearest Wife,

I feel sure this has been a most notable day in my life and in that of the Union. General Lee has surrendered his army and we will no longer be fighting. Me and some of my regiment have been guarding Rebel prisoners until they are paroled. The ones I have talked to are mighty glad to stop fighting and want to get home in the worst way.

My regiment is now in Washington, D.C., still guarding prisoners and dealing with paroles. I do not know when I will have time to get this letter out to you—which is why I have crossed through the date--as this city is in great turmoil. President Lincoln died yesterday morning after having been shot as he watched a comedy at Ford's Theater. I hear they have caught the man who shot him but rumors fly like feathers in the wind in this city.

I, like that Rebel soldier, so wish to come home to you, but this war is not yet over despite Lee's surrender. At least I am no longer dodging bullets.

Please write and tell me all the little things. Miss Madge sounds like she is a pistol of a woman as does Mame, in a different way.

Sending you all my love,
Your Benjie
(I think today is April 24)

Lissie read her first letter as Miss Madge napped, but held the second one for later as a bedtime treat.

May 5, 1865

Dearest Wife,

The hurley-burley of life in this city makes me long for the countryside. Everyone is in a hurry to get somewhere, but there are no smiles on the faces of people you meet. I believe the death of President Lincoln has set back the healing of the Union in a terrible manner. I was able to attend a church service Sunday, the first since leaving your side. The minister reminded us of Lincoln's plea this past January in his Inaugural Address. He asked that fellow citizens would not hold malice in their hearts toward anyone.

The Confederacy continues to fight although word reaches this city occasionally of those generals and army leaders who have surrendered their forces.

Thank you for your sweet letters, dear wife. Your droll descriptions of some of your tasks for Miss Madge give me a chuckle when there is nothing here to laugh about. My life is no longer in danger, but it is dreadfully boring. Dare I say I miss the former adventure, but not the danger?

You have asked when I might be coming home. My contract is for a year so I may well be stuck in this city for some time yet. There are several Rebel forces still fighting or who have not heard they can surrender and obtain parole.

I have been assigned to the quartermaster who supervises supplies and provisions. For that reason I shall not be suffering from hunger for the remainder of this war, although our vittles resemble nothing like the wondrous food your Aunt Jane spreads before her family each day.

I should be able to get this sent to you tomorrow as the chaos here seems more orderly now. I know not whether this is true or that I have become accustomed to it. At any rate, I send you all my love,

Your loving husband
Benjie

Lisse read Lew's letter with a sense of gratitude mixed with the dread that she might not see him for several more months.

The remainder of spring flowed into summer and Lew did not come home although he wrote regularly. He told Lissie in one letter "the quartermaster said yesterday, he would not mind keeping me here until Christmas. He can see I am an honest man and not afraid of hard work. I thanked him but told him I had a wife back home I was missing something terrible. He nodded, and said no more."

Lissie was proud that Lew's honesty and good work ethic was obvious, but she wished that was not such an unusual trait.

As for her, Miss Madge's demands changed somewhat in the summer months because she enjoyed "taking in the air" during the pleasant morning temperatures. She also loved her flower garden and taught Lissie the care and cultivation of daffodils, iris, sweet peas and gladiolus. There were two lilac bushes in the corner of the backyard as well as several rosebushes.

Lissie remarked on the lovely variety. "My Aunt Jane has some rosebushes at the front door of the farmhouse, but I have never seen such lovely, large blossoms as these." She had been told to pick some to fill a vase in the Morning Room and Miss Madge told her a bit about the bushes.

"In my younger years, I became known for the beautiful flowers in my garden. Always furnished fresh flowers for Sunday mornings at church. Whenever Father travelled, he kept an eye out for unusual or beautiful flowers. Many of the rosebushes you see came from his travels. Of course, that was before I had to deal with my lumbago," she added in a bitter tone.

Lissie felt a twinge of pity for the elderly woman. "I am glad you still have so many flowers you can enjoy during the summer. Their fragrance is lovely and the colors are glorious." The sun became overbearing and she helped Miss Madge walk back into the cool house where Mame had a tray of frosty sweetened ice tea with some freshly baked sugar cookies.

July came and went and as the heat of August settled in, Lissie began to despair of seeing Lew any time soon. The middle of the month was near when a knock came on Miss Madge's front door in mid-afternoon. It did not rouse that lady from her doze, so Lissie ran to find out who their visitor might be.

She opened the door to a tall, muscular young man with a nicely trimmed beard who looked somewhat familiar.

"Hello, Wife," came Lew's voice, although in a deeper timbre than she remembered.

There was a second of stunned silence. Then she leaped at him, hugging him with all her might as she cried, "O Lew, O Lew," into his chest—since she could reach no higher.

In turn, Lew reached down and picked up Lissy, kissing her hard on the lips as her feet dangled helplessly above the doorstep.

After a moment, the two came up for air and Lissie gulped in a breath. "Perhaps you should set me down, Lew, and come inside."

By this time, Miss Madge had awakened from her nap and demanded, "Where are you, Girl? Did I hear someone at the door?"

Pulling Lew by the hand, Lissie drew him to the Morning Room to meet her employer. "Mercy me," said the old lady. "How came you in, sir?"

"I opened the door to him, Miss Madge. This is my husband, Lew Reber, come home from the war." Lissy felt like her face would crack as her smile threatened to stretch all the way to her ears.

"Mercy me," the old lady repeated. "You are a tall one, are you not? Well, sit down over here." Then to Lissie, "Go get some tea, Girl, while I get acquainted with your young man. Husband, huh?"

Lissie almost ran to the kitchen dreading the quizzing Miss Madge was no doubt giving Lew. She had mentioned once that she was married to a soldier, but Miss Madge had seemingly paid no attention to her statement.

She returned with the tea trolley laden with scones as well as fig paste tartlets. Mame had piled on the delicacies due to the reason behind Lissie's request for tea for three.

Lew conversed with Miss Madge, quite at ease while Lissie

mostly just listened. The elderly lady posed intelligent questions about the state of the nation's capitol once she discovered Lew had been stationed there for the past three months.

I cannot stand this, thought Lissie. *I want my husband to myself, not visiting with my employer.* She wanted to scream at Miss Madge and fling herself once more into Lew's arms.

As Lissie inwardly pouted, she heard the last of a question Miss Madge aimed toward Lew. "…do, now that you are home?"

"I aim to take my sweet wife on a wedding trip to Ohio," he replied.

Lissie squeaked as her hands flew to her mouth and she felt her eyes widen in astonishment.

"Well, Girl, looks like I will have to search for a new companion, eh? When do you intend to leave on this wedding trip?" the old lady pried.

"I think Monday," Lew replied. "Seeing as how this is Friday, it will give me a chance to visit my family tomorrow and Lissie can spend some time with her family on Sunday after church. I hope that allows you ample opportunity to find a new helper, ma'am," he said respectfully.

"I doubt that highly," fired back the old lady. Directing her gaze at Lissie, she said, "I need you to go to Florence's house and tell her I am being left high and dry after Sunday. She needs to find me a companion or come tend me herself."

Lissie sat there, nodding, but Miss Madge was ready for action. "Go on now. You can drink your tea later if you've a mind to."

Lissie answered, "Yes, Ma'am," and immediately set down her glass, rose and headed for the door.

"Thank you for tea, ma'am" Lew said politely as he rose and followed Lissie.

All he heard in reply was, "Humph."

Once outside the cottage, Lew grabbed Lissie in a bear hug and kissed her again. "How long can you be gone on this errand to Mrs. Braintree's house? I did not think on how we might not be together once I am back home."

Lissie knew he was feeling emotional because his English still became somewhat tangled at such times. And she loved him that much more because of it. Grabbing his arm close to her and beginning to walk, she replied, "I think we can safely stretch the walk to a quarter hour and then of course, I must tell Mrs. Braintree the reason for our visit and she will question you. So an hour sounds reasonable to me," and she smiled up at him.

In answer, he leaned down and kissed her again.

Sure enough, Mrs. Braintree was full of questions, once Lissie told her the reason for her visit. She invited the young couple in because Florence Braintree was a very patriotic woman, and Lew looked quite the handsome soldier despite his youth.

"You have pleased Aunt Madge with your attention to her needs, Lissie. I fear you will be difficult to replace." She sighed. "And of course, I shall need to watch over her until I find someone else."

The young couple said goodbye amidst well wishes from the lady and went on their way—as slowly as possible.

"Lew, whatever made you think of going to Ohio? Who do you know there"?"

"A buddy from the army, Jack Sparling, knew I was married, and when he was mustered out, he made a special point of inviting me, us, to come visit him. I have money from my soldier wages which will pay for the trip. Say, Lissie, how much money is left from my bounty money?"

"All of it, Lew. I felt like that should be our nest egg to get started in our life together. Maybe buy a little house somewhere…"

At that, Lew picked her up and whirled her around. Lissie squealed, "Put me down, Lew. My bonnet is liable to fly away," and she clutched at the strings which had come undone.

Lew hugged his young wife to him and said, "I am so proud of you, Lissie, for not spending that money. I did not know I was married to such a thrifty little wife."

"I daresay there are many things you do not know about me," and Lissie smiled up at him. "And vice versa, of course. At any rate, the reason I took the job with Miss Madge was to help pay expenses when we set up housekeeping."

The rest of their walk was spent talking about the future. *What would their little house look like? What splendors might they see on their wedding trip? What might Lew do for a living now that he was no longer a soldier?*

At Miss Madge's door Lew said, "I cannot think we can be together tonight so I will say goodbye until Sunday."

"Where will you stay this night," asked Lissie, troubled that her

Lew had no place to lay his head.

"I have a room at the hotel," he grinned, "for I am now a man of the world with money in my pockets. And a lovely little wife I wish I could tuck in one of those pockets and whisk away with me," he added in a whisper.

The two embraced and kissed goodbye. Lissie went to tend Miss Madge, and Lew retired to his lonely hotel room to dream of his sweet little wife.

Saturday night after Miss Madge was situated comfortably in her bedroom, Lissie ran upstairs to do her final packing. She left out her new dimity gown, bought from her earnings, hanging it in the chiffarobe. Everything else was carefully folded and packed with the exception of what she would need in the morning.

She hugged herself with excitement at the prospect of seeing Lew the next day and, please God, not to be parted again. Lissie did not ever remember being this excited, not even on her wedding day. But then of course, Lew was heading for the battle field, so no wonder this excitement felt so much more lighthearted. She kissed his ring and was asleep soon after her head rested on the pillow.

Lissie got Miss Madge settled in her pew at church alongside Mrs. Braintree and her husband, the mayor. "I will pick up my trunk this evening when Lew and I return from the Holtschlag's," she promised.

Then she made her way back to Lew who was sitting with her family. Aunt Jane made room for her so she could sit by Lew and after greeting her aunt and uncle, Lissie settled comfortably into the curve of Lew's arm.

He leaned over and whispered in her ear, "I really would like to kiss you but they might throw me out of the church."

Lissie looked up at him and giggled, then promptly covered her mouth with her hand.

They were a merry crowd as the Holtschlag family, including little Jennie and the newlyweds, drove to the farmhouse. Aunt Jane had fried chicken and made potato salad earlier, and the girls had the table set. With a freshly sliced loaf of bread and butter and a huge lettuce, cucumber, onion salad and sliced tomatoes, the family set to eating with great appetite. For dessert Jane fetched apple pie from the pantry.

As an extra special treat Edgar promised, "There is home-made ice cream to be had by mid-afternoon if I can get any help turning the crank." A chorus of male voices assured him of ample assistance.

Jane, Lissie and the two younger girls had washed and dried the dishes, putting the kitchen and dining room to rights and joined Edgar and Lew in the parlor. The younger children ran out to play croquet in the front yard and the conversation turned to the forthcoming wedding trip.

"I do not remember hearing of anyone in our family taking a wedding trip," remarked Aunt Jane. "What made you think of it, Lew?"

He put his arm around Lissie and said, "Just before I was mustered out in Washington, a friend of mine stopped by to visit and said I must be sure to look him up in Ohio. Then as I was riding the train from Washington to Cressona, I realized Lissie had never ridden on a train and had never been out of the state of Pennsylvania. So I figured there would never be a better time for us to set out on an adventure together—and call it our wedding trip."

Lissie snuggled into him a little closer and asked, "Do you know how long we will be on the train before we get to wherever it is we are going?"

"Two days or thereabouts," he replied.

"Sounds like you will have to sleep sitting straight up," remarked Uncle Edgar.

"This is true," replied Lew, "but if the train is not too crowded, we can find facing double seats and stretch out on those at night."

Lissie shuddered. "I have never slept in front of anyone but family. I think perhaps I shall sleep sitting up," she said with a determined tilt to her chin.

Just then Manfred rushed into the parlor. "Pa, we have finished our croquet game. Is it time to make ice cream yet?

"I suppose we have shaken down our dinner enough to make room for it," his father replied. "Fetch a pan from the kitchen and we will go down to the icehouse and chip enough ice from that block we used for our iced tea today."

Jane headed for the kitchen to beat up the milk, sugar and egg mixture—a recipe she had begged from a friend in Philadelphia several years before. Lissie watched her aunt intently, memorizing every detail. She had eaten ice cream occasionally but had never thought about how it was put together or the process of getting it to its icy, delicious state.

Jane poured the creamy mixture into the inner cylinder as Edgar layered ice and rock salt between the cylinder and the wooden walls of the freezer. Many hands truly did make light work and as soon as one set of arms tired of turning the freezer's crank, another was ready to take over.

Soon the cylinder refused to turn which signaled the icy dessert had solidified and was ready to eat. Carefully removing the paddle from the cylinder, Jane began spooning the ice cream into bowls.

"Can I have the paddle, Ma?" blurted Manfred. The younger children often bickered over who got to clean off the contrivance that moved the creamy mixture around to freeze it.

"Yes, dear," came his mother's answer as the other children groaned in disappointment. They soon forgot their disgruntlement with the first mouthful of ice cream. A satisfied "M-m-m" hummed around the porch area which was where everyone had congregated, sitting on the swing, on the steps, or on the railing.

"Jane, what is the sweet flavor? It is not any fruit I can identify," asked Edgar.

"I grated some vanilla bean into the mixture before I poured it into the canister," she replied.

Lissie's ears perked up as she had missed seeing that step in the process of the dessert preparation. She had eaten ice cream with strawberries but never this flavor, and she liked it.

Stomachs now feeling pleasantly full—once again, the freezer was emptied of salt water on the gravel drive and turned upside down to dry, its inner parts washed as well as bowls and spoons. Lew and Lissie got ready to leave for town and their impending wedding trip.

"Shall I hitch up the horse and buggy?" asked Uncle Edgar.

"No need," said Lew for he was accustomed to walking many miles in a day. Then he remembered Lissie had not had that same experience. "Do you mind walking to town, Lissie?" he asked.

She smiled. "My legs are short but I can walk that far." She squinted at the sun and remarked, "Besides that, a breeze has come up and lowered the humidity."

They said their goodbyes and Lew assured the Holtschlags they would be back in two weeks or less.

So it was that the "newlyweds" set off for their hotel room in Cressona, hand in hand, alone at last.

"Do you realize this is the real beginning of our life together?" Lew looked down at his petite wife and then kissed her nose as she looked up at him.

"Yes, Benjie, that very fact has occurred to me," and she giggled.

They walked in companionable silence for a few minutes and then Lissie spoke. "Husband?"

"I hear a question in your voice, Liebchen," replied Lew.

"Would you agree that your legs are somewhat longer than mine?"

"Yes, dear heart, I believe that is why I am more than a head taller than you."

She thought carefully and then said, "I know you are accustomed to marching here and there, not wasting a moment to reach your goal, but do you suppose you could shorten your stride just a bit. I find I am becoming quite breathless and that lovely breeze back at the farmhouse seems to have disappeared."

Lew halted, looked at his now-quite pink-cheeked wife and laughed. Then he picked her up around the waist, kissed her squarely on the lips and then set her down carefully. "I am sorry, Lissie, and you are right. I *am* accustomed to marching rapidly. I believe it is now time for me to…. I cannot think the word."

"Amble?" suggested Lissie. "Or stroll. However, we do want to arrive in Cressona before nightfall so perhaps we should walk with a purposeful stride. But not too long a one on your part," she said, looking up at him sideways with a twinkle in her eyes.

Chapter 11

February 1, 1921
Palmyra, Missouri

ANNALIESE OPENED HER eyes with a start, awakened by the sun directing its waning beams into her face through the west window. "Mercy sakes," she said to Tabby Cat who had climbed onto her lap at some point in the afternoon. "The day is most gone." She stretched and yawned. "I must truly be in my dotage to remember back so many years. 'Twas good we were so young when our adventures started, Lew," she murmured. She shrugged and then thought, *I'm glad Landis doesn't mind leftovers because that's what the poor boy is getting for supper.*

The "poor boy" seemed not to mind the leftovers one whit. "Mashed potato cakes and ham slices are always fine and you know I prize your cornbread, Mother, be it fresh or a few hours old."

Annaliese inquired about his afternoon which consisted of preparing harness and equipment for spring planting in a few weeks. "What of you, Mother? The day was a sunny one, but nippy. Did you write letters or take a nap?"

"No letters, just a nap. Or more like, a trip through my past, dear. That seems to be a habit when I sit down to rest my eyes."

"I see no harm in that, Mother. You had enough adventures with Papa you could fill a book five times bigger than the one he wrote."

"I prefer to remember things, not write them down," she replied. "Just thinking about all the moves we made makes my bones ache."

The next day was sunny and even warmer so Annaliese decreed it wash day. Lew had purchased a washer complete with dasher and wringer about five years after they moved to Missouri. At the time Annaliese was still strong enough to fill her wash and rinse tubs but now Landis, her stalwart, willing worker, had to help her. Working together they soon had the clean clothes pinned to the line outside before dinner time.

Annaliese had put a vegetable soup to simmer before she began the laundry task and the vegetables had melded their flavors nicely by dinner time. They ate their fill accompanied by thick slabs of bread she had baked earlier in the week. The slices, slathered with fresh-churned butter and strawberry preserves from last year's crop, made a fine finish to their meal.

As they ate, Annaliese reminisced about her very first wash day as a young wife. "In those days I had to pump the water, pour it into a kettle to heat, then dip the boiling water back out into the bucket as I did not dare try to remove the kettle and carry *all* that hot water. Next I pounded the clothes with a bat to get the hot, soapy water thoroughly into the material. When the soapy water had cooled enough to put my hands into it, I wrung out each piece of clothing."

"Even Papa's shirts and pants?" interrupted Landis.

"How else would the soapy water get removed?" remarked his mother, with a wry twist to her mouth.

"Then the clothes went into the rinse tub to remove additional soapy water, and finally, they were pegged to the line to dry—unless I felt they needed a second tub of rinse water."

"Well, today's laundry task was certainly easier and faster than what you just described," said Landis, "but I would still rather plow a field than do laundry." He grinned and rose from the table. "Thanks for the grub, Mother. I need to go work in the barn."

"And I am heading for my rocker once I've straightened my kitchen," said his mother.

Annaliese rocked gently, the summary of laundry day woes she had told Landis leading her back again to her earlier years and the wedding trip to Ohio.

Chapter 12

Late August 1865
Cressona, Pennsylvania

THEY ARRIVED AT the hotel in less than an hour's time and Lew proudly showed Lissie their home for the night. She had never been in a hotel before and was somewhat awed by the large reception area with huge fireplaces at either end of the room, adorned with marble mantels and artistically tiled surrounds.

Lissie was less thrilled with their bedroom for she could not help but compare her room at Miss Madge's house, with this cramped, drab chamber. It contained a bed with a chair beside the one window draped in cheap muslin. A small wardrobe hugged one corner. She sat on the bed and discovered it was surprisingly firm, not at all like the feather beds at Aunt Jane's or Miss Madge's.

"Come down the hall," Lew prompted, sounding excited. He opened a door four rooms from theirs and she could see what appeared to be a large bowl on legs and a strange chair-like form apparently bolted to the floor. "This is true luxury, Lissie. An indoor privy and water coming through pipes when you turn this handle," and he demonstrated.

Lissie gasped and clutched Lew's arm when she saw the water gush from a pipe into the bowl. "I believe I prefer Miss Madge's pitcher of water and washbowl on the wash stand," she squeaked.

"Then you will like even less using this commode," he grinned. Opening the lid of the strange chair, Lissie realized it was like a chamber pot. Then Lew pulled a chain above the seat and water whooshed out and the receptacle began to refill with water.

Lissie was struck totally silent and then in a timid voice she asked, "Lew, does the hotel have regular chamber pots?"

"Not that I am aware of, dear. Never fear. I shall hold your hand while you use the facility," this said with a comical twist to his mouth.

"You will do no such thing!" And she swatted his arm.

Back in their room, Lissie opened her trunk to pull out a fresh blouse to wear for their trip the next day. She hung it in the wardrobe hoping the wrinkles would fall out and then said, "Might we go to the dining room and order a bowl of soup?"

"I will never refuse the possibility of eating," Lew said with a grin and down the stairs they walked, arm in arm, Lew taking care to limit his stride to match that of his wife's.

Pleasantly filled by the savory potato chowder sprinkled with bits of fried ham accompanied by a healthy slab of warm, crusty bread slathered with butter, the two young lovers decided to walk to the city park since it was not yet dark. As they walked, they talked—Lissie with many questions, Lew, answering as best he could.

"How does this wedding journey go, Lew? How do we know we can get a seat on this train and when does it arrive? I have never ridden on a train before, you know." She looked up at her young husband in a reproving manner, as she could see smile crinkles edging from his eyes.

He hugged her to him. "Ah, Liebchen. How I love to be the fount of wisdom and experience for my sweet wife." She sputtered but he ignored it and continued. "This wedding journey will begin with us sleeping together tonight…."

He was interrupted by Lissie's scandalized, "Lew!"

And continued, unperturbed, "and being glad for it, as we will most likely be sleeping sitting upright in train seats tomorrow night. All of which means I shall do well to even steal a kiss from my sweet wife without others' prying eyes.

"But back to the beginning of our train ride. I have already bought tickets at the depot for the train heading to Pittsburgh and from there we shall travel on to Dayton, Ohio to meet up with my friend, Jack Sparling. We will board the train around 10:30 tomorrow morning and should arrive in Dayton Tuesday morning, according to the timetable, at 9:45. We will hire a hack after we have collected your traveling trunk, and make ourselves known to Jack and his family."

"Is he also married?" Lissie felt she would be happy to compare notes with another young bride like herself.

"No. He lives with his father and mother and younger brothers.

His father owns a livery stable and since I have had experience working with horses, perhaps I can get hired on."

"Lew, are we not coming back home?" Lissie suddenly felt a fearful shadow clutch at her heart, reminding her of when she had heard that Lew had been killed in battle.

"Lissie, I need to find work to support us." His voice was a bit unsteady but he pressed on with resolve. "You know we cannot return to my father's farm and your Uncle Edgar does not need any additional help. Truthfully, I do not yearn to be a farmer although I enjoy animals and being out of doors. If I could travel this country of ours and still make a good living for us, I would think myself the most fortunate of men."

"I do not know of such work," replied his practical little wife. "Perhaps something will cross our minds as we make this wedding trip or discover something when we arrive at your friend's home." She had already grasped the sense of his statement and suddenly realized, *Home is wherever Lew is.* She found that thought to be a great comfort and actually began to anticipate all the "firsts" she would soon be experiencing.

The moon was shining through the trees lining the street as they neared the hotel. The night sky seemed to make Lissie aware of her fatigue. The frightening thought of that indoor privy down the hall—she noticed the words "Water Closet" painted on it as they walked by—made her shiver and then stiffen her backbone. *Might as well deal with this 'first' right now,* she mused and headed for what she thought of as her nemesis.

She had packed a bar of Castile soap Aunt Jane had given her for a wedding gift wrapped inside a flannel washcloth along with her comb. Armed with her toilette articles, Lissie felt ready to do battle with the dread Water Closet.

Lew arched an eyebrow and asked, "Are you sure you do not want me to hold your hand?" for it was obvious where Lissie was going.

Her only answer was a haughty curl of her lip and a flip of her skirt as she flounced out of their room.

She decided to tackle the less frightening item first and gingerly turned the handle to run water over her washcloth. She startled and then scolded herself. *This is not that much different from pumping water at the farm. Just less work.* After washing her face and the rest of her body she deemed in need of cleansing, she turned to the commode.

Lifting the lid, she peered into the white porcelain bowl. She spied the chain Lew had pulled earlier and followed his example. Whoosh went the water. "Eek," came Lissie's muffled squeak. Again, she compared this seat, this commode, to the chamber pot at home. *I shall lift my skirts, sit down, and do my business,* she thought. She discovered the wooden seat was actually quite a bit more comfortable than using a chamber pot, although she trembled a bit at first, envisioning a ghostly hand pulling the chain and sucking her down into some hellish pit in a violent stream of water.

Mentally shaking herself in disgust, she went about her business, then stood, straightened her skirts—and pulled the chain. Once again, startled, she thought, *I should never become accustomed to such a contraption, although it would be nice never having to empty another chamber pot again.*

Gathering up her belongings and feeling much refreshed, she returned to their room, ready to report on her bravery. "I fared quite well without any hand holding," she said sprightly. "Now it is your turn."

As soon as Lew left the room, Lissie began undressing, hanging her clothes as neatly as possible in the wardrobe and folding the blouse she had worn all day, putting it in the trunk. She pulled out her nightdress and hairbrush. She had decided against trying to comb her hair in the water closet because the curls tangled and ratted so. It was time to take down her coronet of braids anyway and give her hair the one hundred strokes Aunt Jane always recommended.

She was brushing the wavy brown locks over her shoulder as Lew walked in. The look on his face made her turn away in embarrassment. He stripped to his drawers, sat down next to her and enclosed her small hand with his, effectively stopping the brush in mid-stroke. "You are so beautiful," he whispered in her ear as his other arm encircled her shoulders and he began nibble-kissing that same ear.

"Lew, I am not finished brushing my hair," Lissie protested. But her giggle when his lips reached the ticklish spot under her jaw belied her stern tone.

The hair brushing came to an abrupt end.

The sun shining through the muslin curtains was bright enough to wake them. Lissie was the first to rouse, or so she thought. As she turned to look at her husband, her hazel eyes met his brown ones and the next minute two sets of lips also met.

Lissie broke away first saying, "Oh Lew, I did not think to get water for the wash basin last night. Can…"

"You need not even ask, my love," he replied. Pulling on his trousers, he was up, grabbing the washbowl and out the door before Lissie could draw another breath. He returned in about the same amount of time. Setting the basin down, he turned and whisked the covers off Lissie. "Rise and shine, love," he grinned. "We have a train to catch and an adventure to share."

Dressed, breakfasted, and full of excitement, the two walked hand in hand down the boardwalk toward the train station. Lew had ordered a cart to carry Lissie's trunk and it was already there, awaiting their departure. Lew had his knapsack over his shoulder, and Lissie had packed her immediate necessities for the train ride in a carpet bag Aunt Jane had loaned her.

It was not long before the train pulled up alongside the depot, engine belching smoke and ashes. A maelstrom of passengers, mailbags and baggage finally sorted itself out with items and people properly deposited in the railroad cars. Meanwhile, their opposites coming from as many different directions were scattered onto the boardwalk in front of the train station.

Lew led the way to a vacant seat with Lissie following him, trying to familiarize herself with all the strange surroundings they would be riding in the next two days. He situated his wife next to the window where she was surprised to find thick crimson velvet curtains. Next she poked an inquisitive finger at their seat and discovered it felt very much like Aunt Jane's horsehair sofa in the parlor at the farmhouse.

Lissie carefully removed her bonnet, a straw from Miss Milligan's Millinery Shop. The creation boasted a jaunty peacock feather, cleverly curled around the crown. Lew settled her carpet bag and his knapsack comfortably around them almost as if nesting in their own little piece of the world.

The next moment the train whistled and jerked, Lissie squealed and grabbed Lew's arm, and they began to move. By the time the train had travelled well beyond Cressona, the trees and fences seemed to blur with the speed of their passing.

"I have never ridden this fast, Lew," gasped Lissie. "Even Uncle Edgar's fastest stallion does not run so rapidly."

"I should think not," and he grinned down at her. "We are likely traveling at forty miles per hour."

"Oh my goodness." She put her fingers to her lips in consternation. "What is to keep us from flying off these tracks at such a speed?"

"As long as we are riding on the straightaway, there should be no problem," assured Lew. "When we come to curves, the train will go much slower."

"I do hope so," replied Lissie, as she continued to peer through the glass almost pressing her nose against it.

Within an hour the train had stopped at another town to load and unload passengers, baggage and mail. It continued in this fashion until they came much closer to the Allegheny Mountains where the train slowed, as Lew had said, for curves.

One minute Lissie was gulping in fright at the sheer mountainside reaching down to a tiny stream many feet below her window. The next, she was exclaiming at the mountainous peaks on the horizon. "What an awesome landscape we are seeing in comparison to the rolling hills at home."

"It is an exciting experience," agreed Lew, "but I am glad to be experiencing it in a train car rather than on foot."

Lissie shuddered at that thought. "Did you have to climb mountains when you were soldiering, Lew?"

"No, but after marching for ten miles on an empty stomach, a small hill seemed mighty like a mountain to me," he sighed. "I am glad those days are over."

"I am also glad, very glad," and Lissie snuggled closer to her husband.

He kissed her cheek and then said, "Talking about marching reminds me that we have not eaten since breakfast," and he pulled out two apples and some smashed cookies from his knapsack. "I bought these at the restaurant while you went back upstairs to take care of last minute things," and he winked at her.

"I am glad you did," replied Lissie, "for I was so excited about riding on this train, every other thought flew out of my head."

They had soon eaten Lew's luncheon and drank from his canteen while Lissie marveled at his forethought. "I am so impressed, Lew. You seem to have thought of everything." He grinned, perfectly willing to accept her praise.

By this time, they had passed the mountainous area and were nearing Pittsburgh. The train stopped there for an hour which gave them time to get off, stretch their legs, use the facilities—Lissie felt quite the experienced traveler by this time—and bought some more apples and a couple of meat pies from a vendor.

"I declare I cannot eat any more," stated Lissie, but the tantalizing smell of sausage, onion and cabbage tempted her to eat a few bits. Lew had no trouble finishing the rest of her pie as well as his own.

They heard the "all aboard" call so made their way back to their car. They had been joined throughout the day by other passengers sharing their space in the facing bench seat, but the last one had disembarked in Pittsburgh and the young couple now had the little cubicle to themselves.

"Once we get moving, I suggest we settle in on our "beds" and perhaps we will not be called to get up and share our space until tomorrow," said Lew.

"Are you telling me I must lie down in full view of whoever walks by?" Lissie's face paled at the idea.

"You need not remove your clothes, Lissie," came Lew's dry reply. "In fact, I wish you would not. At least not here," he added in a much lower voice and wriggled his eyebrows.

"Oh, Lew!" She swatted at him and giggled.

He prepared the cubicle, first by drawing the curtains at the window, then situating Lissie's carpet bag at her head for a "pillow" and covering her with her cloak which had been of little use until now. "Are you comfortable?" he asked in a tender tone.

"As comfortable as I can be in such a circumstance," she murmured. "Thank you, Benjie." He leaned over and kissed her and then went to work on his own "bed."

Once he was situated, Lissie looked over at him and said, "I guess you have made many a bed something like this in the past months."

'Yes, I have, although they were not this comfortable, nor were they accompanied by a lovely woman lying just a foot or so from me."

"I do not suppose these seats would hold two of us," Lissie sighed. "I truly miss my husband lying close."

"I fear one of us would soon be on the floor," he laughed, "and that after having been smashed together flatter than a pancake."

The click-clack of the rails became a soothing rhythm and both were soon asleep.

The next morning the young couple was awakened by the train whistle, a jerk and screech of metal against metal followed by a sudden stop, throwing Lissie on the floor in a flurry of petticoats and much pained surprise.

Lew was up in a flash, hair bristling in all directions, looking dazed as he saw the empty bench seat and then realizing Lissie was on the floor. "Are you injured, Lissie?" He knelt down beside her, checking her head and stroking her hands.

She withdrew one of her hands from his grasp and held onto her right side. Wheezing, she slowly said, "My…side…hurts. It feels like the time Frederick ran into me when we were playing tag back in schoolyard days."

He carefully helped her sit up and then get back onto the seat. "Are you feeling any better now?" She loved that concerned look on his face.

"Yes, Lew, I am fine now. I was just not expecting to be awakened by a fall to the floor. I think the shock knocked the breath out of me as much as the tumble." Changing the subject, she asked, "What could have caused that sudden stop and horrible noise?"

Just then the conductor came through their car inquiring if everyone was all right. Answering the same question fired at him by many voices, he said, "A large cow wandered onto the track and refused to move. The engineer tried to stop the train when he saw her, but it had too much momentum."

"Do we get steak for dinner?" asked one impertinent fellow. He was shushed and dirty looks directed at him by the women from across the aisle.

"Is the engine damaged?" asked another.

"It does not appear to be," replied the conductor, "but the dead animal has to be disentangled from the front of the engine."

"The cowcatcher," snorted the first speaker who had received the original dirty looks and was now the recipient of additional ones.

"Yes. Well, if no one is inconvenienced, I shall continue on to the next car," announced the conductor, seemingly flustered by the comments he had encountered.

Lissie had smoothed her skirts and her hair and was sitting beside Lew when the train started to move again. "What an unusual way to begin our morning," she remarked. "Do you predict any more exciting events that might occur during my first train ride, dear?" She leaned against Lew, looking up at him and rapidly batting her eyelashes.

He spluttered with laughter and said "No," kissing her a delighted good morning.

The remainder of the trip was completely uneventful. They arrived in Dayton early in the afternoon. Lew's friend, Jack, was waiting for them in a horse and buggy, full of questions as to why their train was late. The telegraph had only let the stationmaster know there would be a delay but did not give any details. So Lew gave his friend a blow by blow report of colliding with the unfortunate cow.

"Almost sounds like the days of riding Grant's railroad, doesn't it, Lew?" joked his friend. "I remember us hanging on for dear life as that flatbed car bounced and jounced over the rutted fields in Virginia."

"Yes," replied Lew. "The locomotive reminded me of a bucking stallion as it dipped and reared over those hillocks."

The men laughed while Lissie sat quietly, looking out at the streets of Dayton, a mixture of mean cabins and further on, well kept homes surrounded by white picket fences.

It was at one such house that Jack halted the buggy and said, "Here it is. My folks' house as well as mine. And now yours for the time being." He jumped down and offered a hand to Lissie with a flourish.

Jack's parents were gracious hosts, but Lissie felt uncomfortable knowing she and Lew were displacing younger members of the household when it came to bedtime. Lew spent the next day with Jack checking out job possibilities and housing options while Lissie tried to be of assistance to Jack's mother.

After Lissie had washed and dried dishes from breakfast the next morning, Mrs. Sparling got out her ironing board. Lissie was accustomed to Aunt Jane using a large blanket wrapped board braced on two kitchen chairs for her ironing surface. Mrs. Sparling's contrivance intrigued Lissie as she watched the lady unfold the board which came to a rounded point at one end and stood on its own wooden supports. As Mrs. Sparling set to work, she waved Lissie to a chair saying, "Please sit at the table and tell me about yourself."

It so happened Mrs. Sparling grew up on a farm outside of Dayton, and it was not long before she was sharing stories of farm life and all Lissie had to do was listen.

That evening after supper was over, the dishes washed, and the family sitting in the parlor, Mr. Sparling commented on the malaria outbreak reported in the newspaper that day. "I even heard a greater number of people getting sick than the newspaper account," rumbled the barrel-chested man. "Two fellows came into the livery stable today saying that a multitude of folks have come down with malaria in Miami County."

"What seems to be the cause?" asked Lew.

"I hear it is the soil," replied Mrs. Sparling. "So much of that area is swampy-like."

"Do you mean the ground, itself, gives off noxious vapors?" asked Lissie.

"Seems so," was the answer.

Lissie and Lew looked at each other, uncertainty in their eyes.

That evening in bed, Lissie said," Lew, I do not think I want to live in a state that has poisonous air arising from the ground."

Lew laughed, but with an uneasy sound. "I do not really think there is anything to that explanation, Lissie." And with that he turned over and was soon snoring softly. Lissie did not find it that easy to go to sleep for she felt uncomfortable in these surroundings and found the news of this malarious sickness to be disquieting. She knew Lew was hoping to find employment here where he was acquainted with people, but she had nagging doubts about the wisdom of setting up a home here so far from her family.

The next day was pretty much a repeat of the previous one with more people being reported ill. That night Lissie asked, "Lew, have you drunk any of the water in this city?"

He hugged her and nuzzled her neck before answering. "Come

to think of it, I only drank tea and coffee today. Do they count?" and he kissed her under her ear.

She squirmed away and looked at him in a serious manner. "I started to drink a glass of water this morning and felt the need to gag."

"Really?" He looked at her quizzically.

"Yes," came the emphatic answer." I walked to the dining room window where Mrs. Sparling keeps her African violets and poured the water into the plants."

"Better check the plants tomorrow for survivors," Lew snickered. She swatted at him and he continued in a more serious tone. "I will take a drink of the water tomorrow and see if I wish to gag."

The next night Lissie was ready with her question. "Did you taste the water?"

Lew was startled as it was the first thing out of Lissie's mouth once they had closed the bedroom door. "What? Oh. Yes I did, and the violets got another drink this afternoon." He grinned at her. "I have to say the taste of Dayton water ranks right up there with the water from the Rappahanock River when I filled my canteen. And believe me. The only thing in its favor was that it was wet!"

"Lew," and Lissie took a deep breath, "can we go home?"

By this time they were sitting on the bed but not yet ready to lie down. Lew said, "Lissie, I had hoped to find work here but Mr. Sparling has no need of help in his livery stable, and the town seems to be full of returning soldiers just like me. But in their case, they have connections with friends and family. It does not look very promising for me."

"If we go back home, you would have the same sort of connections because it is your home area," pleaded Lissie. "And besides, the soil here makes people sick. And I would not be surprised if the terrible tasting water does too," she added.

"You win, Wife," Lew grinned as he pinned Lissie flat to the bed and started kissing her face. His free hand began working on buttons.

The next morning they thanked their hosts for their gracious hospitality and headed for the train station. Once they were settled in their seats, Lissie hugged Lew's arm and said, "I truly enjoyed all the 'firsts' on our wedding trip, but I hope there will be no more excitement for a while."

"I cannot guarantee where the cows might wander," he teased. But their return to the east was completely uneventful.

They arrived in Cressona at dusk making it too late to search for a boarding house, so the couple headed for their former residence at the Regent Hotel. A meal of soup and slabs of bread and butter in the hotel restaurant filled their stomachs comfortably as they discussed the agenda for the next day.

"Shall we look for a boarding house after breakfast tomorrow?" asked Lew.

"Our nest egg is dwindling rapidly at this rate," declared Lissie. "Surely a boarding house would not cost as much as this fine hotel. With its indoor privy," she whispered, a twinkle in her eye.

"Yes, back to the life of the much less wealthy," remarked her husband. "Once we have a room, I shall leave you to settle in and I shall go in search of work."

Back in Room 201, settled comfortably in bed, Lissie yawned and said, "I find it comforting to have a sort of schedule for tomorrow. I felt uneasy at the Sparlings because I did not have any tasks to do other than care for our clothes and keep our bedroom tidy."

Lew hugged her close and said, "That may well be what you will be doing tomorrow too, but if I can find work, we can begin hunting for a little house to rent or buy."

Lissie shot straight up to a sitting position. "Oh Lew, do you mean we can have our own little house!" She had visions of a white picket fence with green grass in the front, a small vegetable garden in back and a clothesline stretching from the trunk of a large tree to the corner of the house.

"Lie back down, Lissie," he soothed. "We cannot live in a boarding house forever because…" He stopped and swallowed. "You want to have children, do you not? I cannot imagine dealing with a baby in a boarding house."

"Yes, Lew," said Lissie. "I want very much to be the mother of your children." By this time she was lying against him with one arm across his chest. "Our own little house," she murmured, and thought, *I wonder how long it takes to start a baby?* She went to sleep on the thought.

Chapter 13

AFTER BREAKFAST THE young couple began their search for a boarding house. There were several to choose from, but the first house looked so ill-kempt, Lissie shuddered and said, "Let us look further. I can imagine neither the floors nor the bed linens to be clean at that place."

The next dwelling advertising itself as a boarding house had been whitewashed and there were even two rockers sitting on a porch that ran along the front of the house. Mrs. Bradley, who managed the boarding house, was a friendly, buxom woman of about forty.

"Yes, I have a vacant bedroom that would do well for you," she announced. "Come upstairs and see for yourselves."

The room reminded Lissie a little of her bedroom at Miss Madge's, although not so luxurious. It appeared to be clean and when Lissie went to the window, she stealthily checked for dust on the sill and smudges on the glass. Nothing there. At the sight of Lissie's smile signaling approval, Lew asked, "How much does this room cost?"

"For a couple, it will cost $7 per month. But bear in mind that includes three meals a day for the two of you."

"I must say that amount took me aback somewhat until you mentioned the meals that sum includes," admitted Lew. "We would be pleased to rent your room, Mrs. Bradley," and he shook her hand.

The next order of business was to get their belongings to the boarding house, so Lew arranged for a cart and they were soon checked out of the hotel and settled into their new residence. It was barely mid-morning so Lew set off to see what jobs might be available. Lissie bustled around her new abode, trying to somehow make the room look homey and not feeling very satisfied with her efforts. She was soon downstairs again, sitting in the parlor when Mrs. Bradley came through on her way to the kitchen.

"Mrs. Bradley?" Lissie's voice was soft because she felt quite timid approaching their landlady.

"Yes, Mrs. Reber," the buxom lady replied. "Are you in need of something?"

"Well, in a manner of speaking," and Lissie smiled at the woman. "I need something to occupy my hours while Lew is off on his job search. Do you suppose I might help you in the kitchen?"

The woman looked startled but then said slowly, "I never had a boarder make a request like that before." And then she grinned back at Lissie. "But I never had a young wife stay at my boarding house before, either. It has always been men. And they certainly never asked to help with anything unless it was to help themselves to more grub at dinner time.

"Yes, if you ain't too good to wash and dry dishes, I can use your help," and she exited the parlor, going through the dining room to the kitchen with Lissie following her. She discovered Mrs. Bradley had ten mouths to feed including her new boarders, herself and her two children who were at school. It took about an hour for Lissie to finish the dishwashing, drying and putting away.

Mrs. Bradley was paring potatoes for the afternoon meal which was to be a hearty vegetable and mutton stew. Lissie asked if she might help with the vegetable preparation so she took over the potato peeling. The landlady started roasting the mutton so it would be tender as it simmered with the vegetables closer to dinner time.

Lissie set the dining room table for eight since the children took their lunch to school. As the grandfather clock in the parlor struck one, a stream of footsteps was heard entering the house. Lew arrived along with the last man and caught sight of Lissie serving coffee to the men already seated at the table.

He walked over to her and said, "Looks like you set yourself to work mighty quick."

She smiled up at him. "I could not abide sitting in our lonely room with nothing to do, so Mrs. Bradley kindly allowed me to busy my hands in her kitchen. Now, Husband, if you would take your seat at table and see that I have a spot beside you, I shall fetch the bread to go with this delicious stew."

After all were comfortably settled and the dining room became relatively quiet, except for the clanking of eating utensils against dishes, Mrs. Bradley introduced the Rebers to their fellow boarders.

When the majority of the diners were finished, she brought in two dried apple pies and a bread pudding. These were passed around among murmurs of appreciation.

Lew swallowed a bite of bread pudding and asked, "Do any of you know of some small houses to rent?" There was a chorus of "no's" and "don't believe so'" but Mrs. Bradley had a more positive answer.

"I do, indeed," she replied. "About two blocks north of here there are some houses facing the railroad tracks. The people at City Hall could maybe give you some other addresses in town. Old Dan Haxson owns a good part of the town, and since he is a councilman he might be there in his office today.

The young Rebers did not waste much time at the table after that pronouncement, but thanked their hostess and bidding their fellow boarders adieu, set off on a house search.

"Lew, what did you find out about work here?" Lissie looked up at her husband to see a frown cross his face.

"I can work at Michelson's Livery Stable," he said. "The pay is four dollars a week to start and could increase to five dollars after I have worked there for thirty days—if they like me."

"Well, of course they will like you," declared his little wife in a vehement tone. "Will you take the job?"

"I must first speak to the road master at the train station, I think," he said slowly. "I like trains, I like the smell of the metal and oil and smoke, and I like the idea of how they can carry so much freight and so many people. Trains help me to dream," and he laughed.

Lissie said nothing to that as her thoughts on trains were that they were nasty, smelly, noisy contraptions, but she saw no need to pit her ideas against Lew's idyllic view.

By this time they had reached the block of small houses Mrs. Bradley had mentioned. As they walked slowly down the pathway in front of the houses, a freight train roared by. The train whistle made Lissie jump and some ashes flew through the air from the smokestack and landed on her sleeve. Brushing at it left a smudge.

"Lew, look at my dress sleeve," she fussed. He looked down at it and then at her with a quirked eyebrow.

"I do not believe we need go further," she said in a decisive tone. "How could one ever hang out laundry to dry and be able to know the clothes would not be covered with soot and ashes?"

"I see your point, Wife," agreed Lew, doing his best not to grin at Lissie's indignation. "Let us turn at this corner and walk to the center of town and find this Mr. Haxson at City Hall."

The councilman was in his office and invited the young couple to sit down. After Lew explained they were looking for a small house to buy or rent, Mr. Haxson reeled off a list of houses and locations.

"We are not interested in any houses in close proximity to the railroad," insisted Lissie.

"That is a shame," puffed the elderly man, speaking around a noxious cigar. "I do have a three room house for sale at $600—fenced all round with trees in the back yard located one block over from the town square."

"That is a bit steep for our pocketbook," Lew said slowly. "Do you have anything in the same area for rent?"

Haxson stubbed out his cigar in an ashtray by his desk edge and said, "I have a two room house a block further from the square that just became vacant. I would be willing to rent it to you for $4.50 per month since you are a war veteran."

"May we see that house, please?" requested Lew.

"You are welcome to look it over," replied the councilman. "The door is not locked."

After getting the directions to Ambergris Avenue, Lew and Lissie set out with high hopes of possibly seeing their new home.

The little structure was situated on a street of sorts, along with four houses of similar size and mostly ill-kempt. Lissie was silent as they walked up to the door on a sandy path and entered. Standing just inside the front door Lissie could see dust motes riding the beam of sunlight coming through the streaked window at the side of the room.

She heaved a large sigh and Lew squeezed her hand, saying, "At least it has a wooden floor instead of dirt."

"Oh Lew, do you think we can make this livable?" Lissie asked with a sob in her voice. She could not help comparing the cheery Hotschlag farm house and Miss Madge's little home with this depressing structure.

"Let me pace this off to see how big it really is," replied her husband. After counting his strides to the far wall from the front door and then doing the same with the width of the building, he said, "This appears to be about twenty-two feet wide and sixteen feet long." He twitched a dusty sheet that hung toward the back of the dwelling and said, "I guess this marks out the second room Mr. Haxson was talking about." And he sneezed.

"I am feeling quite disheartened," said Lissie, "but let us check the back yard."

The back door was off center of the back wall, closer to the shelves on the outer wall that Lissie was already thinking of as the kitchen. It opened to a grassy plot with a privy situated about three feet from the alley and a mid-size maple tree casting its shade from the opposite side of the lot. A pump stood a few steps from the door.

"Too bad we cannot live outside," Lissie sighed.

Lew laughed and asked, "Does that mean you are ready to take this on, Wife?"

"Let's see what the water tastes like first," she replied, thinking back to the nasty tasting liquid they had been served in Dayton.

Lew worked the pump handle several times and finally got a stream of water. Cupping his hand, he caught some and drank it. "Tastes all right to me."

Lissie followed suit as he continued to pump and she approved the taste. "If Mr. Haxson allows us to put up a clothes line back here, I am ready to face this task," she said with a determined tilt to her chin. "Perhaps Aunt Jane will have time to help me one day next week as I begin to work on this place."

And so the young Rebers obtained their first home. They lived at Mrs. Bradley's boarding house until the little house on Ambergris Avenue was ready to inhabit. Lissie continued to help Mrs. Bradley in the kitchen most mornings and that grateful lady lowered their boarding fee to $5.50 because of it. After each afternoon meal, Lissie would head for Ambergris Avenue and work on their little house.

Lew was hired as a baggage/freight clerk with the railroad, much to his delight. His starting salary was $5.50 per week which seemed a princely sum to the young couple until they began to buy furnishings for their home. Aunt Jane provided a rocker but the young couple needed to purchase a table and chairs, a bed and kitchen utensils and dishes. All the money saved from Lissie's work at Miss Madge's was now gone, but Lissie felt it was well spent.

Starting with a thorough scrubbing from floor to ceiling, Lissie whitewashed the walls and then hung cheery gingham curtain at the now-gleaming windowpanes—two flanking the front door, one on the side wall next to the cook stove and the last in their bedroom. That "room" was marked off by sheets also donated by Aunt Jane, which hung from wire running in an L shape supported by hooks screwed into the ceiling.

Uncle Edgar donated a bench for seating in the living room area against the far wall and Lissie fashioned pillows with goose down and feathers from the farm to be used as seat cushions on the bench or to put at one's back, depending on what was most needed.

She had crocheted brightly colored rag rugs, an oval one for the front door entry, one to rest in front of the living room bench, and two small rectangles for either side of their bed. By the end of September the young couple was ready to move into their new home.

The last Monday of the month Lissie told Lew she thought the house was ready to live in. Lew arranged for a wagon to carry their belongings to the little house after work the next day. Lissie had helped Mrs. Bradley with her morning chores for the last time and after eating dinner, bade her farewell and headed for Ambergris Avenue.

When Lew arrived with their things, he entered a cheery room with blue and white gingham curtains at the windows and a matching cover on their little table which was laid for two. Since it was dusk, Lissie had lit a lamp in the corner of the living room which rested on a small wooden crate, also covered with gingham material and situated beside the rocker. That, along with the lamp she had placed in the center of the kitchen table, lent ample light to the room.

Lissie directed Lew and the drayman where to put the trunks in their bedroom area. After the man left, Lew walked to Lissie and putting an arm around her shoulders, he kissed her on the forehead and said, "What is that delicious smell?"

Lissie giggled as she detected a rumble in the region of Lew's stomach. "I knew you did not have time for dinner today so I put on a pot of potato chowder and baked some biscuits."

"Ah, Wife, marrying you was the smartest thing I ever did,"

groaned Lew in ecstasy as Lissie served him a savory bowl of potato, onion and milk seasoned with salt, pepper and butter.

Comfortably full from supper, Lew moved to the rocker, stretching out his long legs while Lissie cleaned up the kitchen area from their meal. She felt quite housewifely—and yes, rather tired, too. She began to pull a chair from the table so she might sit beside Lew but his voice stopped her.

"Come, sit here," and he patted his knees. She giggled, but did so. As he settled her comfortably in his arms, he nuzzled her neck and said, "You have made a most dismal house into a cozy little home, Wife."

She looked up at him and said, "I did not do it alone. Aunt Jane helped and so did you, Benjie."

"True, but you did the bulk of the work and it was you who placed items precisely—and fed my hungry appetite." He smiled and kissed her again. "As you arranged your little house just so, can you think of other things this little house needs?"

"If more shelves could be built so I could have more food preparation space, it would be helpful. Right now, there is barely room to put my dishpan and rinse pan, not to speak of an area for dishes to dry."

"I will purchase lumber tomorrow and perhaps some oilcloth like Jane has in her kitchen work area. But enough of labor, mein leibchen, let us retire." And Lew rose with no seeming effort and carried Lissie to their bedroom.

Lew built additional shelves in the kitchen area and designed counter space for the dishpan and food preparation. Utilizing the maple tree as one end of support for the new clothesline, he dug a deep hole for a sturdy pole with a crossbeam so that two lines could be strung. Lissie felt she was truly ready to set up housekeeping. That is, until washday came around and she faced it alone, for the first time in her life.

As soon as Lew was off to the rail yard and breakfast cleaned up, Lissie set to work. She had already filled her largest pot with water and it was heating while she fixed breakfast. She stirred up the embers in the cook stove as the water was not yet steaming and then tried to think through the next steps. *I must fetch the two tubs, one for washing and one for rinsing. Oh yes, I must get the lye soap Aunt Jane gave me.*

She arranged the tubs to her liking in the back yard and then asked herself, *How shall I manage this when the weather gets colder?* She decided to worry about that later and returned to the house to check the water temperature. It was steaming so she gathered the clothes that needed to be washed and piled them on the ground outside along with the washboard she had purchased the week before.

Lissie discovered getting the hot water into a bucket and then to the tub outside was a scary, as well as a heavy, task. By the time her washtub was full enough, her hair was escaping from her braids and into her eyes, and she was decidedly perspiring. And no clothes were yet washed! She had remembered to put some soap in the tub after the first bucket of hot water, so she began loading in the dirty clothes.

Lissie started to grab one of Lew's shirts and thought better of it because the water was still so hot and then she remembered the thick dolly stick Uncle Edgar had fashioned for her, copying the design of Aunt Jane's. She could use that to push the clothes around in the tub without burning her hands. She spied a greasy spot on one of Lew's shirts and as the wet garment cooled she scrubbed at it on her washboard and was gratified to see the spot disappear.

By the time she had run a total of three wash tubs full of clothes, wrung them out, rinsed them, wrung them out again, and hung them over the clothesline—she had forgotten to buy clothes pegs—her apron was remarkably damp and she was totally exhausted. As she transferred a pair of Lew's denim pants to the rinse tub, the pants owner opened the back door and said, "Oh, there you are." And in the next breath asked, "What are we having for dinner?"

Lissie was sure she had never sent such an angry look to her husband. "I have had no time to prepare a meal," she stated, spitting out each word separately.

Lew took a more careful look at her and realized the error of his ways. "I will cut some slices of bread and cheese. That should serve me well until supper time."

"You do that, Husband," came her decidedly unfriendly reply.

When she had finished hanging all the clothes, emptying the tubs, bucket by bucket into the alley and propping them against the house to drain and dry, Lissie staggered inside and flung herself on the bed. *How am I going to be able to do such work, over and over and over, again, year after year?* And then dread thought. They would likely have at least one child which meant diapers and more clothes. *Oh, Lord, what have I gotten myself in to?*

Lissie woke the next morning knowing it was ironing day. She had left the clothes on the line as they were not totally dry at nightfall. As she began warming her flatirons on the stove top, she went to fetch the clothes. She took a moment to bury her nose in the clean garments. *Ooh, they smelled so fresh and clean.* Piling them on the rocker and on the sitting room bench, she spread a flannel blanket on the table and prepared to iron the clothing and other items she had laundered the day before.

She discovered it was not an easy task to get the irons' heat just right. She flicked some water on one of the irons which immediate spat back at her. She flinched, realizing it was too hot. That would scorch even the roughest of Lew's shirts. Once she deemed the proper amount of heat, she began her task.

The day was a warm, fall day and normally, Lissie would have enjoyed the musky scents of autumn leaves. But shut up in her tiny house, smoothing piece after piece of clean clothes and household linens with a hot, heavy iron proved to be the dreaded twin of the previous day's laundry. Mopping her face occasionally, Lissie persevered throughout the morning. All the pieces were ironed and folded on their bed but not yet stored away when Lew arrived for dinner.

"I fear you must make do with bread and cheese once more," she sighed. "Tomorrow I shall go to market and bake bread and pies," she promised. "That is, if I can use my right arm," and she winced as she rubbed her shoulder.

"Truly, I had no idea of the labor it takes to run a household, even such a small one as ours," Lew remarked. He had helped himself to most of the left-over dried-cherry pie Lissie had baked on Saturday. "Time to go back to work," and Lew was out the door, leaving Lissie to straighten her kitchen and put away her clean laundry. Despite her aching back and arm muscles, she felt deep satisfaction in having come through what she considered her first major step as a housewife.

Days turned into weeks and Lissie continued feeling more at ease with her homely tasks although washday and ironing day were always grinding chores. But, oh, how rewarding it was to inhale the scent of clean clothes fresh from drying outdoors and the satisfaction of folding and putting away their belongings.

The young couple enjoyed several Sunday dinners with the Holtschlags. Lissie remarked more than once, "I should so love to feed your family a meal Aunt Jane, but I do not know how we should fit everyone in our tiny house.

"Not to worry, dear," replied Jane. "The time will come when you will seat many around your table and think nothing of it."

The beginning of that prediction heralded its start as the calendar flipped to November. One morning Lissie woke as she heard Lew shaking down the ashes and stirring up the coals in order for her to start preparing breakfast. As she sat up and turned to put her feet on the floor, her head felt woozy and suddenly she had a violent urge to vomit. The first retch was a dry heave, but by the time she had crawled to the chamber pot under the bed, the remnants of last night's supper had evacuated.

Lew heard the unusual sound and rushed to his wife's side. "Lissie, whatever is wrong?" He had the presence of mind to wet a flannel washcloth in the kitchen wash basin and return, wiping Lissie's forehead and then her mouth. Hugging her to his side, he asked, "Do you want to try to sit at the table or lie back down?"

"I think perhaps lie down. My head felt so strange when I sat up." He gently helped her back to bed, covering her as she curled into herself.

After Lew fixed his own breakfast, checking on Lissie every few minutes, it was soon time for him to go to work. He went to her bedside but found her still sleeping, so left, wondering what malady had struck their house.

When he arrived at home for the afternoon meal, he was surprised to see Lissie bustling around, just then pulling biscuits from the oven to accompany roast pork with carrots and potatoes from the Holtschlag farm.

Amazed at her miraculous recovery, Lew kissed her cheek and said, "You certainly look healthier than when I left this morning. How did you manage that?"

"I do not know, Lew. But when I woke again, I felt quite well, except for a very empty stomach." She grinned at him. "It would seem something at supper disagreed with me greatly." She went to fill their plates. "I am just thankful that you did not suffer the same illness."

Supper that night was a delicious stew using the leftovers from dinner. Later, Lissie sat darning a hole in one of Lew's socks while he read to her from the Gospel of Matthew. This sort of activity had become a favorite custom after supper. Lissie loved to hear Lew's deep voice intone the Shakespearean sound of the Scriptures. "I like to go to sleep with the sound of your voice in my head, speaking of God," she explained.

The next morning Lew was up first, as usual, shaking down ashes, stirring the coals, and preparing for coffee making. Again, he heard a retching sound coming from their sleeping area. Rushing to Lissie's side, he found her on her knees beside the chamber pot, forehead leaning against the mattress. "Liebchen," he whispered as he knelt beside her, holding her against him. "What can be causing this sickness?"

"I do not know," came her weak answer. "Please help me back to bed."

Lew's morning was a repeat of the previous one. Checking on Lissie just before he left for work, she appeared to be resting comfortably although her face was pale.

He could hardly believe his eyes when he opened the door that afternoon and once again beheld his little wife giving a last minute stir to hearty chowder, thick slabs of bread already cut and on the table, ready for his arrival.

Lissie turned to him at his entrance. "Oh, Lew, I am so glad you have not caught this wretched disease I have contracted."

He kissed her cheek and then sat down at the table. "I, too, am very grateful to be free from this mysterious malady. I had enough of retching and stomachaches back in the war." Then he grinned at her over a spoonful of chowder. "I believe you must be rebelling against preparing breakfast, Wife."

"Not at all, Husband," Lissie insisted. "This morning sickness is truly much too unpleasant to stage a charade like that."

At her statement, both of them gasped and said in unison, "Morning sickness. Morning sickness?"

Lew reached across the table to grasp both of Lissie's hands. "Lissie, could you be carrying our child?" Before she could frame an answer, he stood, upsetting his chair as he rushed around the table to pick up his petite wife, laughing and twirling around.

"Lew, put me down," she protested. "I have enough whirling in my head of a morning. You do not wish me to regurgitate my dinner down your shirt front!"

That put an instant stop to the twirling and Lew set her back down as carefully as if she were a crystal figurine.

It was difficult to curb their excitement but Lew had to finish his meal and return to work. "Must this sickness continue the entire time you carry our babe?" he asked.

"I sincerely hope not," Lissie replied. "The idea of spending nine months in this fashion is even more daunting than the thought of spending a lifetime doing laundry." She giggled but felt some trepidation at the thought. "I can only hope Aunt Jane will have some advice since she has endured the birthing of three children."

Chapter 14

THAT NEXT SUNDAY as Jane was visiting with Lissie after church, the younger woman said softly, "I have spent my mornings this past week feeling decidedly ill. As I searched my memory I realized I have missed my monthly flow. I believe I am with child." She looked down, embarrassed and blushing to have said such a thing, even to her aunt.

"What wonderful news, my dear." Jane patted Lissie's hand. "So you are feeling queasy, eh. Are you able to eat any breakfast at all?"

"No," admitted Lissie, "but I feel better by mid-morning, though somewhat weak, and am able to eat with Lew at dinner and supper."

"That is good," pronounced her aunt. "You need to keep up your strength. Remember, you are now eating for two. Maybe keep soda crackers beside your bed and nibble one before you even try raising your head from the pillow at dawn. This morning sickness will likely go away in a week or two, so try not to worry about it. Worry is not good for either you or the babe," Jane cautioned.

Lissie was somewhat fearful at the comment that morning sickness would *likely* be gone soon, so she decided that might be a good thing to pray about. Wash day was coming and she needed all the strength she could muster for *that* task.

The remainder of November sped by, and, gratefully, so did Lissie's morning sickness. By Christmas she presented a blooming presence, the picture of health, although beginning to find her Sunday Meeting skirt a trifle tight at the waist.

The Sunday after Christmas day, the congregation was mingling after church and Eliza spied Lissie. "Lissie," she called in a schoolmarm's voice. Lissie excused herself from conversation with Aunt Jane and her neighbor, and ran to her friend. Grabbing hands and kissing each other on the cheek, they headed for a nearby pew and sat down.

"Lissie, you are absolutely blooming. I do not think I have ever seen you look so well. I declare, marriage truly suits you," Eliza said, arching an eyebrow.

"It does, indeed," replied Lissie in a sedate tone but with a twinkle in her eye. She leaned forward and whispered her latest news to Eliza.

"Oh, my dear, how truly wonderful," gasped her friend. Then in a low voice, "Are you frightened of the coming ordeal?"

"Perhaps. A little," admitted Lissie. "But I shall have Aunt Jane to help and Lew will be there to cheer me on. Enough about me. Tell me about Philadelphia," for she knew Eliza had returned to the city as a beginning instructor at the Finishing School where she had been a student not too long before.

"Life is not so gay as when John was alive," sighed Eliza, "but now that the war is over we have no shortage of young ladies wanting to be 'finished,' and indeed, many of them need a great deal of it," she added, drily.

"Such a martinet you are," laughed Lissie and she playfully pinched her friend's arm.

"'Tis true. Many of our young ladies come from the frontier and have no idea how a proper table is to be set or appropriate topics of conversation.

"I fear you may have become altogether too elegant for me," stated Lissie.

"No, you will always be my forever friend," stated Eliza solemnly. "Please write to me as you have time, for I envision you as living real life while I live vicariously by virtue of my students' lives."

Lissie impulsively hugged her friend. "Have you given up on the idea of love, marriage, and a family?"

Eliza's face showed great sadness in one so young, as she replied, "When John died, a piece of me was torn away. I cannot think another man might ever make my heart sing again. There will never be another man like my gallant John," and she sighed.

Just then Lew called Lissie for they were to eat dinner with the Holtschlag family. "I must go," said Lissie as she rose, giving her friend another hug and kiss, "but I shall certainly write. And you must do the same." With that she was off to join Lew and the rest of the family.

Winter passed and spring arrived along with all sorts of physical changes for Lissie. "None of my clothes fit anymore," she fussed. Lew had just come home for dinner and kissed his little wife as he gently patted her baby bump. It now rounded out her apron in a way not to be ignored.

Lew soothed her by saying, "Shall we go shopping for dress goods to cover my beautiful wife who is obviously with child?"

Lissie wriggled out of his arms and laughed, her discontent forgotten. "I am perfectly capable of shopping for myself, Husband. Sit down at table and let me feed you."

As Lew returned to work, Lissie set off for The Mercantile. She came home with some hunter green calico and a length of peach striped linen. Lissie had to remind herself to purchase adequate material to allow for an ever increasing waist band and waist tops with ample room for her blossoming bosom. She also purchased lightweight cotton for underclothes as her chemises had become uncomfortably snug.

In addition to sewing new clothes for herself and baby, for whom she had bought lengths of flannel, Lissie had determined back in the winter to plant a vegetable garden. She prevailed upon Lew to spade up a six foot square plot next to their property line on the opposite side from the maple tree.

Near the end of March as the days became longer, Lissie asked, "Do you feel like breaking up those dirt clods with the new hoe you bought? I think it is time to plant my vegetable garden."

"I reckon I can do that, Wife," replied Lew. "Will this vegetable garden also be considered mine?"

She laughed and swatted his shoulder. "Of course, you big silly." As he picked up the hoe from the back corner of the kitchen and went out to work, Lissie washed the supper dishes, thinking of what vegetables she wanted to plant. *We need carrots, onions, beans, spinach, squash, beets, and seed potatoes*. With that list in mind, she gave her dish towel a satisfied shake as she dried the last dish and put it away.

The next morning she walked to The Mercantile to purchase the seeds she needed for the Reber garden. Back home she lined out her rows using twigs from the maple tree at each end of the plot to help her keep the rows straight. She dragged the hoe along, pressing down into the dirt Lew had loosened the previous evening.

Bending over her newly made rows, Lissie dropped in the bean seeds first and then covered them, patting the dirt gently with the hoe head and marking her row. On to the carrots, she followed suit in the same manner, straightening up and feeling a decided pain in her back. *I shall just go sit on the bench by the back door and rest a bit,* thought Lissie. Lew found her there when he came home for his afternoon meal.

"Lissie, are you ill? I would joke about it being no longer morning, but I think I should not," he said, sitting down and putting an arm around her.

"I am so tired, Lew," she said, barely able to get the words out.

"Let me help you to bed," replied her worried husband. "I think I must send word to your Aunt Jane."

Settled in bed, Lissie fussed in a weak tone. "Please do not bother Aunt," but that said she drifted off to sleep.

Getting a message to Jane Holtschlag posed a challenge for Lew. But fortunately, he saw Hiram on Main Street the next morning and was able to get word to Lissie's aunt asking her to check on her niece.

That morning had started normally for Lissie but by the time she had a row carved in the dirt for her onion sets, she barely had ample energy to put a hand to her back and straighten her frame. As she slowly made her way to the back door to let herself into the house, she heard a knock on the front door.

"Just a minute," she called. It took more than that but excitement at having a caller fueled her steps. She opened the door to see Aunt Jane and almost literally fell into her arms. "Oh, Aunt, I am so tired—and so glad to see you."

The older woman entered the house and led Lissie to her rocker. "Sit here, my dear and rest. I have some bone broth with me that I shall heat up on the stove. A cup of that will perk you right up," she soothed.

Whether it was the broth or the comforting presence of Aunt Jane, Lissie did feel more energetic after drinking a cup of the hot beverage. After downing it all in a very short period, Lissie asked, "Why am I so tired of a sudden, Aunt? Is this part of being with child or have I contracted an illness of some sort?"

"You do not seem ill," replied Jane, "for I feel no fever heat rising from your body. I have heard tell of child bearing women having thin blood and my granny always swore by bone broth to build blood strength and energy.

The bone broth apparently solved Lissie's lack of energy after a week or so. She eventually managed to plant her garden which prospered well. Almost too well, for she had a bumper crop of beans which she was picking the day Baby Reber made his appearance into the world.

That morning Lissie surprised herself at the sprightly feeling she was experiencing despite the bulky baby bump protruding from her front. She kissed Lew goodbye as he set off for work and she commenced giving their living area a good sweeping complete with shaking the four rag rugs from various locations.

Then she decided to go check the garden. The inch-long beans from a few days before had grown several inches and were ready to be picked. Lissie had filled her apron, looping up the corners to form a sort of bag below baby bump when a pain sliced through her back, strong enough to make her stagger.

"Oomph," went Lissie, and she looked over her shoulder thinking some strange object had struck her from behind. *No.* Then another grinding pain chiseled at her body, this time from the direction of her groin. Pressing her beans to her belly, Lissie limped to the outside bench.

I must be having labor pains. Oh, dear God, I am having my baby and no one is here to help me. Tears began to roll down Lissie's face, her sobs were fueled by fear. Then she remembered Pastor Yost's voice reading the 23rd Psalm during last Sunday's sermon. "Though I walk through the valley of the shadow of death, …Thou art with me." A sense of peace settled over her like a warm blanket. Her tears dried and her fear was gone.

Suddenly Lissie realized she had experienced no more of those pains. Looking down she saw her apron still full of beans so she slowly stood, and went inside to get a pan. She intended to stem and snap the beans into small pieces and cook them for dinner. As she prepared the beans for cooking, she felt grinding pain occasionally in her stomach and back somewhat like menstrual cramps. *How long will I have these pains before Baby arrives,* she wondered.

Lew came home for dinner and while she was setting the food before him, she said, "You may be a father by the end of this day,

Lew."

"What!" He was up in a flash, putting his arms around her. "Should you not be resting instead of working here in the kitchen?"

Lissie rested her hand on his chest to reassure him. "The pains have not yet come hard and I hear tell first babies take their time a-birthing. Although, I would wish this little one might not take too much time arriving," she muttered.

Lew sat back down and ate at a rather more rapid pace than usual. "Shall I send for Jane?" he asked.

"Perhaps this evening you can rent a buggy and horse at the livery stable," she answered. "Aunt Jane is expecting to get news of this impending birth. She told me this past Sunday she has everything packed for when I needed her."

The afternoon went on normally with contractions coming a little more regularly and when Lew came home after work, he found Lissie sitting in the rocker, sewing another flannel gown for Baby. He came over and kissed her. When she smiled up at him, it turned into a grimace.

"Ugh. That was a nasty one," she said in a weak voice.

Lew immediately turned back to the door. "I am off to fetch Jane," he said.

Lissie was spent from the last contraction, so she just nodded her assent.

After he left, she decided she should start heating water. As she opened the back door to pump the pail full, her water broke. "Aiee!" she yelped, grateful later that she had the presence of mind to rush on outside so she would not have to mop her kitchen floor. Right then, the thought of doing any kind of additional work seemed decidedly distasteful.

She did get her water bucket partially filled, dealing with another contraction, before she was back in the house. Ladling water into a large pan, she set it to heat, poking up the fire and adding a few sticks of wood. Then she decided to lie down. Lew and Aunt Jane found her curled up around baby bump.

"My water broke, Aunt Jane." Lissie's voice had a tremulous note.

"It should not be too long, Lissie," Jane assured her.

Then the contractions started in regularly. "Can I do anything to help, Jane?" asked Lew. He was pacing from one end of the tiny house to the other.

"No, Lew. I suggest you go walk off your nerves by pacing up and down the street four or five times."

The fifth time he neared his house, Lew heard a baby cry. Rushing in, he met Jane at the bedroom. "Meet your new son, Lew. What name will you call him?"

"A son." With that, Lew flopped into the rocker as if his legs were made of rubber. "Oh, we shall call him Elmer. A good sturdy name, do you not think?"

"I do, indeed," answered Jane. "Here, acquaint yourself with young Elmer while I get Lissie cleaned up and more comfortable," and she handed the baby over to his father.

Baby Elmer lay content in Lew's arms and the rocking of the chair seemed to soothe both father and son. But all too soon, eyes flew open as well as a tiny, rosebud mouth, and little Elmer let his world know he needed—something.

Lew arose from the rocker wondering what was wrong with this child. He had been around babies since he had three siblings younger than himself, but he had never taken care of them.

Jane met him as she came from Lissie's bedside. "That young man has a rare set of lungs. I predict a fine preaching style from him in later years," she remarked. "But for now, I predict he might well be hungry."

Lew followed Jane as she returned to Lissie's side. She was sitting up, propped with pillows and prepared to nurse the squalling baby. Fortunately, he was soon quieted at his mother's breast.

"Draw up a chair, Lew, so you two can visit," Jane advised as she bustled off to straighten the kitchen and put more wood on the fire.

Lew picked up Lissie's hand from the coverlet and kissed it. "Oh, my sweet Lissie. I thank God for your safety and our strong baby boy."

"I, too, Benjie," and she scooted over on the bed to lean against his shoulder.

He was watching her and his tiny son with intense interest but noticed her wince when she moved. "What is wrong, Liebchen? I saw pain cross your face."

"I am just sore from the birthing," she answered. "Our babe is not over-large but I can tell you his arrival felt much like I was birthing something as big as a log."

"Perhaps a sapling," he teased.

"Little do you know, Benjie," she scolded him in a tired voice.

He held her until both she and little Elmer were asleep. Then he gently laid her back, curled protectively around their little son.

Eighteen-year-old Lissie bounced back quickly from childbirth. She sang to baby Elmer as she fed him and changed diapers. Lew got a smile and a kiss every time he came home from work. Mopping floors, doing laundry—which increased by a large proportion with a baby—or preserving fruit and vegetables seemed a never ending task, but Lissie thrived on it all. She even salted down some hams from the farm. Lissie loved to sit with Elmer on the back bench while Lew dug potatoes and spaded up carrots and onions, feeling quite rich in the bounty God had provided them.

Lew remarked to Lissie one day, "I remember our farmhouse had a root cellar where we stored garden produce through the winter. The next time we visit your Uncle Edgar we must ask what he might suggest for us. I am at a loss as to know how to keep our garden produce from freezing before we can use it."

The next meal at the Holtschlags, Lew asked his question as they sat around the table, visiting.

"I once had a neighbor who dug up an area of his garden, buried his vegetables there and they were able to use their produce all winter," Edgar commented.

"How large an area should I dig for our little patch?" asked Lew.

"You had a good crop of potatoes and other root vegetables," replied Edgar. "I judge a three x four foot area would be ample. Dig down at least six inches, spread out your root crops and then cover them with dirt and leaves. Newspapers would make good insulation--I'll give you all our back issues--and then cover them with another four inches of dirt."

Lissie had been listening in on their conversation so she wasted no time in arming Lew with their spade for she did not want any of her gardening labor to be in vain.

Elmer was an active child and not generally fussy. Lissie took him outside with her when she worked in the garden or did laundry. Jane had given her a large basket with a carry handle spanning the middle. When it was time to venture outside, Lissie would scoop up little Elmer, already swaddled in linen sheeting or flannel, depending on the weather. "We are going outside for some fresh air, my sweet boy," she would say, nuzzling his soft neck. He would gurgle at her, trying to catch a stray lock of brown hair that had loosed from around her face.

As colder weather set in, such outings halted, but Elmer was generally satisfied by watching his mother bustle around in the kitchen. She would prop him up in his cradle which she pulled out of their sleeping area each morning. That idyllic phase did not last long, however, because young Elmer had learned to rock his own cradle. One fine day in late November he rocked himself right out on to the wooden floor.

Lissie was horror-stricken. "Oh my sweet baby. Dear God, have I killed my child?" She ran from the vegetables she was preparing to roast for dinner and fell to the floor beside her wailing baby. Picking him up and nestling him to her, she began to sing "Hush a bye, don't you cry, go to sleep my little baby." Apparently, the excitement of his fall plus the lulling of his mother's voice soon quieted the child enough that he went to sleep.

As Lissie laid Elmer back in his cradle, she could see a purple lump forming on his forehead. "O Lord, please do not let that fall hurt our baby son." She knew she could do nothing more and turned aside to continue peeling the potatoes for Lew's dinner.

Elmer awoke at his father's homecoming, and as Lew picked up his little son, he noticed his wife's tear-stained face. She explained what had happened and Lew said, "I see a small, purple spot on Elmer's forehead. Believe me, sweet wife, this is nothing to what he will experience as a growing boy." And he laughed.

Lissie could not find it in herself to even smile. "Please help me figure out what to do, Lew," she pleaded. "I can no longer prop our bumptious youngster in his cradle as I go about my work."

By this time they were sitting at the table and as Lew ate, he sorted through possibilities. "Why not fold up a blanket or two along with a pillow and spread them on the floor with young Elmer in the midst. That way he can watch you work, play with his rattle or sleep. And he will have no place to fall but over on the blanket pad."

"That should work fine, Lew." Lissie jumped up, getting blankets and a pillow before Lew had eaten another bite.

Their active baby boy often provided chaos to Lissie's orderly household, but that was nothing compared to what was coming.

Chapter 15

LEW ARRIVED HOME one evening brimming with excitement. As soon as they sat down for supper, he said, "I heard today of a step upward job for which I can make."

Lissie knew Lew well enough by now she could tell when he was excited because his English came out upside-down and sideways.

Little Elmer was sitting on her lap and as she edged the bread out of his reach and closer to Lew, she teased her husband gently. "Please tell me about this step upward job."

One look at her face and Lew knew he was being mocked. "Wife," he grinned while arching one eyebrow, "Hezekiah 46:39 says 'Thou shalt not tease thy husband.'"

"Husband, there is no such book in the Bible," retorted Lissie. "Now tell me about this exciting job."

Amidst their laughter, Lew proceeded. "The stationmaster told me today that the depot in West Reading is looking to hire a train supervisor. He said he would give me a recommend if I was interested. The salary is $7.50/week with a dollar raise after three months of satisfactory work."

"What would you be doing, Lew?"

"I for sure will not be hefting bags and boxes onto a baggage car," he replied. "It sounds like I will be checking tickets of passengers and manifests of freight. What do you think, Lissie?"

"I think we will be forty or fifty miles away from Aunt Jane," said his wife in a troubled tone.

"We are almost twenty years old," chided Lew. "Surely that is old enough to brave a move to a new town. It is not like we are heading west to Kansas or some such foreign place."

"You are right, Lew. I should be as brave as my soldier husband. Apply for the job and if you are hired, this branch of the Reber family will move."

Lew applied for the position, was hired, and left for Reading to work and find a house to rent. Lissie notified the Hostschlags, wrote Eliza her news and prepared to move.

Uncle Edgar agreed to drive a wagon with the young family's belongings. Lissie and baby Elmer would take the train at no charge since Lew was an employee of the railroad.

It was now December and the weather seemed not to know whether to rain, snow or shine. The day Uncle Edgar chose to move the Reber household goods was cloudy, but the men--Hiram came in to help--were cheerful as they loaded table, chairs, benches, bed frame, treasured feather bed mattress, a cradle and of course, the wash tubs.

Lew had uncovered the produce he had buried in the garden patch and Lissie packed potatoes, onions, carrots and beets in wooden boxes layered with sawdust.

As she waved goodbye to her uncle, he said. "I should pull up to your doorstep in Reading some time Wednesday."

Aunt Jane had come into town in the buggy after getting her children and Jennie off to school.

"Aunt, I do not know what we would have done without your help." Lissie tried her best to keep her voice steady as Jane helped her pack three valises and the large basket in which young Elmer would nestle for most of his first train ride.

"I hate to see you leave us so close to Christmas," remarked Jane, "but this is actually a good time for Edgar to help you move since all the crops are in." Her matter of fact tone belied the sheen in her eyes.

As Lissie shut the door of her first home as a married woman, she gave a little pat to the door casing, then turned with a resolute tilt to her chin and joined Hiram, Jane and baby Elmer in the buggy.

The trip to Reading was uneventful although Lissie dreaded making the journey without Lew. The clack of the wheels on the rails and the sway of the train coach seemed to lull baby Elmer. As long as his tummy was comfortably full and his diaper dry, he was a happy baby.

Lew was waiting for his little family when the train pulled into the station. "Welcome to Reading." Lew kissed Lissie's cheek and then grabbed the large cloth bag she was carrying. "We will get your trunk and other bags and then to our new home we go."

Lissie was too tired to smile at Lew's excited, tangled English.

Indeed, she was too tired to even think, for the early rising in Cressona and the stress of leaving Aunt Jane had drained her energy.

Soon they were on their way in a buggy Lew had rented from a nearby livery stable. He stopped in front of a nondescript building very much the size of the house they had left behind in Cressona. But there was at least one very large difference.

Lew opened the door with a flourish and Lissie walked in holding Elmer. Looking around in the dusty twilight, Lissie turned to her husband. "Lew, we cannot stay here."

"Why ever not?" he demanded.

"Our furniture has not yet arrived," half sobbed Lissie. "Where would Elmer sleep? Where would *we* sleep?" She looked at Lew's sleeping bag in the corner with disdain. "I did not sign up to be a soldier," and she erupted into tears which in turn upset the baby, who wasted no time in adding his cries to his mother's.

"Ach, liebchen, I am such a dumkopf," came Lew's sad tones as he embraced his little family. "I was so excited to have a house for you I forget Edgar will not arrive until tomorrow—maybe. You are tired and so is baby. Let us go to the boarding house where I have been staying and rent my room for another night. I have not been living here," he explained, "but just today told Mrs. Bloomberg I was leaving because my family was arriving."

Fortunately, the landlady had not rented out Lew's room and was more than happy to see it rented for that night.

The next morning Lew set off for work and once Elmer was fed and changed, Lissie walked to her new home. First, however, she prevailed upon Mrs. Bloomberg to lend her a broom, because Lissie wanted to sweep as much dirt as possible from the floor before Uncle Edgar arrived with their belongings.

She told Lew later, "I am sure I was quite the sight marching down the boardwalk with a broom in one hand, a bag for Elmer over a shoulder, and a basket holding Elmer in the other hand."

The night's rest had done her good and she was ready to face the task of cleaning this unfamiliar house which would soon become their home. The sun shone down on mother and child as she marched with energetic step, reveling in the crisp air and the challenge that lay before her.

Lissie opened the front door to their new home and spied the flicker of a mouse tail as it disappeared into a crevice beneath the floor. "Eeoo," was her pronouncement as she walked in, her nose snatching unwelcome scents of mustiness, dust and other smells she declined to identify. "I can see it is time to find a tabby cat for the Reber household," she declared, as she sat Elmer's sleeping form on the floor, still snugly secure in his basket.

She walked around the little house, trying not to think of the snug nest they had left behind in Cressona. Lew had mentioned last night at supper that this place was somewhat larger—twenty-two feet square—but at first glance she was not impressed. The sleeping areas were separated from the living areas by a wall that ran almost to the back door. She discovered a dark little cranny at the back which was shelved and apparently meant for a pantry.

She opened an inner door to the side of the pantry space and discovered she was in a small bedroom. She moved some curtains aside, sneezing as dust was dislodged from the movement and saw a slightly larger room adjoining with its one window opening out to the street. This room had an actual door to one side and opening it, she found she was back in the living area. Almost directly across the room sat the only source of heat, a dirty black hulk of a stove which, of course, was cold as the grave at this point.

Lissie blew a wisp of hair from her eyes and said to Elmer, who was now awake and waving plump little fists in the air, "Mother has her work cut out for her today, my fine boy."

Lew had arranged to meet her there at dinner time, and they walked back to Mrs. Bloomberg's laden table, hungry as the proverbial bear. When they had finished eating, they excused themselves and hurried back to their house. Upon arrival, Lew attempted to make a fire in the stove to take the chill from the dwelling.

Soon, Lissie's nose began to itch. "Lew, something is burning." The next instant she spied tendrils of smoke curling from the joints of the stovepipe connecting the firebox to the chimney. Screaming, she ran to the window closest to the stove, opening it to let out the smoke.

Meanwhile, Lew had run the opposite direction, grabbing a bucket on his way out the back door. He pumped some water so he could douse the wood and smother the flames.

In the midst of all this hubbub, little Elmer decided to add his voice to the excitement. Soon all three Rebers were coughing and/or crying as smoke continued to billow into the house.

"I cannot work in here," declared Lissie, as she attempted to flap the smoke toward the open window with the apron she had shrugged off..

"I must go back to the station," stated Lew. "When the smoke has gone, close the window and return to the boarding house. I will come back here after supper and clean the soot from this stovepipe."

"How will you cover the floor?" she asked.

"That need had not crossed my mind," he admitted. "I intended to dismantle the stovepipe sections, carry them outside, dislodge the soot and reassemble them."

"I do not see it being that simple, and you most definitely must cover the floor," declared Lissie.

Lew left the house shaking his head at his wife's picky ideas. But as he talked with a fellow worker, it became clear he had best heed Lissie's words.

"Cleaning a soot-laden stovepipe has to be one of the messiest jobs I know," stated Jake Duncan. He was a mail clerk on the run from Philadelphia and had disembarked for a few minutes to get some fresh air as well as a smoke. Jake and Lew had struck up an acquaintance the week before.

"You need some sort of floor covering because it is next to impossible to keep from dislodging soot before you are ready even if it is only a short distance from the stove to the outside door. And wear your worst clothes. Soot seems to be lighter than air and when it alights, it can always be depended upon to leave a smudge."

All that dire advice led Lew to look on the coming task with much foreboding. He gathered up a pile of old newspapers that had been sitting in the far corner of the station since he had begun work there. Feeling quite proud of himself as he carried the stack of papers, he had covered almost a block when he realized night had fallen and he needed a lantern. He ran back to the station, grabbed a lantern off a shelf in the supply room, told the night supervisor he needed to borrow it and was off again.

Jake's prediction held true, for despite Lew's best efforts, soot escaped, much of it landing on him. *I am* so *glad our furniture has not yet arrived. If Lissie had freshly laundered curtains at the window, I might well be sleeping at Mrs. Bloomberg's for the rest of the year!* As it was, Lew did his best to clean up the mess, including himself. He brushed off his shirt and trousers outside and washed his hands and face, His efforts were less than effective for when Lissie took one look at him upon his arrival back at the boarding house, she started to giggle.

"How can you laugh, Wife," he growled. "I have wrestled with the mighty stovepipe and I vow I won the battle."

"Perhaps so, Husband," Lissie gasped, "but you have come home looking like a raccoon," and she turned him to face the mirror hanging above the wash stand.

Lew took one look and joined in her laughter. Then, mischief in his eyes, he turned and said, "I think this raccoon would like to kiss his wife."

"Do not even consider it," Lissie warned him as he edged closer to her. "Lew, I shall run downstairs, screaming," she threatened.

"Very well," he sighed in resignation and returned to the wash basin to eradicate the black circles around his eyes. His next comment was a typical Lew Reber one. "I wonder if Mrs. Bloomberg has any leftovers from supper."

The next morning Lissie and Elmer were back at the little house. She had started a fire in the stove and it appeared to be drawing properly, so she soon had the dirt and cobwebs out of the corners and into the dustbin outside the back door. She was grateful to see that Lew really had cleaned up after himself from the stovepipe debacle of the previous night.

Lissie was washing window panes and ledges when she heard a knock on the door. Throwing it open, she beheld Uncle Edgar and his wagonload of Reber belongings.

"Oh, Uncle, I am so happy to see you," she squealed, throwing her arms around him. "Do come in. Although I have no chair to offer you," she added.

Edgar rumbled his hearty laugh and replied, "I been sitting these many miles except for bedding down at night, Niece. Let me start unloading your things and perhaps you can make a cup of tea while I work."

Lew had once again made plans to meet Lissie at the little house and he joined Edgar in unloading the wagon, soon making a finished job of it.

"I shall go to the inn down the road and buy some hot beef and cabbage pies," said Lew. "You can set things to right and serve us more tea when I come back, Lissie."

Things were far from set to right in Lissie's eyes when Lew returned, but at least the table was set, chairs in place and the stove was keeping them warm as the teakettle warbled happily on top.

"Edgar, I have paid for this night's lodging at Mrs. Bloomberg's. I suggest you take our room there so you can set off fresh tomorrow to go back home. Lissie, Baby, and I will settle into our new little home here."

As if he had settled the cares of the world, Lew was off to work, with a shake of a hand and a grateful grasp of Edgar's shoulder.

Lissie was a bit more practical. "Uncle, if you will help me place the bed and trunk just so in the bedroom, we can make you known to Mrs. Bloomberg and you can settle in your room for the evening. Her cooking is not equal to Aunt Jane's but you will have plenty to fill your stomach, pleasantly."

After Edgar was satisfied that Lissie had all the heavy boxes and furniture in place, he agreed to journey to the boardinghouse where Lissie introduced him to Mrs. Bloomberg and explained the switch of renters for that evening.

"That is fine by me," exclaimed the lady, "for the room is paid for this night and I am pleased to meet the relative of Mrs. Reber."

Uncle Edgar gave Lissie and Elmer a ride back to the little house. "I will come by in the morning before I leave," he promised.

"Rest well, Uncle," and Lissie hugged him. Edgar returned to his horse and wagon and Lissie turned back to the work at hand. Settling Elmer into his basket with a little gourd rattle that fascinated him, Lissie bustled around emptying boxes and heating a pot of dried vegetables to re-absorb water so they could have soup for supper. Aunt Jane had wrapped a couple of loaves of bread in dish towels and they could eat bread and strawberry preserves for a treat marking the first actual meal in this new home.

Having made their bed, Lissie was hanging clothes on hooks lining the bedroom wall when she heard Lew come in from work.

"Have I walked into the wrong house?" he asked. "No, there lies my son shaking his rattle. Who might be the fairy who waved her magic wand bringing forth soup on the stove and a table set for supper?"

"Here I am," sang out Lissie. "Wash your hands, Husband, and let us sit at table. I, for one, am starving."

"You have done wonders with this place, Lissie," remarked Lew as he sopped up the last drop of soup with a piece of bread.

It did help for Uncle to put furniture and boxes in the places where I needed them," said Lissie, giving credit to Edgar.

After the table was cleared off, Lissie fed Elmer, readied him for bed and then rocked him as Lew read from Proverbs 31. "Who can find a virtuous woman? For her price is far above rubies. The heart of her husband doth safely trust in her; so that he shall have no need of spoil."

"That was lovely, Benjie," sighed Lissie. "I declare, I am so tired, I fear I shall fall asleep rocking Baby."

"Tuck him in and then ready yourself for bed, liebchen. I will bank the coals and join you directly." He rose as she did and stopped her progress with an embrace that enveloped both her and Elmer. Then he tipped her chin upward and kissed her mouth. "Welcome home, Mrs. Reber," he said in his warm baritone and released her.

If Lew had any intentions of christening this new home by making love to Lissie that night, he was out of luck. By the time he was ready to turn out the lamp and crawl into bed, Lissie was curled up in her own little hollow of their feather bed, tiny breaths parting her lips. Lew smiled, blew out the lamp's flame and crawled into bed, his face against her shoulder and arm across her stomach.

The next morning was similar to the mornings back in Cressona with Lew leaving for work after breakfast and Lissie caring for Elmer's needs and doing normal housework. Of course, added to what was normal, was the task of unpacking boxes and putting things away.

At mid-morning Uncle Edgar arrived to make his farewell. There was still leftover coffee from breakfast so he had a cup before he left. "We will miss you and Lew at Christmas, this year," he said, "but I can guarantee there will be a box of goodies of all sorts from your Aunt Jane coming your way in a couple of weeks. I declare, this train does make it easy for a body to travel. What do you think about having Jennie come see you for a day or two after Christmas?" he asked.

"We shall be well settled by that time," Lissie declared. "Having Jennie here will be like a breath of fresh air from home. Do you think she will be brave enough to travel alone?"

"Well, we will just have to test the waters," and he smiled. "I must be off, Niece. You and your man have landed on your feet and there is no doubt this youngster is a fine feller." Edgar kissed Lissie on the forehead, stroked Elmer's soft cheek with his calloused index finger and was out the door.

Lissie waved until he was out of sight, the finality of this move now firmly settled. She could feel tears building and tremors in her stomach but gave herself a stern talking to. *You are a lucky girl, Lissie Reber. A handsome husband who has a good job, a beautiful baby boy and...* "Eeoo!" She caught a flicker of a mouse tail as she turned around.

Heading for the bedroom and warm outer clothes, she told the baby in her arms, "You and I are wrapping up and visiting Mrs. Bloomberg. Perhaps she knows where we can get a cat who loves to catch mice."

The day after Christmas Lissie sat in her rocker holding Elmer, a tiger-stripe cat purring at her feet on the rug. The young cat was still somewhat scrawny but much healthier than it had looked when it joined the household two weeks before. Lissie had seen a tiny bit of gray fur but no more glimpses of the tiny beasts nor evidence of their presence shown by shredded paper and droppings. With table scraps and a proper hunting skill, Tabby, Lissie's name for the cat, would soon be a plump rug-sitter.

Lissie dozed as did Elmer and the cat. She had a stew simmering on the stove top so she could relax until Lew arrived home from work. She roused as she heard voices outside and then the front door opened. In bounced her ten year old sister, Jennie, followed by Lew bearing a large crate on his shoulder.

Cries of welcome and joyous tears greeted Jennie who was soon seated in the rocker holding Elmer. "He has grown quite huge, Lissie," exclaimed the girl.

"As have you, sweet sister. When I kissed you hello I could see your eyes were level with mine."

"'Tis true, Lissie," laughed Lew, "but your height is not all that high. Whoa, careful. Can you not see I come bearing gifts from the Holtschlag farm?" He dodged Lissie's attempted pinch on the arm.

Pulling up a chair from the table, he said, "Let us see what wondrous things Jane has sent."

"We all helped," interjected Jennie. She was as excited as the adults to see the gifts unearthed.

Out came red and black striped wool socks and a matching scarf, mittens and a stocking cap for Lew which he immediately put on—except for the socks—much to Jennie's delight.

"I knitted the scarf, Sally made the cap, and Aunt Jane did the socks and mittens for she said size was important for them."

"Nicely done, Jennie," said Lew and Lissie hugged her little sister.

Next emerged a beautiful cambric apron edged with lace as well as a more practical one of red gingham. "Must be for you, sweet wife," announced Lew as he handed them to Lissie with a flourish.

"So beautiful," Lissie sighed as she smoothed the glistening white material. Her fingers found a lump in the pocket and when she pulled it out she discovered a tiny bag of potpourri. Holding it to her nose, she closed her eyes and inhaled the fragrance. "How thoughtful of Aunt Jane. She has shared some of her favorite lavender potpourri. Did you and Sally help prepare it, Jennie?"

Her sister was more than eager to tell of picking the lavender, crushing the cinnamon and watching Jane pour just the right amount of oils to meld the fragrance and substances together.

While the sisters were discussing potpourri, Lew was busy extricating the next item from the Christmas crate. "Ah, I believe this can fit none other than Master Elmer." He held up a quilted outerwear bunting lined with soft blue flannel. "Once we button our boy into this, he will be snug as a bunny in its burrow." He reached in again, "What have we here? I believe it is a stuffed likeness of your dog, Rover, Jennie."

She giggled and nodded her head vigorously. "Aunt Jane made me a doll too, but she said it would be my last for I am getting much too old for dolls. I have it packed in my valise. Do you want to see it?"

Without waiting for an answer, she ran to her bag and pulled out her latest baby doll. "I think she looks like you, Lissie," she confided, and indeed the doll had brown yarn braids and greenish-brown eyes. "And see, she is wearing a dress made from scraps of your red gingham. I really like this doll because she reminds me of you when I start to miss you."

That brought the tears pricking at Lissie's eyes, but she just hugged her young sister close and kissed her, saying, "I have missed you, too, Jennie."

The remainder of the crate was filled with wonderful foodstuff. Lissie unearthed a garland of onions, a small ham, a tin of tea, another tin containing sugar, a small jug of molasses, and tucked away in a corner, one of Aunt Jane's delectable fruitcakes.

"Such a feast we shall have," cried Lissie, eyes sparkling as she spied the fruitcake.

The time with Jennie sped by all too fast and five days later Lew was handing her up into the train car, Lissie waving and willing her tears not to fall. At least until the train pulled out of sight.

By January Elmer was pulling up to the chairs at the table and crawling everywhere as fast as he could put hands and knees to floor. Lew had fashioned a sort of wooden-barred pen placed on top of the pallet in the living area. Soon Elmer was walking and by the time they celebrated his first birthday in July, Lissie had missed three months of her menstrual flow. Young Elmer was going to be joined by a new brother or sister sometime around Christmas!

The young couple's friends were mainly the fellows Lew had become acquainted with at the rail yard. Lissie was so busy with housekeeping, childcare, and gardening--for she had prevailed upon Lew to spade up a patch of dirt at the back of the house--that she had no free time to drink tea with a neighbor.

Lew worked six days a week at the train station, and the young couple worked together on their little home on Sundays rather than attend church. Lew built extra counter space and shelves for the kitchen while Lissie crocheted bright new rugs for the living area and sewed new clothes for Elmer as well as the expected addition to the family.

In a short note to Eliza, Lissie wrote:

I find these short times when Elmer naps to be a prize possession. Never did I think when growing up at Uncle Edgar and Aunt Jane's that a few moments of silence and inactivity would be so precious. I do love this baby boy but he insists on being underfoot every waking moment it seems. And to think, another will soon join him!

Yes, little Elmer will soon have a brother or sister around Christmas or New Year's. Aunt Jane has promised to come help me during the birthing. (I pray we are not far off from the correct arrival time.) Having her here will be such a comfort and she feels confident leaving the house in the hands of Sally and Jennie as Sally is now fourteen and well able to tend a home of her own.

Please write and tell me of the exciting doings in Philadelphia.

Your forever friend,
Lissie

Mid-October arrived and Lissie remarked during a meal, "It is time to harvest and store our root crops, Lew. Can you spade up some of the garden plot for a sort of root cellar as you did in Cressona?" She said this while serving Lew's dinner plate, at the same time deftly defying Elmer's attempt to grab the tablecloth.

Lew sighed and remarked, "It seems time flies. How can it have been almost a year since we left there? And, yes, of course, I will dig the same sort of dirt protection as we had in Cressona. Although it is too bad we were not able to see if it actually afforded protection for the vegetables all winter."

"I do not see us moving again this year, do you?" replied Lissie. The mere mention of another move made her tired. This baby seemed to be heavier than Elmer at this stage, but perhaps it was because she had more work to do keeping track of a toddler.

Chapter 16

March 1, 1921

Palmyra, Missouri

LANDIS CAME IN from the mailbox with five birthday cards for Annaliese—from Elmer, Howard, Lewis, Martha and her sister-in-law, Emma. "James came by the barn yesterday afternoon on his way to town and said we were to come to their house for your birthday party tonight. Anna will be there as well as Harvey and Tillie with little Jessie."

"That should prove to be quite the party," remarked Annaliese. "Do you suppose I shall have to blow out seventy-three candles in one great puff?"

"Very likely, Mother, although that many candles might clean out Woolworths," and he grinned.

"Be respectful to your aged mother, boy," she growled in mock anger.

Party time came and Landis wrapped Annaliese snugly in blankets before getting into the buggy. March had roared in like a lion but at least the skies were dry. They were greeted by cries of "Happy birthday," by all assembled.

Amid much talk and laughter, the birthday presents were laid in Annaliese's lap. James and his women gave Annaliese a cameo brooch and Tillie had crocheted a soft, multicolored scarf. Landis had etched and colored a rose on a small, oaken box he had made and lined with burgundy velvet scraps filched from his mother's ragbag. "It's to hold your brooch and other trinkets," he explained.

Annaliese was quite as ready to head for bed as little Jessie once the birthday cake had been served. "Thank you for this lovely angel food cake, Louisa. And I'm almost as grateful that it held only seven candles instead of seventy-three."

She smiled at her daughter-in-law who laughed infectiously. "I felt it was much more merciful to have a candle to mark the decades. I declare, I can't imagine a birthday cake when the candles mark much beyond ten years."

Thanking everyone again, the travelers made ready to leave. As they trotted toward their little house, Annaliese yawned, "That was truly delightful, gifts and all, but the best thing was being with family. I am so blessed."

It took Annaliese no time at all to fall asleep but as she slid into slumber, again the scenes from years past took over her subconscious mind.

Chapter 17

December 1867

Reading, Pennsylvania

CHRISTMAS DAY 1867 neared and Lew brought home an evergreen that fit nicely on the small table beside the rocker. "Beautiful, Benjie," cried Lissie, as she twirled a fascinated Elmer in a circle around tree and rocker. "It is a perfect size and shape. I shall start popping corn after supper is cleared away. When you come home for dinner tomorrow, you will see your tree garlanded and perhaps a few tiny candles placed just so."

As she glanced at him, Lissie saw that Lew's eyes were glistening in the lamp light. "Is something amiss, Benjie?"

Lew sat down in the rocker and pulled her into his lap, hugging Elmer along with his wife. "The sight of that little tree reminded me that I have not enjoyed a Christmas tree since I was fourteen, the Christmas before Mother died." He gulped and raised a free hand to wipe his eyes. "As I gaze at this little house you have made so warm and inviting and I see our lively son squirming to remove himself from this 'Reber sandwich'," he laughed and continued, "I realize how God has blessed this farm boy-soldier turned railroader." He caressed Lissie's apron-covered baby bump with a gentle hand.

Christmas arrived and departed and Lissie realized that her baby had dropped lower in her abdomen. "This baby has kicked more than Elmer," she told Lew, but of a sudden it is much quieter with this change in position."

"Shall I send word to Jane?" Lew's face wrinkled into worry lines.

"I should feel much comforted if you did," agreed Lissie.

Jane arrived on December 28 and James Franklin arrived late in the evening of December 29, 1867, a compact youngster with a strong voice.

Elmer was curious about this new addition to the family. He poked at his eye when Lissie had laid James in the cradle after his morning feeding. "No, Elmer, you must pat baby brother gently and just on his tummy." Elmer was not much of a talker at this point, but he understood tone of voice and could obey instructions—if he wanted to. At the moment, he realized his mother was not pleased with him so he immediately began to cry.

"There, my little man," soothed Lissie. "Let me show you how to pat baby brother," and she took his hand and showed him how to touch James gently.

"Baby," stated Elmer, looking up at his mother, his adorable face with tiny tear beads clinging to his lashes.

Elmer became his younger brother's guardian, sometimes to the disgust of James, for he was a rough and tumble youngster, generally fearless, much to Lissie's disquiet.

Two years later Elmer became guardian to another little brother, Linneus, born in December. Despite his young age, Elmer had accumulated a sizeable vocabulary. At the sight of the tiny new addition to the family, he stated, "Mama, we have an early Christmas present."

Lissie had explained to the two little boys that they would soon have a new little baby sister or brother, this after Elmer had remarked, "Mama, your tummy looks like my big ball." He was referring to a prized treasure he had received for his third birthday that past July from Uncle Edgar and Aunt Jane.

Elmer was excited to speechlessness when his father brought home a little tree and set it on a side table. "I 'member little tree and popcorn." He was jumping around with joy, James joining in the activity although he had no clue as to the reason for his brother's ecstasy.

"I am surprised that you remember our Christmas tree last year, Son," remarked Lew.

"Do you remember the popcorn garland you helped me make for the tree?" asked Lissie. She had allowed him to hand her the popcorn as she strung the kernels on a stout thread before draping their little tree.

"Yes, yes. May I help with the garland this year, Mama?"

"Me help, Mama," echoed James.

"Yes, you may help," answered Lissie, but right now I must put supper on the table. I shall pop the corn later and we can string the garland tomorrow."

The next day Elmer solemnly sat beside his mother handing her just the right popped kernel as she strung the corn. James did his part by choosing just the right kernel—and popping it into his mouth.

"James," protested Lissie, "the popcorn is supposed to go on the tree, not in your mouth."

He just looked at her with mischief in his eyes as his little hand delved into the bowl of popped corn. "Me help," he giggled, and put another kernel in his mouth.

It was a little more than two weeks before Christmas when Lissie sensed baby #3 might well make its appearance before the New Year dawned. They had lived in Reading long enough by this time that Lissie had become acquainted with a midwife who lived about ten blocks from their little house.

On the morning of December 12 Lissie was standing in the kitchen preparing Lew's breakfast of pancakes and sausage when the activity started. "Aiee!. Lew! Bring me a towel." He rushed out of their bedroom, shirt half on but clutching the requested item.

"What is happening, Lissie?"

"My water just broke," and she raised her skirt and mopped at her legs with the towel he handed her. Then she grabbed at her back and headed for the nearest chair. "I think you had best finish dressing, Lew, and go fetch Midwife Leukenig. This baby is preparing to arrive faster than either James or Elmer."

By the time Lew had dressed, Lissie had put the coffeepot on between back spasms. She handed him a cup of coffee which he gulped down after blowing on it a bit.

Lissie was rocking as she sat protectively holding her stomach when Lew arrived back home with the midwife. "I have hot water ready Nurse Leukenig, and protective sheets are on the bed." Lissie gasped as a contraction hit.

"You have done well, M'am. Now it is time for me to do the work for which your husband called me," and she sent Lissie to lie down. Turning to Lew she asked, "If you are working today, who is there to watch over these youngsters?" She nodded in the direction of Elmer and James who were playing with blocks beside the front window.

"I must work today," he replied, "although I intend to plead my case of ensuing fatherhood and perhaps my supervisor will at least let me leave early. Mrs. Manton, our next door neighbor, agreed to watch our boys if we had such a need as this. Come boys, help papa put on your coats and hats so you can go visit the Cookie Lady."

Lissie had become friendly with Melissa Manton early in the spring. Melissa's two little girls, aged seven and nine, loved to play with the little boys next door. Melissa was an excellent baker and always had fresh cookies at her house. This led Elmer to decide she should be known as the Cookie Lady.

Lew only needed to utter the words, "Cookie Lady," and the boys were clamoring at the door, Elmer minus a glove and James, having no idea where his other shoe had gone.

The house quiet, Lissie and Mrs. Leukinig got down to the business of birthing Baby Reber. Within an hour's time the child was born. When the baby's cry was finally heard, the sound was not the lusty one Lissie remembered from her older boys.

"Is something amiss with my baby?" she asked the midwife.

"He seems healthy enough," the woman replied as she lay Lissie's newest son next to her breast, "but he is small. I judge him to weigh about six pounds. Remember too, by our calculations, he is close to a month early. Little boys born early sometimes need extra time to strengthen their lungs. I am sure with your good mother's milk he will thrive."

Lissie bounced back from this third birth with her usual vigor, but little Linnneus failed to show signs of the boisterous good health Elmer and James had exhibited as infants. Lew was thrilled at having another son, but as he observed the tiny babe at Lissie's breast one evening, he said, "Our little Linnie seems to remain quite small and quiet." The baby seemed to lack even enough energy to fuss and his color remained waxen.

Lew could see hints of unshed tears in Lissie's eyes as she whispered, "I cannot help comparing this little one to James and Elmer at this age—and it seems he is barely alive. All we can do is love and care for him and pray God will make him strong."

Little Elmer, not quite four, felt he was guardian of baby Linneus just as he had been told he was James' big brother. Elmer took his responsibility seriously and could be trusted to rock the baby's cradle if he made a peep of unhappiness.

As for James, curious two-year-old that he was, he would have poked baby brother in the eye and pinched his mouth, if not stopped by a horrified Lissie. After that episode, Elmer was given the task of keeping James occupied when Linneus was out in the living area in his cradle.

March 1870 blew in like a lion and the little house on Arbutus Lane seemed to put all its drafty crevices on exhibit. Lissie stuffed rags around door and window casings. The drafty house caused her great concern, particularly because Linneus did not have strong lungs. Despite all her efforts Lew came home from work with a dreadful, racking cough and Elmer caught the bug next, although his lungs were healthier than his father's.

It was the end of that week when Lissie awakened to the wheezing sound of baby Linneus struggling to breathe. Up in a flash, she grabbed her night robe, a warm gift from Jane that Christmas, and picked up her little son, cuddling him to her chest. Tapping his small back gently and humming to him, she began to rock him as she stood by his cradle. "Oh God," she prayed. "Please heal my sweet baby." She prayed it over and over, tears raining down her face until she realized the small form she was hugging to her heart, no longer breathed.

Lew slept deeply throughout the night. He had finally gotten some respite for his cough with hourly doses of lemon juice and honey. When he awoke the next morning, he saw Lissie's spot next to him, empty, and the cradle, empty as well. Going out into the living room, he spied Lissie sitting in the rocker, head drooped over baby Linneus.

He shook down the ashes and stirred the coals, loading in more wood so he could put the coffeepot on. When he looked over at Lissie again, she was staring at him. *No*, he thought, *it was like she was staring* through *him.*

"Little Linnie is gone." Her tone was as lifeless as the fact she uttered.

He rushed to her side and knelt, one hand on her arm, the other touching the baby's neck. Cold. The baby's skin was as chill as the air around him and the emotion within. "Oh, Lissie. When did this happen?"

She recited the circumstances in the same flat, lifeless tone of a few seconds before.

Lew rose from his knees. Impulsively picking up Lissie and the eternally sleeping form of little Linnie, he sat in the rocker, holding them both close to his heart. Resting his chin gently on the top of her head and slowly rocking, he said brokenly, "I am so sorry you dealt with this alone in the dark watches of the night, liebchen. So sorry. So sorry." His arms tightened around her.

They sat and rocked for some minutes until little James came into the room, crying because he had wet his pants and it was cold and uncomfortable. His wailing had awakened Elmer who soon joined the little family group, tousled and rubbing sleep from his eyes.

"Mama,why are you sitting on Papa's lap and holding Linnie?"

Lissie heard her son's question but could think of no answer. In fact, her mind seemed to be totally blank and her tongue thick and unable to form words.

Lew came to the rescue. "Lissie, give me the baby and tend to James' wet pants."

That young man had continued his wailing. "Elmer, you may fetch the porridge bowls from the shelf and set them at our places at the table." He had recently been given this task and seemed quite gratified at accomplishing this big-person job at their meals.

Lissie came back through their bedroom with a dry and comforted James, and saw Lew, tears streaming from his eyes, smoothing the downy, cool cheek of their dead baby. She set the two little boys to playing with their blocks in the warm corner by the stove while she made porridge and sliced bread for toast. Waiting until the last possible moment so Lew might mourn his son in solitude, she finally called him to the table.

The boys settled to eating their porridge and she asked, "How do we do this—this death thing?"

"What is death, Mama?" questioned Elmer.

"We will speak of it later, dear. Finish your porridge."

"I will go to the undertaker's on the way to work," replied Lew. "The boss may allow me to leave work once things are put in order."

Later that morning a grim-faced Lew wrapped his dead baby son in a sheet and carried him to the mortuary. There was an array of various sized pine boxes, sadly, several quite small. Lew picked one and laid the lifeless body of his son in it. "I will speak to Pastor

Holofern when I leave here to ask if he will say a few words at the graveside. Will your gravediggers have time to do this so we can hold the service tomorrow afternoon?"

He was assured that all would be taken care of so he went back home and was greeted with joy by his little boys and questions from Elmer.

They both had crawled into his lap as he sat in the rocker. "Papa, little Linnie is gone from his cradle. When I asked Mama, she said death took him." Then came the big tears rolling down his chubby little cheeks. "I want baby Linnie back. He belongs here in his cradle."

Lew swallowed hard and thought fast. "Baby Linnie has gone to heaven to be with Jesus."

The boys had heard Bible stories from their parents so the name of Jesus was not foreign to them. However, Elmer was not feeling generous. "Jesus not need baby Linnie. I am the big brother. I take care of Linnie."

Lew sighed. "Well, son, Jesus decided it was time for Linnie to come home to heaven."

"But *this* is home, Papa."

"This is our home, right now, but our forever home is with Jesus in heaven, if we love Him.

"I do not love Him because He took baby Linnie. 'Member, you told James and me we should share. Jesus should share."

"He did share, Elmer. He gave baby Linnie to us for a while, but Jesus loved him so much He decided it was time for him to come to his forever home."

Elmer's lower lip trembled but the tears had stopped as his little mind mulled the hefty philosophical tenets his father had laid before his almost four-year-old mind.

By this time James had scooted off Lew's lap and was back playing with blocks and Elmer soon joined him. Lew got up from the chair and walked to Lissie who was stirring a big pot of vegetable stew simmering on the stove. He kissed her cheek and hugged her, asking, "Are you well?"

Lissie's eyes felt like holes in a piece of material singed by flying sparks. "At this moment, my chest feels like a leaden piece lies within." She turned back to the pot she was stirring as if it was of world-shaking importance.

Lew had never seen his sweet Lissie so lifeless and it worried him.

That evening after the little boys were tucked into bed, Lew saw Lissie's eyes dart toward the empty cradle as she gulped back a sob. He tenderly guided her to bed, tucked her in like a child and climbed in beside her. Hugging her to his chest, spoon fashion, he kissed her neck and whispered, "I pray the Lord will grant us rest in our grief. It helps me to picture our little one nestled in Jesus' loving arms." He could feel sobs shake her body and as he drifted off to sleep, he realized his tears were making his pillow wet.

Lew arose first, shaking down the ashes and stirring the coals in preparation for coffee making. His eyes were drawn to the empty cradle and he hurried over and carried it to the pantry, out of sight for the moment. When Lissie came out of the bedroom, he guided her to the rocker and handed her a mug of coffee. He pulled up a kitchen chair alongside her and took her empty hand.

"Can you get Melissa to watch the boys this afternoon? I have made arrangements for a graveside service at three."

Lissie sobbed once and then looked at him with tear-filled eyes and nodded.

Lew left for work and the little boys finally woke up hungry as bear cubs. Lissie was grateful for the everyday needs of her youngsters. The activity helped keep her mind from the pain she knew lurked within if she gave it the least bit of encouragement.

After cleaning up the boys from breakfast, she said, "Time to put coats on, boys. I need to speak with Mrs. Manton."

"The Cookie Lady," they screeched, laughing and tumbling over each other.

When Lissie explained to Melissa why she needed help in watching the boys for an hour or so, her neighbor folded her into her arms. "Oh my dear, of course I will watch the boys. I am so sorry to hear about little Linnie."

Elmer with the big ears heard that and explained, "Jesus took baby Linnie. Jesus must learn to share," he explained with a very earnest expression, "just like James and me has to share. Sometimes James grabs my blocks," he stated in a confiding tone.

"Perhaps we can talk about that," said Melissa looking questioningly at Lissie, "after we have some cookies."

"Yes," shouted the little boys who could hardly wait to get out of their coats and go sit at the table.

Lissie was grateful for the direction change in Elmer's line of thinking and hugging and thanking Melissa, took her leave to join Lew and say a final goodbye to their sweet baby boy.

The minister, his wife, a head deacon and his wife accompanied Lissie and Lew to the Reading cemetery. The men employed by the undertaker carried the tiny casket to its final resting place. Lissie could hear the minister's voice, but his words ran together as a backdrop to scenes of coaxing little Linnie to eat, trying to interest him in a rattle, and days of worrying why her baby did not thrive as their two older sons had. What had she done wrong? Why was God so angry at her that He would take their little son? The questions and the blaming whirled in her head until she became literally dizzy and felt her knees begin to buckle. Lew sensed the movement and put his arm around her to steady her.

"Chin up, Lissie. You can get through this," he whispered as the minister finished his short homily. Lew continued to support Lissie as they walked by the casket and Lissie stopped for a moment, resting her hand on it.

Lew hugged her even closer and whispered, "Our little one is in Jesus' arms now—safe and warm and healthy."

She lifted tear-filled eyes to his and said, "How I wish I could believe that."

Life returned to normal in the little house for all except Lissie. She would find herself listening for Linnie's weak little cry which would make her milk come, in turn drenching her shirt front and bringing tears. Eventually, those incidents happened less and less and Lissie once again found loving comfort in Lew's arms as he soothed his wife's pain as only he knew how.

Chapter 18

IN AUGUST OF that year Lissie turned to Lew one night as they lay in bed after making love and said, "Lew, it appears that I am once again with child."

"Ach, Liebchen. How wonderful!" He kissed her lips and smoothed her hair as it lay in curls on the pillow.

Then changing the subject, abruptly,"I have noticed that you no longer call me Benjie as you once did during our tender moments. Why is that?"

Lissie sighed. "Your pet name seems to belong to the days of our youth, even though we have not many years, presently. Children birthed and dying have a way of aging a person."

She sighed again. "I am fearful, Lew," she continued. "What if this little one is tiny and fails to thrive as did our sweet little Linneus?"

"We shall pray for God's favor—and see that you put some meat on your bones," he stated in mock sternness hugging her tightly.

Sure enough, at least to Lissie's mind, God did look upon her with favor and Abraham Landis was born that next year in April, a strong little boy with lusty cries from the beginning as well as a healthy appetite.

Elmer was delighted that Jesus had sent him a new little brother, quite positive that "Jesus must have learned to share even though Landis does not quite look like little Linnie."

Landis' birth was followed by Howard's a little less than two years later. Once Lissie was back on her feet, she proposed a startling need to Lew one evening after supper.

"Lew, this house is too small for us. I have little boys underfoot all day long in the winter and I suppose we shall soon need to purchase another trundle bed to slide under Landis' crib, just as we have for James and Elmer. Howard will outgrow the cradle and need to move into James' crib bed. That tiny room will be bulging with little boys and the older ones will wake the younger ones whether going to bed or waking up. May we please begin looking for a larger home?"

Lew felt fortunate he was sitting in his rocker—they now had two of them—because he was totally flabbergasted at Lissie's request. She had finally gotten all four boys down for the night, but the noise from the direction of the children's tiny room let him know the boys were not ready to settle in for a good night's sleep.

He grinned at his wife and said, "My quiver is truly filling up, Wife. I suggest a visit to look at the possibilities this Saturday afternoon when I get off work."

"How will we know where to look?"

"I will ask around at work and go by the newspaper office tomorrow after I eat a bite of dinner. Property owners may well have advertised houses for rent as that has become a profitable enterprise."

She nodded, satisfied.

Later that evening after snuggling together under the covers and the aftermath of such snuggling, Lew heard Lissie muffle a giggle.

"What is so funny, Wife?" he asked in a mock stern tone.

"I was just wondering how many rooms you might be thinking of for our new house" she replied. "Our lovemaking appears to bear rapid fruit for I seem to resemble Mother Eve after she and Adam were evicted from the Garden of Eden. Although I pray God I will not bear children for the next several hundred years the way she did." They both snorted with laughter at the thought and were soon asleep.

By the time Howard was sitting up in his cradle, ready for Landis's crib, the young parents had found a house to their liking which also fit their budget. It consisted of two stories, three bedrooms upstairs with the staircase leading to the bedrooms and dividing the front half of the house. To the right, was the parlor, a room shut off for the most part, unless the pastor or deacons came or if the Holtschlag family came for a visit after the harvest was in.

To the left of the stairs was the family living area incorporating the eating area and the kitchen and pantry. Lissie was delighted with the spacious feeling this new house gave her. There were windows on each side of the house, the one on the west lighting the parlor which also had a window facing the street as did the family area.

"The only thing I fear is the stairs and little boys falling down them, cracking their heads."

"I can assure you, Wife, that little boys will likely suffer worse calamities than tumbling down stairs. I am well able to attest to that, having been a little boy, myself, at one time." He tweaked a curl that had escaped the bun at the back of her head and hugged her to him. "If it will make you feel better, we can make it a rule that once the boys come downstairs, they stay down here. In that way you can shepherd them as they descend and ascend each day.

"I feel sure, however, that Elmer and James will be spending all their waking hours in the back yard during this warm weather. "

Lew's prediction proved true and to add to his young sons' enchantment with their new back yard, he built a tree house for them, a platform about five feet above the ground, girdling the trunk of an old maple. Elmer and James were delighted to "help" Papa construct a ladder to clamber up to their "house" which took on varying identities as a fort, a castle, a church, or whatever else their fertile imaginations could conjure.

Lissie soon met her neighbors, one of whom, Mary Ann Baker, was married to a blacksmith and had three little girls. Lissie sometimes wondered what it would be like to have little girls rather than boisterous little boys and when she discovered early in 1874 that she was pregnant again, she guardedly wished for this baby to be a daughter.

That September her hoped-for Louisa turned out to be a strong, gusty-lunged Lewis. With five little boys Lissie was grateful every day for the larger living space in this house.

Enjoying an unusually warm November day, Mary Ann and Lissie were chatting over a cup of tea. The older children played outside and the little ones were busy exploring the Rebers' living area, making sure to stay close to Mother, or in Lewis's case, dozing in Lissie's arms.

"Lissie, we are going to have some revival meetings at our church starting this Sunday," stated Mary Ann. "We would like for you to come with us, if you are interested."

Lissie set her tea cup down on its saucer and answered in a wistful tone. "Lew and I used to go to church regularly in Cressona, the Lutheran church. In fact, I took organ lessons from the pastor's wife who was the organist. But since we have moved here, we have attended church very little. Now with five little boys I do not see how we can attend a worship service for my children do not easily sit quietly."

"I can understand that," replied Mary Ann. "My parents attend the same church we do and are great help in keeping the girls entertained."

The subject was dropped as the women's conversation drifted to prices of yard goods at The Mercantile, their favorite shopping place for most household items.

An awesome turning point came in the lives of Lissie and Lew in the spring of 1875. One Sunday morning as Lissie was feeding breakfast gruel and mugs of milk to the four boys old enough to sit at table, Lew announced, "I feel led to go to church this morning."

Lissie looked up from mopping young Howard's chin and said in an aggrieved voice, "It is impossible for me to go with you with so little notice, Lew. Have you considered how the boys could be kept quiet in a church service?"

"No," he answered, as a strange expression crossed his face. "I must admit this impulse has just come upon me, but I feel I must go." He was soon ready and left the house, brushing a kiss across her cheek as he headed for the door.

Lissie busied herself around the house, settling boyish squabbles, preparing a nice roast and the trimmings for dinner and then allowing herself to sit for a moment with a cup of tea in front of her. As she did so, she thought, *how strange that Lew should decide to attend church this morning.*

Many months ago they had ceased the habit of Lew reading from the Bible after supper was over. *In fact,* she realized, *we have not read the Bible since we moved to this house. At least, not read aloud. I remember Lew reading it to himself two nights ago as I was busy mending a tear in James's trousers. That child* will *try to outdo everything his older brother attempts.*

Just then the door was flung open and Lew rushed in. But instead of stopping to greet her or tousle the heads of his boys, he rushed upstairs and she heard their bedroom door slam. She had the distinct impression that, as he rushed past her, tears were streaming down Lew's face. Her tea forgotten, Lissie ran up the stairs to check on her husband.

She found him face down on their bed, shoulders shuddering from great sobs. "Lew, what is wrong? Are you ill?" She went to sit by his head and gently smoothed his quivering shoulder nearest her.

"Ah, Lissie, I am the most abject of sinners," came his muffled reply. Finally when he had managed to quell the sobbing, he turned over and explained what had happened. "You remember I told you earlier this morning I had this great urge to go to church."

She nodded and he continued. "As I neared the front door, I could hear children's voices singing and I thought I was listening to the very angels of heaven. I entered the church and sat down at the back. As the service began, so did my weeping. I could not stop and the weight of the world seemed upon me. Then something the preacher said pierced my very soul, and I could see my sin debt weighing down Christ's shoulders as he hung on that Golgotha cross."

He sat up and dashed the tears from his eyes. "I could take no more of the emotion and as the closing prayer was being prayed, I ran from the church to our house, weeping as you have now seen me."

Lissie pulled a handkerchief from her apron pocket and handed it to him. "Dry your eyes, Lew, so you do not frighten the children." She placed her hand against his forehead, wondering if he had contracted some sort of brain fever. "Dinner is almost ready to put on the table. Do you feel like coming down soon?"

"Yes," he sighed. He got up to pour water from the pitcher into a wash basin on the small dressing table. Lissie left him to wash his face and comb his hair as she descended the stairs to set the table for dinner.

Lew spent the afternoon quietly reading his Bible while Lissie tended the children. After supper he said, "I feel I must return to the church service tonight or I shall never have peace."

Lissie patted his shoulder, kissed his cheek and sent him on his way, wondering what sort of thing God might be doing to her husband's brain. She put the children to bed, sat down in the rocker doing nothing but thinking about the strange happenings to Lew this day. *Dear God, please protect Lew from brain fever for that is all I can think of. Please grant him peace.*

She had almost dozed off when Lew got back from church. He bounced into the room, the taut lines erased from his face, his eyes sparkling. "What a wondrous experience, Lissie. God has shown Himself in awesome love and compassion and forgiveness."

"What has brought this marvelous change, Lew? You are the most joyful I think I have ever seen."

"I'm saved, Lissie! Forgiven of my sin, freed from worry and doubt—and even the bad feelings I have harbored against my father these many years." He kissed her fervently and pulled her down on his lap for she had risen to meet him and he had taken the rocker after his exuberant outburst. He continued. "I feel like a new man. I *am* a new man because according to the scripture, 'If any man be in Christ, he is a new creation.' Oh Lissie, do you not want this same thing for yourself?"

She smiled and made a noncommittal sound, but thought, *Whatever should happen to the children if God were to put upon me this spiritual brain fever,* for that is what she silently called Lew's new-found religious fervor.

Several weeks later, Lissie was awakened by Lew sitting up in bed, shouting "Praise God."

"I'm sorry for waking you, Lissie. I dreamed I was preaching a sermon and could not contain the joy I felt." Lew turned over and went back to sleep, but Lissie was not so lucky. That night after supper, when the children had been tucked in, Lew said, "Lissie, I think God wants me to be a preacher."

She looked at him in a mixture of amazement and horror. "How can that be, Lew? You have a young, growing family. How can you become educated for the ministry?"

He nodded, a sad look on his face. "I know. My education is sadly lacking, and I see no recourse for it." Then he looked at her more closely. "Lissie, what exactly did you mean by a 'growing' family?"

A smile touched her lips as she replied, "It appears that a new little Reber will be joining us sometime in September."

He kissed her tenderly and said, "Are you feeling well? You have not mentioned being sick in the morning."

"No, I have not really suffered morning sickness since before Elmer's arrival. I find it hard to realize he will be ten years old this July."

"Six children. We will soon have this house, too, filled with children. I shall need to build another bunk atop Landis's bed as I did for Elmer and James."

Another thought hit Lew but he did not voice it, just grinned.

"What was that grin about?" demanded Lissie.

"Oh, you will find out soon enough," and his smile widened.

With that mysterious statement, Lew lay back down and Lissie followed suit.

Several days later, Lissie heard a commotion at the front door. Opening it to check on the noise, she discovered Lew directing four hefty fellows carrying a large wooden box while he held a round stool.

Before she could say anything, he called out, "Hold the door open wide, Lissie, and be sure there are no young'uns underfoot."

As she did his bidding, she finally shot out, "What on earth are you bringing into our parlor?" for that was where Lew was leading the men.

"I have a birthday present for you, Lissie, although it is several weeks early." The men helped Lew peel away the wooden boards making up the box and there stood—

"An organ? Oh Lew, wherever did you get it? How can we afford it?"

He waved off her queries, thanking the men as they finished maneuvering the instrument into the perfect spot. From there the sun shining in through the front window could light up the music on the stand above the keyboard.

"Sit down and play, Liebchen," Lew said, so excited he was almost dancing.

Lissie could scarce take it in. "I fear I can remember nothing from my lessons for it has been more than ten years since I have played an instrument," she said. But the utter joy of once again making music overcame her reluctance. First, she merely played a C scale with trembling fingers.

The unusual sound brought their boys from every conceivable part of the house for the older boys had sat down waiting for supper. "Why do we have a little organ in our parlor?" asked James and Elmer in unison. They had begun attending Sunday School at the church where Lew had experienced his encounter with God and had heard and seen the organ in the church sanctuary.

Three-year-old Howard headed straight for the bellows pedal, fascinated by his mother's foot movement and reaching for the keys in curiosity. Five-year-old Landis stood some distance away assessing the situation while Lewis, the toddler, decided he wanted Mama's attention and burst into tears at the unusual sound.

Lew scooped up his youngest and shushed his older sons. "Listen to your mother play," he admonished them as Lissie had launched into "A Mighty Fortress Is Our God" picking out the melody with very few stumbles.

When she had finished, she twirled around on the stool and said, "Thank you for a wonderful birthday present. Boys, this pump organ is not your toy. Mother will try to play it in the evenings before bedtime, but otherwise, it is not to be touched." As she said that, she wondered if such a restriction would be somewhat akin to God telling Adam not to eat the fruit of the tree in the center of the Garden.

The boys were so excited about the new organ, they found it difficult to eat between bits of conversation. Dishes were washed, dried, and put away courtesy of Elmer and James while Lissie tended to their younger brothers.

"May we hear the organ again?" asked Elmer.

"After I read a Bible passage and we have prayer," replied his father.

"I do not know any other songs," pleaded Lissie.

"We do not care," clamored the boys. "Please just play the organ."

That night in bed, Lissie turned to Lew and said, "Your gift is certainly of great interest to the boys. Really, Lew, whatever possessed you to buy the organ?"

"Do you not like it?" Although she could not see his face in the dark, she realized she had hurt her husband's feelings.

"I *do* like it," she said, kissing him. "It was just so unexpected. And, I fear, expensive."

"It actually cost very little," he replied. "A family in town had shipped it here from the estate of a deceased relative in Philadelphia and then the lady of the house decided it did not fit her décor. It sat in the baggage area until a note was put up on the bulletin board offering it for sale at the price of transporting from Philadelphia to Reading. As soon as I saw the advertisement, I knew I must get it for you."

She kissed him again and said, "I shall gain much joy from

playing the organ, Lew. Thank you," and she kissed him a third time. However, as she rolled over later to go to sleep, the thought crossed her mind, *When shall I ever have time to practice an organ with five sons, a husband, and a baby on the way?*

Fortunately, Lissie discovered she *could* find time to practice and was delighted to find a small hymnal secreted under one of the candleholder shelves. Elmer and James were now attending school but once they arrived home, she turned over the care of their three younger brothers to them and practiced playing her organ. The boys seemed to enjoy the sound of her playing, mistakes and all, so the thirty minutes she allotted herself most days proceeded smoothly.

The year 1876 was an auspicious one for the Reber family and for the country. The Fourth of July was commemorated as the centennial day of independence, and Reading celebrate with great fervor since their sister city, Philadelphia, was a central player in the struggle for independence.

Elmer felt quite special because his July 31st birthday marked his tenth year. And during the first week of September Lissie began feeling premonitions of the coming birth of her child.

Annie Eliza Reber arrived bright and early on September 6 and was greeted with great fanfare by her five brothers and an awestruck father.

"She looks like you, already, Lissie," he whispered as he knelt beside her. Lissie lay on their bed, suckling her newborn daughter and gazing at her with loving eyes. The baby had brown ringlets and later her blue eyes turned to hazel just like her mother's.

Annie was a delightful baby, even-tempered and seemingly unafraid, a useful trait since she had five older brothers.

Lissie enjoyed a respite from most of her household chores for the first week after Annie was born because her sister, Jennie, came to help. Jennie had first come to assist after Howard was born and at seventeen, she proved a great aid to Lissie. Now, at almost twenty, Jennie was seriously interested in Henry Wilhelm, one of Manfred's friends. While the two older boys were in school and the three younger ones napping, the sisters enjoyed visiting and Lissie delighted in the extra time she could devote to her baby daughter. She used this relaxing time to write Eliza, telling her of her namesake.

The week after Jennie returned to the Holtschlag farm, a letter accompanied by a small package arrived from Eliza.

Dear Lissie,

What exciting news. To think that you now have a daughter. I prophesy she will be the most spoiled little girl in the state of Pennsylvania! How sweet of you to name her for me. I find it particularly fitting that part of your name and mine are joined in hers.

My life is a steady round of teaching etiquette with some relief provided by attending concerts and educational lectures. I am now at the age where I chaperone young ladies at cotillions rather than dance at them myself.

I am sending along a small token for Miss Annie Eliza. Perhaps I can come see her next summer between school terms.

Friends forever,
Eliza

Lissie opened the small package and unpacked a little box padded in satin upon which rested a silver spoon initialed with an AE. It was just the right size for a tiny mouth once Annie was eating table food.

Chapter 19

ONE DAY IN late fall, Lew arrived home from work looking more weary than normal. Lissie shushed the boy's clamor at the supper table saying, "Papa's head is hurting. Please speak softly and play quietly before bedtime." Elmer and James were working on spelling words and arithmetic sums so they had no problem staying quiet and soon the younger boys were readying for bed.

The next morning Lissie awoke and realized Lew was still lying beside her. That was unusual as he always stirred up the coals and started the coffee. She turned over and breathed his name. He opened his eyes but made no move to get out of bed nor did he speak.

"Lew, are you ill?" She reached up and put her hand against his forehead. "Dear heavens, you are burning up."

His mouth moved but all she could discern was, "..so dry."

She hurriedly dressed, ran downstairs after checking Annie, sleeping in her cradle, stirred the coals and fed the fire so the coffee could begin to brew. Then she poured a dipper of water into a cup and ran back upstairs to give Lew some fresh, cool water. She sponged his face and hands with a flannel cloth after pouring water from the bedside pitcher into a basin.

By that time, the schoolboys were up and asking for breakfast. "Papa is sick in bed with a fever, boys, so I need your help. Elmer, please prepare the oatmeal like I showed you last week. James, I need you to carefully cut six slices of bread and toast them in the skillet over the stove top lid.

The boys questioned their mother as they went about their tasks. She assigned Landis the job of setting the table since he had come downstairs and joined his older brothers.

"I shall need to run to the depot to tell the stationmaster your father is sick and cannot get out of bed. If the two 'Littles' wake up before I return, help them get dressed and feed them some toast." The family referred to two-year-old Lewis and three-year-old

Howard as the "Littles" in a sort of verbal shorthand.

Lissie did literally run to the depot and explained to Mr. Hughes, the stationmaster, "Lew appears to be having a recurrence of the sickness he contracted during the war. He was burning up with fever when I left the house and barely able to drink some cool water." She went on to explain that he had had a couple of recurrences of the sickness during the eleven years they had been married. "I feel sure he will be well enough to come back to work on Monday," she assured Lew's boss.

She returned home just in time to keep the oatmeal from scorching and poured out helpings for all five boys, the three youngest sporting jam-smeared faces. She sat down with them after toasting a piece of bread for herself and pouring a cup of coffee. "Elmer and James, you did a fine job of getting breakfast on the table. When you finish eating, go tidy yourselves and get ready for school."

After the schoolboys left, Lissie settled the younger boys to playing with blocks, five-year-old Landis in charge. By this time Annie was making it known to the world that she was hungry and wet. As Lissie sat on a stool by the dresser, nursing her baby daughter, she sent worried looks toward her sick husband who occasionally moaned as he tossed and turned. *I wonder if I should move Annie's cradle from our bedroom,* she mused.

The boys arrived home from school, overjoyed at freedom from schoolwork for the next two days as it was Friday, and ravenous as only growing boys can be. Lissie was exhausted from running up and down stairs and realized she must have help as Lew's fever had not broken and she dare not sicken in such a household of children.

Summoning Elmer to her side, she asked, "Do you remember where the telegraph office is, just two buildings down the street from Papa's workplace at the train station?"

"Yes, Mama," he replied. "Why do you ask?"

"I need to send a telegram to your Aunt Jennie asking her to come help us while Papa is sick. Do you think you can be my brave boy and take a message to the telegraph office?"

"I can, Mama," he replied, "though I think I should feel braver with James by my side."

She laughed and tousled his hair. "I think that would be fine."

Saturday dawned and Lissie was doubly glad she had sent for

Jennie, as Lew had not improved over the night. After feeding her brood, including Annie, she settled the boys into various activities, leaving Elmer in charge. Bundling up Annie, Lissie went next-door to ask Mary Ann to care for the baby while she went to fetch the doctor for Lew.

She walked the ten blocks to the doctor's house and office thanking God silently when she found the doctor at home.

"Mrs. Reber, how is that fine baby girl we delivered not too long ago? I hope you are not here on her account."

"No, Doctor. It is my husband, Lew. This is the second day he has been in bed with a fever and nothing I have tried will lessen it for any amount of time. I am hoping you have a miracle hidden away in your doctor's bag." She smiled, but knew it was a weak attempt.

"I shall come right away," he announced. "With a house full of children, you must do your best to guard them from whatever your husband is dealing with." He called for the stableman to hitch up his carriage and assisting Lissie into it, she rode back to her little home in comfort.

After the doctor had checked Lew, he gave Lissie instructions on preparing willow bark tea and assured her she was doing all that could be done for Lew at this point. "This could be a return of that malarial sickness he contracted during the war," he pronounced, "or it could even be smallpox."

At her gasp of dismay, he said, "Your husband is a strong and generally healthy man. If it is smallpox, do not despair. But prayer would not hurt," he added. "I will return on Monday to check on our patient but call me if he seems to worsen. And I suggest you move the baby's cradle out of this room. I do hope you can get someone here to help you, ma'am. Fatigue from caring for your husband and seeing to your children, could cause you to become ill—and we cannot have that."

"Yes, Doctor. I telegraphed my sister asking her to help with the children and the household. She was the one you met when my Annie was born."

"Ah, yes. A very worthwhile young person. Well, I hope she may soon arrive."

"As do I," murmured Lissie. She saw the doctor out and then put on her coat. "I need to go next door to fetch Annie," she told Elmer.

Lissie thanked Mary Ann for caring for the baby, gave her friend a brief summary of what the doctor had said, and returned home.

The next evening as Lissie was preparing supper, someone knocked on the door. "James, please answer that," she called.

He opened the door and shouted, "Ma, it is Aunt Jennie!" and pulled his aunt into the room, immediately telling her, "Pa is very sick, and Ma is plumb wore out, and we big boys are the men of the house and…"

Jennie laughed and gently put her gloved hand over his mouth. "James, I will hear all this very soon, but please be a man of the house and help me with my bags and boxes."

Jennie, who had become a very resourceful young woman, had not only packed the clothes she thought she would need, but had raided Aunt Jane's pantry—with her aunt's urgent suggestions. Elmer, not to be outdone by his younger brother, ran out to help and between them, the boys carried in a large wooden box sporting a handle on each side and covered by a hinged lid. Jennie paid the carriage driver and they entered the house.

Lissie threw her arms around her younger sister. "Oh, my dear," she whispered, "You cannot know how grateful I am to see you."

She directed Landis to set the table for supper and she fed Annie as Jennie made herself comfortable in the rocker beside her sister.

"Miss Annie looks to be gaining well," her aunt remarked.

"Yes, I pray that continues. I do not know what I shall do if she or the boys catch this fever Lew has contracted."

"I want to hear all the details," asserted Jennie, "but first, let us eat. I am starving and by the drawn look on your face, you need to sit still and eat a bite in peace."

The boys all loved their aunt and were accustomed to having her around, so it did not seem strange to them for her to take charge, leaving Lissie to finish caring for Annie and then take some thin gruel and tepid tea to her ailing husband.

When she came back downstairs, Jennie had directed the older boys to clean up the supper dishes and straighten the kitchen. They were then free to play a game or read while the two younger boys were readied for bed.

"I have made up a cot for you in the Littles' bedroom," Lissie informed her sister. "Unfortunately, Annie's cradle is in there too as the doctor advised removing it from the sickroom."

With the children all settled in bed, the two sisters rocked in welcome quiet as Lissie told Jennie what had transpired a few days earlier. "The doctor said he would return tomorrow to see how Lew fares. I believe his fever has lessened but the poor dear just lies there hardly conscious, it seems."

The next morning Lissie felt almost joyful as she descended the stairs to find Jennie ready to pour some coffee, the living area warm and inviting, and the smell of heated cinnamon-apple sauce wafting from a pan atop the stove.

"Jennie, you have lifted a great burden from me," exclaimed Lissie as she hugged her sister. "The aroma of some of my favorite breakfast smells when I lived at Aunt Jane and Uncle Edgar's is almost too much joy to bear." Tears glistened in her eyes as her emotions threatened to overtake her.

"Sit, Lissie," commanded her sister. "I fear you did not rest very well as I do not ever remember you becoming tearful over applesauce and coffee." Lissie sniffed and smiled while Jennie continued. "How is Lew this morning?"

"I truly believe the fever has lessened, but he still seems to be very uncomfortable. It is quite difficult for him to use the chamber pot and I think he has not ingested adequate liquid. And, in these four days, I fear he has lost much weight for his wrist bones stick out from his arms and his cheekbones jut so that his face looks hollow."

They both agreed that it was fortunate Dr. Anders would be coming to check on Lew.

The doctor arrived and went upstairs with Lissie to look in on his patient. "How do you feel today, Lew?"

"My tongue feels thick and I find it hard to swallow," he whispered.

"Let me take a look," said the doctor. After checking Lew's tongue and peering at his throat, he looked up at Lissie who stood nearby, silent. "Just as I feared. Lew appears to have smallpox."

She gasped, her hand flying to her mouth, her heart filled with fear. Lew moaned but said nothing.

"He will soon show a rash which in turn will exhibit bumps. These will break open and then scab over. From this point on, Lew is quite contagious. When you tend to him, Lissie, you must wear gloves. Wash his bed clothes in very hot water keeping them separate from the rest of the household's. You have done well to move the baby from the room for the children must not come into contact with Lew until the pustule scabs fall off. Once all the scabs are gone, he is no longer contagious."

"How long does this illness last, Doctor?" whispered Lissie.

"You are looking at roughly four weeks of caring for Lew. And I cannot stress strongly enough, Lissie, how important it is for you to guard your health by using protective garb."

"I have been inoculated against small pox," stated Lissie. "May I not sleep in the same room as Lew, even if not in his bed?"

Dr. Anders hesitated and then answered, "If you are certain you can remember to put on gloves when you care for Lew, no matter what hour it might be, I suppose you could put a cot in here. However, you are still nursing the baby and if she were to catch this disease, it would kill her. I leave you to make up your own mind on that."

Lew lifted his hand in a weak gesture. "Lissie, I do not want you to take any chance with Annie. Please do not sleep in our bedroom until this dreadful disease has run its course—or I die."

She made a cry of dissent and reached out to him.

"Stop!" barked the doctor. "You are not gloved nor do you wear a protective apron. Maybe now you can see the detriment of you sleeping in here at night, Lissie."

"Please listen to him, Lissie," mumbled Lew and he closed his eyes in exhausted finality.

After the doctor left, Lissie and Jennie discussed the situation. "Since you have been so good to come and help in our dire circumstance, I feel my first responsibility is to Lew. I must see to his comfort and guard against contamination to the children as none of them have been vaccinated," stated Lissie.

"I am comfortable with caring for the children and the house while you tend to Lew," replied Jennie. "It is truly providential Aunt Jane saw to it that we children all received the smallpox vaccination soon after we moved to Uncle Edgar's farm."

"Yes," laughed Lissie. "I remember the fright at being stuck by that needle as well as feeling rather sick the day after. But Aunt Jane assured me I would soon feel better, particularly since I need never worry about catching the dread disease. I had heard her speak of her sister's neighborhood in New York and the many that died in a smallpox epidemic there."

The sisters worked well in tandem and the household moved into a different rhythm fairly easily although Lewis and Howard could not understand why they were not allowed to see Papa.

The third week of Lew's illness saw Lissie needing to visit the market to buy milk for the children as well as eggs and cheese. When she went to the bowl where she kept her household money, she saw that her marketing would use all the coins she had put aside from Lew's last pay packet.

As she walked the five blocks to The Mercantile, all she could think of was *what shall we do for food when we run out of these supplies? Even worse, how will the children and I survive if Lew dies?*

She paid for her order and started the trek home, anxiety building in her chest, almost feeling like she might suffocate. It was then that she heard a quiet voice in her head reminding her, *My grace is sufficient for you, for My strength is made perfect in weakness.* She gasped as she realized it was a verse in 2 Corinthians chapter 12. Lew had chosen to read that passage the last evening they had had family devotions after supper.

As Lissie neared her house, Mary Ann was coming home from the other direction and greeted her. "Lissie, how is Lew? Has he returned to work?"

"Oh, no, Mary Ann. It will be at least two more weeks before Lew is no longer contagious. And then it will take him some time to regain his strength. He is just now beginning to sit up for an hour at a time and is quite wobbly on his feet."

"My goodness, I had no idea it took so long to recover from smallpox. Tonight is prayer meeting and I shall ask those present to pray for you." She patted her friend on the arm and headed toward her front door.

Lissie directed her steps to her own front door, thinking, *Lord, thank You for these folks adding their prayers to mine. But do You think You might nudge them to bring us food or money?* She immediately felt ashamed and murmured, "Please forgive that last sentence, Lord," as she opened the door.

Jennie was rocking Annie when she entered the room, and asked Lissie, "Who were you talking to just now?"

"Uhh. Oh, I met Mary Ann just outside and she was asking after

Lew." Lissie did not want to admit she was talking out loud to God Almighty. *Such presumption,* she scolded herself as she put away her purchases.

The next day an acquaintance from church knocked on her door mid-afternoon with two loaves of freshly baked bread and a crock of cottage cheese. "I just heard of Mr. Reber's sickness," she said. "It was baking day and I threw in a little more yeast and flour for some extra loaves."

Lissie thanked her profusely but it felt strange to accept food from people other than family. When a large bag of coal was discovered on their doorstep the next morning as the boys left for school, she pulled it into the house, sat down on the rocker and burst into tears.

"Whatever is wrong?" asked Jennie from the kitchen.

"I was so afraid when I discovered our money would be gone with my last trip to the market," confessed Lissie. "I prayed as I walked to The Mercantile and told God I did not see how we should live until Lew is back on his feet—provided he does not have a setback," she added. "God spoke to my mind and reminded me His grace was sufficient for our dilemma. And now He is proving that to me," and she burst into a fresh torrent of tears.

Jennie, by now standing alongside her sister, patted Lissie's shoulder and replied in her common sense fashion, "Dry your eyes, Sister, and shout for joy. The Creator of heaven and earth has put hands and feet to your needs. Go share this good news with Lew."

Lissie did not waste any time in doing so. Lew's intermittent fever was now gone but he was very weak. Every day she helped him walk around their bedroom, take care of his functional needs and change his bed clothes when necessary. As she told him of their needs being supplied, she remarked, "When Mrs. Jackson from church brought us bread and cheese, I felt like a beggar. I find it very hard to accept needed provisions like that."

Lew had tears in his eyes as he said, "I lie on my bed praying to God daily that He will provide so that our boys will not have to go out and beg. I believe He has answered that prayer. I am so grateful to people like our mysterious giver and Mrs. Jackson, and you must be, also, Lissie. Be willing to let God use these people to be generous, for He will bless their generosity through it."

From that day forward, until Lew was once again able to return to work, the Reber family did not lack for food to eat, coal to heat their home or money to pay the rent.

Six weeks after she arrived, Jennie was returning home to the Holtschlag farm, this time escorted by a healthy Lew. By now he had heard of her wedding plans and said, "This portion of your family will come and wish you and Henry congratulations, and Lissie will be prepared to play the Bridal March for your wedding ceremony."

Serenity reigned in the Reber household for the next year or so—if a house containing five boys ranging from age three to ten could be judged serene. At any rate, there were no broken bones to mend and only boyish squabbles to arbitrate with Annie teething and then learning to walk.

They celebrated Annie's one-year birthday on September 6, 1877 and that night, Lissie told Lew, "I have some news for you, Husband."

"What news might that be, sweet wife?" he asked, nuzzling her neck in a favorite spot."

"I am once again with child," she sighed. "Your quiver will soon be fit to bursting at this rate. It seems like you need only *look* at me and I conceive another babe."

He kissed her with exuberance and caressed her cheek. "Ah, liebchen, you have given me many fine sons—and sweet little Annie," he added. "I shall be overjoyed to add another fine daughter to our home or another strapping son."

Lissie made a face at his proud tone and replied, "Let us hope he will not be *too* strapping for I can assure you, Husband, if you were bearing these children, you may well have stopped the process after Elmer!"

He laughed and kissed her again which led to more intimate activities. Afterwards, he whispered in her ear, "At least tonight I am not responsible for fathering a child."

She giggled and retorted, "No sir, the mischief has already been done."

Chapter 20

LISSIE'S PREGNANCY WAS an easy one with no morning sickness. Since the boys each knew their responsibilities in the household, all progressed well.

That is, all was well on the home front, but the Long Depression, initiated by the Panic of 1873, was making itself felt severely in the United States. The nation had joined the rest of the western world in changing the basis for money from silver to gold. The decision was wreaking havoc the world over and railroads as well as banks and other businesses were going bankrupt or laying off employees at an alarming rate.

By the time Linnaeus was born on March 31, 1878, rumors of additional layoffs by the Reading Railroad were spreading like wildfire. One evening toward the end of April Lew arrived home, walked through the kitchen to hang up his jacket and cap, kissed Lissie's cheek as she was slicing bread for supper, and murmured, "We must talk after the children are in bed."

Lissie shivered with apprehension. The last time Lew had said that, their landlord had raised their yearly rent. They had had to decide whether to somehow stretch their budget and stay at 345 Coaldust Avenue or try to find another place for the same annual rent that would house their growing family.

Once everyone was fed, the children tucked in and Lissie free to sit in her rocker, Lew began telling his painful news. "We have been told the railroad will close its office here in Reading at the end of June. The rolling stock will be housed in Philadelphia as the company is closing all offices outside of that city in order to cut back on expenses."

"Lew, how shall we feed our family and pay rent on our home?" Lissie's voice was terrified.

He reached out and patted her arm. "I am an able bodied worker, experienced with animals as well as other occupations. I am sure I will find work. However, I must be diligent and question my brother, Gideon, who has homesteaded in Michigan. His last letter spoke of work at sawmills in the area. I believe it is wiser to not put all our faith on employment in Reading."

Lissie nodded in agreement. Later, as she lay sleepless beside Lew, who was snoring softly, she wondered, *however shall I manage moving so far away?* Her heart sank as she thought of the miles that would separate her from Jennie and Aunt Jane. She swiped furiously at the tears that were running into her ears, flopped over on her side and determined to sleep.

The next morning, tired to the bone because she had slept very little, Lissie was snappish to the older boys as they dawdled, getting ready for school. Baby Linn's crying set her teeth on edge and the "Littles" seemed to excel at staying underfoot the entire day. By the time all the children were fed and bedded that evening, she did not know whether to scream at Lew, cry hysterically or throw the coffeepot through the window to show the world how vexed she was.

Lew seemed preoccupied after supper and Lissie did not feel able to lift his spirits since hers had been in the cellar all day. He absently kissed her cheek as they went to bed and Lissie's throat convulsed at the thought of another sleepless night.

The next evening, Lew spoke quietly with Lissie after the children were asleep. "I made some inquiries today." He had cut his dinner time short at noon, saying he had to see to some errands.

"What sort of inquiries, Lew?"

"Checking into job opportunities. I do not relish looking for work, hat in hand so to speak, once I am laid off from the railroad."

"What did you discover?" Lissie felt a leaden lump form in the pit of her stomach.

"I asked some discreet questions at The Mercantile and telegraph office. They require experience and the pay does not seem commensurate with the training needed. Then I checked at Ogilvie's Stable. I know horses and could qualify as a driver and deliveryman. The pay is nowhere near railroad wages, but nothing is. And of course, such wages will soon be non-existent."

"So what are your plans for work, Lew?"

"I believe I shall finish this month at the railroad and start work at Ogilvie's at the beginning of next month. We can live on that wage but likely not save money as we have done in the past." They had managed to save a healthy "nest egg" in hopes of buying a home in Reading. That was obviously not going to happen.

Lew's transition from railroading to livery stable appeared seamless with the exception of him wearing a different type of clothing for his work. Instead of a suit, he now wore denim pants with flannel or wool shirts. Elmer and James noticed the difference but paid little attention to the change since their parents downplayed it themselves.

Lissie promised herself she would not worry about this change in their circumstances, but her sleep was troubled. She sometimes caught herself speaking sharp-edged tones to the children and when the realization hit, she felt ashamed.

Letters began to pass monthly between Lew and his brother, Gideon, who had urged his younger brother to come homestead a plot of land in the area of Michigan where he had settled.

Lissie could see the tight lines in Lew's face as he brought home his weekly wages and placed it in the decorative sugar bowl Miss Madge had given Lissie for a wedding gift. A useless gewgaw, with its gilt edges and hand-painted roses on porcelain, it hardly fit with their sturdy china plates and bowls. It did, however, seem a fitting receptacle for Lew's wages, especially now that there was nothing extra to place in a savings account at the bank.

Lissie found it difficult to stretch those wages to feed and clothe a household of two adults and seven children ranging from an infant to an almost-thirteen year-old boy. She soon realized she needed to plan for an impending move--even if Lew had not yet accepted the idea.

One wintry November afternoon as she sat rocking little Linn, the "Littles" napping and the three older boys in school, Lissie realized the mental weight she was carrying. Anxiety hit her, almost like a blow to her mid-section. Tears began streaming down her cheeks, her mind a vortex of fear and doubt.

"Lord, am I going mad?" she murmured. Then she realized she had spent very little time talking to Him the past few months, letting childcare and worry over finances take the place of any quiet time with God.

As she sat, rocking her sleeping child, she sensed a peaceful presence pose the question, *what do you trust in more, Lew's wages or My provision for you and your family?* Fresh tears gushed forth as Lissie realized she *had* depended on Lew's salary instead of trusting God to provide for their needs. "Please forgive me, Lord," she prayed.

She was dozing, totally relaxed, when the children arrived home from school. Their boisterous actions now seemed like lively joy to her and Lissie realized she was looking at the world with brand new eyes. *Thank You* she thought as she kissed the baby, brought the "Littles" downstairs to greet their brothers and began putting together the evening meal.

After supper, Lew chose to read the sixth chapter of Matthew. As he read the words of Jesus, telling his disciples not to worry about their daily life, Lissie sensed those words were spoken to her. Jesus was saying His heavenly Father took care of the birds, and His disciples were of much greater importance than a tiny sparrow.

That night Lissie slept better than she had in months. The next morning when she went outside to pump a fresh bucket of water, she heard the sound of birds chirping. Looking over at the maple tree she saw a flock of sparrows, some fluffing their wings in a puddle of water from yesterday's rain, others busy eating grass seed. Then she remembered the gist of Lew's reading last night. "Look at the birds of the air, for they neither sow nor reap nor gather into barns; yet your heavenly Father feeds them. Are you not of more value than they?"

She breathed a "Thank You, Lord, again" as she turned back to her pail of water and went inside. Seeing that flock of tiny birds gave Lissie confirmation that God was going to take care of her family. *I just need to remember those sparrows every time I get anxious,* she thought.

By the time little Linn turned a year old, Lew had decided to move his family to Michigan and try his hand at homesteading. "Gideon has been checking around the area and heard that a fellow has given up his claim. It is about three miles from Gideon's homestead acreage and maybe seven miles from Sherman, the county seat."

Lissie began planning what household articles she absolutely must have in the wilderness and Lew made inquiries into how he would transport a family of nine along with said necessities. He remembered the vouchers he received as a bonus during the years the Reading Railroad was prosperous. Checking the dates he discovered they should still be honored. He used part of his dinner hour one day to check with the stationmaster, who had been reinstated, but now functioned as ticket master, supervisor, and even floor sweeper when necessary.

"It is truly dismal at the station," Lew shared with Lissie that evening. "Mr. Hughes said he would not have hired back on but he had too many family obligations not to do so. The good news for us is that we can travel by train to Dayton, Ohio from here in Reading. That is as far as my bonus vouchers will take us.

"Remember our wedding trip, Lissie? I intend to contact that same Army buddy, Jack Sparling. I hope he will allow us to stay the night with his family. The next day I plan to buy a wagon and a team of horses so we can finish our journey to our new home in that fashion. We will need a wagon and team anyway so it is not as if the purchase would be a waste."

Lissie had her doubts about converging on any woman with nine overnight guests, but merely remarked,. "When you contact Jack, be sure to tell him how large our family has become. The last time he saw you, we were only two." She smiled at him then. "I am so grateful not to have to travel the entire seven hundred miles to Michigan by wagon. My sit bones still remember how it felt by the time we got to church in Cressona after riding from the farm in Uncle Edgar's wagon."

After much discussion and sorting and then sorting again, the family made the hard decision of what to keep and what must be given away. "For a family not particularly blessed with great wealth, we certainly own a great many things," sighed Lew.

Each child able to hoist a knapsack on his shoulder was guided in his choice of belongings to travel with him. Lissie packed two large crates with foodstuffs and kitchen items, three trunks with clothes and linens as well as filling the cradle with linens. "So you think to add more arrows to my quiver," joked Lew to his tired wife the evening before they left Reading.

"Not any time soon," she snapped. And then seeing the hurt on his face, Lissie reached out to him. "I am sorry for my sharp words, Lew. My very bones ache with the tiredness."

As Lew went to bank the coals in the stove for the night, he glimpsed Lissie in the parlor, stroking the keys of her organ. The organ had been sold to Deacon Bradbury so at least they would get some money for it. But the idea of leaving it behind was a sore subject, and the older boys were quite vocal about it.

"I think it is truly unjust that Mother cannot take her organ," stated twelve-year-old Elmer in a loud voice.

James stamped his foot and added, "We are leaving all our friends behind and now we cannot have Mother's music. It is *not* fair!"

"We will have music," soothed Lissie. "We do not need an organ to sing and perhaps we can buy a mouth harp and you boys can learn to play it."

At that prospect, the discussion turned to who would be the first to play it and the storm subsided. As Lissie caught the puzzled look on Lew's face at their boys' stormy statements, she wondered if he had stopped to think of how this move was affecting their sons, especially the older ones. Reading was the only home they had ever known and now their world was changing in a matter of days. Before she had a chance to speak of this to Lew, Linn began crying, letting her know he was unhappy about something.

The day arrived for the young family to start their Great Adventure as Lew had begun calling it. The title fascinated the children while the mere sound of the phrase made Lissie's heart ache. Lew had rented a wagon to carry their belongings to the depot. Elmer and James helped their father load the trunks and two large crates containing sacks of flour, rice, and beans, cooking pots, washtubs and an item Lissie would guard with her life. That prized possession was a clothes wringer purchased two years before. No longer did she have to wring out every piece of wet laundry by hand. The cradle was the last item loaded and by that time Lissie had settled the five younger children in the wagon ready to head for the train station.

Once aboard the passenger car they would inhabit for the next three days, they settled in, filling four bench seats, two on each side of the aisle. Lissie sat with part of her brood on one side and Lew sat across the aisle from her with the remainder. Excitement at their first train ride made for shrill screams and loud chatter.

Lew leaned across the aisle and murmured in Lissie's ear, "This is certainly a different trip than the one we last took to Dayton almost fourteen years ago."

"Truly, Husband," replied Lissie with a wry twist to her lips just before turning to settle a squabble. Landis and Howard were already fighting over whose turn it was to sit by the window.

Lissie had brought two lengths of oilcloth to lay on the floor between the facing seats. This fashioned sleeping space of a sort as she had brought blanket rolls with them. Elmer and James were allowed to each sleep on facing bench seats with Landis and Howard on the floor between them. Lissie and Lew each stretched out on the facing bench seats across the aisle from their four boys. Annie and Lewis were on the floor between them with Linn nestled in his mother's arms.

The family managed quite well with the apples and jerky Lissie had packed in addition to the food and drink they were able to purchase at stops along the way. However, all were overjoyed to arrive in Dayton.

Jack Sparling met them at the train station. "Just like old times," Jack laughed as he slapped Lew on the shoulder and doffed his cap to Lissie.

"Not quite," countered Lew. "A pair of Rebers has become a veritable flock."

Jack laughed again and said, "Come, let us get all these bags and boxes loaded and we shall head for home. Mother is most anxious to see all of you." Jack had never married and was still living with his mother, his father having died two years before.

That kind lady oohed and ahhed over the Littles and congratulated Elmer, James, and Landis on their fine appearances. "You must be starving after traveling all those miles," she declared. "Come and wash up and then we shall sit down to a lovely roast I bought at the market just yesterday."

It was indeed a fine roast and the potatoes, carrots and onions which had been cooked alongside the meat brought a shiver of taste delight to Lissie as she chewed and swallowed the first tender mouth full. "Mrs. Sparling, I believe heaven must serve up such delicious meals as this," she declared.

"'Tis true," echoed Lew. "If I were not so hungry, I should love to just sit here and inhale the wonderful aroma of this fine meal."

"Oh, I am sure you are just tired of the smell of coal smoke from that train. That would make any food inviting," declared the lady, but Lissie could see she was well pleased by their compliments and gratitude.

That night the Rebers all slept in one big bedroom, Lew and Lissie curled around little Linn and Annie, the other five stretched out in comfort on a carpeted floor.

After breakfast the next morning, Lew went with Jack to buy a wagon and team of horses while Lissie helped Mrs. Sparling wash the dishes and clear away the disarray of feeding nine extra mouths.

Lew was back before noon with his new purchases and loaded up his family and all their belongings. Thus began the second half of the Great Adventure which Lissie chronicled in a letter to Eliza two weeks after they alighted on their homestead land.

June 28, 1879

Dear Eliza,

Do not look shocked at the postmark of this letter as I have not taken a trip around the nation. Or, perhaps you should join me in the shock of realizing that our family has moved to the back of beyond some five miles from Sherman, Michigan where we now find ourselves nestled in a dense forest of pine trees.

Employment paying adequate wages to support our family is unavailable in Reading so Lew decided to leave Pennsylvania and join his brother, Gideon, in a homesteading venture. We are taking over an abandoned homestead plot adjoining Gideon's acreage, albeit two miles away from his family's cabin.

The four Littles and I stayed with Gideon and Fannie the first week we arrived while Lew and the three older boys took our covered wagon to live in while they re-worked the lean-to the previous settlers had erected. I must say, Eliza, after seeing that lean-to and having traveled 400 miles or so in that wagon, I was more than grateful to sleep in a clean, dry bed without several little, squirming bodies pressed next to me. I love my children but after five weeks of enforced proximity, I am more than willing to send the older portion of our boys with Lew.

I will spare you the details of our trip after we left Dayton other than to remark that we experienced rain, wind and even hail. No sand storms or snow although Gideon says it has snowed here in May!

I do hope it will not be too long before the lean-to emerges into a well-built cabin such as Fannie's, boasting a loft where the older boys can sleep.

After closing pleasantries, Lissie signed the letter, sealed it and gave it to Fannie who added it to a small pile of mail that would be taken to the post office next week when they bought supplies in Sherman.

It was late afternoon when Fannie drove their wagon containing her three younger children along with Lissie and the four Littles into the forest to the newest Reber homestead acreage. They could hear the sound of axes ringing against wood and boyish shrieks of laughter before they spied the clearing.

Gideon and his older son had spent the day with Lew and his older boys and the group had made great strides on building the cabin. The lean-to had been dismantled but included in the twelve by sixteen foot dwelling. Logs had been cut, notched and raised to a height of five massive logs all the way around.

"I hope to put the final two logs in place tomorrow," stated Lew. "We have the logs cut and we will notch and remove the bark in the morning."

"John and I will come on over as soon as we get the chores done," said Gideon. "We should have your cabin up and roofed by Saturday."

Three additional days were added to Gideon's prophecy, first because Lissie insisted on a loft as sleeping quarters for the older boys. Lew decided he needed two more rows of logs "so I shan't have to walk with my head bent throughout the house," he explained.

The next challenge was figuring out how to get the last few logs hoisted above their heads. Thanks to a rope and pulley they rigged up, the top logs were slipped into place. The men had also pondered about the procedure of getting the rafters situated. The loft floor solved that problem since it gave them a platform from which to work.

As long as it did not rain, the loft floor would serve as a roof. "If it looks stormy, we can always spread the canvas from our wagon over our sleeping area," Lew declared. He intended to haul some logs into the sawmill at Sherman to make roof planks. Then they would fasten the bark strips onto the planks as shingles.

"I had no idea this cabin building process was such an immense operation," Lissie told Lew as they snuggled up on the floor of their new home. The boys had gathered pine boughs and Lew tied them together while Lissie placed linen sheets over them as well as extra blankets in case it got chilly before sunrise.

Amidst soft breathing sounds from the children, Lissie wriggled closer to Lew and whispered, "The wind blowing through the trees sounds like rushing water."

"'Tis a soothing sound, yes?" he added.

Just then a mournful howl tore through the air. Soon the single howl was joined by several more. "Are there many dogs out here on the homesteads?" asked Lissie. "I did not think we were so close to neighbors." She knew Gideon and Fannie had a large Irish setter, but they kept him inside at night.

"Those are wolves," pronounced Lew. "If they get any closer, I shall have to fetch my rifle."

"Lissie shuddered and whispered, "I pray they will not decide our horses would make a nice meal."

"Go to sleep, Lissie, There are plenty of deer in these woods to fill the wolves' stomachs," he assured her.

The next morning Lew was up at dawn, building a fire and brewing coffee. Lissie had become a professional at cooking over a campfire and she had ham frying by the time the children began to stir.

First up was James and she set him to slicing a loaf of bread she had baked at Fannie's earlier in the week. Lissie had placed a short plank of wood on two stumps and that functioned as kitchen workspace when she needed it.

The family was soon fed. The four older boys, including six-year-old Howard who was deemed big enough to help as an errand boy, began trimming the logs meant to travel to the sawmill in Sherman. Lissie tied a sheet over the wagon bed and set the three younger children to playing house with five-year-old Lewis in charge. "I shall be Mama with Linn our baby," declared Annie as the children crawled under their shelter.

Lissie set to work preparing a haunch of venison to roast along with potatoes, carrots and onions in a dutch oven that she buried in the ashes of the fire. *I shall certainly be grateful to at least have a fireplace inside our cabin and some workspace besides a plank on two stumps* she grumbled silently. As soon as the thoughts arose, she was convicted of her ingratitude. *Sorry, Lord. I know I should be thankful I can fill my family's stomachs with food.* Her mind then flitted to the dwindling foodstuffs she had brought from Reading.

By nightfall two of the trees had been cut down. With the children settled in bed, Lissie snuggled close to Lew. "You and the boys made great progress on felling trees today,' she whispered.

She looked up to see moonlight streaming through the loft floor, bathing their sleeping children with soft rays of light. She sighed in content as Lew hugged her tightly to him, saying in a drowsy voice, "I hope to fell two more trees of that size tomorrow. Then I can make the trip to the sawmill and finish roofing our home." He kissed her face and was asleep almost immediately. *How tired he must be,* thought Lissie, and then she, too, fell asleep.

When Lew let Gideon know their roof was completed, Gideon and his oldest son came over to help build their fireplace. Gideon had worked for a stone mason one summer as a youth and having built the fireplace for his own cabin, Lew counted himself lucky to have his brother's assistance.

As the cabin was being built, the men had left an opening for the fire box. Then using the rocks gathered by Lew and his boys, Gideon commenced to build the chimney.

Meanwhile, Lissie worked bits of bark and twigs into clay and dirt for the men to use as mortar between the stacked stones. By mid-afternoon the chimney was as high as the roof line. "Is that high enough now?" she questioned.

"'Tis a fact that a chimney needs to be higher than the roof. Learned it the hard way when our cabin filled with smoke after I built our chimney. Fannie threatened to move to town that night if I did not find a way to take care of the problem."

Gideon laughed, his expression somewhat rueful. "I asked my neighbor for advice the next day, after eating a cold breakfast that morning served by an unsmiling wife. He told me about the additional height helping the chimney to draw out the smoke. And it did solve the problem," he added.

Gideon left instructions on how to coat the firebox with clay, being sure to reach as far up the chimney as possible. Since the chimney was actually outside the cabin there was less danger of fire and it did not take any of the much needed space inside the small dwelling.

By the next day the fireplace had been completed. To add a touch of coziness, the men had built a stone hearth raised a few inches above the dirt floor so the children could sit and warm themselves on a cold morning.

Now it was time to test their creation. As the boys gathered branches and twigs for the event, Lissie had visions of that stove back in Reading, belching smoke and soot the first time a fire was lit. "I believe I shall take the Littles outside and watch from the doorway," she declared, a slight wobble in her voice.

"Ah, do you not trust my mudding technique, Wife?" teased Lew. He turned to Elmer and stated in a ceremonious tone, "Come strike the flint and let us light our first fire in our log cabin home."

The older boys oohed and ahhed as a wisp of smoke appeared, then caught the tinder, and flared into a strong flame. Lissie realized she had been holding her breath. She sighed with gratitude as the Littles clapped their hands and jumped up and down in delight, not sure for the reason, other than the joy of their elders.

Chapter 21

March 2, 1921
Palmyra, Missouri

"HOW DID YOU sleep after all the birthday festivities last night, Mother?" asked Landis.

"All I can remember is dreaming," she replied. "Not particularly restful, as I was birthing babies, tending your father when he had smallpox and building a log cabin." Annaliese sighed, and began cooking breakfast.

She felt very tired and decided to nap after feeding Landis dinner. She cleaned up the kitchen and headed for her rocker, wondering *does one merely become more fatigued by marking the completion of another year*? Sitting down and leaning her head against the tall chair back, Annaliese thought of other birthdays and remembered one not celebrated but rather cloaked in sadness.

Chapter 22

Summer 1879
Michigan Homestead

LEW AND HIS three older sons began clearing their land in earnest because they needed to get in at least one crop of oats before winter came. "There is enough cleared land close to the cabin for a garden, Lew," pronounced Lissie as he and the boys sat on a stump eating their dinner of venison and boiled turnips. "We may well run out of food stuffs before winter comes at the rate our supply is shrinking."

"I'll hitch up Daisy to the harrow before supper tonight," replied Lew. "We will likely have to use some of our "nest egg" to buy vegetables until ours mature."

Lissie's garden got planted, Lew's field of oats began to poke green heads through the rich loam, and the clearing of the land continued. It was arduous work often taking Lew and the two older boys an entire day to fell at least two trees.

Lew was not unhappy when the heavens opened and sent them rain for a day. During such times, he, Elmer and James built bed frames and bunk beds because they had left all their furniture back in Reading. Lissie would have liked to be anywhere but crowded inside a twelve by sixteen foot cabin trying to prepare food with the four Littles underfoot while Lew and the older boys sawed and pounded boards overhead.

The beds in the loft had to be constructed in place as there was no space to maneuver a finished product into the loft. As for reaching their sleeping area, the four older boys considered it great fun to clamber up the ladder at the back wall. Five year old Lewis begged to join the big boys but Lissie feared his short legs would not manage the steep trip. "Perhaps by the time we bring in the pumpkins, your legs and arms will have grown strong enough to climb the ladder." He would turn six toward the end of September and joining the Big Boys was his goal.

That November as the snows not only fell but arrived with bluster, Lissie was glad she and the children had persevered in mixing a mess of clay, dirt, twigs, and bits of bark to fill the cracks between the logs of their cabin. Their garden had yielded a good crop of beans, carrots, potatoes, and onions. And thankfully, the pumpkins and squash grew well as did little Lewis's arms and legs for he was now sleeping up in the loft with the Big Boys.

The months passed in a blur of backbreaking toil and Lissie realized there would be another Reber child before 1881 came to a close. She wept as she told Lew the news. "I fear for myself and this child," she told him. "I have no energy to do my work." As he made comforting sounds, she continued. "Howard and Lewis and even little Annie have learned to wash and put away dishes and sweep the floor, but it seems I can barely summon the strength to put one foot in front of the other come nightfall."

"You have always been very tired during the first months of a pregnancy," he reminded her.

"Not like this," she sighed. Tears soaked her pillow as she suddenly realized her 33rd birthday was the next day—but there would be no celebration of her birth, just the endless drudgery of cooking for a husband and seven hungry children--and then cleaning up after them.

Lissie's energy level waxed and waned but mostly remained at a low. When Fannie heard the news of another Reber arriving, she nagged at her sister-in-law. "Lissie, you must keep your strength up. What if you fall ill? Or even worse, die? Lew cannot care for all these children on his own."

"You truly do not dance around the point," Lissie answered with a shaky laugh. "Do you perhaps know of any tonic I could take? Or perhaps herbal teas?"

Fannie thought for a moment and then said, "I remember my mother giving my older sister, Reba, a soup of chard cooked in bone broth, seasoned with garlic. She was said to have tired blood."

"I have chard growing in my garden," replied Lissie. "I have no garlic but I noticed wild onions already grown in a meadow near where Lew and the boys have been clearing land."

Fannie nodded her head in assent to the recipe and their

conversation wandered on to the children's schooling and the leave taking of the current schoolmaster.

Lissie did not have the chance to make Fannie's blood-strengthening recipe. Later in the week she was out in the garden harvesting spinach and radishes when a stabbing pain lanced through her. She dropped her basket and fell to her knees, clutching her stomach.

"Lewis," she called. "Go get Papa and tell him I am sick." When his lower lip began to tremble and he started to question her, she spoke as sternly as possible, "You must go—now!"

"Papa, papa!"

Lewis's panicky little voice struck fear into Lew's heart as he looked up, ax in mid-swing. He had been trimming the large branches from the oak he and the boys had felled earlier in the day.

Running to meet his little son, Lew knelt on one knee and clasped his shoulders gently. "What is wrong, Son?"

"Mama," gasped the child, out of breath and full of fear. "Mama fell on the ground in the garden and said I must come get you."

"You are a brave little man, Lewis. Boys," Lew addressed his work crew, "continue trimming these branches and roll the log to the pile over there with the others. If I do not return before you finish, come to the cabin and start the chores."

"Yes, Pa," said Elmer.

"But what can be wrong with Mother?" asked James.

"I know not, but I must go to her aid." Lew picked up Lewis and tried not to run until he was out of sight of the older children. When he rushed into the cabin door, he found Annie playing with Linn.

"Mama is sick in bed," she announced. "She told me to play house with Linn."

"You are a good helper, Annie," Lew said as he tousled her hair. By this time he had set Lewis down.

"Can I not help, Papa?" he asked in a wobbly tone.

"Yes," replied Lew. "You helped by coming to fetch me and now you can help by playing you are the papa with Annie and Linn."

The little boy sniffed back tears but obeyed his father as Lew opened the sheeted "doorway" to his and Lissie's bedroom. He saw Lissie clutching her stomach as a contraction hit and she bit back a moan.

"Oh Lew," she wept. "Our little one is arriving much too early." He held her close, as sobs and another contraction shook her body.

"My brave little wife," he whispered. "Do you think we can do this together?

"So tired," she whispered. "Send for Fannie."

After holding her through the next contraction, Lew rushed from the bedroom. "Lewis, please fetch all the big boys and tell them Papa wants them to come home."

The boys arrived at a run with James carrying Lewis piggyback.

"Elmer, ride Daisy over to Uncle Gideon's and ask Aunt Fannie to please come help your mother with childbirth." Lew knew Fannie would realize something was amiss this early in Lissie's pregnancy.

"The rest of you Big Boys start tending to chores. I must see to your mother until Aunt Fannie arrives."

Lew was not squeamish about blood. He had seen plenty of it during the war, but seeing Lissie lying there in blood-soaked sheets, frightened him worse than any battle he could remember.

With a loud groan, Lissie delivered a tiny baby girl. There was no lusty cry, just a limp little form the size of Lew's palm. He wrapped the tiny morsel in one of his handkerchiefs and returned to Lissie's side.

"The baby came?" Her eyes looked huge in her pale face.

"She did," he replied, and hugged Lissie as they wept together.

Lew's concern grew as Lissie continued to bleed, slowly. With a weak grunt she finally delivered the placenta but the blood kept seeping. Lissie's face was as pale as bleached flour.

"Are you in pain, Liebchen?"

Her whisper, "Tired," was so soft he could barely hear it.

A noise at the door announced Fannie's arrival along with Gideon. Her calm demeanor eased Lew's fear and her expertise soon stopped Lissie's bleeding. Lew disposed of the blood-soaked bedding and then stayed by Lissie's side. Fannie made supper and then put the children to bed, checking on Lissie occasionally. After she had cleared up supper, she summoned Lew and Gideon. "You must bury the tiny mite that was birthed this day."

The two brothers dug a burial spot under a maple sapling at the far corner of the garden. Kissing the tiny babe that barely covered his hand, Lew placed his daughter into the earth and gently refilled the hole, weeping all the while.

Fannie stayed with Lew and the family for two days but could not be away from her own household beyond that. It soon became evident that Lissie was not well enough to get out of bed, let alone take care of her household. Lew hired a spinster sister of another neighbor two miles west of their homestead. She rode in each morning and left before nightfall.

Jemima Forbes, the mother's helper Lew had hired, was a no-nonsense female. She fed the family dinner, straightened and swept the cabin, watched over the Littles and left a meal ready to be served in the evening. However, Lew and the older boys had to tend to nightly household chores in addition to caring for the livestock and chickens after working hard labor in the field.

As Lissie lay in bed those first few days, her heart felt as heavy as her weak body. Thanks to Jemima's nourishing meals, Lissie began to heal and her near comatose state turned into awareness—and depression. Thoughts of dreading pregnancies, railing at herself for being such a weakling and an unfit mother, Lissie spent a good part of two days in the doldrums.

Her mind began to clear away some of the feelings of failure and Lissie realized she had not prayed for two weeks. *How could she have hoped to weather another pregnancy without her heavenly Father at her side?*

As she wept again, a voice only she could hear said, "I have always been with you, Lissie." She wiped her eyes because she recognized that voice. It was the voice that had spoken to her back in Reading when Lew was so sick. "I will *never* leave you.," she was reminded.

And then Lissie remembered one of her favorite comfort scriptures where Jesus said, "Come unto me, all ye that labor and are heavy laden, and I will give you rest."

"Thank You, Lord," she whispered, and sank into a deep sleep. When she awoke, she felt almost energized. Or at least able to sit up in bed and call for the Littles to come in and visit their mama.

Jemima would not allow her out of bed for more than a few minutes a day but Lissie insisted on whittling away at the pile of mending that she knew had to be accumulating. "Just prop me up with pillows and bring me some socks to darn. They should not be too heavy for me to lift." She knew there would never be a dearth of holey toes and heels to be darned despite the fact that the younger children ran around barefoot this time of year.

Lissie was amazed at how tired she felt after just sitting and darning socks for a short time. "Right now I am grateful you forbade me sitting in the rocker to work on the mending," she murmured to Jemima a few days later. Jemma, for she had asked Lissie to call her that, had brought her a bowl of nourishing vegetable and venison stew after feeding the hungry Reber family their noontime meal.

"At the risk of saying, 'I told you so,'" said the younger woman with a grin, "I think this nurse knows best. Despite your enforced bed rest, Lissie, I must say you have made great progress on that basket of holey socks. There were only four socks left after I brought you that last batch."

The next day Lissie started mending the pile of shirts and trousers sporting rips and three-corner tears. Once again she was grateful for the lighter weight socks she had worked on earlier in her recuperation, thinking, *I am astounded at how weak I still seem to feel.* She mentioned the fact to Jemma.

"Lissie, Miss Fannie told me how much blood you lost when you birthed your baby. You are lucky you lived through it." She continued in her matter of fact voice. "The nurse-midwife I apprenticed to some years ago saw to it all her ladies who bled large amounts, only slowly added to their activities, all the while eating plenty of colorful vegetables and bone broth. You cannot expect your body to rebuild itself in just a few days."

Jemma was an excellent cook, and she saw it as a personal mission that Lissie should regain her strength through good food. Three years younger than Lissie, her good humor reminded Lissie of her dear sister, Jennie.

"You have spoiled me dreadfully, dear Jemma," sighed Lissie several weeks after she had suffered her miscarriage, "but you have accomplished the task of getting me back on my feet as well as caring for this brood of mine."

"'Tis true. You are almost hearty enough to take over all this work once again," stated her new friend. "I will come over here a few days more as I still see dark circles under your eyes and your hands are a-tremble after you have been on your feet for a time."

"I daresay you should put out your shingle as a nurse," noted

Lissie with certainty. "You have truly saved this family as we are far from any relatives able to help out as you have."

"It has been a joy to assist you. And your idea of my nursing has merit. I had given up the notion after Ma was sick for so long. I could not seem to stir myself to look for others to care for. Nursing would surely pay my way, me being a spinster and all." She tossed her head and grinned.

Lissie laughed and said, "As your nursing reputation spreads, I doubt your spinsterhood will remain much longer, if you so wish."

Life resumed normalcy but Lew and the older boys had a new respect for all the work Lissie did for her family, every day, without fail, and thanked her often for a good meal or mended clothes.

Summer 1881 was unique for the family. The children, especially the Littles, clung to Lissie more than ever before. She did her best not to rebuff them but also used their desire to please to teach them family responsibility. Annie, almost five, now dried dishes and put them away as well as doing other simple household tasks. Lewis, two years Annie's senior, was his mother's Big Boy helper, carrying water, toting ashes from the fireplace and generally being a willing gofer. Both older children were gentle with their youngest brother, Linn, who was a loveable child and rarely fussy.

But all three were never happier than when Lissie would take a rare moment to sit down with them and sing "Jesus Loves Me." Then Lissie would tell them a Bible story like young David and his slingshot killing a bear or brave Daniel in the lions' den.

Lissie's garden was not as fruitful that year because she was in bed or recuperating when much of the garden tending needed to take place. Jemma could not be expected to tend garden while she nursed a weak woman back to health as well as seeing to the daily needs of a family of nine. Of course, Lissie expected all of that, and more, of herself. But after all, she had had a chance to become accustomed to the work and had her own efficient shortcuts.

Consequently, the Reber family had to buy some food stuff before it was time to garden once again. Lew and the boys were able to harvest a few shocks of oats and wheat but clearing their land of trees was slow and difficult. The trees they felled were used in a lean-to barn sheltering Daisy and Mac, their team plus Sukey, the milk cow Lew bought from Jemma's brother, Ned. They also used the smaller limbs to construct a chicken house which needed to be tight and secure against wild animals who would prize a tasty bird.

Lissie had insisted on buying chicks earlier that spring of 1882 rounding out the flock of five hens and a rooster. "I think it is time to turn that one old hen into fried chicken," she stated one day at dinner. "She refuses to lay eggs and bullies the other pullets and hens."

Even the rooster seems to be a-feared of her," announced Howard whose job it was to gather the eggs and feed the fowls. "I know I do not like the hateful ol' biddy," he blustered, showing a scratch on his wrist where she had pecked him.

After a particularly hard week of blistering hot weather followed by three days of precipitation ranging from a steady drizzle to a slashing rainstorm, Lissie could see despair written in her husband's eyes.

"This rain is coming at the absolute worst time," he stated in a flat tone. Wet clothes were hung over chairs steaming by the fireplace. "We have lived three years on this land, Lissie, and all I have to show for it is a handful of acres cleared and no money to get ahead."

"If we can hang on, we will own this land, right?" she questioned.

"That is the problem. I do not see how we *can* hang on. The nest egg we came with is almost completely gone and I imagine we shall have to dip into our savings at least as much as last year.

"You are right," she sighed. And the older children need new winter clothes because they have outgrown everything they own. Actually, the younger children also need new clothes because the hand-me-downs are all mostly in tatters."

He laid a hand on her knee as they sat on a bench next to the far wall. "Despite all the toil and scrimping, you are looking mighty fine, Wife." He smiled, leaning over to kiss her cheek.

She looked at him with a hint of concern. "Yes. Well. There is something I need to tell you. It seems that my blooming cheeks and rounding body heralds the advent of another child to our family." She glanced away, curious about the way he would take this news.

"Ah, my sweet Lissie. Another strong son will you give me?" Then sobering. "Perhaps a sweet girl like our Annie. Or the tiny one we lost," he whispered.

"I know not, but I pray for a healthy baby," she whispered in return, eyes glistening with tears. "At least for this pregnancy I go into it feeling full of energy as I did with most of our babies."

The evening conversations regarding their future continued almost daily as they discussed their situation. "Where shall we move and what shall you do to make a living," asked Lissie one September night as they sat outside the cabin enjoying a harvest moon.

"I think we might move to Cadillac. It is now the county seat of this area, and James, Elmer and I can find work there at a sawmill."

"Perhaps," she sniffed. "But it is high time the boys get some more schooling." It had been pretty sporadic for the three older boys, and now Howard and Lewis were old enough to start going to school, too.

"You are right," he agreed. "I have often felt the lack of formal schooling for myself, especially during our years in Reading."

She knew he could have been promoted to better jobs on the railroad if he had had an eighth grade certificate of completion.

However, that was not what he was referring to. "I could have been following God's call to preach if I had had an education," he said wistfully.

"I had forgotten that time in our lives," she said in a flat tone. She had bad memories of that time with Lew indulging in fantasies of God speaking to him while she dealt with a house full of noisy children either crying or rough housing, all needing to be fed, soothed, or cleaned up.

They decided to move before the winter blizzards snowed them in. Gideon lent his time and team-drawn wagon to help his brother's family make their exodus. Each child was responsible to fill a bag with their clothes. Lissie was grateful she did not have an infant to care for in addition to packing linens, dishes, pots and foodstuffs.

She and Lew had found a house to rent in Cadillac reminiscent of the one they had last lived in four years ago in Reading. As she bent over her rounded stomach to fill a crate with kitchenware, she thought, *I am so glad I can deliver this child in a real house with a midwife ready to help.* She knew Lew was disappointed that their homesteading attempt had not worked out, but the thought of having a stove to cook on, sporting an oven to bake in, rather than a fireplace or a fire built outside when the weather was sweltering, was Lissie's idea of a little piece of heaven.

The family was settled in with the older children attending school and Lew working at Parson's Sawmill. He started work sorting and stacking lumber but when Mr. Parsons learned Lew had experience with bookwork both at the end of the war and also during his days with the railroad, he was given the responsibility of keeping the tally book and filling orders from house and boat builders.

They visited three churches in town and by Christmas, Lew decided to cast his lot with the Free Methodists. Soon he was actively starting Sunday School classes and praying with the sick. In the midst of all Lew's extra activities and Lissie's normal household duties, her labor pains began.

On February 27, 1883 tiny Charles Wesley Reber was born. "You have a son," pronounced the midwife, but it was several minutes before Lissie heard the welcome sound of her baby's cry. And that sound was more like a very weak mewling. Little Charles could not seem to catch on how to nurse so Lissie dripped sugar water into his tiny mouth.

Three days later Lissie woke with a start, alarmed at the silence from the cradle beside the bed. Up like a flash, she held her swaddled infant to her breast, bending her head to rest her cheek on his forehead.

Cold. Her warm hand caressed his cheek. It felt icy cold. Then she realized his tiny form was stiff. Grief pierced her chest as she realized her baby was not breathing, and judging by the lack of warmth as she touched his chest, he had likely ceased living some time in the night. Her tears anointed his head as Lissie began to sob, rocking the tiny body as she cried.

"Lissie, what is wrong?" Lew's voice was ragged with sleep and then grief as he hugged his wife and baby son with trembling arms. His tears were added to Lissie's but after a few minutes of silence broken by sobs he said, "I will take care of breakfast and prepare the children. We must arrange for a burial spot so I will speak to Pastor Armstrong after I notify Mr. Parsons I cannot come to work today."

Lissie wrapped baby Charles in a soft green flannel bunting after cleaning his tiny body for burial. She then went to her rocker by the window and gathered the children around her. It was a Saturday so the older children were not in school and the boys looked at her, doing their best to keep emotions in control.

However, Annie, who at six years was already Mama's helper, sobbed noisily at her mother's knee because she considered Baby Charles her real, live doll. Four-year-old Linn did not quite understand what was going on, but followed Annie's suit, crying loudly. Lissie spoke to the children quietly, and their grief calmed.

Several hours later, Lew returned from his necessary errands. "Children, Mother and I must take Baby Charles with us to the church. Elmer, you and James are in charge of the family. Boys, do your studies and Annie and Linn, please amuse yourselves with the building blocks." The two youngest children were elated at that statement because the blocks were only played with during special occasions.

Later that night when all were in bed, Lew drew Lissie close to him and once, again they wept together. "Lew, I do not know how I can bear this awful emptiness I feel. If this is to be my lot, bearing children only to have them die, leaving my arms and my heart empty, I wish to die, myself."

Lew's voice was as raw sounding as Lissie's. "Oh my love, Do not say that. I cannot imagine life without you. And I know I speak for the seven children, healthy children, who are asleep in this house with us."

Lissie stirred from his arms and reached for the square of flannel she had used to wipe her eyes earlier. "You are right, Lew. That was a selfish, weak statement. I have much to be thankful for and much to be responsible for." She turned back and kissed him, snuggling into the crook of his arm and resolutely shut her eyes. Exhaustion fueled her sleep for she was only three days past bearing a child, but the sleep was fitful and interrupted by the remembrance of waking and finding her baby, dead.

The next morning after breakfast and before Lew left for church, Lissie asked him to move the cradle from their bedroom to the back storage area. "I do not wish to have that reminder of sadness while our grief is so fresh," she explained. Privately, she was hoping the absence of it by her side of the bed would aid in her rest.

Despite her sadness, Lissie's body rebounded surprisingly well and her family prospered in the town of Cadillac. Lew had joined the Free Methodists and was soon totally involved with church activities, even holding extra prayer meetings during the week at the Reber home.

When Lissie questioned Lew about holding meetings at their house, he replied, "Lissie, God has allowed us to have this roomy home and I feel led to share it."

"That is quite commendable, Lew, but where are we to stow seven children during a prayer meeting?"

"Why should they not learn to pray along with the rest of us?" His mouth smiled but his eyes were serious. He knew Lissie did not share the same religious exuberance that he felt.

Most of the children were excited about being included in the "big folks" prayer time. James was less than interested, but Lissie overheard Elmer persuading him that he needed to curb his unwillingness, "if only to please Papa."

One evening Lew came home from a church meeting filled with excitement. In fact his German overtook his English. "The Exhorters License I have now been granted. Liebchen, to preach I am now allowed." He clasped Lissie round the waist and twirled her in a dizzy circle.

"Lew, put me down," she cried. Then she promptly ran to the slops bucket beside the back door and vomited.

"My dear wife, what has sickened you?" He reached her in four long strides, instantly sobered and helped Lissie sit at the table. Then, moistening a cloth in a basin on the kitchen counter, he wiped her face gently. "What has sickened you, Liebchen?" he repeated.

'Oh Lew, I am not ill. I am just with child—again." She broke down, weeping silently. He hugged her tightly to his side, stroking her hair back from her face.

"I know not how this can be…um,well, yes, I *do* know. But I do not understand why the Lord has seen fit to send more children. And this so soon after little Charles Wesley. But Lissie, this one thing I do know. This child is a gift from God. Perhaps to soothe our grief from the loss of our tiny babe. So let us be thankful.

"Can we be thankful?" he asked, bending down to look in her eyes. She began to smile through her tears and he spoke again with certainty. "Yes. We shall be thankful." With that, he lifted Lissie in his arms and carried her to bed. “You are to get rest this night, Little Mother,” he grinned. “I go and take care of readying the house for the night.”

And so it was that Lissie bloomed in her pregnancy and Lew worked day and night. “All week during the days I work for my family,” he said with pride. “On Sunday and many evenings I work for my Lord.” That statement worried Lissie for she wondered how long his health could stand up to such a schedule. “Not to worry, Wife,” he assured her. “God will give me the strength to do what He has called me to do. Can I do less than obey Him?”

Lew was soon preaching often, filling in on a circuit near Cadillac. Unfortunately, the Rebers did not own a horse, so Lew walked to his preaching points. “God has given me long, strong legs. And I learned to do plenty of marching during the War,” he added.

Nevertheless, Lissie worried. Michigan winters were not kind and she remembered well Lew’s propensity to catch colds—what the old doctor in Reading called “deep” colds with coughing that caused his entire body to shake.

Chapter 23

SHORTLY BEFORE CHRISTMAS 1884, Lissie sat down to write a long overdue letter to Eliza.

My Dearest Friend,

I pray this very tardy message finds you well and anticipating a lovely Christmas holiday with your parents and other family members. A sudden longing for the Holtschlags and her sister, Jennie, knifed through Lissie, but she immediately tamped down the emotion.

Much has happened since I last wrote for as you can see, our address is now Cadillac, Michigan. We have lived here for two years now--a bittersweet time. I say that because our tiny Charles Wesley was born at the end of February 1883 only remaining on this earth for three days.

The bitter was replaced by sweet when Robert Francis was born in June of this year. His temperament is much like Linn's as he is a sweet child, not fussy or colicky. His blond hair and blue eyes will apparently remain that color. My mother had blond hair and blue eyes so he's not a changeling as Lew laughingly suggested one day. He dotes on the attention from his brothers and sister and does his best to converse with Linn when he tells Robbie all the adventures they will have just as soon as he learns to walk and run.

Annie is determined to be a little "mother hen" to her baby brother. I must say, it is helpful that the older children are willing to join in. 'Tis hard to believe, but Linn is now six and Annie turned eight in September. The older boys help with chores, of course, but they are not particularly interested in baby brother as are the younger two.

The other exciting, but somewhat frightening, news is that Lew has been licensed as an Itinerant Preacher. We joined the Free Methodist Church not long after we moved to Cadillac and Lew became very active in the church. He has wanted to be a preacher since our sojourn in Reading but lacked education. Apparently, the Free Methodists now rank Zeal as equaling Education, although Lew did have to take some examinations to be granted this license.

I call this move of his exciting, but frightening, because we now must depend on the kindness of the people to whom he ministers on his circuit. They are mostly new settlers, therefore, not well off. There is no parsonage or church building on this circuit so we must continue to pay rent. Elmer is now eighteen and James will soon be seventeen so they do odd jobs but need to continue their schooling as our years of homesteading gave them very little time at formal education.

Thank you for reading of my fears with kind eyes as I know your words would be comforting and encouraging if you were sitting here in my kitchen listening to my voice . And how I wish you could be doing just that, dear Eliza. I know this experience is an opportunity to trust God to provide, but I so wish He would let me see Him and hear Him say, as Uncle Edgar often did, "Things will work out just fine, Lissie."

Oh my, this letter will give you eye strain, sweet friend, so I must draw it to a close. Please do write back much sooner than I did.

Affectionately,
Lissie Reber

The winter of 1884-85 was a cold, blustery one. Lew received a letter from his district superintendant in mid-January. Lissie heard him groan as he sat down in his rocker after supper to read the mail.

"What is wrong, Lew?" She was busy cleaning up after the meal, but she glanced over at him to check his well-being.

"Nothing is wrong—exactly," he answered, his voice toneless. "It is just that the quarterly meeting is next week in Colfax and I am expected to be there. Particularly because I have been elected secretary," he added, with a wry twist to his mouth.

"Merciful heavens," Lissie exclaimed. "The snow is three feet deep in places and we have no horse. On top of that, Colfax is twenty-seven miles from here and we have no money for train fare!"

With a "I have spoken" flounce, she climbed the stairs to check on Linn and Annie's preparation for bed.

When she returned to the sitting room, Lew patted the chair beside him. "Come sit, sweet wife. Would you agree to pray with me for this need of train fare? I should like to have you with me on this trip. We can take little Robert Francis with us, and the older children can take care of themselves for three days. You have trained them well and Annie can take Linn to school with her on Thursday and Friday, as we will leave Thursday and return Saturday."

"You seem quite certain of the outcome, Lew, even down to the disposition of the children while we are gone." Lissie's voice held a sharp edge but Lew ignored it.

A smile turning up the corner of his eyes, he replied, "God called me to this ministry, Lissie, and I must be ready to obey. He will provide the money for both of our fares. We must just pray, believing He will do so."

The matter became a topic of family prayers, nightly. But no money appeared. Lew was not visiting any of the settlements on his circuit that week because of the unbearable weather. He did odd jobs around town, shoveling snow and working at the livery stable, but his pay at the end of the week did not come even halfway close to buying his ticket, let alone Lissie's.

The next Tuesday night Lissie asked, "Did God send your train fare today?" She was pretty certain nothing like that had happened. When Lew answered in the negative, she continued, "Well, I guess you had better give up on the idea of going to the meeting at Colfax. I certainly have."

Wednesday, Lew did not go out on any odd jobs. Instead he spent the day doing small repair jobs around the house—and praying. Lissie was watching him and counted seven separate times he went to their bedroom and prayed. She knew that was what he was doing because she peeked inside to check on him the second time he entered the room.

The sun had finally come out that afternoon although the temperature was still in the single digits. The children came home from school with a great flurry of noise and shedding of outer garments. Elmer had stopped by the post office to get the mail. "Papa," he said in a loud voice, "you have a letter from Jack

Sparling."

Elmer handed him the letter as Lew sat in his rocker and slit it open.

He began to read aloud.

Dear Lew,

I have been prompted to send you this bank draft and I suppose God must be at work. You and your family were constantly on my mind all day Sunday. I did not have ease until I went to my bank Monday to withdraw this amount and mailed it to you. Monday night I slept the best I can remember.

Sincerely,
Jack

"How much did he send, Papa?" Howard's impatience was obvious.

"Forty-five dollars," replied Lew with a dazed look on his face. "Forty-five dollars, Lissie." His tone was much stronger the second time. He jumped up and twirled her around much to the children's delight. "We both can attend the meeting, stay in a nice room and eat in the dining room rather than take our own food. Do you realize what has happened, children?" Without waiting for their answer, Lew gave it. "God answered our prayers! And He did not just send my train fare. He sent your mother's fare too and enough to be comfortable while we are away from home."

It was difficult for the children to settle down for the evening meal but by family prayer time, the excitement had diminished somewhat.

"Papa," said Linn with a very earnest look on his face, "I do not understand why you say God sent the money. I thought Mr. Jack sent the money?"

The older children giggled or snickered, but Lissie shushed them as Lew answered, looking very serious. "That is a very good question, Linn. God could have sent us the money in a fish Mother bought at market to cook for our dinner." The younger children giggled at the thought of filleting a fish and finding gold coins inside.

However, Lew was not finished with his spiritual lesson yet.

"Remember the story you heard Pastor Armstrong speak on last Sunday when Jesus' disciple, Simon Peter needed some money to pay taxes? Jesus told him to go catch a fish and he would find the money inside. Simon went to the seaside, caught the fish, and when he went to clean it for their evening meal, there was the money."

He had their attention now. Their eyes were glued to their father's face as he continued. "God often uses people to be His hands and feet, to be His helpers. Just like He used Mr. Jack to provide the money your mother and I needed to attend the quarterly conference."

Understanding bloomed on faces big and little as the children murmured amongst themselves. "I want to be God's hands and feet," piped up Annie.

"I have no doubt you will be just that when you get a bit older," said her father as he reached down and caressed her cheek. "In the meantime you can make God smile when you help your mother dry the dishes."

Later, when all were bedded down and the house was quiet, Lissie said, "Lew, your prayers were surely answered. And I am sorry I doubted your relationship with God. I had been thinking how I wished God would show Himself to me. Your explanation to the children tonight made me realize He did exactly that."

"Exactly what, Liebchen?"

"Show Himself to me," she half-sobbed. "I think I need to pray some 'please forgive me, Lord' prayers."

Lew hugged her close and was soon asleep. Lissie, however, was awake for some time, talking to the Lord and asking forgiveness for her doubting and unloving attitude. She drifted off to sleep with visions of a Kind Being, looking somewhat like Uncle Edgar, beaming at her in approval.

Before the end of February, Lissie's pantry shelves were showing many bare spots. One evening when she set a watery mixture of peas, barley, tiny pieces of dried onion and the last fragments of the chicken dinner they ate at noon, there was much murmuring among the children.

"Mother, there is not even enough bread for each of us to have a whole piece," grumbled Howard.

"I am sure there is good reason, Son," replied Lew, sending a questioning look at his wife.

"Yes, there is good reason," said Lissie in a flat tone. "My pantry contains enough flour to bake one more batch of bread. We have no meat as of tonight and the dried vegetables are in very short supply. Try to balance that small amount of victuals and the hollow legs of growing boys and full-grown men, and the equation comes out sadly unbalanced." She was unable to keep a treacherous wobble from her voice at those last few words for she prided herself on feeding her family well.

The children were struck silent because their mother never spoke about these things in such an emotional fashion.

Lew cleared his throat. "I look at this as another opportunity for God to show His love by providing us victuals. Finish your soup with a grateful heart and then we shall pray as soon as you take your bowls to the counter." Then he repeated, " And eat your soup with a thankful heart. There are some, even in this township, who would be grateful for such a flavorful stew to give them strength."

As the family prayed, thanking God for the food they did have but beseeching Him to refill Mother's pantry, James' stomach growled. There were sounds of muffled snickers, but "perhaps it was an added plea to God's ears," said Elmer after prayer time was over.

Breakfast was porridge and coffee with milk substituted for the two youngest children. No one mentioned the absence of toast and butter, but the thoughts hung in the air. The students trooped off to school, wrapped in their warmest clothes because the winter weather was still in force. Lew, also wrapped in his warmest clothes, set out on a seven mile walk to check on a sick member in his circuit. Lissie set Linn to playing with Robert Francis while she cleaned up the kitchen and eating area.

Holding the baby in her lap after feeding him, Lissie heard a knock at the door and arose to answer it, still holding her little one. She opened the door to a man she had never met although he looked familiar.

"Miz Reber, my name is Jake Wilson."

"How do, Mr. Wilson. How can I help you?"

He stood on the doorstep, twisting his cap in both hands and looking decidedly cold and somewhat embarrassed as he said, "Mayhap I can help *you*."

"Come in out of the cold, Mr. Wilson and have a seat. Would you like a cup of coffee?"

"No thank ya, ma'am."

For a moment the room was silent save for Linn talking to himself as he clicked blocks together, and then the man began his story.

"I am not a churchgoer, ma'am." His cap was contorted into a corkscrew as he continued, "So my story really makes no sense."

Lissie had sat down in her rocker across from him holding a drowsy Robert Francis. She gave Jake an encouraging nod.

"Last night I woke up with a strong thought in my head that I was to bring Preacher Reber a ham. The idea was so real I woke my wife and told her. She laughed at me and said I was a fool to think such a thing. She does not hold with church going either," he said in a sheepish tone.

"Well, I turned over and went back to sleep, but not for long. Here comes this strong idea I needed to take a ham to Preacher Reber. I never was able to get back to sleep. After breakfast I hitched up my horse and wagon to come into town. I was down the lane a little ways and the thought hit me, *You forgot the ham!* Well, it seemed to me like I was to bring you folks a ham whether you needed it or not.

"Say, Miz Reber, how are you folks gettin' along?"

"Why, we are all fine, sir," answered Lissie, quite mystified by this time.

"No, ma'am, that is not what I mean," insisted Mr. Wilson. "Are you in need of food?"

Lissie generally answered questions in the manner in which they were asked, so since Mr. Wilson had asked very plainly, she answered the same way. "Since you ask, sir, we *are* in need of food as I have no meat left in my pantry and very little flour. As a matter of fact, we prayed for God's provision and it would appear He has used *you* to answer our prayers." Her eyes were twinkling but she only allowed a hint of a smile at the corner of her mouth. "That is to say, if you are still willing to give us the ham you brought with you."

"Oh yes, ma'am." And Jake was out of his chair like he'd been sitting on a coiled spring. He exited the house, soon to return with the largest ham Lissie had ever seen.

"Thank you, Mr. Wilson," she said as she directed him to place the huge ham in the middle of the table. "This is a very fine ham."

"I brung the biggest one," he said and went into the finer points of raising hogs in their part of the state. "Now, I want you to let me know if ever you are in need again. No family shall go hungry if Jake Wilson knows of it," he declared. "Even if Mr. Reber *is* a preacher," he added, a grin splitting his face.

There was much rejoicing in the Reber household that evening as the larger meal that night was supper, a hearty ham chowder. Lissie had used the last of the flour to bake a batch of bread, in faith that their supply would be replenished soon.

Her faith was rewarded the next morning when the boys opened the door to go to school and stumbled over a sack of flour as well as a tub of butter.

Those frigid months of 1885 became etched in Lissie's memory as Jehovah Jireh months, meaning the God Who Provides. Lew's assigned circuit was comprised of mostly new settlers in the region who had little cash money to help sustain their preacher. The distances he must cover meant he could only shepherd his scattered flocks once every three weeks.

Again, the pantry shelves of the Reber household were looking alarmingly bare and Lissie began to wonder what small bits of food she might add to hot water to feed her hungry family. Even Lew's stalwart faith seemed to falter. Then he got a message from the leader of the class in a village on his circuit asking him to visit in two days time. The leader said he would have a sum of money gathered from the faithful to give their preacher.

Despite the subzero weather and the snow which lay two-three feet deep, Lew was willing to walk the 11.5 miles to Deacon Hodge's house to gather their offering for his family's sustenance.

Upon reaching the Deacon's home, Lew found no one there. Apparently, the appointment had been forgotten. Lew recounted his experience to the family later that night. "I was sorely troubled," he sighed. "After having walked that distance to not be greeted and given an offer of rest and drink, *and* not be given any payment for the time and care I have poured out on those people, was too great a load for me to bear. I told the Lord I could no longer do this circuit preaching. The people's hearts are hard and my work not appreciated.

"Then the strangest thing happened, Lissie." She looked at him, questioningly. "I heard a voice call my name. I had not seen a soul my entire trip home. 'Lewis dear,' the voice said. And it sounded like my mother's voice the way she used to call me when I was a child. I turned around quickly, but of course no one was there. Then I realized if the Lord loved me enough to send me the sound of my sainted mother's voice, He would surely provide for me and my family.

"I have to admit it was still hard to walk up on our doorstep knowing I returned with empty hands."

"But then you opened the door and we told you the good news," shouted Lewis, eager to get to the best part of the story.

"Tell how God provided for our needs," said Lew. He knew the essence of the story but he wanted them to hear it again.

"You tell it, Mother. You say it best," the children urged.

With a nod from Lew, Lissie began. "Along about mid-morning Miz Benson from the Presbyterian church came knocking on the door. Remember Lew, she came to a prayer meeting here more than a year ago and surrendered her life to Jesus?"

He nodded, remembering also that Mr. Benson owned The Mercantile. Lissie continued. "I offered her a cup of coffee and she asked how it was going with you itinerating and not having a steady job anymore. I could tell she was sincerely interested, not just being nosey. So I told her things were pretty tight right now, but you had gone to Hartwick to pick up a sum of money the class leader had gathered from the folks there.

"She told me she had been impressed to visit us and check on our welfare. We chatted about our children and she commented on how Robert Francis had grown. Then she left."

Annie could not hold in the rest of the story. "Papa, it was not two hours before we heard another knock on the door and two men from The Mercantile said they had some things for us. They brought in two sacks of flour, a keg of lard, a side of mutton, turnips, squash, carrots and onions. Oh, and a cask of molasses!"

"Look, Papa," whispered Linn. "I never seen such before, but it smells wondrous." In each hand he held an orange.

Lew reached out and hugged him, "I have seen oranges only a few times, myself. You are right, Son. They *do* smell wondrous."

The next evening after a sumptuous meal of mutton stew laced with onions and carrots accompanied by slabs of fresh bread with butter, they heard a knock at the door. Howard was sent to open it and there stood Brother Chatham, a steward of the Free Methodist Church in Cadillac.

After greetings were exchanged, he declined to stay and visit but stated his reason for coming. "I just received this sum of money from our treasurer given as a love gift from our church. We thank the Lord for the distances you travel to preach the Gospel to homesteaders in this part of the country." Handing a bag of money to Lew, the churchman said his goodbyes and left.

"Papa, count the money," insisted James, so Lew sat back down at the table. Everyone watched as he carefully sorted gold coins and paper bills.

Lissie sensed she was holding her breath and suspected some of the children were doing the same. When he finished sorting and began totaling up the amounts, Lew looked over at Lissie with a dazed expression.

"I dare hardly believe what I am seeing with my own eyes," he exclaimed, emotion breaking his voice.

"How much, Papa? How much?" asked the children like a Grecian chorus.

"The Lord has lain on the hearts of His people to give us enough money to pay the rent, buy food as we need it, and even have enough to buy readymade clothes for us, at least those of us who are wearing pants more holey than righteous." He grinned and pointed to a patch on his knee that had worn through.

Family devotions were once again full of devout praise and the rendition of "Showers of Blessings" was sung with a tremendous amount of fervor by all, including little Robert who did his best to mimic his siblings.

It was difficult to settle everyone down for sleep but finally the house was quiet. Lissie and Lew snuggled into their feather bed and reviewed the last two days worth of providential miracles. Finally, Lissie yawned and said, "Truly, our cup runneth over. May it continue so, Lord."

Chapter 24

April 1, 1921
Palmyra, Missouri

AS SPRING BEGAN to warm the earth, Annaliese sensed new life and energy enlivening her arthritic joints. *Good thing,* she thought as March exited meek as a lamb *because I have a birthday party to plan for Landis. Gracious sakes, how time flies. Seems like just yesterday he was a little tyke trying to keep up with Elmer and James. Now he's due to turn fifty years old in two days.*

James' wife and daughter, Louisa and Anna, helped her get word to the neighbors and they ended up having a joint birthday party for young Carl Disselhorst who was born on April 3, also.

The neighbors thronged the little house because Landis was well thought-of, particularly as he had stayed on and helped his mother after Preacher Reber died. Annaliese baked a three layer cake covered with red rosettes and candles—fifty of them. Master Carl and Landis mounted a joint assault on the blaze when all the candles were lit and managed to snuff them out in a might blast of air.

After everyone left, Landis remarked, "That was a jolly party, Mother. I never heard such music played, or songs sung, or stories told. And I may not sleep for all the cake and ice cream I ate," and he rubbed his stomach in part discomfort, part bliss.

Annaliese had even been coaxed into playing her pump organ and with one fellow's violin and another neighbor's flute, the parlor had been filled with voices and instruments alike. The selections ranged from "A Mighty Fortress is Our God" to "The Battle Hymn of the Republic."

Annaliese was exhausted by the time she climbed into bed, but as she stretched out, trying to relax tired muscles and joints, her thoughts turned to her birthday ten years earlier when James and Lew had given her the pump organ that now stood in the parlor.

When she saw the men moving it in, for James had called two neighbors plus Landis to help move the crate from the wagon to the house, she was speechless.

Lew teased her. “You weren’t so quiet when we brought in your first pump organ back in Reading. Remember? As I recall, you gave me quite the tongue lashing about not being able to afford it.”

Annaliese looked at him and said, “I probably should give James the tongue lashing this go-round.”

“Now, Mother,” James had said with a stern look on his face, “I remember how bad we boys felt when you had to leave your organ behind when we left to homestead. I have always wanted to replace it, and Father said he thought you would enjoy it, so here it is. May you have many hours of joy playing it.”

“Thank you, Son.” Annaliese walked to him and hugged him tightly. “You were always my sweet boy,” she whispered.

“Let’s have a tune, Wife,” coaxed Lew.

“I warn you, my fingers are stiff and my brain does not remember much,” but jokingly, she picked out the melody of “Happy Birthday” amid much laughter and before she had finished, the men were all singing in her honor.

“Oh, Lew,” she murmured. *How good it was to hear his voice.* And then she woke with a start, saw the moonbeams dancing through her sheer drapes and realized she had been dreaming. She turned over, sighed, and went back to sleep.

April had always meant Spring Housecleaning Month to Annaliese, at least when she had lived in an area that saw a normal spring season. This April 1921 was no exception and she decided to start by going through drawers in her desk with a wastepaper can nearby. As she sorted through old receipts and letters that had long been answered, she spied her journal nestled at the bottom of the desk’s middle drawer.

She picked up the thick leather-bound book and opened it to the front page. *To Lissie,* it read, *To record your thoughts and activities in this new land where we may at last take root and settle down.*

Merry Christmas 1898 from your loving husband, Lew.

Annaliese smoothed the cover and thought of all the places they had lived and all the times Lew had fallen ill prior to the writings in this journal. She remembered thinking it was appropriate to start recording her thoughts at the time Lew had given her this gift. She would not have had time in earlier years.

Her mind wandered back to those years as she settled comfortably in her chair with the journal open on her lap.

Chapter 25

March 1885

Cadillac, Michigan

THE MONTH OF March exited like a lion with blustery weather and many people contracting harsh colds that easily became pneumonia. The entire Reber family caught and shared the bug with each other, except for Lissie and James. Lew, Robert Francis and Annie were the ones hit hardest. At times, Lissie despaired of bringing little Robert through, but her prayers and steam tents finally broke up the congestion in his little chest.

Not so for Lew. The weak chest he seemed to have developed during his war years made him susceptible to every cold possible to catch. It did not help that he had walked many miles in the worst kind of weather so his constitution was weakened at the outset when this virulent bug hit the family.

Lissie tried all sorts of medicines in an attempt to soothe Lew's throat for even slight speech brought on a severe coughing attack. At times he barely lacked the energy to make it to the table to eat a meal with the family.

Lew finally decided he must resign his circuit. "I feel such a responsibility to preach the Word to those settlers so far away from any Godly influences. Someone must go!" He ended his declaration with a spasm of coughing.

Lew's Chairman refused his resignation and wrote him, *I recommend you retain your circuit. I will see to it that someone takes care of the folks on your rounds until such time as the Lord sees fit to heal you.*

School finished mid-April, and Elmer and James went to work at a sawmill about a mile from the house. This was necessary as Lew was still very weak and spent much of each day wrapped in a blanket, rocking as he read his Bible and dozing. Lissie tried every remedy she had ever heard of to get Lew back on his feet. Nothing worked and she began to despair of ever again seeing the virile man he had once been.

In July Lew received a letter from a young man in Hartwick who wanted to have some revival meetings there toward the end of the month. I *will see that you have a preacher but I am not well enough to preach*, wrote Lew in a return note.

The town of Cadillac celebrated the Fourth of July with a parade, food in the City Park and fireworks in the evening. That morning Lew got out of bed, seeming to move with greater ease and much less coughing. "Shall we take the children to see the parade?" he asked Lissie as he sat, drinking another cup of coffee, and while she cleaned up around him.

"Yes, Papa. Please Mother," pleaded the younger children. It was a foregone conclusion for the four older boys.

"Are you sure you are up to an outing like this, Lew? Must I remind you about your exhaustion at merely walking two blocks and sitting in church for two hours on Sunday?"

"I do seem to have an extra supply of energy today, Lissie," Lew said, and then he began to cough. When he could catch his breath again, he grinned at her with a weak attempt at humor. "Well, I *did* have some extra energy."

The family went to the parade but only the four older boys were allowed to enjoy the remaining festivities downtown. That night the younger children tucked in bed and the sound of firecrackers blasting in the distance, Lissie asked, "What made the difference in the way you were feeling today, Lew?"

He was quiet for a moment and then answered, "Perhaps it was my Hartwick parishioner urging me to attend the meetings at the end of this month. He ended his letter with *Come to the meetings and get healed.* If my health continues to mend, I may just go up there. It would be so good to see those folks again."

"I suppose time will tell," replied Lissie, but she did not put much hope into the idea that her husband would have adequate energy to make the journey and attend the meetings. She did not intend to go since there were too many children left at home who needed her.

The last week of July neared and Lew became all the more determined to go to the revival meetings and renew contact with the folks on his circuit. "It is true that your health has improved from when you first sickened, but I think it extremely unwise that you make this trip," protested Lissie.

"Have faith, Liebchen," said Lew. "I am riding to the meetings in comfort because one of the speakers I have procured is coming through town and I shall ride with him in his buggy."

At least you are not walking *to Harwick,* Lissie murmured to herself as she waved goodbye to Lew. The grumbling thoughts continued as she finished her housework that morning. *I do not know why Lew is so stubborn. He should know by now at age 38 he is not immortal.* She shuddered at the memory of his illness during The War and then the bout with smallpox some years later.

By nighttime she had managed to worry herself into an absolute tizzy. As she lay in her lonely bed, she began to think of what it would be like if Lew sickened further and died. She could not get comfortable and began to cry as she envisioned Lew's side of the bed being forever empty.

Perfect love casts out fear.

She wiped her face and thought, *Fear is normal. What if Lew remains an invalid and I have all these children to rear? What shall I do?*

Come to me with your load, Lissie, and I will give you rest. Perfect love casts out fear.

"Is that really You, Lord?" she whispered. There was no audible answer or any further mental message, but Lissie felt a sense of peace slowly pass over her and she knew all was well. Sleep then came without effort.

Lissie was outside hanging up laundry in the back yard when she heard Annie scream, "Papa is home! Papa is home!

Leaving her wet laundry Lissie hurried inside, somewhat apprehensive as to Lew's state of health. He had bent over and picked up little Robert, tickling him with his beard. When he directed his gaze toward Lissie, her jaw dropped in amazement for his brown eyes were clear. Where were the dark circles under them? His shoulders were not slumped in fatigue and his back was erect. When he stepped toward her to kiss her in greeting, still holding Robert, his stride appeared effortless.

"Lew. Your illness has gone!"

He kissed her soundly and smiled. Putting Robert back down,

Lew embraced Lissie, kissed her again and whispered in her ear, "You see before you a man touched and healed by God."

At family devotions that night, Lew read a scripture and they sang a hymn. Then Lew told his family of his miraculous healing. "I know that even you younger children realized I have not been well for several months." The Littles began to speak of his symptoms as the older boys merely nodded.

Lew quieted the youngsters and continued. "Your mother felt I was most unwise to attend the revival meetings at Hartwick, but I felt I must, particularly as I had been coughing less a few days previous. It turns out I made the right decision for the longer I was there, the better I felt. Brother Jones asked me if I felt like preaching one evening and I got through my entire sermon without coughing once. And to add to that joy, several people surrendered their lives to Christ, accepting His salvation."

"That was a ''citing part, huh, Papa?' interjected five-year-old Linn.

"Yes, son, that was the greatest decision they will ever make. But there is more excitement to the story," and he continued before another youngster could interrupt. "Sunday night after meeting was over we went back to Brother and Sister Zeigler's house where we had been staying. I was conducting family devotions and during prayer time I had this very strong impression to lift my hands.

"Now I have never lifted my hands to pray and I did not see any reason to do it then. However, that strange urge to lift my hands persisted, so I did. Immediately, I felt something like a jolt of electricity strike my head and I realized it was the power of God. Then I had the sensation of oil running all over me, penetrating all parts of my body. After five or six more jolts of spiritual electricity, I realized I was feeling like a brand new man. 'Glory to God,' I hollered. 'I am healed!' You can be sure there was a lot of praising God that night. It was like the entire room was filled with His glory. I doubt any of us will ever forget that experience."

The children were very quiet and then Annie walked to her father and patted his chest. "Even the hurt here?"

"The hurt is all gone, Annie. Your Papa is no longer sick, having to sit in a chair and doze all day."

"I am so glad, Papa." She hugged him, kissing his cheek, and then went back to her spot on the floor.

That night the children's prayers were especially heartfelt in thanking God for giving back their father's health. Lissie shed tears of joy as she listened to their sweet prayers of praise and added her own.

To lend credence to his miraculous good health, Lew went with Elmer and James the next day and was hired to sort and stack lumber at the sawmill. In addition, Lew resumed his circuit preaching, going out on Saturday to a preaching point and returning late Sunday night.

Lissie attended the Fall Conference with Lew, accompanied by the four younger children. She was gratified to hear her husband praised by several. The most outstanding remark was made by Superintendent Roberts, himself. "Brother Reber has done an exemplary job this past year, doubling the membership in his circuit and leading numerous souls and backsliders to the Lord. And that was accomplished despite the fact he was an invalid for a good quarter of the time."

Lew was shifted to a different circuit at that conference, Big Falls, a large circuit he shared with another itinerant preacher named Smith. Lew was responsible for the preaching points of Hungerford and Brush Lake. The distance was too far for him to travel from Cadillac so he put out some feelers for possible places to live.

The day after they returned home from Conference, Lew received a telegram from Preacher Smith. "Lissie, listen to this," Lew all but shouted. "Smith has spoken to a member of the church in Big Rapids who owns several pieces of real estate. This Brother Turner is willing to allow us to live in one of his houses rent-free. Once again God has provided for our needs."

Lissie smiled, but thought, *I must needs be grateful, Lord. But I surely hope the roof does not leak and mice are not overrunning the rooms.* She was surprised to find a pleasant house large enough to hold her numerous offspring. The bonus of living in a rent-free dwelling during their sojourn in the area also added to its attractiveness. After a week in their new home, Lissie remarked to Lew, "I am quite happy with this new home as well as the ease of this move compared to the one when we moved to Cadillac from the log cabin."

They were sitting side by side in their rockers during an unusual quiet moment, children either sleeping or busy in their rooms. Lew reached over and patted her knee. "The longer I know you, the more efficient I see you become, Liebchen. You have done an admirable job of training our children to help others as well as to be self-sufficient."

Lissie prized the warm and affectionate feeling of his hand on her knee. He continued. "I saw Annie helping Linn pack his knapsack and Howard, Lewis and Landis needed no instruction at all in packing their belongings. As for Elmer and James, our two oldest are now as strong as full-grown men and just as responsible."

Lissie arose, discomfited by Lew's praise, and changed the subject. "Do you realize our eldest two are now older than when we were first married?"

"Are you wishing to marry them off?" joked Lew.

"No, I am in no hurry to see them leave home." She made a face and swatted at him. "I was just comparing ages and how the times have changed."

The house continued to prove comfortable and life hummed along pleasantly. By January 1886 Lissie realized she was pregnant once again. She told Lew of their impending addition and added, "I do not feel so fearful carrying this babe since our sweet little Robert was born a stout child and continues so. Even though I *shall* be thirty-eight when this child is born," she sighed.

Martha Amanda was born on August 12 and was soon surrounded by a crowd of adoring siblings. "I declare, I shall have to demand you draw lots as to whose turn it is to rock little Marti," laughed Lissie. They marveled at her curly brown hair very much like Annie's which gave that young lady great pride.

The birth was an easy one for Lissie and she bounced back to her normal level of energy within the month despite the demands of such a large family. This was indeed fortunate because at the close of the Fall Conference, Lew came home with news.

"I have been given the circuit of Evart, Chippewa and Forks," he stated with a happy face.

"I dread leaving here, Lew. The people of this circuit have shown much kindness to us."

"This has been a wonderful work this past year," he declared. "We had sixty souls come to know Christ and surrender their lives to him during that series of meetings last winter."

"And perhaps best of all, Elmer surrendered his life to Christ," Lissie reminded him.

"Yes, I cannot imagine a better year's work. However," he continued, "I feel the Lord is calling me to another mission field. This circuit is well on its way to having an actual church building in which to worship and the present membership are willing to support their earthly spiritual shepherd. The solid foundation of this past year's circuit leads me to feel my work here is done. This, no doubt, was a factor in the decision to place me in a new circuit."

"It is quite a distance from Big Rapids, is it not?"

"Yes, Lissie. As soon as I can find a proper dwelling, we must pull up stakes and move to Evart," he replied.

Her heart sank. This had been a comfortable home for the family and she liked the town and her neighbors. *Why do we have to move? Will we ever put down roots again?* Those thoughts as well as other rebellious ones churned in her mind, but she willed herself to blank them out so she could sleep come bedtime.

The home Lew found was adequate to house their family of eleven but showed itself to be exceeding drafty. This was not apparent when the family moved, in mid-October. But when the November winds began to howl, Lissie scrambled to find enough blankets to hang over windows at night and rolled up burlap bags to wedge into the door thresholds.

Severe respiratory ailments, including whooping cough, spread throughout the region. Adults and children--no one was immune--and those with weak chests were especially vulnerable. That meant, for the Reber family in particular, Lew and little Robert.

Lew came home from Chippewa one Sunday evening at the end of December and was sick in bed afterward for a week. Howard came home from school in mid-January, sneezing in every direction. Between the two, the entire family caught some version of the sniffles. Lissie kept the older children away from baby Martha as soon as a sneeze or sniffle developed, but everyone but the baby caught some version of respiratory distress, including Robert Francis. His lungs had been weakened by the pneumonia he had suffered the year before which made it very difficult to fight this bout of illness.

By April of that year everyone had sniffled and coughed their way back to health—except for little Robert. His tired cough could be heard throughout the night for Lissie had fixed him a little pallet close to Martha's cradle. Lissie had coaxed Robert to drink potions of herbal tea and cups of bone broth but nothing seemed to help him breathe easily for long or strengthen his little body.

On the 21st of April, 1887, their golden-haired little boy looked up at the face of his mother, smiled, and stopped breathing altogether. She had been rocking him and singing his favorite song, "Jesus Loves Me." Lissie stopped rocking and just whispered, "Oh, my sweet Robbie." His little mouth continued to hold the smile as her tears slid down her cheeks and kissed his face.

A black shadow seemed to hover over the family as they mourned their little brother for he was a great favorite. After his burial the next day, Lew gathered the family together and said, "We must somehow give our sorrow to God as we grieve for little Robbie. Scripture tells us that we may be unaware when angels are among us. Perhaps our Robbie was actually an angel sent to live with us for a short time." His voice broke and he fished a handkerchief from his pocket. "Let us take turns speaking of something special about Robbie that brings you joy."

Silence. Then Elmer, as oldest, spoke. "I loved the sound of his laughter when I swept him up on my shoulders and carried him around. Whenever I came home from school, he would run up to me and throw up his arms, shouting, 'Horsie, Elmer. Horsie, Elmer!"

Soon, all the children had thought of at least one wonderful memory of Robbie, ranging from his sweet little voice singing with the "big children," his gurgles when someone tickled him, to his adorable attention to baby Martha, urging her to "hurry and grow up so we can play."

Neighbors and church friends were kind and Lissie was surprised to learn that Lew had been assigned to a different circuit several miles east of his present one when the next Fall Conference arrived.

"Some members from Chippewa even came to Conference asking the committee to reconsider and allow me to continue ministering to their circuit, but the authorities decreed that I should go to Clare and Farwell circuit." He sighed. "It is a strong circuit and I suppose they believe the strong membership will make it an easier year for me."

It proved to be the very opposite.

Lissie felt she had the job of moving her household fairly well fine tuned. Elmer and James were now young adults and could lift and carry furniture as well or better than Lew. The three younger boys were now teenagers so Lissie need not do any heavy lifting at all. Annie, at eleven, was a good little housekeeper and mother's helper. Nine-year-old Linn was not stout, but his slender frame held a willing heart and when Annie was busy helping her mother cook and clean, he was willing to amuse little Marti, who was now beginning to walk.

The new circuit boasted a church and parsonage just built. But after the first night spent in their new home, Lissie had much to say about it to Lew, first making sure all the children were tucked away in bed. "Lew, I thought our last home was full of drafts, but it was built before we were born so I granted it some grace." This was stated with a straight face but a quirk to the corner of her mouth. "I declare, though," she continued, "I do not see how a brand new dwelling can have so many spots for the wind to blow through!"

It became apparent that the house had a sheathing of clapboard on the outside fastened to long studs with a coat of plaster applied to thin laths on the inside. Lissie had discovered this when a bunk bed in an upstairs bedroom bumped into the wall and a chunk of plaster plopped on the floor . The house was a mere shell and air entered around windows and doors without any impediment.

The first morning the temperature descended to the single digits, it was not much warmer inside the church parsonage. "Mother, the water pail is frozen almost solid," Elmer called. Being the first one up that morning, he was intending to start the coffee brewing. Obviously, the water would have to be thawed first.

"That is not the only thing frozen almost solid," remarked his father as he emerged from the bedroom. His mustache was coated with frost and as he brushed it with his hand, the frosty ice crystals shone in the sunlight from the front room window. "Perhaps we shall become snowmen before this winter is over."

Lissie was not amused. The membership of the circuit seemed to think their preacher did not need to be fed well since this lovely new home was provided for his family. "I do not understand how these people can be so paltry in their giving," she railed at Lew one evening as they sat huddled in their rockers, swathed in blankets extending from the tops of their heads to their toes.

"I have made some inquiries," he said, slowly. "It seems that building the church house as well as the parsonage has left the circuit heavily mortgaged. People in the community pledged money but have not made good." Lissie shook her head in disgust. She could not understand building a house without having the money in hand.

The winter seemed to go on forever. Lissie tended sick children constantly for it seemed at least one child or another was down with a bad cold for a solid three months. "And it is no wonder, Lew," she scolded, "because the children do not have enough warm clothes. And that problem would include living in this dreadful house!" she added.

She knew it was not Lew's fault that work was scarce so that the older boys could not help with finances. She also knew Lew could do nothing about the financial morass the circuit had gotten itself into with the heavy mortgages on both buildings. Life suddenly seemed too heavy, but there was no way out. Lissie could hear her voice sharpen in tone if the older children did not obey her immediately or if little Marti made a mess.

One night after Lissie had roundly scolded everyone who crossed her path, including her husband, Lew met her at the bottom of the stairs after she had seen the children to bed. "Come sit by me, Lissie," he coaxed. She sighed, thinking of the mending that continued to pile up daily in her sewing basket. "I wish for you to tell me what is bothering you, liebchen."

At his term of endearment, she burst into tears. Lew stood, picked her up, and sat back down holding her on his lap. "Now then, liebchen. Speak." He proceeded to pull out his handkerchief, offered it to her, and kissed her forehead. "Yes?" he urged.

Lissie blew her nose, wiped her eyes and tried to stiffen her spine. "This is most unbecoming of a mother of nine. Eight," she corrected herself, and began weeping again.

"Ah, my dear Lissie. Such a heavy burden you carry." Lew rocked her silently, holding her against his chest for her head fit nicely under his chin. After the sobs subsided, he tried again. "Do you feel like talking? What is weighing on you so heavily, dear wife?"

Lissie tried to gather her thoughts into some semblance of order but then just decided to blurt out whatever surfaced first. "I am so tired, Lew. Tired of moving each year, tired of sickness, tired of being poor, tired of death. Oh, Lew, whatever shall I do if *you* sicken and die?" She began to weep again and he hugged her even closer.

He was silent until her tears subsided, then he said, "Our wedding vows we promised to each other and God. Are they still true?" She looked at him, puzzled. "Remember? For better or worse. In sickness or health, poverty or wealth. Can you still find truth in those vows? Trust our love and God to whom we also promised?"

"I want to, but I feel I am very close to breaking apart," she whispered.

"I will share what I have learned," he stated. "First of all, remember God is always walking beside us. He promised in His word He would never leave us or forsake us. That promise gives me strength when I am so tired I can barely put one foot in front of the other as I walk from one appointment to the next. Or when I stand beside the headstone of my child who has just died." His voice trembled and his arms tightened around her.

"Do you believe God has called me to preach the gospel, Lissie?"

"So you have said," she replied in a hesitant voice.

"Do you resent that calling?"

She hesitated a moment and then answered. "I was quite proud to think of you as a preacher. At least at first. I must admit, I had no idea what it would mean for our family." Her last statement ended in a whisper. "So yes, perhaps I do resent this calling. Why, I wonder?"

They sat quietly as Lew allowed his wife to come up with the answer to her own question. "I believe my resentment is rooted in fear and loneliness. I am afraid of being left alone with all these children to rear. And," she paused to ponder, "I feel lonely because you are gone so much of the time to preaching appointments leaving the children and me behind. Which of course is out of necessity," she added.

"I am unsure of the answer to the loneliness you describe, but I am glad to be aware of it. I promise to do my best to alleviate your loneliness." He kissed her temple. "As for your fears, I can sympathize for I am well acquainted with fear. It started with the death of my mother and the strange aloofness of my father. Then I was shot at in the War and have been sick unto death more times than I like to remember. Presently, I continue to dread preaching in front of men much more educated than I. My fear runs the gamut from physical to mental and back again. When those fears come at me, I remember that God says to me, 'Fear not, for I am with you.' When the Creator of the universe reminds me of that, how can I be afraid?"

At that moment Lissie recognized the impassioned preacher of the gospel that Lew had become. She turned and pulled his head down to kiss him, slipped off his lap and said, "Let us go to bed, Husband. Your wife feels much healed," and she smiled.

The Fall Conference of 1888 saw Preacher Reber moved to the strong circuit of Luddington, Custer and Free Soil. Lissie was delighted despite the fact she was moving her family again. As they shut the door of the parsonage in Clare, Lissie remarked, "This house actually makes our cabin seem like a snug, comfortable little home," alluding to their homesteading days. She was looking at Lew when she said it and caught a grin lurking at the corner of his mouth. "You know better than to say anything," she teased. By the end of their stay in the woods, Lissie had made no secret of how she detested the tiny, primitive cabin.

It took six days to move the family and belongings to their new home. Lew had rented a large wagon and a team from the livery stable and the children treated the trip as a lark. Listening to the younger children laughing as they played tag the second evening they had stopped for supper,

Lissie remarked, "The beans and biscuits seem to taste better out in the open air." She sat shoulder to shoulder with Lew on a quilt next to a wagon wheel. Martha had gone to sleep in her father's lap and he smoothed her curls as he said contentedly, "The apple cobbler you baked in that dutch oven would make a scrumptious finish to any meal, sweet wife."

Lissie delighted in having Lew at her side during the trip and she could tell by the children's actions and comments they felt the same. "God seems to be smiling on this trip," she remarked midway through the journey. She was riding on the wagon seat beside Lew, lifting her face to the autumn sun as a light breeze blew some curls loose from her chignon. "I can smell leaves getting ready to turn beautiful colors," and she inhaled, deeply.

Reality returned as they moved their belongings into the rented house in the village of Custer. "This house looks able to grant us some breathing room," Lissie remarked to Lew. With three bedrooms upstairs to house the children, Lew and Lissie occupied the bedroom downstairs.

The main floor had an actual parlor and a large eat-in kitchen with no walls to separate the eating area from a comfortable sitting area. There the family could gather around a second stove positioned to also heat the parlor, separate from the cook stove in the kitchen.

"We need to build another bunk bed," stated James.

"Yes, with Marti moved into Annie's bedroom, Linn has joined us big boys," grinned Lewis.

Once they were settled in to their new home, it was time to get the children enrolled at the school. Lissie walked her brood to the village schoolhouse, minus James and Elmer, and met the two teachers.

After family worship had finished the night before, James had said, "I intend to look for work in Luddington. It is a port city and I should have no trouble finding a job." He had finally attained his eighth grade certificate the year before, and Lissie knew he saw no need for further formal education.

James continued with what Lew later called his emancipation proclamation. "I should like to live here at home while I'm working, but I will help with expenses." He had observed his mother's frugal ways and knew at least some of the hardship involved in feeding so many children. "I intend to give you half my wages, Mother."

Lissie felt pride swell in her chest at the thought of their son making his own way in the world, even if he did live at home.

Elmer decided this would be a good time to break his news to the family, also. "I, too, am looking at new opportunities," he stated. "I have discovered a business college located on the outskirts of Luddington. In exchange for work as a tutor, I can get room and board. I have saved an adequate sum from preaching and work at the lumber mills to pay for my tuition."

So it was that Lissie kissed her firstborn goodbye, tears lurking but knowing he could come home if necessary. James got work as a general laborer on the docks and Lew did not have to build another bunk bed after all.

Chapter 26

THE FIRST FULL week of school brought almost unnerving quiet with only one child at home. Lew was responsible for six preaching points on this new circuit. Consequently, he was gone a great deal of the time although he came home each evening if the distances permitted.

By mid-January, Lissie became quite concerned about her husband's health. "Lew, do the people feed you dinner when you visit sick members or counsel with troubled families?"

"Yes, they often do," he replied, removing his shoes as they were preparing for bed by this time.

"Did you eat dinner today?"

"Why, I do not believe I did. But I quite made up for it tonight at supper," he was quick to remind her.

"I think not," came her sharp reply. "You were so tired, you near had to be awakened while eating your stew. Young Annie had to ask you twice about getting a kitten for a pet."

"You worry too much, Lissie." He stretched out in bed, pulled up the covers, kissed her and was asleep in a matter of minutes.

The Free Methodist church in Luddington had asked Lew to hold a series of meetings during the first part of February. The previous week he had walked beyond Free Soil, a five mile trek, to pray with some sick church members. When he returned home and opened the door, Lissie gasped at the sight of her husband, snow clinging to him and frost coating eyebrows and beard.

"Lew, you look like a snowman," she scolded as she peeled him out of his wet clothes, wrapped him in a blanket and sat him in his rocker pulled close to the stove.

"I reckon I may feel like a snowman, or at least one who is melting," he joked as he began to shiver and thaw. "The storm hit soon after I left the Jordan's," he explained. "I kept hoping it would let up but it did not and I knew I must get home."

The children were already in bed so after Lissie had dosed Lew with hot tea laced with honey, she greased his chest liberally with goose grease and turpentine and they went to bed.

He woke with a congested head and chest but declared himself able to fulfill his promise to hold meetings at the Free Methodist church in Luddington in two days time.

"I know well your perseverance," stated Lissie, "but does not God's word say 'tis wrong to tempt the Lord? Seems to me you are just daring God to kill you dead or do a miracle," she sniffed.

"I do not wish to do any such thing, Wife," he replied, "and to show you, I shall rent a horse for the duration of the meetings, just so I may cosset myself."

Lissie glimpsed the mirth in his eyes, but she saw no humor in the situation. "'Tis better than nothing," she allowed.

The third evening Lew came home after preaching "looking like death itself," Lissie declared later. The entire household was quietly slumbering when Lew began shivering so hard the bed shook and woke Lissie.

She sat up and tried to get some response from Lew, but he could not speak. She flung off her covers, put on a robe and ran upstairs to fetch James. Shaking him to wakefulness, she whispered, "Go get Doctor Price. I think your father is dying!"

She knew of the doctor because Howard had fallen while playing in the snow several days earlier and had to be carried to the doctor so his head wound could be plastered to stop the bleeding.

Lissie stoked up the fire and started heating water. She also pulled quilts out of the blanket chest and began warming them. She tucked them around Lew, who continued to shiver convulsively and still could not speak.

Doctor Price arrived, checked Lew, and then spoke gravely. "His heart has slowed dangerously and his chest is much congested." He approved of the warmed blankets and set Lissie to work massaging Lew's hands and arms, propping him up on pillows to aid his breathing. Once he was conscious enough to swallow, the doctor dosed him with something to "startle his heart into greater activity." The main thing it did was cause Lew to choke so Lissie guessed it must have tasted vile even in Lew's half-conscious state.

The doctor and Lissie worked over Lew for the remainder of the night and by daybreak, Dr. Price stood and yawned. "I believe we have your husband over the worst of this, Mrs. Reber. Feed him as much broth and other warm liquids as he will take."

Lissie instructed James to fetch Elmer from college at the end of the work day. The younger children went off to school, and Lissie and little Marti tended Papa. By that evening, Lew was able to speak a few words to Elmer, who had come home with James.

"I need you to finish out the meetings at the church in Luddington," he whispered. Then he sank back on his pillows, exhausted from that tiny bit of exertion.

Elmer returned the next evening to report to his parents. "I explained your sudden sickness to those gathered, and they seem well pleased to have me finish the week of meetings."

Lissie was not surprised at Elmer's enthusiasm at the thought of preaching. He delighted in elocution at school and had preached at various times starting soon after his conversion at the revival in Clare two years earlier.

Lew recovered slowly over the next two weeks. His first wobbly venture to stay up for any length of time was at family devotions when he reminded them that God is Jehovah Rapha, the Healer. Lissie felt he should take it slower but Lew said, "He has called me to work until I wear out." He eventually regained his strength and was able to tend his circuit for several months by the time Fall Conference came around.

Much to Lissie's joy, Lew was appointed for a second year to the Luddington, Custer, Free Soil circuit. The house was comfortable, the younger children liked their classmates and teachers and both James and Elmer were making their way in the world.

Then Elmer came home with surprising news. "I have been offered a teaching position in Mississippi. Professor Cadwell told me of it and the school board accepted my application. I am guaranteed lodging and the stipend I receive will cover food and other needs."

Lissie was quite perturbed at the idea of her son moving far away. "Elmer, it has been *many* years since I looked at a map of our country. What is the distance to Mississippi?" Then, without waiting for his answer, she stated with finality, "As I recall, it is all the way at the *bottom* of the map." And she pursed her lips at the idea.

"Not to worry, Mother. I believe the Lord will entirely provide for my needs."

Lissie could tell by Lew's pleased expression he approved of Elmer's move to a distant land, but this news twisted in her chest.

"I wish you would be pleased for me, Mother," stated her son.

"I shall be pleased for you, my dear," Lissie said. "I just dread the thought of you living so far away."

Lew patted her knee. "He will never be far away from his heavenly Father and you know He will be watching over Elmer."

"It is not the same," sniffed Lissie. In her heart she knew she could trust God for Elmer's wellbeing. She would just like to have a little more control over the situation.

So that winter saw no change in the inhabitants of the Reber house nor the location, but Elmer's cheerful countenance was sorely missed on weekends and holidays. Ever the letter writer, Elmer wrote glowing reports of opportunities to preach and he started a campaign urging Lew and family to journey South.

January and the following winter months of 1889 saw as bitter weather as the previous year. Lissie guarded Lew's health as best she could but she was helpless to lift the despondency that bowed his shoulders even as exhaustion darkened the circles under his eyes.

"I believe it is time" Lew stated mysteriously to Lissie one evening when he had arrived late from a preaching point.

"Whatever is the matter, Lew?" exclaimed Lissie as she hastened to help him with his outer wear, settle in his rocker, and bring him a cup of hot tea.

"Several members of the group meeting near Custer have been telling lies about others," he said in a weary tone. "I have tried for weeks to arbitrate between the two factions and have gotten nowhere. I see no signs of penitence or forgiveness and young believers in the faith are being hurt as a result." He rested his head in his hands and then looked over at Lissie. "All my work there has come to naught these two years. I am ready to tell my District Superintendent I must resign the circuit."

Lissie hugged him and replied, "You are exhausted right now. We must pray about this matter before you take any action."

Lew rested at home for most of the next day and then went to The Mercantile to buy some cheese and eggs for Lissie. He returned with more than groceries. "Lissie, you will not believe the conversation I just had with Jason Pressman."

"I am sure I shall not, especially if you do not tell me," she said, reaching for the items in his bag. The eggs were meant to be included in a cake recipe she had begun when she discovered she was minus one egg. What should have been a short trip to the store for Lew had turned into an absence close to an hour.

Lew managed to be oblivious to her impatience and proceeded to tell her his news. "Jason complimented me on my preaching, but wondered if I would consider settling down on forty acres of his land, building a home there. He knew of my many bouts of sickness and thought perhaps I could just rest and farm as I was able, preaching when pulpits needed to be filled, and generally getting myself healthy again."

"Do you mean he would *give* you the land?" asked Lissie in disbelief.

"That is what he said."

"Do you not see, Lew? God has already answered our prayers." Leaving her much desired eggs, Lissie ran to Lew, hugged him and jumped up to kiss his cheek.

"Not so fast, Lissie," replied her husband. "This has all come about too quickly. For some reason I do not have peace about the offer."

Lissie felt like the offer had come straight from heaven, but she said nothing more at that point.

Another letter arrived from Elmer the next day.

Dear Family,

I pray this missive finds you well, particularly you, Papa. I know the winters in Michigan take a toll on your health and I truly believe you should consider moving here. The weather is so much warmer and the pilgrims here are in much need of an ordained preacher such as you. I have ample opportunity to preach but cannot offer ordinances such as the Lord's Supper and several converts are in need of baptism.

I beg of you to seriously consider coming to this part of Mississippi. Truly, the harvest is great, but the laborers are very few.

Your loving son,
Elmer

Jason Pressman again approached Lew about building a house on his land, this time coming to the Reber home in Custer. After seeing their guest comfortably settled in a rocker with a cup of coffee and a slice of fresh-baked dried-apple strudel, Lissie busied herself in the kitchen with a sharp ear tuned to the men's conversation.

"What have you decided to do about my offer of land, Brother Reber?" asked their visitor as he forked the strudel into his mouth.

Lew rocked for a moment and then spoke. "I have prayed a great deal about your generous offer, Brother Pressman. At first, the prospect of working only when I felt I had adequate energy was very appealing. As that thought crossed my mind, I was convicted by the Apostle Paul's statement of how God's strength shows itself perfect in our weakness. That was the point at which I realized God is not yet ready for me to give up actively and regularly preaching the Gospel.

"So I thank you, very sincerely, for your generous offer, but I cannot accept it."

Pressman's rocker stopped in mid-motion and his cup rattled against its saucer. "I must say, I am quite surprised," he said in a tight voice. Then he smiled, but Lew could see there was no mirth in his eyes. "I certainly am not one to argue with the Almighty."

Their visitor soon wished them farewell and was gone. Lissie showed her displeasure by banging spoons against pots as she prepared supper. Her unhappiness was not lost on Lew. He got up from his rocker and walked over to his disgusted wife. Putting his arms around her, he said, "Come sit for a moment, Lissie."

"I need to prepare supper." Her tone was curt.

"Just for a few minutes," he coaxed.

Her step dragged but she complied. Sitting stiffly in her rocker, back straight, feet planted firmly on the floor, Lissie glared at her husband.

"Would you want me to disobey my Lord, and not continue preaching?" he asked in a gentle tone.

"You would not have to stop preaching," she replied. "And we would have had a house and land. And not have had to homestead to get them," she added in a low tone.

"That is true, Lissie, but think of this. Every time Jason Pressman saw me or drove by the house we might have built, he could likely be thinking, *this is where* my *preacher lives, on land that* I *gave him.* I believe the Lord has shown me it is not healthy, spiritually speaking, for me—or Jason Pressman—to build a home on land he has given me."

"You speak wisdom," said Lissie in a grudging tone. "You cannot know how I should like to have a house of our own. But as we talk, I can see how that yearning could be a sign of not trusting God, and perhaps even a bit of pride." She rose from her chair. "I am over my 'mad,' Lew, and I really *do* need to prepare supper for we shall soon have a horde of hungry children descending upon us." Lissie's anger was gone, but her sadness remained.

By the time Fall Conference arrived, Lew had decided to resign from the Michigan Conference and make his way to Mississippi. "My heart is broken over my inability to lead the members to beg forgiveness as well as forgive," he told Lissie. "Perhaps these needy pilgrims in Mississippi will have more open, loving hearts sensitive to the Lord's direction."

Lissie was not particularly excited about taking her large family cross country to an entirely new environment. However, she dreaded even more Lew having to weather another Michigan winter making the rounds of his preaching circuit.

The Michigan Conference did not want to lose Lew entirely from their group. They arranged for him to obtain a certificate of transfer to the Louisiana Conference, there being none any closer to Mississippi.

As Lissie directed the children to pack their personal belongings in knapsacks and valises, she was reminded of their trek from Reading to the Michigan woods. They were selling all their furniture except foodstuffs Lissie deemed necessary to get them through the winter since it was already October.

They traveled three days by train, beginning the trip in winter clothing and ending it shedding overcoats and wielding fans. There were only five older children this trip, ranging from twelve-year-old Linn to nineteen-year-old Landis. Even little Marti at four years was able to pack her own belongings. As the family embarked on their southern adventure, Lissie's heart ached. The family felt incomplete for James had left home the previous month.

"I see no prospects for myself in Mississippi," he had stated, after family devotions when Lew announced plans for the family's move. "I have been considering moving to Missouri and working for Uncle Albert."

Albert was Lew's younger brother who had immigrated to southern Missouri and built a sawmill. James had met him during one of his visits to see his brothers, Gideon and Lew, during the homesteading years.

James had left two days later, but not before expressing bitterness to Lissie. "I cannot believe Papa is dragging the family all the way to Mississippi. Are there not enough unbelievers up here in the North?"

"Try not to think badly of your father, James," soothed Lissie. "He is merely following what he believes is God's will."

"I still say it makes no sense," fumed the young man as he prepared to go out the door.

"Remember, God's ways are not always our ways," cautioned Lissie. "Will you not wait for your father's return before you go to the train station?

"I think not," he replied. "I do not wish to leave Papa saying harsh things, even if I only think them. It is better I go now." He kissed his mother's cheek and left.

So now they were journeying toward Elmer and leaving James far behind. From Michigan to Louisiana, then to Mobile, Alabama and finally Gulfport, Mississippi. Elmer had arranged for them to live in a small house not far from his school. When Lissie saw it, her heart sank. It consisted of two bedrooms, a kitchen, and a commons area where they must eat, have family devotions, and do homework.

The weather was a welcome change from Michigan's wintry bluster, but the humidity remained high most of the time and laundry took an eternity to dry.

Lew preached at every opportunity whether in schoolhouses or private homes. He baptized several and found the people to be poor but very friendly.

As for Lissie, after making some visits with Lew, she came home to her cramped house with gratitude. "I declare, Lew, how do these people live? That cabin we just came from had no windows at all and the floor was just hard-packed dirt! Can you imagine what it must be like when it rains?"

The Reber children went to school except for Martha and they were less than thrilled with their teachers. "In the first place, I can hardly understand Mr. Pickens, and secondly, he made a mistake in the answer to an arithmetic sum," sniffed Lewis, who was the student of the family.

"Why are we not allowed to go to Elmer's classes? " asked Annie. "That would be ever so much more fun."

"He is teaching classes in higher grades," Lew answered.

"Well, I wish things were different," was Annie's retort.

By the end of the school year, everyone, including Lew, was ready to head back north. They hated the bugs and critters, they were impatient with the slow-moving, slow-talking populace, and the believers in the area were so poor they could not pay Lew in cash but only in varied produce. Lissie was having great difficulty feeding her family with an occasional chicken or side of pork. Especially when that family contained four growing boys.

July 1891 found Lew and Lissie headed back north with their brood. "From yellow pine forests in Mississippi to hickory and evergreens in the Pennsylvania mountains," remarked Lew to his wife as trees pressed in on both sides of their train car. The engine was slowly winding its way up the mountain to Waynemart, the closest depot to Berlin, Pennsylvania where they would be living until—*who knows when?* pondered Lissie. *I guess God knows, but He has not dropped a hint to me.*

The air was refreshing as a cool mountain breeze blew a wisp of hair across Lissie's cheek. "This is truly a welcome change from the heat and humidity we left back in Gulfport five days ago," she sighed.

Lew had shown her the letter from his new District Superintendent for Lew was now part of the New York Conference. His circuit included Berlin and Beech Pond extending into the mountains of Pike County.

Being the preacher he was, Lew had a phenomenal memory of interesting quotes. When he told Lissie about Pike County, he quoted Horace Greeley's description of that area: "It is a land noted for rattlesnakes, democrats and bad whiskey." Lew grinned and said, "You watch out for the rattlesnakes, Lissie. I will be on guard for those indulging in bad whiskey."

"Oh dear," moaned Lissie. "Have we jumped from the frying pan into the fire?"

Her fears were soon eased. Despite their short sojourn in the area, Lew found devout believers and Lissie, friendly neighbors.

Fall of 1892 Lew was appointed to the Free Methodist pulpit in Allentown, PA, a city of 35,000. The family was soon moving south from the mountains of Pike County.

What a change for the Rebers. Lew no longer travelled long distances on foot to minister to church members, the children attended a large school and Lissie thrived on city life. Landis and Howard, at 21 and 19, respectively, declared they were done with school and wished to find work. This left three children in school and six-year-old Martha still at home.

One late October evening after family devotions, Lissie announced, "A letter came from James in today's post. His news is absolutely marvelous," and she waved the missive in the air.

"We already know he is married, Ma," stated Howard. "He wrote and told us that last year."

"Out with it," commanded Lew, "so we do not need to wait and read the letter ourselves."

"We are grandparents, Lew!" shouted Lissie. "And you children are now aunts and uncles. James and Louisa have a little daughter, Anna Frances."

"I wonder where they got the baby's names?" asked Landis.

"From me, of course," sniffed Annie.

"James does note they chose names from each of their sisters, so I guess you are correct, Annie. Louisa must have a sister named Frances."

"What is an aunt and uncle?" asked little Marti.

Lissie felt a pang when she realized they had moved so many times during Martha's short lifetime, she had never known an aunt or uncle. "When your brothers and sister have children, their daughters become your nieces and their sons are known as your nephews. So now you are Aunt Marti to your new niece, Anna." Martha beamed from ear to ear and hugged her cornhusk doll even closer.

How I should love to see them," continued Lissie in a wistful voice.

Later, after the household was bedded down, Lew read the letter from his son. “It seems strange to have never met this wife of James, but the tone of his letter seems to be happy enough.”

Their second son had written only once, about a year before, saying he had married a young woman named Louisa Walter. He had met her uncle, August Bogner, when James made a special delivery of walnut from his Uncle Albert’s lumberyard. August mentioned he needed a farm hand and it turned out his niece was an excellent cook. James tested her cooking and found both food and cook to his liking. The young couple married and built a small house about a mile down the road from the Bogner farmhouse.

Lew held a revival meeting in January, several folks surrendered their lives to Christ, and the membership was revitalized and increased. Much to Lissie’s joy, the trustees decided to build a parsonage and by the end of June, a fine, three story brick house became home to the Reber family.

On their first night, settled into their new place, Lissie sat in her rocker and listed the wondrous time-saving amenities included in this new home. “No longer do we need to carry water from outside. There is a pump and a sink with a drain in the kitchen. And we now have an indoor privy! Do you remember that marvelous bathroom on our wedding journey?”

“How could I forget?” Lew teased. “You squealed like a little girl seeing her first mouse.”

She slapped his knee. “I am sure you jumped in surprise when you first saw the water rush into the commode.

“I never thought to have such luxury in my house,” She sighed in contentment.

“Do not become too accustomed to such fine living,” cautioned Lew. “Remember, it is unusual to be appointed to the same location two years in succession.”

Changing the subject slightly, Lissie asked, “Do you suppose I could take Martha to see Aunt Jane and the family back in Cressona. Your salary has been steady this year and we may never be this close to Cressona again. I should so love to see her once more.”

“I think that is a capital idea.” Lew’s answer came without hesitation.

"Oh, thank you, Lew." Lissie swooped over and kissed him. "I can plan the menus and Annie is well able to prepare them even if she goes to school each day. The boys have been trained to help and I shall give each their marching orders. I am *so* excited," and she twirled around in the middle of their sitting room to Lew's laughter.

A letter went off to Jane the very next day and within a week, a telegram arrived at the Reber household. It was from Jane. "Please come. Looking forward to your arrival third week of October."

Mother and young daughter duly embarked on the train out of Allentown to Cressona for a long day's journey. Marti glued her nose to the window on this trip, "for I am a grown girl," she declared. Lissie knew the trip to Mississippi was a blur in Marti's mind, but she was old enough now she would likely remember all the details of this journey.

Manfred met them at the station and drove them to the farm. He filled Lissie in on some of the family events while Martha sat between them on the buggy seat, clearly awed by the speed of the matched team.

"Father died five years ago," he said, and Mother invited my family to move from our small house on the east side of our land to the main farmhouse to live with her.

"I am so sorry to hear this news about Uncle Edgar," said Lissie. She did not mention the sorrow brought by little Robbie's death that same year.

The speedy buggy ride made the trip to the Holtschlag home seem almost momentary and soon Lissie and Marti were following Manfred to the front porch where Lissie and Lew had courted under the watchful eye of Uncle Edgar many years earlier.

The sound of their footsteps on the porch alerted Jane to open the door. At the sight of Lissie, Jane's arms opened wide and she hugged her niece tightly."Dear Lissie, I thought I might never see you again when you left Pennsylvania." She kissed Lissie on the forehead for despite her slightly stooped stature, Jane was still a head taller than her niece.

"And this young lady must be Miss Martha," exclaimed Jane.

"No, ma'am, I am Aunt Martha," explained the little girl, mindful of her new status in life.

At Jane's puzzled look directed at her, Lissie said, "I will explain later," and smiled. Then she said to Martha, "Say how-do to your

Aunt Jane, Marti."

The little girl beamed in delight. "How wonderful. I also have an aunt. How-do Aunt Jane. If you are my aunt then I am your niece."

"This is true, Martha," said Jane in a grave tone, doing her best not to break into laughter.

"Come on in and sit for a bit as soon as we get your coats and bonnets off and hung up. I have left Alice in the kitchen finishing supper. Manfred, please go fetch her for introductions and then we shall soon be sitting down to a meal. I imagine you are starved."

Manfred returned with a young blond woman and said, "This is my wife, Alice. We have a two-year old son and a four-year-old daughter, but they are already in bed."

"How-do, Alice," said Lissie, smiling. "I smell something delicious from the direction of the kitchen. Might it be chicken potpie and apple strudel for dessert?"

Alice smiled and nodded while Jane said, "You always were a good one with the nose, Lissie. As I remember, you could smell when a pastry was ready to come out of the oven before I ever checked it."

"I think my appetite has always had a strong tie to my sniffer, Aunt Jane," laughed Lissie.

Supper was put on the table in a very few minutes which was fortunate because Martha's eyes began to flicker after three or four bites of the delectable pastry-enclosed chicken dish.

"I must excuse myself for the moment and take care of my girl," Lissie stated.

"Take her up to your old room," said Jane. "You can join her there later tonight."

Lissie returned and finished her meal, telling of their journey from Allentown, and then went to bed herself.

The next morning, having breakfasted and acquainting Martha with her newfound cousin, Nancy, Lissie settled on the front porch with Jane, both of them hulling peas as they visited.

"What of family events, Aunt Jane? Manfred told me of Uncle Edgar's death five years ago but we had no time for other news. Obviously, Manfred has a fine family, but what of Frederick and Sally? And my sweet Jennie," she whispered. "I have had no letter from her since before Marti was born."

"I shall answer your questions in order," stated Jane. "Frederick had decided before he finished school in Cressona that he wanted to go to New York City and make his way in the business world. My people had connections in the City so he resides there. He has never married and the last time I saw my boy was when he came home for Edgar's funeral." Jane dabbed at the corner of her eye with the edge of her apron.

"Sally married Jason Verona, the livery stable owner's son. Do you remember Jason?"

"No," answered Lissie, but a girl by that last name was two grades below me at school."

"His sister, Gina," explained her aunt. "At any rate, Sally and Jason have one little boy. They live in Reading but since both sets of parents live in this area we see them once or twice a year. We take turns on holidays," she added, "and that works well."

"And Jennie," prompted Lissie.

"Ah, our sweet Jennie," murmured Jane. "She married her beau after she came and helped you during Lew's smallpox bout. They moved to Philadelphia, I think about the time your Lew turned Free Methodist."

Lissie smiled, knowing Aunt Jane was a staunch Lutheran who considered the Methodist faith to be somewhat close to heresy."

"At any rate," resumed Jane, "that is the last I heard from Jennie."

Lissie felt a great wave of sorrow pass over her at those words "Such news brings me much grief," she said.

"You are no stranger to grief, my dear," replied her aunt, "starting with the loss of your mother. And, according to Jennie, when she returned from helping you back in Reading days, she mentioned an infant son who lived only three or four months."

Now it was Lissie dabbing at her eyes with apron edge, but then she looked up with a smile at her aunt and said, "Life has not been all sorrow. Living with Lew will always be an adventure and we have six sons and two daughters to spice up the journey."

"My word," exclaimed Jane. "Eight children?"

"Plus the three God saw fit to call home early," replied Lissie, a weak smile tugging at her lips.

"And what of this brood of children you have raised to adulthood—almost," pressed Jane.

"Oh, first a delightful tidbit of news. We are grandparents!"

Jane tsked. "Seems like you and Lew were youngsters courting on our front porch just last year. How did you become grandparents?"

"I suppose the usual way," giggled Lissie. At her aunt's stern look, she sobered. "Oh you mean, w*ho* made us grandparents. James. He immigrated to Missouri two years ago, apparently met and married the farmer's daughter, or in this case, niece."

"Well, Lissie, you never did anything by halves," murmured Jane. "So where was Elmer with all this Missourian state of bliss?"

"He was, and is, teaching and preaching in Mississippi.."

"And where is that? One of those secessionist states, as I recall," said Jane, her tone acerbic.

"The War is over, Aunt Jane, and yes, it is a southern state, way at the bottom of the United States map."

"As I recall from your travelogue last night at the supper table, your adventurer husband took the family to tour the country down there."

"Just Gulfport, Aunt. And we all agreed it was too hot, humid, and poverty-stricken to live there for long."

They had nearly finished their pans of peas when Alice appeared with two more baskets to hull.

"I will trade you," she said, a grin bringing a dimple to one cheek. Jane groaned, and then laughed. "You are a slave driver, dear. But yes, we will trade. Let us stand and stretch, Lissie, before we start in on shelling this bountiful harvest.

Once they were settled again, Jane asked, "What of the other children, I am up to date on your two older sons and have met your sweet little Martha, but what of the others. I do not even know their names."

"I must start with sweet baby Linneus Robert who lived with us for almost four months." Lissie pressed on, determined not to weep at the thought of that sweet babe. "Then came Landis who is now twenty-two and Howard, who is twenty. They are working at lumberyards in Allentown at present. Our Lewis, at eighteen, is the student of the family, excepting Elmer, of course," she added.

She took a breath and reached for another peapod. "And then we have sweet Annie, who is now sixteen."

Jane interrupted her with clapping. "Finally, a daughter."

"Yes, and she is a true blessing to all," bragged her mother.

"Everything she does is done well and with no complaint. I sometimes doubt she could have such a mother as I, for I well know my complaining ways."

Jane sniffed and said, "Apparently, you turned from wicked ways and taught her well. In fact, I see very few strands of gray in your chestnut locks so I surmise you have your brood quite well organized. Else you would be in an insane asylum down in Scranton."

"The years when they were all small children were difficult ones. I daresay the gray strand you see came from that time period," smiled Lissie. Then she resumed her narrative. "Our dear Linn is now fourteen and such a sweet, gentle boy."

"Then comes a great painful gap," Lissie said slowly. "There was a tiny girl babe who died before she had a chance to live. Next came Charles Wesley who graced our family for only three days. The last grief of that time was our sweet angel Robert Francis, or Robbie, who lived for three years. If Marti had not been born the year before he died, I think I, too, might have died from the grief. Our house was one of sadness for many days and we truly believe he must have been an angel sent by God to bless us for a while. You know, 'entertaining an angel unawares'?"

"Quite the narrative, my dear. I believe it is time for some tea even if we have not quite finished shelling all these peas."

Lissie felt drained after reciting her family's history as well as hearing Jane's narrative. She would not trade this time with her aunt for anything though, she realized.

One day of visiting remained and Jane decreed they would have homemade ice cream even if it was not Sunday. Manfred groaned at his mother's determination but was good natured about being the lone turner of the crank on the ice cream maker.

That night as Lissie put Marti to bed, the little girl said, "I really do like meeting aunts and playing with cousins. Do you think we can come back again, Mother?

"It would truly be lovely, Marti, but it may be a long time before we can return. Do your best to remember all the good times and sights and smells.

"And the good food," added the little girl.

"Especially the good food," her mother laughed.

The goodbyes were bittersweet the next day. As Lissie hugged

Jane, she knew it was likely the last time she would see her on this earth. "I love you, Aunt Jane. Thank you for being mother to me."

Unshed tears shone in Jane's eyes as she spoke. "I am proud of you, Sarah Annaliese, and your mother would be too."

Thanks extended to all present at their departure and hugs all round, Lissie and Martha climbed into the buggy as Manfred made ready to drive them back to the station.

Chapter 27

FALL CONFERENCE ARRIVED and to Lew's amazement, he was once again appointed to the Allentown church. Lissie was totally delighted because she felt as if she were living in luxury—and she was, compared to some of the houses they had occupied.

Unfortunately, this year at Allentown was nothing similar to the previous one. There was no revival and a misunderstanding between two families in the congregation resulted in many of the members taking sides, essentially splitting the church.

Lew came home one Sunday night after services as silent as Lissie had ever remembered. "What is troubling you, Lew?" she asked, as she helped him off with his coat and settled him in his rocker with a cup of hot tea.

"I have never dealt with such a stubborn, rebellious bunch," he sighed. "The Mastersons, who paid for the stained glass windows on the west side of the sanctuary, are unhappy with the subjects chosen by the McAllisters, who purchased the windows on the east side. I have tried my best to reconcile the two factions but at least three families have sided with each group. They now refuse to speak to each other. There can be no compromise where communication is lacking," he said with downcast face.

Lissie knew he had been suffering with headaches and now she suspected why. The following week Lew contracted a severe cold which he had great difficulty throwing off.

As the winter wore on, Lissie could see Lew losing muscle tone and looking quite beaten down. "I declare," she said in a sharp tone, when she discovered how Lew's trousers had to belted up to the last notch to keep them from sliding off. "If these church members do not soon bury the hatchet, they may soon be burying their preacher, Lew. How I wish you did not take their foolishness so to heart. Especially, as they refuse to listen to any words of arbitration."

Lew soothed Lissie's indignation with a hug and soft words. "God has the solution for these warring children of His. If I cannot lead them to reconciliation, He will surely bring someone who can.

As summer came on, Lew's outlook seemed to brighten and his health to improve. "I have finally been able to leave my burden of these unhappy people with the Lord, and He has given me peace. In fact, I believe I feel well enough to go on circuit again."

Lissie wrinkled her nose in disbelief at her husband's enthusiastic words, but said nothing.

The 1894 Fall Conference saw Lew appointed, not to a circuit, but to the German church in Newark, New Jersey. "Well, I must say we are seeing the world. Or at least a goodly part of the United States," sniffed Lissie. She was not unhappy to leave Allentown despite the lovely house, for she had come to greatly dislike the people who had given Lew so much heartache with their hard hearts.

In addition to anticipation of a different location, Lissie found the move to be almost effortless compared to earlier years. Martha, their youngest, was now an eight-year-old and the rest of the children were in their mid-teens or early twenties. The move was made by railway as Lew had been paid a regular salary in Allentown so that furniture could be boxed and transported, accompanying the family.

Their rental house was satisfactory although not so luxurious as the parsonage in Allentown. The family settled in quickly with Martha attending elementary school and Linn, in high school.

Annie had achieved her eighth grade certificate and was delighted to find an active Salvation Army society in Newark. She had met Eliza Shirley, a young English woman, while the Rebers had lived in Allentown. Eliza had immigrated to Philadelphia with her parents and as a founder of the Salvation Army in America, had come to Allentown to introduce those interested in the cause of Christ to the Army's goals and ideals.

Annie had heard Eliza conducting some street preaching and had come home to tell her parents. "Papa and Mother, I heard this woman preaching on the street today as I came home from school. It was, indeed, a fine sermon, and the musicians with her played in a stirring manner. I should very much like to learn more about this Salvation Army for she counts herself as a soldier of Christ in this Army."

Both parents were familiar with the Army and did not

discourage Annie to find out more information. Later that evening, Lissie remarked to Lew, "I have thought much about Annie's lot in life. We have moved so often she has not been able to make lasting friendships. And, of course, when I was her age, I was engaged to my soldier-love." She patted Lew on the knee.

"I am overjoyed at Annie's interest in the Salvation Army," he replied. "It has been my dearest hope that more of my children would be called by God to the ministry, but I never dreamed of our sweet Annie being chosen."

Annie's interest increased in the Army and she enrolled in the recruiting classes along with her formal schoolwork. By the time the family left Allentown, she was a bona fide Salvation Army lass. "I feel great pride when I wear my navy jacket and skirt with a white blouse, knowing it is my Army uniform," she told her parents.

Lissie now had an empty house for a good part of the day with her brood off on their various endeavors. The older boys had found work and industrious Lewis was also going to night school, aiming for a teaching degree. Lew did most of his study for sermons at the church because he actually had an office there. Consequently, Lissie had time to start designing quilts, something she had longed to do since piecing the Wedding Ring quilt Aunt Jane had helped her make years ago.

Lew preached most of his sermons in German at first as Newark was filled with German settlers, but he discovered several church members understood and spoke English quite well. "Lissie," he exclaimed with excitement, one noon at the dinner table, "I believe we should start a class in English for the young people. That is the best way for them to make their way in this land of America. I think it was good for our children to know both German and English, but for them to find meaningful work and a living wage, I know, personally, that understanding and speaking English is necessary."

Lissie knew that Lew had grown up in a household where only German was spoken and had to learn English in school which slowed his progress in early years. She smiled at his enthusiasm and said, "When do you intend to start this English class?"

"This Sunday evening," he replied. "I will announce the class and see what sort of interest I receive."

He came home Sunday evening to report as Lissie seldom

attended evening services. "We had a room full of interested folks and most were young people our children's age."

Lew, ever the evangelist, always brought the conversational English around to discussion of God's gift of salvation made possible by Christ's death and resurrection. Revival broke out among the young people in the English class and spread throughout the church.

Lissie was sitting in a pew toward the front when a couple walked the aisle to take Lew by the hand one Sunday morning. In a few minutes she saw him kneel with the couple and pray. Afterwards, at home, she asked Lew about their story.

He replied, "Mr. and Mrs. Burg came to me and stated they had been members of churches wherever his work took them, but they had never learned how to pray. So I had them kneel with me, and just as I taught my own children to pray, I led them to talk to their heavenly Father. What a privilege God has given me in this ministry." His face glowed with ardor directed toward God.

Lissie felt a burst of love for Lew in that moment. He often shared tidbits of his ministry opportunities with her which led her to appreciate her godly husband more and more.

One Sunday evening Lew came home and told her, "Tonight an elderly German lady came forward, crying in despair, certain that she had sinned beyond God's grace. 'Ich bin veloren! I am lost!' After talking with her at length as well as much prayer, she burst into tears of joy and began singing, 'Gott ist die liebe! Er liebe auch mich. God is love. He loves me, too.'"

The membership contained many fine voices and as Lew and his family loved to sing, the praise singing soon extended to thirty minutes before the evening sermon. When the weather was decent, people often came in off the street or crowded around the door of the church to hear those German Methodists sing praises to God. It was a favorite memory of Lissie's during that time in their lives.

The constant work caused by a growing congregation resting on the shoulders of one man, although exhilarating, took its toll on Lew's health. By the end of March 1895 Lissie detected a drag to her husband's steps and an increasing slump to his shoulders. The last day of March Lew took to his bed with intermittent chills, fever, headache and great pain in his arms and legs.

Lissie called the doctor because she began to fear for Lew's life, he was so unresponsive. "He has la grippe or influenza," pronounced the doctor. "Continue dosing him with willow bark tea for the fever and aches and the honey in chamomile tea for his cough. This will just have to wear itself out."

I pray it does not first wear out Lew, thought Lissie. The fever left before the week finished, leaving behind all the pain as well as a dry cough which shook Lew's body and in turn made his head and muscles ache each time his throat tickled.

Lissie was grateful Annie could take care of household chores and Martha was now old enough to be helpful, too. This left Lissie free to tend her very sick husband.

By the middle of April Lew's muscle and joint pain was mostly gone and the cough had subsided. However, his energy was such that he could still barely walk. Slowly, the once-powerful muscles gained strength, but a lassitude seemed to hover over him.

"Lissie," he cried in a weak voice, one morning. "I think I shall never preach again. I struggle for energy enough to breathe, much less think of delivering a message to my congregation. And the thought of even trying to search for a sermon topic, much less gather thoughts in a coherent order seems totally exhausting." He sank back in his chair and closed his eyes.

Lissie had never seen him like this after an illness. His lethargy fed his despair.

Without opening his eyes, he said, "I must relinquish my appointment. When Lewis comes home tonight remind me to dictate a letter of resignation to the District Superintendant. I do not feel strong enough to even lift a pen to paper or clearheaded enough to think the proper words. I trust he can help me." In minutes he was asleep, chin resting on his chest, which was no longer a muscular frame but a sunken cavity.

A pastor came from elsewhere as substitute for Lew. In the meantime, Lissie did her best to nurse her husband back to health, but the progress was slow and painful.

They attended Fall Conference that year held in Dover, an easy journey by rail. Lissie was able to attend the meeting with Lew and was gratified at the Newark Society's request.

"We wish you to continue your appointment at the German Free Methodist Church," stated Brother Miller.. "We realize your health has been very poor but your work there has been so exemplary, we are offering you three months vacation before you need to once again stand in your pulpit."

Lew stood and replied. "I am honored by this request but I fear my health will never return to the robust level I have enjoyed. I feel it would be taking advantage of you, should I accept your kind offer. Therefore, I must formally withdraw from active ministry," and he sat down.

Lissie could feel tremors coursing through his body, for her arm was pressed against his. She so longed to give him a tight hug, but resisted the impulse, furtively squeezing his knee.

Back to Newark they went with Lissie wondering what was to become of them. Here was her husband not yet fifty, more or less proclaiming himself to be an invalid,

Then Lew saw an advertisement in the newspaper about a water cure being touted at a local sanatorium. "Lissie, come sit for a moment and listen to this," he called one afternoon while she was cleaning up after their dinner. He commenced to read. "Nature's remedy for man's ills. Test our mineral baths if you suffer from headache, nervous prostration, gout, heart palpitations or any number of other maladies. We predict miraculous healing for many ailments. Make an appointment without delay."

Lew shook the paper emphatically. "This may be an answer to our prayers for my healing!"

It had been months since Lissie had seen her husband with a spark of life in his eyes and she felt a thrill of elation. However, she merely asked, "How much does it cost, Lew?"

"Who cares how much it costs," he retorted. "Do you not think it is worth trying?"

"I do, Husband," she replied, "but the money in our sugar bowl is nearing bottom."

God's provision came through again, this time from their older sons, for the children were all apprised of the possible help this water cure might have on their father's health.

"We have decided we will, together, pay the cost for this water cure," declared Howard, the others nodding in agreement.

"God bless you, my sons," declared their father. "I feel He has used your generosity to help heal my body."

Lew visited the mineral baths three times a week. At first, he traveled in a rented horse and buggy but by the second week he told

Lissie, "I can feel the strength returning to my legs. I believe I can walk the eight blocks to the bathhouse." Within a month, Lissie was overjoyed to see a renewed vigor in her husband's step and healthy color in his cheeks.

One night after retiring, Lew told Lissie, "Oh dear wife, I fear I have spoken too hastily in retiring from active ministry. My health has improved astonishing much with this water cure. I feel well able to take up my cross for Him again."

She caressed his cheek and then kissed him. "Lew, God has healed you for this season and allowed you to rest. I do not believe His timing is an accident. If you are to return to the pulpit, God will make that plain."

He smiled at her and returned her kiss. "My wise Lissie. No doubt you are right."

In the meantime a letter had come from James in Missouri.

Dear Mother, Father, and Family,

I find myself quite homesick for the sight of you and would so like for you to meet the two fine daughters Louisa has given me—before they grow up and leave home. Sarah Matilda had her first birthday in May of this year and Anna Frances will soon attain completion of her third year.

The railway now runs along the bottom of our property line near the Fabius River so it would be an excellent mode of travel to come see us. Our air here in the Missouri countryside is fresh and clean and perhaps that fact along with the sight of your granddaughters (as well as their mother and father) might prove beneficial to your health, Father.

If you agree to this trip in time for Miss Anna's third birthday, I should be pleased to purchase tickets for you and Mother, Annie, Linn, and Martha. My older brothers are welcome to visit but they can pay for their own transportation.

Your loving son,
James

The children urged their parents to make the trip. "Father, the climate change would do you good," encouraged Landis.

"I should so love to see James' babies," murmured Annie.

"Mother, would it be like going to Aunt Jane's house?" wondered Martha.

"Much further, dear," replied Lissie.

As Lissie lay in bed that night, thinking of tiny girls nestling in her lap, their chubby little arms hugging her, she realized how much she missed having little children around her. *I have spent half my life caring for little ones,* she thought. *How I yearn to hold James' babies and nuzzling their sweet necks.* With a sigh she turned over and went to sleep dreaming of kissing the faces of her little granddaughters.

The next day saw much discussion between Lew and Lissie regarding the pros and cons of such a journey as the children were all at school or work.

"James must be doing quite well to offer us rail tickets," mused Lew.

"Yes, but I believe Martha and possibly Linn can travel at half-fare," remarked Lissie, ever practical.

"Perhaps if we *do* go, my brother, Albert, might come up to Marion County to visit at the same time."

Lissie heard a wistful tone in Lew's voice. She knew he had not seen his younger brother, Albert, since they had homesteaded more than ten years ago. "I should imagine there are lodgings to be had close by," replied Lissie. "James lives near the county seat so there is surely at least one hotel.

"I suggest you write to James accepting his kind offer of transportation and ask him to extend an invitation to his uncle Albert to visit while we are there. By the way, how long should we plan to stay?"

"I judge the journey, itself, to take three days, so perhaps a ten day visit," Lew answered with a hint of a question in his tone.

"That amount of time sounds satisfactory to me," said Lissie, smiling. "I do hope five extra mouths to feed for that period of time will not prove a hardship, however."

"Truly, if James can pay for our transportation, I doubt it will be a problem for his wife to feed us."

"Louisa will have Annie and me to help," murmured Lissie. "I believe there should be no problem."

And so it was settled. The older boys chose to stay home and work and Lewis, especially, did not want to miss two weeks of night school.

The trip went smoothly and Lissie could not help comparing all the trips by rail she had experienced in her lifetime. This was, by far, the least stress filled. When the train stopped after crossing the Fabius River, there was James, waiting with a horse and wagon to transport his guests to his home.

The foliage was flaunting fall colors and as the team and wagon slowly made it way up the tree-line track, gold and scarlet leaves floated into the wagon, one red-orange maple leaf alighting on Martha's dark brown curls. Lissie inhaled the scent of woods in the fall, remembering with fondness Uncle Edgar's woodlot on the farm near Cressona.

It took less than thirty minutes to make the trip from the train stop at the bottom of the large hill to James' little frame house nestled at the northern edge of the woods they had just traversed. The little house was situated at the end of a short lane with a windbreak of small cedar trees.

"I will take care of the team after you meet Louisa and the girls," said James as he helped Lissie from the wagon. Everyone else clambered out with a bag or valise. Louisa was at the door to greet them with Matilda in her arms and little Anna clutching the folds of her mother's apron, part of her face hidden in the material.

"Welcome, Mother and Father Reber," said Louisa in a vibrant tone. "Can you say hello to your Mawmaw and PawPaw, Miss Anna?" She tousled the little girl's curls as the child hid her face, totally.

After greeting Annie, Linn and Martha, Louisa said, "Please come into the parlor and rest." She led them into the house while James returned to his team and wagon.

Lissie smelled a delectable aroma of roast beef and roasted vegetable with an undertone of yeast rolls newly taken from the oven. Annie had begun making friends with her tiny nieces while Martha looked on in awe, for she was not accustomed to small children since she was the baby of the family.

Lissie liked the looks of this new daughter—wife of James. Louisa was a tall woman, perhaps taller than James, and strongly built. As she asked about their trip, Lissie could see that this was a woman who could laugh easily. In fact, her impression of Louisa was a woman at ease with herself and the world, despite the fact that she was far from beautiful. *Pretty is as pretty does*, thought Lissie. She smiled at the sight of Annie and now Martha, on the floor with the little girls, playing with dolls and talking at a great rate.

James came in from the back door and Louisa rose. "I shall get supper on the table. You are likely hungry after being away from Mother Reber's good cooking for three days." She flashed a smile at Lissie, who rose in turn and said, "May I help you in the kitchen? Your table has now more than doubled."

"This evening please sit and visit with James. There will be plenty of time for your help in the kitchen." The younger woman patted Lissie's shoulder and left the room.

The meal was delicious and the hungry travelers did it justice. When the last crumb of dried apple pie had disappeared, the men went outside to sit on the porch while Martha played dolls with Anna and Matilda. Annie and Lissie helped Louisa clear the table and wash the dishes.

"I fear we have wiped the platter clean," announced Annie, merrily. We have no leftovers to cover and cool."

"No matter," announced Louisa. "I love to cook and since you are such obliging eaters, I shall whip up some experimental recipes I have not had reason to try before. Besides," she said with a smile tugging at the corner of her lips, "the recipes we decide are 'keepers' may well be used when James' Uncle Albert comes to visit next week."

"Such good news," Lissie remarked. "We did not know whether Albert would be able to visit. I believe Lew will be overjoyed to see this younger brother as will I."

"I, too, shall be quite glad to meet Uncle Albert," stated Louisa. "Were it not for him, I daresay James and I should never have met." She laughed her hearty laugh and led them to the parlor to sit.

The next day Lissie began to get acquainted with her little granddaughters. She coaxed Anna to tell her about her rag doll baby. The little girl announced its name was Mary Ann. Little Matilda, an endearing toddler, tried to do everything her big sister did. This included conversing earnestly despite no one understanding a single word. "She even speaks with inflection to her 'words,'" remarked Annie to her mother.

The little girls loved all the attention they received from their grandmother and aunts. In fact, Louisa did not mind one or the other of the visitors putting the children to bed, and Lissie soon took over that precious task. Hearing sweet little Anna say her prayers and kissing Matilda's smooth cheek good night gave Lissie's grandmother heart a treasure to cling to long after she ended her visit.

Saturday night was to be a sociable at James and Louisa's house. Invitations had been sent to the neighbors in all directions and Annie and her mother busied themselves helping Louisa bake pies, cookies, and strudel. "And I shall serve fresh, sweetened whipped cream for the pies and strudel," announced Louisa.

"Ooh, that sounds delectable," said Annie. "I have never eaten that before."

"I guarantee you, you will like it," promised her sister-in-law.

The night for the party arrived and soon people were knocking on the door. James introduced all the guests to his family visiting from New Jersey and soon there was an ebb and flow of sound as people talked and ate.

Fortunately, the weather was lovely with a harvest moon shining so bright the out-of-doors was almost as bright as inside the house. Because of that, quilts were spread on the front yard for sitting. People were eating and visiting on the steps and on the porch as well as inside the house.

Lissie noticed a tall, dark-haired young man had taken a fancy to Annie, who did not seem to mind. There were three or four other young people clustered around her and Linn, but this young man seemed to monopolize her attention.

After everyone had filled their stomachs with Louisa's good pastries, as well as that of her helpers, James announced it was time for a sing-along. It turned out that the young man, who had taken a shine to Annie, had brought his violin and another man had brought a flute. Apparently, this was not unusual in get-togethers such as these, and once the singing commenced, the group made quite a fine choir.

Everyone was gone well before midnight as nearly all were dairy farmers whose cows would be ready for milking early the next morning. The party was pronounced to be a fine one and all were delighted to meet James' family. Especially, Robert Maher, the dark haired fiddle player.

Before going to sleep that night, Lew remarked, "That was as fine a singing as ever I heard at our German Church back home, and they are top of the heap in my estimation."

"Yes," replied Lissie, drowsily. "And did you see the young fiddle player? And how he took notice of our Annie? Were we to live here, I believe we should have a romance on our hands," and she smiled in the darkness.

Albert Reber and his wife, Emma, were planning their visit the middle of the next week. Lissie and Annie helped Louisa in the kitchen as well as feeding chickens, gathering eggs, and separating cream after James brought in the milk buckets. Linn followed James around and Lew mostly rested, read, and played with his granddaughters and Martha.

They would be celebrating little Anna's third birthday during Albert and Emma's visit. The little girl had declared, "I want an angel food cake for my birthday."

"That will take twelve eggs," Louisa warned her daughter. "Can you come help me gather those eggs?"

"Yes, Mama," and the little girl scampered ahead of her mother, chattering about the hens.

Lissie watched them through the kitchen window. She could remember gathering eggs for Aunt Jane and dreading the hens pecking at her. She marveled at tiny Anna's fearlessness.

Thursday noon arrived along with Albert and Emma. They had come by train the night before and stayed at a rooming house in Palmyra, then rented a horse and buggy to make the trip out to James' farm.

Lissie could see eyes glisten as Lew and his brother, Albert, embraced in greeting. She had not seen Albert since he had visited during their homesteading days and of course, had never met his wife, Emma. She and Louisa greeted the woman warmly and then they sat down after all introductions were made. Louisa said, "I am very grateful to meet the people who made it possible for James to travel to this part of Missouri. Otherwise, I should never have met him."

"That is right," declared Albert. "I suppose we can take at least some credit in getting you and James together. That is, counting in that load of walnut lumber for the furniture maker in Palmyra," and he laughed.

"Yes," James took up the tale, "and I heard that Louisa's Uncle August was looking for a top hand to supervise his farm as well as his sawmill. I checked out the job the next day. And it turns out Louisa did some checking of her own."

They all laughed and Louisa said, "We need to feed you folks. Give me just a few minutes and dinner will be on the table."

What a meal it was. Fried chicken done to a golden crisp, mashed potatoes with chicken gravy on the side, burgundy-colored pickled beets, green beans cooked in bacon grease with bits of bacon sprinkled throughout and fluffy yeast rolls with golden home-made butter, fresh churned the day before.

The adults groaned at the thought of birthday cake on top of the feast they had just eaten, but James said, "We cannot disappoint the birthday girl. And besides, angel food cakes are mostly air, right?" And he winked at Louisa.

"And a lot of effort going into the beating of that air," she retorted with a grin.

Candles were placed on the cake and lit. "Now take a big breath, Anna, and blow a big puff at the candles," urged her father.

Directing a stream of air from her little lungs, the child blew out her three candles. "I did it!" She jumped off her chair and danced around in a circle.

"Very good," said her mother. "Now, come deliver a piece of cake to your guests as I cut it." Anna very carefully carried a small plate holding a piece of cake to each person. Then she sat down and ate her cake, looking up at her mother when every crumb was gone. "That tasted so good, Mama," she said.

Lissie was sitting across the table and hid a smile. Anna had frosting smeared from one corner of her mouth to the other.

Once she was cleaned up, it was time for presents. Lew and Lissie had brought a small coloring book and a box of colored pencils. Albert and Emma gave her a tiny sunbonnet just her size with a matching apron. And Louisa brought out a white cardboard box with a lid and laid it in Anna's lap.

"Open the lid carefully, Anna," her mother said and she helped steady the box. Inside was a beautiful doll with a bisque face and eyes that opened and closed. Her head was crowned with brown, glossy curls and she wore a blue taffeta dress. The doll had china hands at the end of kidskin arms and her kidskin feet were encased in black net stocking and tiny buttonhole shoes.

"Oh, Mama, she is beautiful," sighed the little girl, as she gently picked up the doll and hugged her.

"Yes, she *is* beautiful," said her father. "And you must take very good care of her."

"I shall Papa," the little girl assured him, and off she ran to introduce her new dolly to her rag doll baby, the other presents forgotten.

Albert and Emma spent another day visiting, coming out in the morning in their rented buggy and team, returning to the boarding house in the evening after supper.

Lissie and Lew with their three, left the following day, James driving them down the hill to the train stop the opposite way they had come ten days earlier. Lissie found the thought of leaving Anna and Matilda a painful one. As she hugged and kissed the little girls goodbye, she also felt a lump in her throat at saying farewell to Louisa. She had come to love this jolly wife of James during the time they had spent with his family.

There was a flurry of goodbyes as they boarded the train and they all waved to James until the train rounded a bend and he was no longer visible.

Chapter 28

April 15, 1921
Palmyra, Missouri

ANNALIESE STRAIGHTENED HER back and rubbed at her eyes, suddenly realizing she had dozed and dreamed away a good part of her day. Landis had left for Palmyra after breakfast to get the team shod and take care of other errands that had piled up and could no longer be ignored. He wasn't planning to be back until chore time.

Good thing, thought Annaliese. *Here I've sat mooning over the past and sleeping on the job. I would paddle my behind were I my own child* and she smiled. Then she set to tossing old papers and letters into the wastepaper can with great vigor.

That evening after feeding Landis biscuits with sausage gravy and leftover peach cobbler from the night before, Annaliese said, "I started my spring housecleaning today and found my old journal, the one your father gave me for Christmas when we moved here."

Landis grinned and asked, "Did it bring back old times to read it?"

"Yes," she sighed. "Yes, it did bring back old times."

The next day Annaliese asked Landis to take down all the curtains so she could launder them. She smiled to herself as she thought of the ease of laundry as compared to fifty years before. Landis hauled water and filled and drained tubs while she manned the wringer and hung curtains on the line to dry.

Between tasks connected with curtain laundering, Landis' next job dealt with carpets. "Son, please roll up the area rugs in the sitting room and the parlor. Hang them on the sturdiest section of my clothes line and take the rug beater to them." Landis was well acquainted with this task as it had been his job since he moved to the farm to live with his mother six years ago.

"Beat the carpets until…"

"I remember, Mother. I'm to beat the carpets until no more dust flies out of them."

"Good boy," she replied with a smile.

That night two Rebers went to bed, tired from house cleaning. Unfortunately, Annaliese's sleep was interrupted with dreamed memories dredged up from her journal. The memories were a mixed lot, as is life.

As if in time travel, her dreams took her back to the family's return to New Jersey after first visiting James and Louisa in Missouri.

Chapter 29

Fall 1895

Newark, New Jersey

THE TRAVELERS ARRIVED home to find the three older boys eager for news of James and his family but also having news of their own.

As was their custom after family devotions following supper, any family matters were up for discussion. Lissie and Lew had mulled over their next move as there was nothing holding them in Newark. But they were surprised at what Howard had to say.

"Mother and Father, we have corresponded with our friends in Allentown during our time here, and have job possibilities connected with our former employers. What do you think about moving back to Allentown?"

Lissie looked at Lew and they both smiled. Lew spoke up. "Your mother and I have been discussing just such a change. I suspect God is directing the hearts of all of us pointing to this relocation and smiling at the possibility."

"Oh, good!" exclaimed Annie. "I should love to be back with that group of Salvation Army lasses. I have missed them," she said wistfully.

So it was that the family removed itself, bag and baggage back to Allentown, albeit not to the lovely parsonage Lissie had so enjoyed some years before. Their rental home was quite comfortable for them, however, and Lew was well enough to take on a clerking job part time, while the older boys continued to help as they contributed to room and board expenses.

One day in April 1896 Lew received a letter from Superintendant Miller asking him to fill a vacant pulpit at the Masters Street Church in Philadelphia.

Lew announced the news after family devotions that evening, giving the family a summary of Miller's letter. "We shall be leaving here within the week, assuming you can get everything packed, Lissie."

If he expected joy at yet another move, Lew was sorely disappointed. First, Lewis spoke up. "I need to finish my school term Father, or the lessons I have taken this spring will be for naught."

Annie was near tears. "I have so enjoyed being a part of the League of Mercy here in the Allentown Salvation Army. Now I shall have to seek out a new band and leave my friends behind—again."

The other boys were just as disgruntled as Annie and Lewis at the thought of making another move.

Finally Lew said, "I suggest you sleep on your dissatisfaction and see what solutions might emerge." The household was soon in bed, but not necessarily asleep.

The atmosphere in the elder Rebers' bedroom was frosty and it had nothing to do with the weather outside.

"I think you are as unhappy about my decision as the children are, Lissie."

She sniffed but said nothing for a moment. Then a heated question rose from her lips. "Lew, have you any idea how many times we have moved since God called you to preach?"

He chuckled and said, "No, but I daresay you are about to tell me."

His reply was not a wise retort to an upset wife. "We have moved ten times in almost as many years, a good part of those moves including eight small children. We have buried children along the way and many times I thought I might well see you buried also. Yet you *will* insist on returning to preaching despite the toll you know it always takes on your health." Thus relieved, she burst into tears.

"There, there, liebchen." Lew tucked her into his chest, soaking the front of his nightshirt in the process. "I must remind you of a scripture which is a motto for me and perhaps you should claim it, also. Jeremiah told the children of Israel God had a plan for their lives and it was a good plan. This is true for us, too. God has called me to preach His Good News and I must do that as long as I have breath. You are flesh of my flesh, my wife, so you are included in this promise and this calling. God will always provide, liebchen. Is it not so? We have eight healthy children and two sweet granddaughters. Have we ever come close to starvation? Have we ever gone naked? No. Perhaps the details were not what we would have chosen, but here we are, snug in a warm bed with our bellies full. God is good!"

He kissed her, turned over and was soon asleep. Lissie, however, needed to mull over his mini-sermon before she, too, could accept the idea of God's consistent provision and let go of her perceived hardship.

The next day the boys had a proposition for their father. "If we can find a boarding house that will take the four of us (Lewis was including eighteen-year-old Linn), we should like to stay here with our friends, classmates, and workmates."

Lew saw nothing amiss with this plan for he had struck out on his own at an even younger age than his boys. "Find a decent place to live before we move at week's end, and I shall approve of your remaining here."

The boys did find a clean boardinghouse, run by an acquaintance from church days, and moved their belongings to their new home. Lissie felt a mixture of grief and burning anger at the idea of her family being separated, but also felt powerless to do anything about it.

Annie and Martha both moped around their new home in Philadelphia, although Annie soon discovered a very active Salvation Army band. Lissie could see another move in her future when, after they had been in Philadelphia about a month, Lew remarked, "This is a city of many churches, but I find the formality almost stifling."

The family devotion times were quiet and subdued with the absence of the four young males left behind in Allentown. When Fall Conference arrived and Lew was appointed to Phillipsburg, New Jersey, Lissie surprised herself by welcoming the move. She had found the churchwomen in Philadelphia stiff and unfriendly and she missed her boys dreadfully.

The family rented a home in Phillipsburg, but the membership had a nice building in which to meet. After their second week there, Lew reported, "This is a dedicated group of believers but, sadly, the church split some years earlier, and the congregation has not recovered."

At that point, Lissie could not find it in her heart to care overmuch about dissenting church members. She had obtained a railway timetable and discovered her boys in Allentown were only a few short hours away by rail. She wrote them with the information and begged them to consider pooling their money and coming for a visit at Christmas.

Needless to say, the little rented house was filled to overflowing with the addition of four young men ranging in age from eighteen to twenty-five. Annie had obtained a Christmas tree from a vendor and Martha had trimmed it with popcorn interspersed with cranberries and candles carefully placed just so. Lissie saw to it that everyone's favorite dish was included in the menu during the meals they shared with the boys.

Lew read the Christmas story from Luke 2 on Christmas Eve and presents were duly delivered to specific recipients. The boys received scarves, caps and mittens, each in their own favorite colors. However, they had pooled their money and bought group gifts for the inhabitants of the little rented house. For Lew, a pair of fine leather gloves, Lissie, a cameo brooch, Annie, a multi-colored silk scarf, and young Martha, *Little Women* by Miss Alcott.

"Did you know I saw Miss Alcott while she was nursing soldiers in Washington during the War? remarked Lew.

"No, I did not know that," replied Lissie, for even though she had little time to read for leisure, she knew of Louisa May Alcott.

"What did she look like, Father?" asked Lewis, ever the curious student.

"Old," laughed Lew, "but you must remember age comparisons. I was about Linn's age at the time. Now, I am much older than she was then."

Everyone expressed much pleasure at their gifts as well as Lissie's meals. The leave-taking was difficult, but Lissie felt heartened at the relatively short distance between them and their boys. That night at bedtime, she remarked to Lew, "I sensed a bit of homesickness in our boys. Was it just a mother's yearning?"

"No," replied Lew. "Landis remarked more than once how they all missed being at home with us. But I would not have them move here," he said, much to Lissie's surprise.

"Why ever not?" she asked.

"There are no great employment opportunities for them here nor is there a local college or university for Lewis to attend." He sighed. "I find this congregation quite wearing, Lissie. The faithful members are persecuted by those who left, and there is no unity apparent at any level."

The new year of 1897 rolled in and Lissie saw the dark circles under Lew's eyes deepen and his shoulders sag in defeat. He preached his heart out to the congregation but the lack of forgiveness just seemed to increase.

Finally, one day late in June, Lew took to his bed. Lissie sent Annie for the doctor who checked Lew over carefully, asking him a multitude of questions. He pronounced, "I believe you have a case of nervous prostration and in addition, your lung on the left side sounds somewhat congested. I advise at least ten days rest for you, sir.

"I shall call in again within the week," he told Lissie. "I do not want pneumonia to settle in," for he had been apprised of Lew's weak chest.

The doctor kept his word and was back in five days. "Well, Mr. Reber, let us check your lungs." After listening to Lew breathe, the doctor said, "I still hear a rattle in there," and then referring to Lew's general appearance, "and I must say, you still somewhat resemble the owl that resides near my carriage house."

"As in my wise demeanor," joked Lew in a weak voice.

"That may be," replied the doctor with a smile, "but I was referring to the dark circles I still see under your eyes. You know, one's skin and the clarity of the eye is a definite indicator to the state of one's health. From the recital of your medical history, I recommend you to forsake life in the city. The dust and coal smoke, not to speak of the proximity of many bodies, does not lend to health, particularly in the poor health you exhibit, Mr. Reber. Move to the country, sir. Move to the country."

With that exhortation, the doctor took his leave. Lissie, who was sitting beside the bed, reached for Lew's hand. "Would you consider moving to Missouri, Lew?"

The year before, they had discussed how clean the air seemed during their visit with James and Louisa. And, of course, the friendliness of the people in the area was unbounded.

"Yes, Lissie, I truly would consider such a move. But right now I am so tired. Of course, I must resign the pulpit here..." His voice trailed off and his eyes closed.

Within the week, Lew's resignation had been tendered and with that load off his shoulders, Lissie saw him begin to eat better, sit up and read for longer periods, and even joke with her and the girls at mealtimes. His eyes gradually lost the dark circles and his shoulders no longer looked like he carried a good portion of Phillipsburg on them.

As Lew recuperated, more definite plans were discussed regarding the move to Missouri. Letters from the boys in Allentown made it clear they wished to accompany the family for Linn had painted a glowing picture of the visit to James' farm.

As for Annie, she was elated. "Mother, you know Robert Maher and I have corresponded since we came back east. He has revealed his heart to me. And I, to him," she added, shyly. "If we do, indeed, move to Missouri, I believe I shall be wed within the year."

Lissie kissed her daughter's cheek, and said, "I suspected there were feelings between the two of you by the time we left Missouri." Robert had made several trips to see James during their visit with various excuses, each time managing to spend some time talking with Annie.

For the first time since he had been licensed to preach, Lew did not attend Fall Conference. Instead, he sent a letter requesting he not be appointed to a pastorate for the present. The letter was postmarked from Palmyra, Missouri for the Rebers had moved--all eight of them.

Lew found a house to rent in Palmyra from a local judge. It was a two-story frame home with spring water piped into the kitchen so no one need go outside to pump a bucket of water. Landis had gone to work for a blacksmith, Howard was employed at the Land Office, and Lewis had made arrangements to travel further north to LaGrange to finish his college classes. Annie had renewed her acquaintance with her long-distance beau, Robert, and it seemed the Reber family was happily settling in to a new life in a new state.

Lew was still a semi-invalid, but as the weeks passed and he got stronger, Lissie could see he was restless. Especially on Sundays. They attended a church in town but it was not Free Methodist and Lew minced no words to Lissie. "How dare a preacher water down the word of God. I would not have been surprised if the Lord had struck the man down right in his pulpit this morning."

Lissie had noticed Lew clenching and unclenching his hands during the service and she wondered if he was in pain. *I suppose he was,* she thought, *but it was mental rather than physical pain.*

One day Lew came back from a long walk full of excitement. "I found a schoolhouse a mile or so out of town and I have been given permission to start a Sunday School there." For many weeks, he made visits to the farm folk around just as he was accustomed to do on his circuits.

Wedding bells rang, figuratively at least, for Annie as she became Mrs. Robert Maher on March 12, 1898. Lissie wept as she watched the newlyweds drive off in Robert's shiny black buggy pulled by a spirited chestnut thoroughbred.

Lew drew his handkerchief from a vest pocket and offered it to his wife. "Why are you crying, dear? Did I not do a masterful job of marrying off our darling girl?"

"Of course, you ninny." She laughed as she wiped her tears. "Women always cry at weddings and I declare I saw you dab at the corner of your eye when you gave the groom permission to kiss the bride after the 'I do's'."

By this time, Lew's health had visibly improved and he had rented some farm land from one of James' neighbors. Landis, Howard and Linn, remained at the house in Palmyra. Linn had gotten a job with the railroad, having declared himself finished with school at age nineteen. The young men pooled a portion of their salaries in order to pay for rent and food, grateful they were not too great a distance from their mother's cooking.

Lew, Lissie, and Martha had moved into James and Louisa's house because the younger couple had moved into Louisa's aunt's house upon her death the previous year. Lissie and Martha were delighted that little Anna and Matilda now lived just down the road from them and the horse and second-hand buggy Lew had bought with his first crop check was often hitched up and driven to see the little girls.

One day after reading his monthly news magazine "The Free Methodist," Lew shouted, "Lissie! The brethren are nearby. Hallelujah!"

"What on earth are you talking about?" she exclaimed.

"This article states there is a Missouri Conference of Free Methodists. And at least one congregation in Hannibal."

Lissie had not seen Lew this excited since the revival in Newark.

"I must make arrangements to contact the District Superintendent," he said, and immediately got pen and paper to write the letter.

Lissie had to smile to herself as Lew made arrangements to meet "the pilgrims" as he called the membership.

It was not long before Lew was appointed to the Hannibal congregation. "You are like an old war horse," stated Lissie. "Once removed from the battle, there is always the desire to re-enter the fray." She smiled at Lew's announcement but then scowled. "How are you going to guard your health in the winter months, Lew? True, you have recuperated wonderfully in this clean country air, but I fear your weak chest will always be with you."

"I now have a horse and buggy," he replied. "With that provision and God having called me back into ministry, I do not fear illness."

Lissie could do no less than trust God for her husband's well-being.

Annie and Robert had moved to a farm some five miles distant but that did not keep Lissie from visiting. One summer day as the women were stringing beans picked freshly from Annie's garden, the younger woman said, "Mother, I believe I am with child." Lissie clapped her hands and hugged her daughter.

"How long have you suspected, dear?"

"My time of bleeding did not occur last month," Annie replied. "When I checked our calendar this month, I realized the same thing had happened. Or not happened," she grinned.

"Oh, my dear, I am so happy for you and Robert. Have you told him yet?"

"No, I wanted to talk to you first, so I might be sure." She blushed. "I shall tell him tonight."

So on March 10, 1899, tiny Roberta Anne Maher was born. "My quiver is filling with granddaughters," stated a joyful Lissie.

Summer of that year saw Linn moving to St. Louis to take on the position of a streetcar conductor. "I have had my eye on this method of transportation," he stated, "and when I saw an advertisement in the *Palmyra Spectator* about the position in St. Louis, I knew I had to apply for the job."

He had come out to the farm to tell his parents of his decision and eat one more of his mother's delicious meals.

Later that night as Lissie and Lew sat out on the porch, watching the fireflies and listening to the crickets sing, Lissie said, "Our birdies are flying away, Lew. Lewis will probably be leaving soon in search of a teaching job. And really, he has been pretty much absent since we moved here as he has spent at least eight months of each year at LaGrange College."

"You're right, Lissie, but we have raised our children to make their own way. This state offers much opportunity to do that very thing."

The twentieth century arrived, and life appeared to be moving in a rather comfortable fashion for the Rebers. Lew had been re-appointed to the Hannibal congregation, adding the little town of Ashburn, but his health remained stable. Annie and Robert's little Roberta was a healthy child, walking and adding to her vocabulary of mama, dada, and no, daily. Annie became pregnant again and was radiant in her pregnancy.

Then tragedy struck.

It was a November morning and a storm was blowing in from the east as a knock came at the door and Howard rushed in. He was waving a telegram in his hand.

"Linn has been injured in a streetcar collision. He has asked for you to come."

Lissie heard a blast of wind hit the house and she felt fear clutch her heart, squeezing at her chest. It lasted for only a second for then she threw off her apron and tried to think of what she and Lew would need on their journey. "Is there a train out of Palmyra to St. Louis at noon?" she asked as she hurried to the bedroom.

"Yes," Lew replied. "Howard, please help me harness the horse to the buggy. Can you take care of it once we are at the depot?"

"Certainly, Father. The main thing we need to do is get you on the train."

Once settled in their seat in the rail car, Lissie leaned against Lew's shoulder. "Oh how I pray our sweet son will survive whatever injury he has sustained. I cannot help but imagine the pain he must be suffering," and she began to cry.

Lew put his arm around her and kissed her cheek. She could feel the tears on his face, but he cleared his throat and said, “Let us get some comfort from God’s Word.” He pulled a small Bible our of his coat pocket and turned to Psalm 23. “Yea, though I walk through the valley of the shadow of death, I will fear no evil; for Thou art with me.”

He turned to other scriptures of strength and comfort and read them in the baritone voice Lissie so loved to hear. About half way through the trip, she realized her fear was gone and her heart felt at peace for her sweet Linn.

They hailed a hansom cab once they departed the station in St. Louis and headed for the address they had been given. They were shown into the cubicle where Linn lay. A nurse was rising from his bedside and Lissie had seen the woman close her son’s eyelids.

“No,” she cried. “He cannot be gone.”

Lew hugged her to his side, his body trembling. “What has happened?” he inquired, his voice hoarse with emotion.

“I am so sorry,” replied the nurse. Mr. Linn died about two hours ago. We have been dreadfully busy because we are short handed. This is the first I have had time to tend to him.”

“But we were told he asked for us,” sobbed Lissie. “How can he be dead if he was able to ask for his mother and father?”

“He was conscious when they brought him in,” replied the nurse. “I am so sorry,” she repeated. “He was crushed from the waist down. He could never have survived his injuries.”

Lissie walked to her son’s side, took his hand and stroked his face. “He looks so peaceful, just as if he is asleep,” she whispered. “Yet, he must have suffered terribly.”

“I do not believe so,” replied the nurse.”His body was in such a state of shock, he was protected from the pain. And his heart gave out before the shock wore off. Truly a blessing,” she added.

Just then a middle-aged man entered the room. “Mr. and Mrs. Reber? I am John Dunbar, Linn’s supervisor. I am desperately sorry for your loss. Your son was a fine young man. A man of integrity. I am told that he wanted to be sure the money from his fares were safely accounted for, and that despite the fact that he knew he was dying.”

“Yes,” said the nurse, “he stayed remarkably aware according to the assistant nurse who was with him when he died. He asked that his body be taken home for burial so he knew he was dying and yet he faced it bravely, with no apparent fear."

That evening Lissie and Lew returned to Palmyra, this time with Linn's body lying in a casket in the baggage car. "I feel as though I have aged a decade this day," stated Lissie in a dull voice.

"Cling to the comfort that Linn suffered little, my dear," stated Lew. "And most important, he is now with our Lord."

"Along with little Robbie," said Lissie, and then her tears began again. Lew said noting, just held her close.

Life went on as it does in an extended family. Annie and Robert welcomed Florence Eileen into their family, and news from Elmer told of his marriage to a young woman named Carrie Parker from New York. Elmer had returned from Mississippi in 1895, and after additional years of study at seminary had become an itinerant preacher, following in Lew's footsteps, somewhat.

Annie gave Robert another baby named Fannie Josephine. Robert was heard to say in a joking manner, "I now have more than enough dishwashers in the family."

The next year sickness stalked the Maher home. "Mother," Annie said on a visit from Lissie, "I feel so achy, and this headache will not leave me." She passed a shaky hand over her brow as she spoke.

Lissie took little Fannie Jo from her arms and began to rock her as she replied. "You have three children under the age of five, Annie. And on top of keeping up with the two older girls, this little one still seems to be dealing with colic. Robert's elderly father has joined your household and I wonder that you haven't come close to nervous prostration earlier."

Lissie had become quite upset when she saw the disarray her daughter's house had fallen into with the three little children, a sickly, elderly man who did not clean up after himself and a husband who worked night and day, either in the fields, or caring for his animals.

"When will Robert likely come in from the milk barn?" Lissie was ready to give him a tongue lashing and Annie recognized the signs.

"Oh, Mother. Please do not be upset. Robert is doing the best he can. His hired hand quit last week and he is in dire need of an experienced hand before baby animals start arriving."

Lissie went to fill a glass of water from the bucket and took a sip. She promptly walked to the slop bucket at the corner of the back porch and spit it out. "Your water tastes horrible, Annie. Where does it come from?"

"The well is down the hill between the house and the barn. I am so fortunate to have this pitcher pump so I need not go outside to pump water."

"Yes, I recall when we first lived in a house with a pitcher pump. It was quite the luxury."

Two weeks later Lissie visited Annie and discovered that old man Maher had become deathly ill. She was aghast at the sight Annie presented. "You must get some rest, daughter. You are wearing yourself out nursing Mr. Maher. Cannot Robert bring in a nurse to help you?"

"Mr. Maher will have nothing to do with the idea," replied Annie. Her voice and appearance twisted Lissie's heart.

"I have an idea, dear. What would you say to Roberta and Florence coming to stay with us until everyone gets healthier around here?"

"I should think they would be too much of a handful for you and father," the young woman replied.

"We did manage to live with seven of you young rapscallions," her mother retorted. "I assure you, your father and I are quite able to deal with these lively young ladies," she said as Roberta ran through the dining room and into the kitchen.

"Let me talk with Robert about the plan and if he agrees, I will send a message with Mr. Rankin who drives to Palmyra every three days.

The answer was affirmative and Lew came with Lissie to pick up their little granddaughters.

Annie looked even worse, if that was possible.

"How is Mr. Maher today?" asked Lew.

"He is somewhat improved, but I must admit, I truly feel ill. I seem able to admit it now that you have arrived," said Annie with a weak smile.

"Please excuse me for a moment."

She ran out of the room and they heard the back door slam. She was back in a few minutes but moving much slower and Lissie could see she was unable to walk erect. On a pretext of a food matter, Lissie coaxed Annie to the kitchen.

"What is wrong, Annie? You seem unable to stand straight."

The young woman sat down, her head leaning on one hand, the other arm clasping her stomach. "I have a severe case of diarrhea today. It has been coming on for some days but I thought I was improving. Today I can barely care for Fannie Jo so it is good Mr. Maher is some better."

"You need to see a doctor, Annie."

"Perhaps Robert can get away and take me into town on Friday," she said listlessly.

She assured her parents she would be fine, so with misgivings, they left with their two little granddaughters, who were quite excited about going to Mawmaw and Pawpaw's house.

Two days later, Robert was on their doorstep. "Annie is took bad," he said. "She is asking for you, and," he gulped, "I fear she may not live through the night."

"Have you fetched the doctor, man," said Lew sharply.

"I was going to take her into town tomorrow," the younger man admitted.

"I would advise you to fetch the doctor now," urged Lew.

"I dare not. I promised Annie I would return straightaway. Pa is keeping an eye on Fannie Jo but I am not too confident of him staying awake to do so."

Lew hitched up his horse to the buggy and by that time Lissie had gathered what supplies she thought she might need. They made an emergency trip to James and Louisa's and that good woman immediately agreed to care for the little Maher girls.

Robert had galloped on ahead of the Rebers and had soothed Fannie Jo and made Annie as comfortable as possibly. His father had fallen asleep in his chair.

Annie tried to sit up when she saw her parents but was too weak to do so. "So thirsty," she whispered.

Lissie smoothed her forehead and found her skin to be very warm. "I shall boil up some willow bark tea," she declared. "That should take care of the pain and fever," for Annie occasionally clutched at her lower stomach.

The young woman was able to take only a sip or two of the tea Lissie offered her. "Thank you, Mother." Then she whispered,

"Won't I have a good long rest when I get to heaven." She smiled, closed her eyes, and gave a large sigh which was her last breath.

"Gone to rest in Jesus' arms," her father said later.

Lew called Robert and when it had sunk in that Annie was dead, he threw himself atop her, sobbing. Lissie and Lew walked out of the bedroom to give Robert privacy with his grief.

They sat on the horsehair sofa in the parlor and Lissie leaned against Lew's solid shoulder. "My heart feels like a block of ice," she murmured. "This is even worse than losing Linn. What is to become of our granddaughters?"

"Robert has sisters and brothers. I suppose one of them will take the children in. Or perhaps he has a spinster sister or cousin who can come live here and help with the girls."

"Lew," wept Lissie. "We have not just lost Annie. We are losing our granddaughters too."

"Stay away from the what-ifs, Lissie," he warned. They are potholes in life that can bury us before the buggy even nears one."

She sniffed. "You are right. But I do not have a good feeling about this."

Annie's funeral was two days later and her two older daughters clung to their grandparents as they brought them back to their father's farm. When they arrived, a middle-aged woman met them and introduced herself as Robert's older sister. "I will be taking care of Robert and his girls for the next little time," she announced.

As the months continued, it came about as Lissie feared. Robert did not have time to bring his children to see Lissie and Lew. Consequently, the visits were all one-sided and when Robert sold out and moved with his daughters to another county, the visits stopped altogether. Annie's little girls soon forgot their Reber grandparents and Lissie's prophecy came true.

Chapter 30

Mid-July 1921

Palmyra, Missouri

SPRING MOVED INTO summer and Landis helped his mother plant a garden of beans, carrots, onions and radishes, and of course, tomatoes. He helped harvest the yield too because Annaliese had suffered from arthritis in her knees, hips and hands for at least fifteen years.

They were surprised by welcome guests when Martha and her family drove in on a sultry Tuesday. Her husband, Chan, had church administration business in Hannibal that week.

After greeting and settling on the shady porch with glasses of iced tea, Martha explained, "Sarah and I have come to help you pick and can your tomatoes and green beans."

Annaliese looked at her tall, dark-eyed, curly haired granddaughter and smiled in approval. "Are you near finished with high school, dear?

"I have one more year and then I plan to attend college and become a teacher."

"That's a very creditable goal, Sarah," said her grandmother. "Did you know two of your uncles have been school teachers?"

"Why, no, I didn't," stated the girl in surprise. "I knew Cousin Tillie was a schoolteacher until she married. In fact, she's sort of my idol," she said in a wistful tone.

They were interrupted by Chan, Martha's husband. "Mother Reber, where might I deposit this sleepy little boy?" He was carrying his six-year-old who was still half dozing from the auto trip to the farm.

"Take him into the parlor," replied Annaliese. "I'll spread the afghan to make that old horsehair sofa a softer bed."

Chan stayed in the room with his son, sitting in a chintz upholstered wing chair and stretching his legs to rest on the matching footstool.

Annaliese returned to the porch to visit with her daughter and granddaughter. "What do you hear from the rest of the family, Mother?" asked Martha. "James' Anna occasionally writes, but I don't hear much from Tillie since she married and had her baby."

"Anna has moved home from Peoria and Tillie's little Jessie just turned a year old this April. My first great-grandchild," sighed Annaliese.

She continued, "Lewis has moved from South Dakota to St. Joseph, Michigan and he and Tena now have three children. Howard and his wife have a son and a daughter and are living in Benton Harbor, Michigan. Elmer and Carrie now have six children and are living in Ohio."

"The last time I heard from Elmer they were still living in New York," exclaimed Martha. "Time passes so rapidly."

"Yes," replied her mother. "It's hard to believe your David is now six years old. Do the doctors say if there will ever be any chance of him walking? Or talking?"

Martha smoothed a curly wisp of hair back behind her ear, and answered in a tired voice. "No, the last doctor who checked David diagnosed him as having cerebral palsy. He told us to take David home and love him because we may not have him around many more years."

"I call him my sweet boy," chimed in Sarah. "He understands what we say, but he is just unable to make his body do what he wants. And I can generally understand him when he talks, too," she said, decidedly. "I think I would like to teach children sort of like David," she added.

"And so you shall," said her mother, smoothing her curls, fondly.

Annaliese was delighted to have Martha and her family visit. And besides that, the two younger women, for she counted Sarah as a woman, were great help in preserving her garden's bounty. Wednesday evening after they had canned twenty-four quarts of tomatoes, Annaliese complained, "I think I'm getting too old for this. My legs barely seem strong enough to take me from the kitchen table to my rocker."

Martha shook her finger at her mother. "You and Landis have planted a garden large enough to feed a growing family of six. No wonder you are tired! You kept up with Sarah and me and still seemed full of vigor when we stopped picking."

Annaliese sighed. "I think halting that forward momentum caused my downfall, so to speak." And she grinned.

As her guests were preparing to leave that Friday, Annaliese insisted that Martha take half of the product of their work. "No, mother. This is too many jars," protested Martha.

"Do you not like tomatoes, Martha?"

"You know I love tomatoes."

"Well, I see by my pantry shelves that there is more than enough for Landis and me already. So I insist you take these."

With protests, then thank you's, and goodbye hugs and kisses, Annaliese and Landis waved to the baby of the family as she and *her* family started their trip home to South Missouri.

"Babe looked tired this trip," remarked Landis. Annaliese was often surprised by his sensitivity.

"Ah, Landis. I haven't heard Martha called by that nickname since your father died." The sound of Lew's voice resonated in her memory and brought a lump to her throat. "Well, 'twas good to see them. Sarah has grown into such a tall, lovely young lady. And sweet David. My heart aches for them and the thought of his future."

She turned and busied herself in the kitchen, furtively wiping at the corner of her eyes.

The autumn equinox was fast approaching and Annaliese felt like a squirrel storing ample nuts for the coming winter. Probably unlike the squirrel, the arthritis in her joints had been troublesome the entire month of September.

Annaliese had decided to pull out her journal after cleaning up her kitchen this particular evening. She turned toward the back half and the page flipped open to February 19, 1902.

Martha had married "her preacher feller", as one neighbor had phrased it. Annaliese could remember Lew saying, "She's a mite young, but we would have married at her age, if it had been allowed. Besides, it seems Babe was born a young adult because she grew up with siblings much older than she." As it was, Rev. Reber had to sign a form at the courthouse granting his approval for his daughter, Martha Amanda Reber, age 15, to marry Chandos

Smutz, age 27.

Martha had caught sight of Chan a year earlier at a Fall Conference in Hannibal where he was in attendance as the Free Methodist preacher from Chillicothe. As Chan put it later, "Two pairs of dark eyes met, and a spark of electricity lit a blaze that wouldn't be extinguished."

Our children chose well, Lew, mused Annaliese. *Elmer seems very happy with his Carrie and their six. Louisa has made quite a jovial man out of gruff James and even sweet Annie--and even sweet Annie—oh my darling girl, how I miss you even these many years later.*

Annaliese thought of Annie's dashing black-haired Irishman. Robert. Ever the jokester, but doting on the love of his life, Annie, he delighted in the three darling little girls she'd given him. After she died, Robert sold his farm and eventually went to work on his sister's farm so that she might help him raise his three little motherless daughters. *I read he married again but the girls were near grown by that time. If ever I saw a man nursing a broken heart, it was Robert Maher,* she mused.

Annaliese woke herself up when her head dropped suddenly, chin hitting her chest. "I'm to bed, Landis. I just now near broke my neck, so I judge my body is telling my brain 'tis time to rest in a flat position instead of sitting."

He chuckled and said, "Sleep well, Mother."

Annaliese climbed into bed but was unable to go immediately to sleep. *No more reading my journal before bedtime* she scolded herself. *Brings back too many memories that don't lend themselves to rest.*

She started out lying on her back and then turned to her right side. That hip started to hurt so she turned over on the other side. Drowsiness began to creep in and then her mind's eye alit on Annie's casket at the Baptist church in Palmyra and then to the train ride she and James had taken on that cold January day in 1914 to retrieve Lew's body at Martha's house. It was as if Annaliese was re-living the entire experience once again.

She shifted her sit-bones on the hard, horsehair seat, trying to find a comfortable position for her aching joints. As the railroad car jerked along the uneven track, she was grateful they weren't traveling faster. Only last week over in Shelby County a Burlington train had derailed by taking a curve too fast, dumping milk cans, chickens and mail bags besides injuring ten people in the two passenger cars.

The potbellied stove near the front door provided the warmth for the train car, but very little heat reached her seat in the middle. As she tried to look out the window, it had frosted over so she scratched the surface attempting to clear enough area to see where they might be. Through the thick woods, she caught a glint of the Fabius River in the distance. The land still looked unfamiliar.

Turning to her son, James, she asked, "How far are we from home?"

He leaned across her to peer through the window area she'd scraped clear and said, "I'm guessing we still have at least 25 miles to cover before we get to our stop."

Annaliese searched the haggard lines of his face. James had always had a hard time dealing with death starting with the loss of little Linneus forty plus years ago. Now James was escorting his father's body back from Atlanta, Missouri where Lew had planned to preach that Sunday. The Lord had other plans for Lew Reber and he had breathed his last at Martha's home early Sunday morning.

Grief tightened Annaliese's throat at the thought of no longer being able to greet her Lew with a hot cup of tea laced with honey. That was his favorite drink on a cold day such as this. She shivered as she thought of his chilled body lying in a coffin in the baggage car.

Just then the train whistled at a crossing. The mournful sound seemed to lance through her as if marking finality, a major closing in her life's journey.

Many were the battles we weathered, she though drowsily, her mind now back in the present. *A country at war when I thought Lew had been killed. My own battles with drudgery and poverty—laundry with a wash board and pantries nearly bare of food with seven children looking at me over watery bowls of vegetable soup. Lew, deathly ill more times than I dare count, three babies dying with one not even getting to take a breath. Then Linn's tragic death and Annie three years after.*

As she wept in her drowsy state, suddenly a fierce pain lanced through her head. Not quite conscious, she clasped both hands to her temples. Then she heard Lew's voice reading and it calmed her fear and eased her pain.

"…in all these things we are more than conquerors through Him who loved us. For I am persuaded that neither death nor life, nor angels nor principalities nor powers, nor things present nor things to come, nor height nor depth, nor any other created thing, shall be able to separate us from the love of God which is in Christ Jesus our Lord."

"Lew," she whispered, "How I love the sound of your voice." Then she could *see* him. There was little Robbie with Annie and Linn each holding one of their baby brothers.

And Lissie knew she was home.

To My Readers

All the main characters in this story were actual people, with the exception of the Holtschlag family, Lissie's sister, Jennie, and her friend, Eliza. There *were* such people; there is just no record of their names.

FYI: Lissie's name appears in an 1850 census as Sarah Annaliese Facht, but later family information names her as Sarah Angeline Focht. For that reason I have dedicated this book to her memory by the latter name.

Lissie was my great-great grandmother through her second son, James. His second daughter, Matilda (Tillie) was my maternal grandmother. She and her sister, Anna, knew the people in this story quite well. How I wish I had quizzed them about their memories but at least I have Lew's little book. (As a personal sidelight, the doll Anna received on her third birthday is now sitting in a place of honor on my bookshelf.)

My principal source material for *Lissie's Story* was a brief autobiography written by Lissie's husband, Lew, entitled *Sketch of the Life and Labors of Rev. L.B. Reber* published in 1901. In it he describes his early life, his adventures in the Civil War, and God's miraculous provision numerous times as he traveled his circuits as a Free Methodist preacher. My brother and I own copies of this self-published book, which has long been out of print, and we have edited it into a more readable format offering it for sale on Amazon.

Other sources for information on the family were old family newspaper clippings of activities as well as obituaries. The internet also afforded avenues of research on topics like the dreaded chore of laundry, Camp Parole, Grant's Railroad, etc.

I hope you feel like you now know Lissie well and can empathize with the plight of women in the 1800's as they dealt with the drudgery of housework and bearing and caring for many children.

Book 2 in the trilogy "One Woman's War" will feature Lissie's oldest grandchild, Anna Reber, in *The War to End Them All: Anna's Story*. If you are interested in the progress of that story and want to be included on my e-mail list, send your contact information to me at patricia.diehl3@gmail.com. Also please write to me regarding any questions and comments. I love to hear from readers.

Acknowledgements

I am so grateful to my beta readers, Ruth Ann Diehl and Bettie Rundlett who also proofed the copy as they read. Their comments and eagle eyes are greatly prized. Diane Detweiler and Pat Moon graciously read through the final manuscript for spelling and punctuation errors. Members of Writers for the Son, led by Serenity Orr and Christina Foster, shared helpful comments during the writing process for *Lissie's Story.* Others who helped along the way were Peggy Branch, Bob Johnson and Sara McFerrin.

Some research points were aided by Bob Johnson, Marjory Johnson and Mary Snodgrass. Many thanks to all of you.

My older son, Jeffrey Diehl, designed the book cover and my younger son, Brian Diehl, provided the photograph on the back.

I am grateful to God, the Creator of all gifts, for giving me the opportunity to write this book. What a joy to become acquainted with family members from long ago and learn how God provided for them just as He so graciously provides for me.

CPSIA information can be obtained
at www.ICGtesting.com
Printed in the USA
LVHW032323260622
722161LV00004B/350